PRAISE FOR

A MAN CALLED OVE

'Delightful ... there's a bit of Ove in all of us – which makes it the
PERFECT HOLIDAY READ'
Evening Standard

'A warm and tender story about love, loss and second chances, peppered with
memorable characters, wonderful set pieces and some beautifully black humour.
OVE **IS A JOY FROM START TO FINISH.**'
Gavin Extence, author of *The Universe versus Alex Woods*

'*A Man Called Ove* finally rescued all those men who constantly mean
to read novels but never get round to it. Crotchety old git Ove argues
with neighbours, reluctantly inherits a cat, punches a clown and,
BY THE END OF THE BOOK, HAS YOU WANTING TO HUG HIM.'
Spectator

'Each short chapter of *A Man Called Ove* stands alone as a beautifully
crafted short story. Bring them together and you have an **UPLIFTING,
LIFE-AFFIRMING** and often **COMIC TALE** of how kindness,
love and happiness can be found in the most unlikely places.'
Sunday Express

ABOUT THE AUTHOR

Fredrik Backman made his literary debut in 2012 with the global sensation *A Man Called Ove*. He has written seven highly acclaimed novels including *My Grandmother Sends Her Regards and Apologises* and *Britt-Marie Was Here*, two heartfelt novellas about life and love, and one non-fiction book about parenthood. His books have sold more than 18 million copies in 46 languages, and the Swedish-language film adaptation of *A Man Called Ove* was nominated for two Academy Awards.

fredrik.cafe.se
@Backmanland

FREDRIK BACKMAN

A MAN CALLED OVE

Translated from the Swedish by Henning Koch

s

sceptre

First published in Great Britain in 2014 by Sceptre

An imprint of Hodder & Stoughton
An Hachette UK company

This paperback edition published in 2022

1

A CIP catalogue record for this title is available from the British Library.

Paperback ISBN 9781399713269
eBook ISBN 9781444775822

Printed and bound in Great Britain by Clays Ltd, Elcograf S.p.A.

Hodder & Stoughton policy is to use papers that are natural, renewable
and recyclable products and made from wood grown in sustainable
forests. The logging and manufacturing processes are expected to
conform to the environmental regulations of the country of origin.

Hodder & Stoughton Ltd
Carmelite House
50 Victoria Embankment
London EC4Y 0DZ

www.sceptrebooks.co.uk

Dear Neda. It's always meant to make you laugh.
Always.

1

A MAN CALLED OVE BUYS A COMPUTER
THAT IS NOT A COMPUTER

Ove is fifty-nine.

He drives a Saab. He's the kind of man who points at people he doesn't like the look of, as if they were burglars and his forefinger a policeman's torch. He stands at the counter of a shop where owners of Japanese cars come to purchase white cables. Ove eyes the sales assistant for a long time before shaking a medium-sized white box at him.

'So this is one of those O-Pads, is it?' he demands.

The assistant, a young man with a single-digit Body Mass Index, looks ill at ease. He visibly struggles to control his urge to snatch the box out of Ove's hands.

'Yes, exactly. An iPad. Do you think you could stop shaking it like that . . .?'

Ove gives the box a sceptical glance, as if it's a highly dubious sort of box, a box that rides a scooter and wears tracksuit trousers and just called Ove 'my friend' before offering to sell him a watch.

'I see. So it's a computer, yes?'

The sales assistant nods. Then hesitates and quickly shakes his head.

'Yes . . . or, what I mean is, it's an iPad. Some people call it a "tablet" and others call it a surfing device. There are different ways of looking at it . . .'

1

Ove looks at the sales assistant as if he has just spoken backwards, before shaking the box again.

'But is it good, this thing?'

The assistant nods confusedly. 'Yes. Or . . . How do you mean?'

Ove sighs and starts talking slowly, articulating his words as if the only problem here is his adversary's impaired hearing.

'Is. It. Goooood? Is it a good computer?'

The assistant scratches his chin.

'I mean . . . yeah . . . it's really good . . . but it depends what sort of computer you want.'

Ove glares at him.

'I want a computer! A normal bloody computer!'

Silence descends over the two men for a short while. The assistant clears his throat.

'Well . . . it isn't really a normal computer. Maybe you'd rather have a . . .'

The assistant stops and seems to be looking for a word that falls within the bounds of comprehension of the man facing him. Then he clears his throat again and says:

'. . . a laptop?'

Ove shakes his head wildly and leans menacingly over the counter.

'No, I don't want a "laptop"'. I want a *computer*.'

The assistant nods pedagogically.

'A laptop is a computer.'

Ove, insulted, glares at him and stabs his forefinger at the counter.

'You think I don't know that!'

Another silence, as if two gunmen have suddenly realised they have forgotten to bring their pistols. Ove looks at the box for a long time, as though he's waiting for it to make a confession.

'Where does the keyboard pull out?' he mutters eventually.

The sales assistant rubs his palms against the edge of the counter and shifts his weight nervously from foot to foot, as young men employed in retail outlets often do when they begin to understand that something is going to take considerably more time than they had initially hoped.

'Well, this one doesn't actually have a keyboard.'

Ove does something with his eyebrows. 'Ah, of course,' he splutters. 'Because you have to buy it as an "extra", don't you?'

'No, what I mean is that the computer doesn't have a *separate* keyboard. You control everything from the screen.'

Ove shakes his head in disbelief, as if he's just witnessed the sales assistant walking round the counter and licking the glass-fronted display cabinet.

'But I have to have a keyboard. You do understand that?'

The young man sighs deeply, as if patiently counting to ten.

'Okay. I understand. In that case I don't think you should go for this computer. I think you should buy something like a MacBook instead.'

'A McBook?' Ove says, far from convinced. 'Is that one of those blessed "eReaders" everyone's talking about?'

'No. A MacBook is a . . . it's a . . . laptop, with a keyboard.'

'Okay!' Ove hisses. He looks round the shop for a moment. 'So are *they* any good, then?'

The sales assistant looks down at the counter in a way that seems to reveal a fiercely yet barely controlled desire to begin clawing his own face. Then he suddenly brightens, flashing an energetic smile.

'You know what? Let me see if my colleague has finished with his customer, so he can come and give you a demonstration.'

Ove checks his watch and grudgingly agrees, reminding the assistant that some people have better things to do than stand around all day waiting. The assistant gives him a quick nod, then disappears and comes back after a few moments with a colleague. The colleague looks very happy, as people do when they have not been working for a sufficient stretch of time as sales assistants.

'Hi, how can I help you?'

Ove drills his police-torch finger into the counter.

3

'I want a computer!'

The colleague no longer looks quite as happy. He gives the first sales assistant an insinuating glance as if to say he'll pay him back for this.

In the meantime the first sales assistant mutters, 'I can't take any more, I'm going for lunch.'

'Lunch,' snorts Ove. 'That's the only thing people care about nowadays.'

'I'm sorry?' says the colleague and turns round.

'*Lunch*!' He sneers, then tosses the box on to the counter and swiftly walks out.

2

(THREE WEEKS EARLIER)

A MAN CALLED OVE MAKES HIS

NEIGHBOURHOOD INSPECTION

It was five to six in the morning when Ove and the cat met for the first time. The cat instantly disliked Ove exceedingly. The feeling was very much reciprocated.

Ove had, as usual, got up ten minutes earlier. He could not make head nor tail of people who overslept and blamed it on 'the alarm clock not ringing'. Ove had never owned an alarm clock in his entire life. He woke up at quarter to six and that was when he got up.

Every morning for the almost four decades they had lived in this house, Ove had put on the coffee percolator, using exactly the same amount of coffee as any other morning, and then drunk a cup with his wife. One measure for each cup, and one extra for the jug – no more, no less. People didn't know how to do that any more, brew some proper coffee. In the same way as nowadays nobody could write with a pen. Because now it was all computers and espresso machines. And where was the world going if people couldn't even write or brew a bit of coffee?

While his proper cup of coffee was brewing, he put on his navy blue trousers and jacket, stepped into his wooden clogs, and shoved his hands in his pockets in that particular way of a middle-aged man who expects the worthless world outside to disappoint him.

Then he made his morning inspection of the street. The surrounding terraced houses lay in silence and darkness as he walked out of the door, and there wasn't a soul in sight. Might have known, thought Ove. In this street no one took the trouble to get up any earlier than they had to. Nowadays, it was just self-employed people and other disreputable sorts living here.

The cat sat with a nonchalant expression in the middle of the footpath that ran between the houses. It had half a tail and only one ear. Patches of fur were missing here and there as if someone had pulled it out in handfuls. Not a very impressive feline.

Ove stomped forward. The cat stood up. Ove stopped. They stood there measuring up to each other for a few moments, like two potential troublemakers in a small-town bar. Ove considered throwing one of his clogs at it. The cat looked as if it regretted not bringing its own clogs to lob back.

'Scram!' Ove bellowed, so abruptly that the cat jumped back. It briefly scrutinised the fifty-nine-year-old man and his clogs, then turned and lolloped off. Ove could have sworn it rolled its eyes before clearing out.

'Pest,' he thought, glancing at his watch. Two minutes to six. Time to get going or the bloody cat would have succeeded in delaying the entire inspection. Fine state of affairs that would be.

He began marching along the footpath between the houses. He stopped by the traffic sign informing motorists that they were prohibited from entering the residential area. He gave the metal pole a firm kick. Not that it was wonky or anything, but it's always best to check. Ove is the sort of man who checks the status of all things by giving them a good kick.

He walked across the parking area and strolled back and forth along all the garages to make sure none of them had been burgled in the night or set on fire by gangs of vandals. Such things had never happened round here, but then Ove had never skipped one of his inspections either. He tugged three times at the door handle of his own garage, where his Saab was parked. Just like any other morning.

After this, he detoured through the guest parking area, where cars could only be left for up to twenty-four hours. Carefully he noted down all the registration numbers in the little pad he kept in his jacket pocket, and then compared these to the registrations he had noted down the day before. On occasions when the same registration numbers turned up in Ove's notepad, Ove would go home and call the Vehicle Licensing Authority to retrieve the vehicle owner's details, after which he'd call up the latter and inform him that he was a useless bloody imbecile who couldn't even read signs. Ove didn't really care who was parked in the guest parking area, of course. But it was a question of principle. If it said twenty-four hours on the sign, that's how long you were allowed to stay. What would it be like if everyone just parked wherever they liked? It would be chaos. There'd be cars bloody everywhere.

Today, thankfully, there weren't any unauthorized cars in the guest parking, and Ove was able to proceed to the next part of his daily inspection: the bin room. Not that it was really his responsibility, mind. He had steadfastly opposed from the very beginning the nonsense steamrollered through by the recently arrived Jeep-brigade that household rubbish "had to be separated". Having said that, once the decision was made to sort the rubbish, someone had to ensure that it was actually being done. Not that anyone had asked Ove to do it, but if men like Ove didn't take the initiative there'd be anarchy. There'd be bags of rubbish all over the place.

He kicked the bins a bit, swore, and fished out a jar from the glass recycling, mumbled something about 'incompetents' as he unscrewed its metal lid. He dropped the jar back into glass recycling, and the metal lid into the metal recycling bin.

Back when Ove was the chairman of the Residents' Association, he'd pushed hard to have surveillance cameras installed so they could monitor the bin room and stop people turfing out unauthorized rubbish. To Ove's great annoyance, his proposal was voted out. The neighbours felt 'slightly uneasy' about it; plus they felt it would be a headache archiving all the video tapes. This, in spite of Ove repeatedly arguing that those with 'honest intentions' had nothing to fear from 'the truth'.

Two years later, after Ove had been deposed as chairman of the Association (a betrayal Ove subsequently referred to as the coup d'état), the question came up again. The new steering group explained snappily to the residents that there was a new-fangled camera available, activated by movement sensors, which sent the footage directly to the internet. With the help of such a camera one could monitor not only the bin room but also the parking area, thereby preventing vandalism and burglaries. Even better, the video material erased itself automatically after twenty-four hours, thus avoiding any 'breaches of the residents' right to privacy'. A unanimous decision was required to go ahead with the installation. Only one member voted against.

And that was because Ove did not trust the Internet. He spelled it with a capital 'I' and accentuated the '-net' even though his wife nagged that you had to put the emphasis on 'inter'. The steering group realised soon enough that the internet would watch Ove throwing out his rubbish over Ove's own dead body. And in the end no cameras were installed. Just as well, Ove reasoned. The daily inspection was more effective anyway. You knew who was doing what and who was keeping things under control. Anyone with half a brain could see the sense of it.

When he'd finished his inspection of the bin room he locked the door, just like he did every morning, and gave it three good tugs to ensure it was closed properly. Then he turned round and noticed a bicycle leaning up against the wall outside the bike shed. Even though there was a huge sign instructing residents not to leave their bicycles there. Right next to it one of the neighbours had taped up an angry, handwritten note: 'This is not a bicycle parking area! Learn to read signs!' Ove muttered something about ineffectual idiots, opened the bike shed, picked up the bicycle, put it neatly inside, then locked the shed and tugged the door handle three times.

He tore down the angry notice from the wall. He would have liked to propose to the steering committee that a proper 'No

Leafleting' sign should be put up on this wall. People nowadays seemed to think they could swan around with angry signs here, there and anywhere they liked. This was a wall, not a bloody noticeboard.

Ove walked down the little footpath between the houses. He stopped outside his own house, stooped over the paving stones and sniffed vehemently along the cracks.

Piss. It smelled of piss.

And with this observation he went into his house, locked his door and drank his coffee.

When he was done he cancelled his telephone line rental and his newspaper subscription. He mended the mixer tap in the small bathroom. Put new screws into the handle of the door from the kitchen to the veranda. Reorganised boxes in the attic. Rearranged his tools in the shed and moved the Saab's winter tyres to a new place. And now here he is.

Life was never meant to turn into this.

It's four o'clock on a Tuesday afternoon in November. He's turned off the radiators, the coffee percolator and all the lights. Oiled the wooden top in the kitchen, in spite of those mules at IKEA saying the wood does not need oiling. In this house all wooden worktops get an oiling every six months, whether it's necessary or not. Whatever some girlie in a yellow sweatshirt from the self-service warehouse has to say about it.

He stands in the living room of the two-storey terraced house with the half-sized attic at the back and stares out of the window. The forty-year-old beard-stubbled poser from the house across the street comes jogging past. Anders is his name, apparently. A recent arrival, probably not lived here for more than four or five years at most. Already he's managed to wheedle his way on to the steering group of the Residents' Association. The snake. He thinks he owns the street. Moved in after his divorce, apparently, paid well over the odds. Typical of these bastards, they come here and push up the property prices for honest people. As if this was some sort of upper-class area. Also drives an Audi, Ove has noticed. He might have known. Self-employed people and other idiots all drive Audis. Ove tucks his hands into his pockets. He directs a slightly imperious kick at the skirting board. This terraced house is slightly too big for Ove and his wife, really, he can just about admit that. But it's all paid for. There's not a penny left in loans. Which is certainly more than one could say for the clotheshorse. It's all loans nowadays; everyone knows the way people carry on. Ove has paid his mortgage. Done his duty. Gone to work. Never taken a day of sick leave. Shouldered his share of the burden. Taken a bit of responsibility. No one does that any more, no one takes responsibility. Now it's just computers and consultants and council bigwigs going to strip clubs and selling apartment leases under the table. Tax havens and share portfolios. No one wants to work. A country full of people who just want to have lunch all day.

'Won't it be nice to slow down a bit?' they said to Ove yesterday at work. While explaining that there was a lack of employment prospects and so they were 'retiring the older generation'. A third of a century in the same workplace, and that's how they refer to Ove. Suddenly he's a bloody 'generation'. Because nowadays people are all thirty-one and wear too-tight trousers and no longer drink normal coffee. And don't want to take responsibility. A shed-load of men with elaborate beards, changing jobs and changing wives and changing their car makes. Just like that. Whenever they feel like it.

Ove glares out of the window. The poser is jogging. Not that Ove is provoked by jogging. Not at all. Ove couldn't give a damn about people jogging. What he can't understand is why they have to make such a big thing of it. With those smug smiles on their faces, as if they were out there curing pulmonary emphysema. Either they walk fast or they run slowly, that's what joggers do. It's a forty-year-old man's way of telling the world that he can't do anything right. Is it really necessary to dress up as a fourteen-year-old Romanian gymnast in order to be able to do it? Or the Olympic tobogganing team? Just because one shuffles aimlessly round the block for three quarters of an hour?

And the poser has a girlfriend. Ten years younger. The Blonde

Weed, Ove calls her. Tottering round the lanes like an inebriated panda on heels as long as box spanners, with clown-paint all over her face and sunglasses so big that one can't tell whether they're a pair of glasses or some kind of helmet. She also has one of those handbag animals, running about off the leash and pissing on the paving stones outside Ove's house. She thinks Ove doesn't notice, but Ove always notices.

His life was never supposed to be like this. Full stop. 'Won't it be nice taking it a bit easy?' they said to him at work yesterday. And now Ove stands here by his oiled kitchen worktop. It's not supposed to be a job for a Tuesday afternoon.

He looks out of the window at the identical house opposite. A family with children has just moved in there. Foreigners, apparently. He doesn't know yet what sort of car they have. Probably something Japanese, God help them. Ove nods to himself, as if he just said something which he very much agrees with. Looks up at the living room ceiling. He's going to put up a hook there today. And he doesn't mean any kind of hook. Every IT consultant trumpeting some data code diagnosis and one of those non-gender-specific cardigans they all have to wear these days would put up a bog-standard hook. But Ove's hook is going to be solid as a rock. He's going to screw it in so hard that when the house is demolished it'll be the last thing standing.

In a few days there'll be some stuck-up estate agent standing here with a tie knot as big as a baby's head, banging on about 'renovation potential' and 'spatial efficiency' and he'll have all sorts of opinions about Ove, the bastard. But he won't be able to say a word about Ove's hook.

On the floor in the living room is one of Ove's 'useful-stuff' boxes. That's how they divide up the house. All the things Ove's wife has bought are 'lovely' or 'homely'. Everything Ove buys is useful. Stuff with a function. He keeps them in two different boxes, one big and one small. This is the small one. Full of screws and nails and spanner sets and that sort of thing. People don't have useful things any more. People just have shit. Twenty pairs of shoes but they never know where the shoe-horn is;

houses filled with microwave ovens and flat-screen televisions, yet they couldn't tell you which plug to use for a concrete wall if you threatened them with a box-cutter.

Ove has a whole drawer in his useful-stuff box just for concrete wall plugs. He stands there looking at them as if they were chess pieces. He doesn't stress about decisions concerning wall plugs for concrete. Things have to take their time. Every plug is a process, every plug has its own use. People have no respect for decent, honest functionality any more, they're happy as long as everything looks neat and dandy on the computer. But Ove does things the way they're supposed to be done.

He came into his office on the Monday and they said they hadn't wanted to tell him on Friday as it would have 'ruined his weekend'.

'It'll be good for you to slow down a bit,' they'd drawled. Slow down? What did they know about waking up on a Tuesday and no longer having a purpose? With their Internets and their espresso coffees, what did they know about taking a bit of responsibility for things?

Ove looks up at the ceiling. Squints. It's important for the hook to be centred, he decides.

And while he stands there immersed in the importance of it, he's mercilessly interrupted by a long, scraping sound. Not at all unlike the type of sound created by a big oaf backing up a Japanese car hooked up to a trailer and scraping it against the exterior wall of Ove's house.

3

A MAN CALLED OVE REVERSES
WITH A TRAILER

Ove whips open the green floral curtains, which for many years Ove's wife has been nagging him to change. He sees a short, black-haired and obviously foreign woman aged about thirty. She stands there gesticulating furiously at a similarly aged oversized blond lanky man squeezed into the driver's seat of a ludicrously small Japanese car with a trailer, now scraping against the exterior wall of Ove's house.

The Lanky One, by means of subtle gestures and signs, seems to want to convey to the woman that this is not quite as easy as it looks. The woman, with gestures that are comparatively unsubtle, seems to want to convey that it might have something to do with the moronic nature of the Lanky One in question.

'Well I'll be bloody . . .' Ove thunders through the window as the wheel of the trailer rolls into his flowerbed. A few seconds later his front door seems to fly open of its own accord, as if afraid that Ove might otherwise walk straight through it.

'What the hell are you doing?' Ove roars at the woman.

'Yes, that's what I'm asking myself!' she roars back.

Ove is momentarily thrown off balance. He glares at her. She glares back.

'You can't drive a car here! Can't you read?'

The little foreign woman steps towards him and only then

does Ove notice that she's either very pregnant or suffering from what Ove would categorise as selective obesity.

'I'm not driving the car, am I?'

Ove stares silently at her for a few seconds. Then he turns to her husband, who's just managed to extract himself from the Japanese car and is approaching them with both hands thrown expressively into the air and an apologetic smile plastered across his face. He's wearing a knitted cardigan and his posture seems to indicate a very obvious calcium deficiency. He must be close to two metres tall. Ove feels an instinctive scepticism towards all people taller than one eighty-five; the blood can't quite make it all the way up to the brain.

'And who might you be?' Ove enquires.

'I'm the driver,' says the Lanky One expansively.

'Oh really? Doesn't look like it!' rages the pregnant woman, who is probably a half-metre shorter than him. She tries to slap his arm with both hands.

'And who's this?' Ove asks, staring at her.

'This is my wife.' He smiles.

'Don't be so sure it'll stay that way,' she snaps, her pregnant belly bouncing up and down.

'It's not as easy as it loo—' the Lanky One tries to say, but he's immediately cut short.

'I said RIGHT! But you carried on reversing to the LEFT! You don't listen! You NEVER listen!'

After that, she immerses herself in half a minute's worth of haranguing in what Ove can only assume to be a display of the complex vocabulary of Arabic cursing.

The husband just nods back at her with an indescribably harmonious smile. The very sort of smile that makes decent folk want to slap Buddhist monks in the face, Ove thinks to himself.

'Oh come on. I'm sorry,' he says cheerfully, hauling out a tin of chewing tobacco from his pocket and packing in a ball the size of a walnut. 'It was only a little accident, we'll sort it out!'

Ove looks at the Lanky One as if the Lanky One has just squatted over the bonnet of Ove's car and left a turd on it.

'Sort it out? You're in my flowerbed!'

The Lanky One looks ponderously at the trailer wheels.

'That's hardly a flowerbed, is it?' He smiles, undaunted, and adjusts his tobacco with the tip of his tongue. 'Naah, come on, that's just soil,' he persists, as if Ove is having a joke with him.

Ove's forehead compresses itself into one large, threatening wrinkle.

'It. Is. A. Flowerbed.'

The Lanky One scratches his head, as if he's got some tobacco caught in his tangled fringe.

'But you're not growing anything in it . . .'

'Never you bloody mind what I do with my own flowerbed!'

The Lanky One nods quickly, clearly keen to avoid further provocation of this unknown man. He turns to his wife as if he's expecting her to come to his aid. She doesn't look at all likely to do so. The Lanky One looks at Ove again.

'Pregnant, you know. Hormones and all that . . .' he tries, with a grin.

The Pregnant One does not grin. Nor does Ove. She crosses her arms. Ove tucks his hands into his belt. The Lanky One clearly doesn't know what to do with his massive hands, so he swings them back and forth across his body, slightly shamefully, as if they're made of cloth, fluttering in the breeze.

'I'll move it and have another go,' he finally says and smiles disarmingly at Ove again.

Ove does not reciprocate.

'Motor vehicles are not allowed in the area. There's a sign.'

The Lanky One steps back and nods eagerly. Jogs back and once again contorts his body into the under-dimensioned Japanese car. 'Christ,' Ove and the pregnant woman mutter wearily in unison. Which actually makes Ove dislike her slightly less.

The Lanky One pulls forward a few metres; Ove can see very clearly that he does not straighten up the trailer properly. Then he starts reversing again. Right into Ove's letter box, buckling the green sheet metal.

Ove storms forward and throws the car door open.

The Lanky One starts flapping his arms again.

'My fault, my fault! Sorry about that, didn't see the letter box in the back mirror, you know. It's difficult this trailer thing, just can't figure out which way to turn the wheel . . .'

Ove thumps his fist on the roof of the car so hard that the Lanky One jumps and bangs his head on the doorframe. 'Out of the car!'

'What?'

'Get out of the car, I said!'

The Lanky One gives Ove a slightly startled glance, but he doesn't quite seem to have the nerve to reply. Instead he gets out of his car and stands beside it like a schoolboy in the dunce's corner. Ove points down the footpath between the terraced houses, towards the bicycle shed and the parking area.

'Go and stand where you're not in the way.'

The Lanky One nods, slightly puzzled.

'Holy Christ. A lower-arm amputee with cataracts could have reversed this trailer more accurately than you,' Ove mutters as he gets into the car.

How can anyone be incapable of reversing with a trailer, he asks himself? How? How difficult is it to establish the basics of right and left and then do the opposite? How do these people make their way through life at all?

Of course it's an automatic as well, Ove notes. Might have known. These morons would rather not have to drive their cars at all, let alone reverse into a parking space by themselves. He puts it into Drive and inches forward. Should one really have a driving licence if one can't drive a real car rather than some Japanese robot vehicle, he wonders? Ove doubts whether someone who can't park a car properly should even be allowed to vote.

When he's pulled forward and straightened up the trailer – as civilized people do before reversing with a trailer – he puts it into reverse. Immediately it starts making a shrieking noise. Ove looks round angrily.

'What the bloody hell are you . . . why are you making that noise?' he hisses at the instrument panel and gives the steering wheel a whack.

'Stop it, I said!' he roars at a particularly insistent flashing red light.

At the same time the Lanky One appears at the side of the car and carefully taps the window. Ove rolls the window down and gives him an irritated look.

'It's just the reverse radar making that noise,' the Lanky One says with a nod.

'Don't you think I know that?' Ove seethes.

'It's a bit unusual, this car. I was thinking I could show you the controls if you like . . .'

'I'm not an idiot, you know!' Ove snorts.

The Lanky One nods eagerly.

'No, no, of course not.'

Ove glares at the instrument panel.

'What's it doing now?'

The Lanky One nods enthusiastically.

'It's measuring how much power's left in the battery. You know, before it switches from the electric motor to the petrol-driven motor. Because it's a hybrid . . .'

Ove doesn't answer. He just slowly rolls up the window, leaving the Lanky One outside with his mouth half-open. Ove checks the left wing mirror. Then the right wing mirror. He reverses while the Japanese car shrieks in terror, manoeuvres the trailer perfectly between his own house and his incompetent new neighbour's, gets out, and tosses the cretin his keys.

'Reverse radar and parking sensors and cameras and crap like that. A man who needs all that to reverse with a trailer shouldn't be bloody doing it in the first place.'

The Lanky One nods cheerfully at him.

'Thanks for the help,' he calls out, as if Ove hadn't just spent the last ten minutes insulting him.

'You shouldn't even be allowed to rewind a cassette,' grumbles Ove. The pregnant woman just stands there with her arms

17

crossed, but she doesn't look quite as angry any more. She thanks him with a wry smile, as if she's trying not to laugh. She has the biggest brown eyes Ove has ever seen.

'The Residents' Association does not permit any driving in this area, and you have to bloody go along with it,' Ove huffs, before stomping back to his house.

He stops halfway up the paved path between the house and his shed. He wrinkles his nose in the way men of his age do, the wrinkle travelling across his entire upper body. Then he sinks down on his knees, puts his face right up close to the paving stones, which he neatly and without exception removes and re-lays every other year, whether necessary or not. He sniffs again. Nods to himself. Stands up.

His new neighbours are still watching him.

'Piss! There's piss all over the place here!' Ove says gruffly.

He gesticulates at the paving stones.

'O . . . kay,' says the black-haired woman.

'No! Nowhere is bloody okay round here!'

And with that, he goes into his house and closes the door.

He sinks on to the stool in the hall and stays there for a long time. Bloody woman. Why do she and her family have to come here if they can't even read a sign right in front of their eyes? You're not allowed to drive cars inside the block. Everyone knows that.

Ove goes to hang up his coat on the hook, among a sea of his wife's overcoats. Mutters 'idiots' at the closed window just to be on the safe side. Then goes into his living room and stares up at his ceiling.

He doesn't know how long he stands there. He loses himself in his own thoughts. Floats away, as if in a mist. He's never been the sort of man who does that, has never been a daydreamer, but lately it's as if something's twisted up in his head. He's having increasing difficulty concentrating on things. He doesn't like it at all.

When the doorbell goes it's like he's waking up from a warm slumber. He rubs his eyes hard, looks around as if worried that someone may have seen him.

The doorbell rings again. Ove turns round and stares at the bell as if it should be ashamed of itself. He takes a few steps into the hall, noting that his body is as stiff as set plaster. He can't tell if the creaking is coming from the floorboards or himself.

'And what is it now?' he asks the door before he's even opened it, as if it had the answer.

'What is it now?' he repeats as he throws the door open so hard that a three-year-old girl is flung backwards by the draft and ends up very unexpectedly on her bottom.

Beside her stands a seven-year-old girl looking absolutely terrified. Their hair is pitch black. And they have the biggest brown eyes Ove has ever seen.

'Yes?' says Ove.

The older girl looks guarded. She hands him a plastic container. Ove reluctantly accepts it. It's warm.

'Rice!' the three-year-old girl announces happily, briskly getting to her feet.

'With saffron. And chicken,' nods the seven-year-old, far more wary of him.

Ove evaluates them suspiciously.

'Are you selling it?'

The seven-year-old looks offended.

'We LIVE HERE, you know!'

Ove is silent for a moment. Then he nods, as if he might possibly be able to accept this premise as an explanation.

'Okay.'

The younger one also nods with satisfaction and flaps her slightly-too-long sleeves.

'Mum said you were 'ungry!'

Ove looks in utter perplexity at the little flapping speech defect.

'What?'

'Mum said you *looked* hungry. So we have to give you dinner,' the seven-year-old girl clarifies with some irritation. 'Come on, Nasanin,' she adds, taking her sister by the hand and walking away after directing a resentful stare at Ove.

19

Ove keeps an eye on them as they skulk off. He sees the pregnant woman standing in her doorway, smiling at him before the girls run into her house. The three-year-old turns round and waves cheerfully at him. Her mother also waves. Ove closes the door.

He stands in the hall again. Stares at the warm container of chicken with rice and saffron as one might look at a box of nitroglycerine. Then he goes into the kitchen and puts it in the fridge. Not that he's habitually inclined to go round eating any old food provided by unknown, foreign kids on his doorstep. But in Ove's house one does not throw away food. As a point of principle.

He goes into the living room. Shoves his hands in his pockets. Looks up at the ceiling. Stands there a good while and thinks about what sort of concrete-wall plug would be most suitable for the job. He stands there squinting until his eyes start hurting. He looks down, slightly confused, at his dented wristwatch. Then he looks out of the window again and realises that dusk has fallen. He shakes his head in resignation.

You can't start drilling after dark, everyone knows that. He'd have to turn on all the lights and no one could say when they'd be turned off again. And he's not giving the electricity company the pleasure, his meter notching up another couple of thousand crowns. They can forget about that.

Ove packs up his useful-stuff box and takes it to the big upstairs hall. Fetches the key to the attic from its place behind the radiator in the little hall. Goes back and reaches up and opens the trapdoor to the attic. Folds down the ladder. Climbs up into the attic and puts the useful-stuff box in its place behind the kitchen chairs that his wife made him put up here because they creaked too much. They didn't creak at all. Ove knows very well it was just an excuse, because his wife wanted to get some new ones. As if that was all life was about. Buying kitchen chairs and eating in restaurants and carrying on.

He goes down the stairs again. Puts back the attic key in its place behind the radiator in the little hall. 'Taking it a bit easy,' they said to him. A lot of thirty-one-year-old show-offs working with computers and refusing to drink normal coffee. An entire society where no one knows how to reverse with a trailer. Then they come telling him *he's* not needed any more. Is that reasonable?

Ove goes down to the living room and turns on the TV. He doesn't watch the programmes, but it's not like he can just spend his evenings sitting there by himself like a moron, staring at the walls. He gets out the foreign food from the fridge and eats it with a fork, straight out of the plastic container.

It's Tuesday night and he's cancelled his newspaper subscription, switched off the radiators, and turned out all the lights.

And tomorrow he's putting up that hook.

4

A MAN CALLED OVE DOES NOT PAY
A THREE-CROWN SURCHARGE

Ove gives her the plants. Two of them. Of course there weren't supposed to be two of them. But somewhere along the line there has to be a limit. It was a question of principle, Ove explains to her. That's why he got two flowers in the end.

'Things don't work when you're not at home,' he mutters, and kicks a bit at the frozen ground.

His wife doesn't answer.

'There'll be snow tonight,' says Ove.

They said on the news there wouldn't be snow, but, as Ove often points out, whatever they predict is bound not to happen. He tells her this; she doesn't answer. He puts his hands in his pockets and gives her a brief nod.

'It's not natural rattling around the house on my own all day when you're not here. It's no way to live. That's all I have to say.'

She doesn't reply to that either.

He nods and kicks the ground again. He can't understand people who long to retire. How can anyone spend their whole life longing for the day when they become superfluous? Wandering about, a burden on society, what sort of man would ever wish for that? Staying at home, waiting to die. Or even worse: waiting for them to come and fetch you and put you in a home. Being dependent on other people to get to the toilet. Ove can't think

22

of anything worse. His wife often teases him, says he's the only man she knows who'd rather be laid out in a coffin than travel in a mobility service van. And she may have a point there.

Ove had risen at quarter to six. Made coffee for his wife and himself, went round checking the radiators to make sure she hadn't sneakily turned them up. They were all unchanged from yesterday, but he turned them down a little more just to be on the safe side. Then he took his jacket from the hook in the hall, the only hook of all six that wasn't burgeoning with her clothes, and set off for his inspection. It had started getting cold, he noticed. Almost time to change his navy autumn jacket for his navy winter jacket.

He always knows when it's about to snow because his wife starts nagging about turning up the heat in the bedroom. Lunacy, Ove reaffirms every year. Why should the power company direct-ors feather their nests because of a bit of seasonality? Turning up the heat five degrees costs thousands of crowns per year. He knows because he's calculated it himself. So every winter he drags down an old diesel generator from the attic that he swopped at a jumble sale for a gramophone. He's connected this to a fan heater he bought at a sale for thirty-nine crowns. Once the generator has charged up the fan heater, it runs for thirty minutes on the little battery Ove has hooked it up to, and his wife keeps it on her side of the bed. She can run it a couple of times before they go to bed, but only a couple – no need to be lavish about it ('Diesel isn't free, you know'). And Ove's wife does what she always does: nods and agrees that Ove is probably right. Then she goes round all winter sneakily turning up the radiators. Every year the same bloody thing.

Ove kicks the ground again. He's considering telling her about the cat. If you can even call that mangy, half-bald creature a cat. It was sitting there again when he came back from his inspec-tion, practically right outside their front door. He pointed at it and shouted so loudly that his voice echoed between the houses. The cat just sat there, looking at Ove. Then it stood up elab-orately, as if making a point of demonstrating that it wasn't leaving because of Ove, but rather because there were better things to do, and disappeared round the corner.

Ove decides not to mention the cat to her. He assumes she'll only be disgruntled with him for driving it away. If she was in charge the whole house would be full of tramps, whether of the furred variety or not.

He's wearing his navy suit and has done up the top button of the white shirt. She tells him to leave the top button undone if he's not wearing a tie; he protests that he's not some urchin who's renting out deckchairs, before defiantly buttoning it up. He's got his dented old wristwatch on, the one that his dad inherited from his father when he was nineteen, the one that was passed on to Ove after his sixteenth birthday, a few days after his father died.

Ove's wife likes that suit. She always says he looks so hand-some in it. Like any sensible person, Ove is obviously of the opinion that only posers wear their best suits on weekdays. But this morning he decided to make an exception. He even put on his black going-out shoes and polished them with a responsible amount of boot shine.

As he took his autumn jacket from the hook in the hall before he went out, he threw a thoughtful eye on his wife's collection of coats. He wondered how such a small human being could have so many winter coats. 'You almost expect if you stepped through this lot you'd find yourself in Narnia,' a friend of Ove's wife had once joked. Ove didn't have a clue what she was talking about, but he did agree there were a hell of a lot of coats.

He walked out of the house before anyone in the street had even woken up. Strolled up to the parking area. Opened his garage with a key. He had a remote control for the door, but had never understood the point of it. An honest person could just as well open the door manually. He unlocked the Saab, also with a key: the system had always worked perfectly well, there was no reason to change it. He sat in the driver's seat and twisted the tuning dial half forward and then half back before adjusting each of the mirrors, as he did every time he got into the Saab.

As if someone routinely broke into the Saab and mischievously changed Ove's mirrors and radio channels.

As he drove across the parking area he passed that pregnant foreign woman from next door. She was holding her three-year-old by the hand. The big blond Lanky One was walking beside her. All three of them caught sight of Ove and waved cheerfully. Ove didn't wave back. At first he was going to stop and give her a dressing down about letting children run about in the parking area as if it was some municipal playground. But he decided he didn't have the time.

He drove along, passing row after row of houses identical to his own. When they first moved in here there were only six houses; now there were hundreds of them. There used to be a forest here but now there were only houses. Everything paid for with loans, of course. That was how you did it nowadays. Shopping on credit and driving electric cars and hiring tradesmen to change a light bulb. Laying click-on floors and fitting electric fireplaces and carrying on. A society that apparently could not see the difference between the correct plug for a concrete wall and a smack in the face. Clearly this was how it was meant to be.

It took him exactly fourteen minutes to drive to the florist's in the shopping centre. Ove kept exactly to every speed limit, even on that 50kph road where the recently arrived idiots in suits came tanking along at 90. Among their own houses they put up speed bumps and damnable numbers of signs about 'Children Playing', but when driving past other people's houses it was apparently less important. Ove had repeated this to his wife every time they drove past over the last ten years.

And it's getting worse and worse, he liked to add, just in case by some miracle she hadn't heard him the first time.

Today he hadn't even gone two kilometres before a black Mercedes positioned itself a forearm's length behind his Saab. Ove signalled with his brake lights three times. The Mercedes flashed its full beam at him in an agitated manner. Ove snorted at his back mirror. As if it was his duty to fling himself out of the way as soon as these morons decided speed restrictions didn't apply to them. Honestly. Ove didn't move. The Mercedes gave him a burst of its full beam again. Ove slowed down. The Mercedes sounded its horn. Ove lowered his speed to 20. When they reached the top of a hill the Mercedes overtook him with a roar. The driver, a man in his forties in a tie and white cables trailing from his ears, held up his finger through the window at Ove. Ove responded to the gesture in the manner of all men of a certain age who've been properly raised: by slowly tapping the tip of his finger against the side of his head. The man in the Mercedes shouted until his saliva spattered against the inside of his windshield, then put his foot down and disappeared.

Two minutes later Ove came to a red light. The Mercedes was at the back of the queue. Ove flashed his lights at it. He saw the driver craning his neck round. The white earpieces dropped out and fell against the dashboard. Ove nodded with satisfaction.

The light turned green. The queue didn't move. Ove sounded his horn. Nothing happened. Ove shook his head. Must be a woman driver. Or roadworks. Or an Audi. When thirty seconds had passed without anything happening, Ove put the car into neutral, opened the door and stepped out of the Saab with the engine still running. Stood in the road and peered ahead with his hands on his hips, filled with a kind of Herculean irritation: the way Superman might have stood if he'd got stuck in a traffic jam.

The man in the Mercedes gave a blast on his horn. Idiot, thought Ove. In the same moment the traffic started moving. The cars in front of Ove moved off. The car behind him, a Volkswagen, beeped at him. The driver waved impatiently at Ove. Ove glared back. He got back into the Saab and leisurely closed the door. 'Amazing what a rush we're in,' he scoffed into the back mirror and drove on.

At the next red light he ended up behind the Mercedes again. Another queue. Ove checked his watch and took a left turn down a smaller, quiet road. This entailed a longer route to the shopping centre, but there were fewer traffic lights. Not that Ove was mean. But as anyone who knows anything knows, cars use less fuel if they keep moving rather than stopping all the time. And, as Ove's wife often says: 'If there's one thing you could write in Ove's obituary, it's "At least he was economical with petrol."'

As Ove approached the shopping centre from his little side road, he could just make out that there were only two parking spaces left. What all these people were doing at the shopping centre on a normal weekday was beyond his comprehension. Obviously people no longer had jobs to go to.

Ove's wife usually starts sighing as soon as they even get close to a car park like this. Ove wants to park close to the entrance. 'As if there's a competition about who can find the best parking spot,' she always says as he completes circuit after circuit and swears at all the imbeciles getting in his way in their foreign cars. Sometimes they end up doing six or seven loops before they find a good spot, and if Ove in the end has to concede defeat and content himself with a slot twenty metres further away, he's in a bad mood for the rest of the day. His wife has never understood it. There again, she never was very good at grasping questions of principle.

Ove figured he would go round slowly a couple of times just to check the lay of the land, but then suddenly caught sight of the Mercedes thundering along the main road towards the shopping centre. So this was where he'd been heading, that suit with the plastic leads in his ears. Ove didn't hesitate for a second. He put his foot down and barged his way out of the junction into the road. The Mercedes slammed on its brakes, firmly pressing down on the horn and following close behind. The race was on.

The signs at the car park entrance led the traffic to the right, but when they got there the Mercedes must also have seen the two empty slots, as he tried to slip past Ove on the left. Ove only just managed to manoeuvre himself in front of him to block his path. The two men started hunting each other across the tarmac.

In his back mirror, Ove saw a little Toyota turn off the road behind them, follow the road signs and enter the parking area in a wide loop from the right. Ove's eyes followed it while he hurtled forward in the opposite direction, with the Mercedes on his tail. Of course, he could have taken one of the free slots, the one closest to the entrance, and then have the kindness of letting the Mercedes take the other. But what sort of victory would that have been?

Instead Ove made an emergency stop in front of the first slot and stayed where he was. The Mercedes started wildly sounding its horn. Ove didn't flinch. The little Toyota approached from the far right. The Mercedes also caught sight of it and, too late, understood Ove's devilish plan. Its horn wailed furiously as it tried to push past the Saab, but it never stood a chance: Ove had already waved the Toyota into one of the free slots. Only once it was safely in did Ove nonchalantly swing into the other space.

The side window of the Mercedes was so covered in saliva when it drove past that Ove couldn't even see the driver. He stepped out of the Saab triumphantly, like a gladiator who had just slain his opponent. Then he looked at the Toyota.

'Oh damn,' he mumbled, irritated.

The car door was thrown open.

'Hi there!' the Lanky One sang merrily as he untangled himself from the driver's seat. 'Hello hello!' said his wife from the other side of the Toyota, lifting out their three-year-old.

Ove watched repentantly as the Mercedes disappeared in the distance.

'Thanks for the parking space! Bloody marvellous!' The Lanky One was beaming.

Ove didn't reply.

'Wass ya name?' the three-year-old burst out.

'Ove,' said Ove.

'My name's Nasanin!' she said with delight.

Ove nodded at her.

'And I'm Pat . . .' the Lanky One started saying.

But Ove had already turned round and left.

'Thanks for the space,' the Pregnant Foreign Woman called out after him.

Ove could hear laughter in her voice. He didn't like it. He just muttered a quick 'Fine, fine,' without turning round and marched through the revolving doors into the shopping centre. He turned left down the first turning and looked round several times, as if afraid that the family from next door would follow him. But they turned right and disappeared.

Ove stopped suspiciously outside the supermarket and eyed the poster advertising the week's special offers. Not that Ove was intending to buy any ham in this particular shop. But it was always worth keeping an eye on the prices. If there's one thing in this world that Ove dislikes, it's when someone tries to trick him. Ove's wife sometimes jokes that the three worst words Ove knows in this life are 'Batteries not included'. People usually laugh when she says that. But Ove does not usually laugh.

He moved on from the supermarket and stepped into the florist's. And there it didn't take long for a 'rumble' to start up, as Ove's wife would have described it. Or a 'discussion' as Ove always insisted on calling it. Ove put down a coupon on the counter on which it said: '2 plants for 50 crowns'. Given that Ove only wanted one plant, he explained to the shop assistant, with all rhyme and reason on his side, he should be able to buy it for 25 crowns. Because that was half of 50. However, the assistant, a brain-dead SMS-tapping nineteen-year-old, would not go along with it. She maintained that a single flower cost 39 crowns and '2 for 50' only applied if one bought two. The manager had to be summoned. It took Ove fifteen minutes to make him see sense and agree that Ove was right.

Or, to be honest about it, the manager mumbled something that sounded a little like 'bloody old sod' into his hand and hammered 25 crowns so hard into the till that anyone would have thought it was the machine's fault. It made no difference to Ove. He knew these retailers were always trying to screw you out of money, and no one screwed Ove and got away with it. Ove put his debit card on the counter. The manager allowed himself the slightest of smiles, then nodded dismissively and pointed at a sign that read: 'Card purchases of less than 50 crowns carry a surcharge of 3 crowns.'

Now Ove is standing in front of his wife with two plants. Because it was a question of principle.

'There was no *way* I was going to pay three crowns,' rails Ove, his eyes looking down into the gravel.

Ove's wife often quarrels with Ove because he's always arguing about everything.

But Ove isn't bloody arguing. He just thinks right is right. Is that such an unreasonable attitude to life?

He raises his eyes and looks at her.

'I suppose you're annoyed I didn't come yesterday like I promised,' he mumbles.

She doesn't say anything.

'The whole street is turning into a madhouse,' he says defensively. 'Complete chaos. You even have to go out and reverse their trailers for them nowadays. And you can't even put up a hook in peace,' he continues as if she's disagreeing.

He clears his throat.

'Obviously I couldn't put the hook up when it was dark outside. If you do that there's no telling when the lights go off. More likely they'll stay on and consume electricity. Out of the question.'

She doesn't answer. He kicks the frozen ground. Sort of looking for words. Clears his throat briefly once again.

'Nothing works when you're not at home.'

She doesn't answer. Ove fingers the plants.

'I'm tired of it, just rattling round the house all day while you're away.'

She doesn't answer that either. He nods. Holds up the plants so she can see them.

'They're pink. The ones you like. They said in the shop they're perennials but that's not what they're bloody called. Apparently they die in this kind of cold, they also said that in the shop but only so they could sell me a load of other shit.'

He looks as if he's waiting for her approval.

'The new neighbours put saffron in their rice and carry-on like that; they're foreigners,' he says in a low voice.

A new silence.

He stands there, slowly twisting the wedding ring on his finger. As if looking for something else to say. He still finds it painfully difficult being the one to take charge of a conversation. That was always something she took care of. He usually just answered. This is a new situation for them both. Finally Ove squats, digs up the plant he brought last week and carefully puts it in a plastic bag. He turns the frozen soil carefully before putting in the new plants.

'They've bumped up the electricity prices again,' he informs her as he gets to his feet.

He looks at her for a long time. Finally he puts his hand carefully on the big boulder and caresses it tenderly from side to side, as if touching her cheek.

'I miss you,' he whispers.

It's been six months since she died. But Ove still inspects the whole house twice a day to feel the radiators and check that she hasn't sneakily turned up the heating.

5

A MAN CALLED OVE

Ove knew very well that her friends couldn't understand why she married him. He couldn't really blame them.

People said he was bitter. Maybe they were right. He'd never reflected much on it. People also called him 'anti-social'. Ove assumed this meant he wasn't overly keen on people. And in this instance he could totally agree with them. More often than not people were out of their minds.

Ove wasn't one to engage in small talk. He had come to realise that, these days at least, this was a serious character flaw. Now one had to be able to blabber on about anything with any old sod who happened to stray within an arm's length of you purely because it was 'nice'. Ove didn't know how to do it. Perhaps it was the way he'd been raised. Maybe men of his generation had never been sufficiently prepared for a world where everyone spoke about doing things even though it no longer seemed worth doing them. Nowadays people stood outside their newly refurbished houses and boasted as if they'd built them with their own bare hands, even though they hadn't so much as lifted a screwdriver. And they weren't even trying to pretend that it was any other way. They boasted about it! Apparently there was no longer any value in being able to lay your own floorboards or refurbish a room with rising damp or change the winter tyres. And if you could just go and buy everything, what was the value of it? What was the value of a man?

Her friends couldn't see why she woke up every morning and voluntarily decided to share the whole day with him. He couldn't either. He built her a bookshelf and she filled it with books by people who wrote page after page about their feelings. Ove understood things he could see and touch. Cement and concrete. Glass and steel. Tools. Things one could figure out. He understood right angles and clear instruction manuals. Assembly models and drawings. Things one could draw on paper.

He was a man of black and white.

And she was colour. All the colour he had.

The only thing he had ever loved until he saw her was numbers. He had no other particular memory of his youth. He was not bullied and he wasn't a bully, not good at sport and not bad either. He was never at the heart of things and never on the outside. He was the sort of person who was just there. Nor did he remember so very much about his growing up; he had never been the sort of man who went around remembering things unless there was a need for it. He remembered that he was quite happy and that for a few years afterwards he wasn't – that was about it.

And he remembered the sums. The numbers, filling his head. Remembered how he longed for their mathematics lessons at school. Maybe for the others they were a sufferance, but not for him. He didn't know why, and didn't speculate about it either. He'd never understood the need to go round stewing on why things turned out the way they did. You are what you are and you do what you do, and that was good enough for Ove.

He was seven years old when his mum called it a day one early August morning. She worked at a chemicals plant. In those days people didn't know much about air safety, Ove realised later. She smoked as well, all the time. That's Ove's clearest memory of her, how she sat in the kitchen window of the little house where they lived outside town, with that billowing cloud around her, watching the sky every Saturday morning. And how sometimes she sang in her hoarse voice and Ove used to sit under the window with his mathematics book in his lap, and he remembered that he liked listening to her. He remembers that. Of course her voice was hoarse and the odd note was more discordant than one would have liked, but he remembers that he liked it anyway.

Ove's father worked for the railways. The palms of his hands looked like someone had carved into leather with knives, and the wrinkles in his face were so deep that when he exerted himself the sweat was channelled through them down to his chest. His hair was thin and his body slender, but the muscles on his arms were so sharp that they seemed cut out of rock. Once when Ove was very young he was allowed to go with his parents to a big party with his dad's mates from the rail company. After his father had put away a couple of bottles of pilsner some of the other guests challenged him to an arm wrestling competition. Ove had never seen the like of these giants straddling the bench opposite him. Some of them looked like they weighed two hundred kilos. His father wore down every one of them. When they went home that night, he put his arm round Ove's shoulders and said: 'Ove, only a swine thinks size and strength are the same thing. Remember that.' And Ove never forgot it.

His father never raised his fists. Not to Ove or anyone else. Ove had classmates who came to school with black eyes or bruises from a belt buckle after a thrashing. But never Ove. 'We don't fight in this family,' his father used to state. 'Not with each other or anyone else.'

He was well liked down at the railway, quiet but kind. There were some who said he was 'too kind'. Ove remembers how as a child he could never understand how this could be something bad.

Then Mum died. And Dad grew even quieter. As if she took away with her the few words he'd possessed.

So Ove and his father never talked excessively, but they liked each other's company. They sat in silence on either side of the kitchen table, and had ways of keeping busy. Every other day they put out food for a family of birds living in a rotting tree at the back of the house. It was important, Ove understood, that it had to be every other day. He didn't know why, but it just didn't matter.

In the evenings they had sausages and potatoes. Then they played cards. They never had much, but they always had enough.

His father's only remaining words were about engines (apparently his mother was content to leave these behind). He could spend any amount of time talking about them. 'Engines give you what you deserve,' he used to explain. 'If you treat them with respect they'll give you freedom, if you behave like an arse they'll take it from you.'

For a long time he did not own a car of his own, but in the 1940s and 50s, when the bosses and directors at the railway started buying their own vehicles, a rumour soon spread in the office that the quiet man working on the track was a person well worth knowing. Ove's father had never finished school, and didn't understand much about the sums in Ove's school books. But he understood engines.

When the daughter of the director was getting married and the wedding car broke down rather than ceremoniously transporting the bride to the church, Ove's father was sent for. He came cycling with a toolbox on his shoulder so heavy that it took two men to lift it when he got off the bicycle. Whatever the problem was when he arrived, it was no longer a problem when he cycled back. The director's wife invited him to the wedding reception, but he told her that it was probably not the done thing to sit with elegant people when one was the sort of man whose forearms were so stained with oil that it seemed a natural part of his pigmentation. But he'd gladly accept a bag of bread and meat for the lad at home, he said. Ove had just turned eight. When his father laid out the supper that evening, Ove felt like he was at a royal banquet.

A few months later the director sent for Ove's father again. In the parking area outside the office stood an extremely old and worse-for-wear Saab 92. It was the first motorcar Saab had ever manufactured, although it had not been in production since the significantly upgraded Saab 93 had come onto the market.

Ove's dad recognised it very well. Front-wheel-driven and a side-mounted engine that sounded like a coffee percolator. It had been in an accident, the director explained, sticking his thumbs into his braces under his jacket. The bottle-green body was badly dented and the condition of what lay under the bonnet was certainly not pretty. But he produced a little screwdriver from the pocket of his dirty overalls and after lengthily inspecting the car, he gave the verdict that with a bit of time and care and the proper tools he'd be able to put it back into working order.

'Whose is it?' he wondered aloud as he straightened up and wiped the oil from his fingers with a rag.

'It belonged to a relative of mine,' said the director, digging out a key from his suit trousers and pressing it into his palm. 'And now it's yours.'

With a pat on his shoulder, the director returned to the office. Ove's father stayed where he was in the courtyard, trying to catch his breath. That evening he had to explain everything over and over again to his goggle-eyed son and show all there was to know about this magical monster now parked in their garden. He sat in the driver's seat half the night, with the boy on his lap, explaining how all the mechanical parts were connected. He could account for every screw, every little tube. Ove had never seen a man as proud as his father was that night. He was eight years old and decided that night he would never drive any car but a Saab.

Whenever he had a Saturday off, Ove's father brought him out into the yard, opened the bonnet and taught him all the names of the various parts and what they did. On Sundays they went to church. Not because either of them had any excessive zeal for God, but because Ove's mum had always been insistent about it. They sat at the back, each of them staring at a patch on the floor until it was over. And, in all honesty, they spent more time missing Ove's mum than thinking about God. It was her time, so to speak, even though she was no longer there. Afterwards they'd take a long drive in the countryside with the Saab. It was Ove's favourite part of the week.

That year, to stop him rattling around the house on his own, he also started going with his father to work at the railway yard after school. It was filthy work and badly paid, but, as his father used to mutter, 'It's an honest job and that's worth something.'

Ove liked all the men at the railway yard except Tom. Tom was a tall, noisy man with fists as big as flatbed trucks and eyes that always seemed to be looking for some defenceless animal to kick around.

When Ove was nine years old, his dad sent him to help Tom clean out a broken-down railway car. With sudden jubilation, Tom snatched up a briefcase left by some harassed passenger. It had fallen from the luggage rack and distributed its contents over the floor. Before long Tom was darting about on all fours, scrabbling together everything he could see.

'Finders keepers,' he spat at Ove. Something in his eyes made Ove feel as if there were insects crawling under his skin.

As Ove turned to go, he stumbled over a wallet. It was made of such soft leather that it felt like cotton against his rough fingertips. And it didn't have a rubber band round it like Dad's old wallet, to keep it from falling to bits. It had a little silver button that made a click when you opened it. There was more than six thousand crowns inside. A fortune to anyone in those days.

Tom caught sight of it and tried to tear it out of Ove's hands. Overwhelmed by an instinctive defiance, the boy resisted. He saw how shocked Tom was at this, and out of the corner of his eye he had time to see the huge man clenching his fist. Ove knew he'd never be able to get away, so he closed his eyes, held on to the wallet as hard as he could and waited for the blow.

But the next thing either of them knew, Ove's father was standing between them. Tom's furious, hateful eyes met his for an instant, but Ove's father stood where he stood. And at last Tom lowered his fist and took a watchful step back.

'Finders keepers, it's always been like that,' he growled, pointing at the wallet.

'That's up to the person who finds it,' said Ove's father without looking away.

Tom's eyes had turned black. But he retreated another step, still clutching the briefcase in his hands. Tom had worked many years at the railway, but Ove had never heard any of his father's colleagues say one good word about Tom. He was dishonest and malicious, that was what they said after a couple of bottles of pilsner at their parties. But he'd never heard it from his dad. 'Four children and a sick wife,' was all he used to say to his workmates, looking each of them in the eye. 'Better men than Tom could have ended up worse for it.' And then his workmates usually changed the subject.

His father pointed to the wallet in Ove's hand.

'You decide,' he said.

Ove determinedly fixed his gaze into the ground, feeling Tom's eyes burning holes into the top of his head. Then he said in a low but unwavering voice that the lost property office would seem to be the best place to leave it. His father nodded without a word, and then took Ove's hand as they walked back for almost half an hour along the track without a word passing between them. Ove heard Tom shouting behind them, his voice filled with cold fury. Ove never forgot it.

The woman at the desk of the lost property office could hardly believe her eyes when they put the wallet on the counter.

'And it was just lying there on the floor? You didn't find a bag or anything?' she asked. Ove gave his dad a searching look, but he just stood there in silence, so Ove did the same.

The woman behind the counter seemed satisfied enough with the answer.

'Not many people have ever handed in this much money,' she said, smiling at Ove.

'Many people don't have any decency either,' said his father in a clipped voice and took Ove's hand. They turned round and went back to work.

A few hundred metres down the track Ove cleared his throat, summoned some courage and asked why his father had not mentioned the briefcase that Tom had found.

'We're not the sort of people who tell tales about what others do,' he answered.

Ove nodded. They walked in silence.

'I thought about keeping the money,' Ove whispered at long last, and took his father's hand in a firmer grip, as if he was afraid of letting go.

'I know,' said his father and squeezed his hand a little harder.

'But I knew you would hand it in, and I knew a person like Tom wouldn't,' said Ove.

His father nodded. And not another word was said about it.

Had Ove been the sort of man who contemplated how and when one became the sort of man one was, he might have said this was the day he learned that right has to be right. But he wasn't one to dwell on things like that. He contented himself with remembering that on this day he'd decided to be as little unlike his father as possible.

He had only just turned sixteen when his father died. A hurtling carriage on the track. Ove was left with not much more than a Saab, a ramshackle house a few miles out of town and a dented old wristwatch. He was never able to properly explain what happened to him that day. But he stopped being happy. He wasn't happy for several years after that.

At the funeral, the vicar wanted to talk to him about foster homes, but he found out soon enough that Ove had not been brought up to accept charity. At the same time, Ove made it clear to the vicar that there was no need to reserve a place for him in the pews at Sunday service for the foreseeable future. Not because Ove did not believe in God, he explained to the vicar, but because in his view this God seemed to be a bit of a bloody swine.

The next day he went down to the wages office at the railway and handed back the wages for the rest of the month. The ladies at the office didn't understand, so Ove had to impatiently explain that his father had died on the sixteenth, and obviously wouldn't be able to come in and work for the remaining fourteen days of that month. And because he got his wages in advance, Ove had come to pay back the balance.

Hesitantly the ladies asked him to sit down and wait. After fifteen minutes or so the director came out and looked at the curious sixteen-year-old sitting on a wooden chair in the corridor with his dead father's wage packet in his hand. The director knew very well who this boy was. And after he'd convinced himself that there was no way of persuading him to keep the money he felt he had no right to, the director saw no alternative but to propose to Ove that he should work for the rest of the month and earn his right to it. Ove thought this seemed a reasonable offer and notified his school that he'd be absent for the next two weeks. He never went back.

He worked for the railways for five years. Then one morning he boarded a train and saw her for the first time. That was the first time he laughed since his father's death.

And life was never again the same.

People said Ove saw the world in black and white. But she was colour. All the colour he had.

6

A MAN CALLED OVE AND A BICYCLE
THAT SHOULD HAVE BEEN LEFT WHERE
BICYCLES ARE LEFT

Ove just wants to die in peace. Is that really too much to ask? Ove doesn't think so. Fair enough, he should have arranged it six months ago, straight after her funeral. But you couldn't bloody carry on like that, he decided at the time. He had his job to take care of. How would it look if people stopped coming to work all over the place because they'd killed themselves? Ove's wife died on a Friday, was buried on Sunday, and then Ove went to work on Monday. Because that's how one handles things. And then six months went by and out of the blue the managers came in on the Monday and said they hadn't wanted to deal with it on Friday because 'they didn't want to ruin his weekend'. And on the Tuesday he stood there oiling his kitchen worktops.

So he's prepared everything. He's paid the undertakers and agreed his place in the churchyard next to her. He's called the lawyers and written a letter with clear instructions and put it in an envelope with all his important receipts and the deeds of the house and the service history of the Saab. He's put this envelope in the inside pocket of his jacket. He's paid all the bills. He has no loans and no debts, so no one will have to clear up anything after him. He's even washed up his coffee cup and cancelled the newspaper subscription. He is ready.

And all he wants is to die in peace, he thinks, as he sits in the Saab and looks out of the open garage door. If he can just avoid his neighbours he may even be able to get away by this afternoon.

He sees the heavily overweight young man from next door slouching past the garage door in the parking area. Not that Ove dislikes fat people. Certainly not. People can look any way they like. He has just never been able to understand them, can't fathom how they do it. How much can one person eat? How does one manage to turn oneself into a twin-sized person? It must take a certain determination, he reflects.

The young man notices him and waves cheerfully. Ove gives him a curt nod. The young man stands there waving, setting his fat breasts into motion under his T-shirt. Ove often says that this is the only man he knows who could attack a bowl of crisps from all directions at once, but whenever he makes this comment Ove's wife protests and tells him one shouldn't say things like that.

Or rather, she used to.

Used to.

Ove's wife liked the overweight young man. After his mother passed away she would go over once a week with a lunchbox. 'So he gets something home-cooked now and then,' she used to say. Ove noticed that they never got the containers back, adding that maybe the young man hadn't noticed the difference between the box and the food inside it. At which point Ove's wife would tell him that was enough. And then it was enough.

Ove waits until the lunchbox eater has gone before he gets out of the Saab. He tugs at the handle three times. Closes the garage door behind him. Tugs at the door handle three times. Walks up the little footpath between the houses. Stops outside the bicycle shed. There's a woman's bicycle leaning up against the wall. Again. Right under the sign clearly explaining that cycles should not be left in this precise spot.

Ove picks it up. The front tyre is punctured. He unlocks the shed and places the bicycle tidily at the end of the row. He locks the door and has just tugged at it three times when he hears a late pubescent voice jabbering in his ear.

'Whoa! What the hell're you doin'!?'

Ove turns round and finds himself eye to eye with a whelp standing a few yards away.

'Putting a bike away in the bike shed.'

'You can't do that!'

On closer inspection he may be eighteen or so, Ove suspects. More of a stripling than a whelp, in other words, if one wants to be pedantic about it.

'Yes I can.'

'But I'm repairing it!' the youth bursts out, his voice rising into falsetto.

'But it's a lady's bike,' protests Ove.

'Yeah, so what?'

'It can hardly be yours, then,' Ove states condescendingly.

The youth groans, rolling his eyes; Ove puts his hands into his pockets as if this is the end of the matter.

There's a guarded silence. The lad looks at Ove as if he finds Ove unnecessarily thick. In return, Ove looks at the creature before him as if it were nothing but a waste of oxygen. Behind the youth, Ove notices, there's another youth. Even slimmer than the first one and with black stuff all round his eyes. The second youth tugs carefully at the first's jacket and murmurs something about 'not causing trouble'. His comrade kicks rebelliously at the snow, as if it were the snow's fault.

'It's my girlfriend's bike,' he mumbles at last.

He says it more with resignation than indignation. His training shoes are too big and his jeans too small, Ove notes. His tracksuit jacket is pulled over his chin to protect him against the cold. His emaciated bum-fluffed face is covered in blackheads and his hair looks as if someone saved him from drowning in a barrel by pulling him up by his locks.

'Where does she live, then?'

With profound exertion, as if he's been shot with a tranquilliser dart, the creature points with his whole arm towards the house at the far end of Ove's street. Where those communists who pushed through the garbage sorting reform live with their daughters. Ove nods cautiously.

'She can pick it up in the bike shed, then,' says Ove, tapping melodramatically at the sign prohibiting bicycles from being left in the area, before turning round and heading back towards his house.

'Grumpy old bastard!' the youth yells behind him.

'Sssh!' utters his soot-eyed companion.

Ove doesn't answer.

He walks past the sign clearly prohibiting motor vehicles from entering the residential area. The one which the pregnant foreigner apparently could not read, even though Ove knows very well that it's quite impossible not to see it. He should know, because he's the one who put it there. Dissatisfied, he walks down the little footpath between the houses, stamping his feet so that anyone who saw him would think he was trying to flatten the tarmac. As if it wasn't bad enough with all the nutters already living in the street, he thinks. As if the whole area was not already being converted into some bloody speed bump in evolutionary progress. The Audi poser and the blonde weed almost opposite Ove's house, and at the far end of the row that communist family with their teenage daughters and their red hair and their shorts over their trousers, their faces like mirror-image racoons. Well, most likely they're on holiday in Thailand at this precise moment, but anyway.

In the house next to Ove lives the twenty-five-year-old who's almost a quarter-tonner. With his long feminine hair and strange T-shirts. He lived with his mother until she died of some illness a year or so ago. Apparently his name is Jimmy, Ove's wife has told him. Ove doesn't know what work Jimmy does; most likely something criminal. Unless he tests bacon for a living?

In the house at the other end live Rune and his wife. Ove wouldn't exactly call Rune his 'enemy' . . . or rather, he would. Everything that went to pot in the Residents' Association began with Rune. He and his wife, Anita, moved into the area on the same day that Ove and Sonja moved in. At that time Rune used to drive a Volvo, but later he bought a BMW. You just couldn't reason with a person who behaved like that.

It was Rune who pushed through the coup d'état that saw Ove deposed as chairman of the Association. And just look at the state of the place now. Higher electricity bills and bicycles that aren't put away in the bike shed and people reversing with trailers in the residential area in spite of signs *clearly* stating that it's prohibited. Ove has long warned about these awful things, but no one has listened. Since then he never showed his face in any meeting of the Residents' Association.

His mouth makes a movement as if it's just about to spit every time he mentally enunciates the words 'Residents' Association'. As if they were a gross indecency.

He's fifteen metres from his broken post box when he sees Blonde Weed. At first he can't comprehend what she's doing at all. She's swaying about on her heels on the footpath, gesturing hysterically at the façade of Ove's house.

That little barking thing – more of a mutt than a proper dog – which has been pissing on Ove's paving stones, is running round her feet.

Weed yells something so violently that her sunglasses slip down over the tip of her nose. Mutt barks even louder. So the old girl has finally lost her faculties, Ove thinks, standing warily a few metres behind her. Only then does he realize that she's actually not gesticulating at the house. She's throwing stones. And it isn't the house she's throwing them at. It's the cat.

It sits squeezed into the far corner behind Ove's shed. It has little flecks of blood in its coat, or what's left of its coat. Mutt bares its teeth; the cat hisses back.

'Don't you hiss at Prince!' wails Weed, picking up another stone from Ove's flower bed and hurling it at the cat. The cat jumps out of the way; the stone hits the window sill.

She picks up another stone and prepares to throw it. Ove takes two quick steps forward and stands so close behind her that she can most likely feel his breath.

'If you throw that stone into my property I'll throw you into your garden!'

She spins round. Their eyes meet. Ove has both hands in his pockets; she waves her fists in front of him as if trying to swat two flies the size of microwave ovens. Ove doesn't concede as much as a facial movement.

'That disgusting thing scratched Prince!' she manages to say, her eyes wild with fury. Ove peers down at Mutt. It growls at him. Then he looks at the cat, sitting humiliated and bleeding but with its head defiantly raised, outside his house.

'It's bleeding. So it seems to have ended in a draw,' says Ove.

'Like hell. I'll kill that piece of shit!'

'No you won't,' says Ove coldly.

His insane neighbour begins to look threatening.

'It's probably full of disgusting diseases and rabies and all sorts of things!'

Ove looks at the cat. Looks at the Weed. Nods.

'And so are you, most likely. But we don't throw stones at you because of it.'

Her lower lip starts trembling. She slides her sunglasses up over her eyes.

'You watch yourself!' she hisses.

Ove nods. Points at Mutt. Mutt tries to bite his leg but Ove stamps his foot down so hard that it backs off.

'That thing should be kept on a leash inside the residential area,' says Ove steadily.

She tosses her dyed hair and snorts so hard that Ove half-expects a bit of snot to come flying out.

'And what about that thing!?' she rages at the cat.

'Never you bloody mind,' Ove answers.

She looks at him in that particular way of people who feel both utterly superior and deeply insulted.

Mutt bares its teeth in a silent growl.

'You think you own this street or what, you bloody lunatic?' she says.

Ove calmly points at Mutt again.

'The next time that thing pisses on my paving,' he says coolly, 'I'll electrify the stone.'

'Prince hasn't bloody pissed on your disgusting paving,' she splutters and takes two steps forward with her fist raised.

Ove doesn't move. She stops. Looks as if she's hyperventilating.

Then she seems to summon what highly negligible amount of common sense she has at her disposal.

'Come on, Prince,' she says with a wave.

Then raises her index finger at Ove.

'I'm going to tell Anders about this, and then you'll regret it.'

'Tell your Anders from me that he should stop stretching his groin outside my window.'

'Crazy old muppet,' she spits out and heads off towards the parking area.

'And his car's rubbish, you tell him that!' Ove adds for good measure.

She makes a gesture at him that he hasn't seen before, although he can guess what it means. Then she and her wretched little dog make off towards Anders's house.

Ove turns off by his shed. Sees the wet splashes of piss on the paving by the corner of the flower bed. If he hadn't been busy with more important things this afternoon he would have gone off to make a doormat of that mutt right away. But he has other things to occupy him. He goes to his toolshed, gets out his hammer-action drill and his box of drill bits.

When he comes out again the cat is sitting there looking at him.

'You can clear off now,' says Ove.

It doesn't move. Ove shakes his head resignedly.

'Hey! I'm not your friend.'

The cat stays where it is. Ove throws out his arms.

'Christ, you bloody cat, me backing you up when that stupid bag threw stones at you only means I dislike you less than that weedy nutter across the street. And that's not much of an achievement; you should be absolutely clear about that.'

The cat seems to give this some careful thought. Ove points at the footpath.

'Clear off!'

Not at all concerned by this, the cat licks its bloodstained fur. It looks at Ove as if this has been a round of negotiation and it's considering a proposal. Then slowly gets up and pads off, disappearing round the corner of the shed. Ove doesn't even look at it. He goes right into his house and slams the door.

Because it's enough now. Now Ove is going to die.

7

A MAN CALLED OVE DRILLS A HOLE
FOR A HOOK

Ove has put on his best trousers and his going-out shirt. Carefully he covers the floor with a protective sheet of plastic, as if protecting a valuable work of art. Not that the floor is particularly new (although he did sand it less than two years ago). He's fairly sure that you don't lose much blood when you hang yourself, and it isn't because of worries about the dust or the drilling. Or the marks when he kicks away the stool. In fact he's glued some plastic pads to the bottom of its legs, so there shouldn't be any marks at all. No, the heavy-duty sheets of plastic that Ove so carefully unfolds, covering the entire hall, living room and a good part of the kitchen, are not for Ove's own sake at all.

He imagines there'll be a hell of a lot of running about in here, with eager, jumped-up estate agents trying to get into the house before the ambulance men have so much as got the corpse out. And those bastards are not coming in here, scratching up Ove's floor with their shoes. Whether over Ove's dead body or not. They had better be quite clear about that.

He puts the stool in the middle of the floor. It's coated in at least seven different layers of paint. Ove's wife decided in principle that she'd let Ove repaint one of the rooms in their house every six months. Or, to be more exact, she decided she wanted a different colour in one of the rooms once every six months. And when she said as much to Ove he told her that she might as well forget it. And then she called a decorator for an estimate. And then she told Ove how much she was going to pay the decorator. And then Ove went to fetch his painting stool.

You miss the strangest things when you lose someone. Little things. Smiles. The way she turned round in her sleep. Even repainting a room for her.

Ove goes to get to his box of drill bits. These are single-handedly the most important things when drilling. Not the drill, but the bits. It's like having proper tyres on your car instead of messing about with ceramic brakes and nonsense like that. Anyone who knows anything knows that. Ove positions himself in the middle of the room and sizes it up. Then, like a surgeon gazing down on his instruments, his eyes move searchingly over his drill bits. He selects one, slots it into the drill and tests the trigger a little so that the drill makes a growling sound. Shakes his head, decides that it doesn't feel at all right and changes the drill bit. He repeats this four times before he's satisfied, then walks through the living room, swinging the drill from his hand like a big revolver.

He stands in the middle of the floor staring up at the ceiling. He has to measure this up before he gets started, he realises. So that the hole is centred. The worst thing Ove knows is when someone just drills a hole in the ceiling, hit-and-miss.

He goes to fetch a tape measure. He measures from each of the four corners – twice, to be on the safe side – and marks the centre of the ceiling with a cross.

Ove steps down from the stool. Walks round to make sure the protective plastic is in position as it should be. Unlocks the door so they won't have to break it down when they come to get him. It's a good door. It'll last many more years.

He puts on his suit jacket and checks that the envelope is in his inside pocket. Finally he turns round the photo of his wife in the window, so that it looks out towards the shed. He doesn't want to make her watch what he's about to do, but on the other hand he daren't put the photograph face-down either. Ove's wife was always horribly ill-tempered if they ever ended up in some place without a view. She needed 'something to look at that's alive', she was always saying. So he points her towards the shed whilst thinking to himself that maybe that Cat Annoyance would come by again. Ove's wife liked Cat Annoyance.

He fetches the drill, takes the hook, stands up on the stool and starts drilling. The first time the doorbell goes he assumes he's made a mistake and ignores the sound for that very reason. The second time he realises that there's actually someone ringing the door, and he ignores it for that very reason.

The third time Ove stops drilling and glares at the door. As if he may be able to convince whoever is standing outside to disappear by his mental powers alone. It doesn't work. The person in question obviously thinks the only rational explanation for his not opening the door the first time round was that he did not hear the doorbell.

Ove steps off the stool, strides across the plastic sheets through the living room and into the hall. Does it really have to be so difficult to kill yourself without constantly being disturbed?

'What?' fumes Ove as he flings the door open.

The Lanky One only manages by a whisker to pull his big head back and avoid an impact with his face.

'Hi!' the Pregnant One exclaims cheerfully beside him, though a half-metre lower down.

Ove looks down at her, then up at him. The Lanky One is busy touching every part of his face with some reluctance, as if to check that every protuberance is still where it should be.

'This is for you,' she says in a friendly sort of voice, and then shoves a blue plastic box into Ove's arms.

Ove looks sceptical.

'Biscuits,' she explains encouragingly.

Ove nods slowly, as if to confirm this.

'You've really dressed up,' she smiles.

Ove nods again.

And then they stand there, all three of them, waiting for someone to say something. In the end she looks at the Lanky One and shakes her head with resignation.

'Oh please, will you stop fidgeting with your face, darling?' she whispers and gives him a push in the side.

The Lanky One raises his eyes, meets her gaze and nods. Looks at Ove. Ove looks at the Pregnant One. The Lanky One points at the box and his face lights up.

'She's Iranian, you know. They bring food with them wherever they go.'

Ove gives him a blank stare. The Lanky One looks even more hesitant.

'You know . . . that's why I go so well with Iranians. They like to cook food and I like to . . .' he begins, with an over-the-top smile.

Then he goes silent. Ove looks spectacularly uninterested.

'. . . eat,' the Lanky One finishes.

He looks as if he's about to make a drumroll in the air with his fingers. But then he looks at the Pregnant Foreign Woman and decides that it would probably be a bad idea.

'And?' he offers, wearily.

She stretches, puts her hands on her stomach.

'We just wanted to introduce ourselves, now that we're going to be neighbours . . .'

Ove nods tersely and concisely.

'Okay. Bye.'

He tries to close the door. She stops him with her arm.

'And then we wanted to thank you for reversing our trailer. That was very kind of you!'

Ove grunts. Reluctantly he keeps the door open.

'That's not something to thank me for.'

'Yeah, it was really nice,' she protests.

'No, I mean it shouldn't be something to thank me for, because a grown man should be able to reverse with a trailer,' he replies, casting a somewhat unimpressed gaze on the Lanky One, who looks at him as if unsure whether or not this is an insult. Ove decides not to help him out of his quandary. He backs away and tries to close the door again.

'My name is Parvaneh!' she says, putting her foot across his threshold.

Ove stares at the foot; then at the face it's attached to.

As if he's having difficulties understanding what she just did.

'I'm Patrick!' says the Lanky One.

Neither Ove nor Parvaneh take the slightest notice of him.

'Are you always this unfriendly?' Parvaneh wonders, with genuine curiosity.

Ove looks insulted.

'I'm not bloody unfriendly.'

'You are a bit unfriendly.'

'No I'm not!'

'No, no, no, your every word is a cuddle, it really is,' she replies in a way that makes Ove feel she doesn't mean it at all.

He releases his grip on the door handle for a moment or two. Inspects the box of biscuits in his hand.

'Right. Arabian biscuits. Worth having, are they?' he mutters.

'Persian,' she corrects.

'What?'

'Persian, not Arabian. I'm from Iran – you know, where they speak Farsi?' she explains.

'Farcical? That's the least you could say,' Ove agrees.

Her laughter catches him on the back foot. As if it's carbonated and someone has poured it too fast and it's bubbling over in all directions. It doesn't fit at all with the grey cement and right-angled garden paving stones. It's an untidy, mischievous laugh that refuses to go along with rules and prescriptions.

Ove takes a step backwards. His foot sticks to some tape by the threshold. As he tries to shake it off, with some irritation, he tears up the corner of the plastic. When he tries to shake off both the tape and the plastic sheeting, he stumbles backwards and pulls up even more of it. Angrily, he regains his balance. Remains there on the threshold, trying to summon some calm. Grabs hold of the door handle again, looks at the Lanky One and tries to quickly change the subject.

'And what are you, then?'

He shrugs his shoulders a little and smiles, slightly overwhelmed.

'I'm an IT consultant.'

Ove and Parvaneh shake their heads with such coordination they could be synchronised swimmers. For a moment it makes Ove dislike her a little less, although he's very reluctant to admit it to himself.

The Lanky One seems unaware of all this. Instead he looks with curiosity at the hammer-action drill, which Ove is holding in a firm grip, like a guerrilla fighter with an AK-47 in his hand.

Once the Lanky One has finished perusing it, he leans forward and peers into Ove's house.

'What are you doing?'

Ove looks at him, as one does at a person who has just said 'What are you doing?' to a man standing with a hammer-action drill in his hand.

'I'm drilling,' he replies scathingly.

Parvaneh looks at the Lanky One and rolls her eyes, and if it hadn't been for her belly, which testified to a willingness on her part to contribute to the survival of the Lanky One's genetic make-up, Ove might have found her almost sympathetic at this point.

'Oh,' says the Lanky One, with a nod.

Then he leans forward and peers in at the living room floor, neatly covered in the protective sheet of plastic.

He lights up and looks at Ove with a grin.

'Almost looks like you're about to murder someone!'

Ove peruses him in silence. The Lanky One clears his throat, a little more reluctant. 'I mean, it's like an episode of *Dexter*,' he says with a much less confident grin. 'It's a TV series . . . about a guy who murders people.' He trails off; then starts poking the toe of his shoe into the gaps between the paving stones outside Ove's front door.

Ove shakes his head. It's unclear to whom the Lanky One was primarily aiming what he just said.

'I have some things to get on with,' he says curtly to Parvaneh and takes a firm grip on the door handle.

Parvaneh gives the Lanky One a purposeful jab in the side

with her elbow. The Lanky One looks as if he's trying to drum up some courage; he glances at Parvaneh, and looks at Ove with an expression of someone expecting the whole world to start firing rubber bands at him.

'Well, the thing is, we actually came because I could do with borrowing a few things . . .'

Ove raises his eyebrows.

'What "things"?'

The Lanky One clears his throat.

'A ladder. And an Eileen key.'

'You mean an Allen key?'

Parvaneh nods. The Lanky One looks puzzled.

'It's an Eileen key, isn't it?'

'Allen key,' Parvaneh and Ove correct at the same time.

Parvaneh nods eagerly at him and points triumphantly at Ove. 'He said that's what it's called!'

The Lanky One mumbles something inaudible.

'And you're just like "Whoa, it's an Eileen key!"' Parvaneh jeers.

He looks slightly crestfallen.

'I never sounded like that.'

'You did so!'

'Did not!'

'Yes you DID!'

'I DIDN'T!'

Ove's gaze travels from one to the other, like a large dog watching two mice interfering with its sleep.

'You did,' said one of them.

'That's what you think,' the other one says.

'Everyone says it!'

'The majority is not always right!'

'Shall we google it or what?'

'Sure! Google it! Wikipedia it!'

'Give me your phone.'

'Use your own!'

'Duh! I haven't got it with me, dipshit!'

'Sorry to hear that!'

Ove looks at them as their pathetic argument drones on. They remind him of two malfunctioning radiators, making high-pitched whines at each other.

'Good God,' he mutters.

Parvaneh starts imitating what Ove assumes must be some kind of flying insect. She makes tiny whirring sounds with her lips to irritate her husband. It works quite effectively. Both on the Lanky One and Ove. Ove gives up.

He goes into the hall, hangs up his suit jacket, puts down the hammer-action drill, puts on his clogs and walks past them both towards the shed. He's pretty sure neither of them even notice him. He hears them still bickering as he starts reversing out with the ladder.

'Go on, help him then, Patrick,' Parvaneh bursts out when she catches sight of him.

The Lanky One takes a few steps towards him, with fumbling movements. Ove keeps his eyes on him, as if watching a blind man at the wheel of a crowded city bus. And only after that does Ove realise that, in his absence, his property has been invaded by yet another person.

Rune's wife, Anita, from further down the street, is standing next to Parvaneh, blithely watching the spectacle. Ove decides the only rational response must be to pretend that she's doing no such thing. He feels anything else would only encourage her. He hands the Lanky One a cylindrical case with a set of neatly sorted Allen keys.

'Oh, look how many there are,' says the imbecile thoughtfully, gazing into the case.

'What size are you after?' asks Ove.

The Lanky One looks at him as people do when they lack the self-possession to say what they are thinking.

'The . . . usual size?'

Ove looks at him for a long, long time.

'What are you using these things for?' he says at last.

'To fix an IKEA wardrobe we took apart when we moved.

And then I forgot where I put the Eileen key,' he explains, apparently without a trace of shame.

Ove looks at the ladder.

'And this wardrobe's on the roof, is it?'

The Lanky One sniggers and shakes his head. 'Oh right, see what you mean! No, I need the ladder because the upstairs window is jammed. Won't open.' He adds the last part as if Ove would not otherwise be able to understand the implications of that word, 'jammed'.

'So now you're going to try to open it from the outside?' Ove wonders.

The Lanky One nods and clumsily takes the ladder from him. Ove looks as if he's about to say something else, but he seems to change his mind. He turns to Parvaneh.

'And why exactly are you here?'

'Moral support,' she twitters.

Ove doesn't look entirely convinced. Nor does the Lanky One.

Ove's gaze wanders reluctantly back to Rune's wife. She's still there. It seems like years since he last saw her. Or at least since he really looked at her. She's gone ancient. People all seem to get ancient behind Ove's back these days.

'Yes?' says Ove.

Rune's wife smiles mildly and clasps her hands across her hips.

'Ove, you know I don't want to disturb you but it's about the radiators in our house. We can't get any heat into them,' she says carefully and smiles in turn at Ove, the Lanky One and Parvaneh. Parvaneh and the Lanky One smile back. Ove looks at his dented wristwatch.

'Does no one in this street have a job to go to any more?' he wonders.

'I'm a pensioner,' says Rune's wife, almost apologetically.

'I'm on maternity leave,' says Parvaneh, patting her stomach proudly.

'I'm an IT consultant!' says the Lanky One proudly.

Ove and Parvaneh again indulge in a bit of synchronised head-shaking.

Rune's wife makes another attempt.

'I think it could be the radiators.'

'Have you bled them?' says Ove.

She shakes her head and looks curious.

'You think it could be because of that?'

Ove rolls his eyes.

'Ove!' Parvaneh roars at him at once, as if she's a reprimanding schoolmistress. Ove glares at her. She glares back. 'Stop being rude,' she orders.

'I told you, I'm not rude!'

Her eyes are unwavering. He makes a little grunt, then goes back to standing in the doorway. He thinks it could sort of be enough now. All he wants is to die. Why can't these lunatics respect that?

Parvaneh puts her hand encouragingly on Rune's wife's arm.

'I'm sure Ove can help you with the radiators.'

'That would be amazingly kind of you, Ove,' Rune's wife says at once, brightening.

Ove sticks his hands in his pockets. Kicks at the loose plastic by the threshold.

'Can't your man sort out that sort of thing in his own house?'

Rune's wife shakes her head mournfully.

'No, Rune has been really ill lately, you see. They say it's Alzheimer's. He's in a wheelchair as well. It's been a bit uphill . . .'

Ove nods with faint recognition. As if he has been reminded of something his wife told him a thousand times, although he still managed to forget it all the time.

'Yeah, yeah,' he says impatiently.

'You can go and breathe their radiators, can't you, Ove!' says Parvaneh.

Ove glances at her as if considering a firm retort, but instead he just looks down at the ground.

'Or is that too much to ask?' she continues, drilling him with her gaze and crossing her arms firmly across her stomach.

Ove shakes his head.

'You don't breathe radiators, you *bleed* them . . . Jesus.'

He looks up and gives them the once-over.

'Have you never bled a radiator before, or what?'

'No,' says Parvaneh, unmoved.

Rune's wife looks at the Lanky One a little anxiously.

'I haven't got a clue what they're talking about,' he says calmly to her.

Rune's wife nods resignedly. Looks at Ove again.

'It would be really nice of you, Ove, if it isn't too much of a bother . . .'

Ove just stands there staring down at the threshold.

'Maybe this could have been thought about before you organised a coup d'état in the Residents' Association,' he says quietly, his words punctuated by a series of discreet coughs.

'Before she what?' says Parvaneh.

Rune's wife clears her throat.

'But, dear Ove, there was never a coup d'état . . .'

'Was so,' says Ove grumpily.

Rune's wife looks at Parvaneh with an embarrassed little smile. 'Well, you see, Rune and Ove here haven't always got along so very well. Before Rune got ill he was the head of the Residents' Association. And before that Ove was the head. And when Rune was voted in there was something of a wrangle between Ove and Rune, you could say.'

Ove looks up and points a corrective index finger at her.

'A coup d'état! That's what it was!'

Rune's wife nods at Parvaneh.

'Well, yes well, before the meeting Rune counted votes about his suggestion that we should change the heating system for the houses and Ove thou—'

'And what the hell does Rune know about heating systems? Eh?' Ove exclaims heatedly, but immediately gets a look from Parvaneh that makes him reconsider and come to the conclusion that there's no need to complete his line of thought.

Rune's wife nods.

'Maybe you're right, Ove. But anyway he's very sick now . . .'

so it doesn't really matter any more.' Her bottom lip trembles slightly. Then she regains her composure, straightens her neck with dignity and clears her throat.

'The authorities have said they'll take him from me and put him in a home,' she manages to say.

Ove puts his hands in his pockets again and determinedly backs away, across his threshold. He's heard enough of this.

In the meantime the Lanky One seems to have decided it's time to change the subject and lighten up the atmosphere. He points at the floor in Ove's hall.

'What's that?'

Ove turns to look at the bit of floor exposed by the loose plastic sheet.

'It looks as if you've got, sort of . . . tyre marks on the floor. Do you cycle indoors, or what?' says the Lanky One.

Parvaneh keeps her observant eyes on Ove as he backs away another step so he can impede the Lanky One's view.

'It's nothing.'

'But I can see it's . . .' the Lanky One begins confusedly.

'It was Ove's wife, Sonja, she was . . .' Rune's wife interrupts him in a friendly manner, but she only has time to get to the name 'Sonja' until Ove, in turn, interrupts her and spins round with unbridled fury in his eyes.

'That'll do! Now you SHUT UP!'

All four of them fall silent, equally shocked. Ove's hands tremble as he steps back into his hall and slams the door.

He hears Parvaneh's soft voice out there asking Rune's wife 'what all that was about'. Then he hears Rune's wife fumbling nervously for words, and then exclaiming: 'Oh, you know, I'd better go home. That thing about Ove's wife . . . oh forget it. Old bats like me, we talk too much, you know . . .'

Ove hears her strained laugh and then her little dragging footsteps disappearing as quickly as they can round the corner of his shed. A moment later the Pregnant One and the Lanky One also leave.

And all that's left is the silence of Ove's hall.

He sinks down on the stool, breathing heavily. His hands are still shaking as if he was standing waist-deep in ice-cold water. His chest thumps. It happens more and more these days. He has to sort of struggle for a mouthful of air, like a fish in an overturned bowl. His company doctor said it was chronic, and that he mustn't work himself up. Easy for him to say.

'Good to go home and have a rest now,' said his bosses at work. 'Now your heart is playing up and all.' They called it 'early retirement' but they might as well have said what it was. 'Liquidation.' A third of a century in the same job and that's what they reduced him to.

Ove is not sure how long he stays there on the stool, sitting with the drill in his hand and his heart beating so hard that he feels the pulse inside his head. There's a photo on the wall beside the front door, of Ove and Sonja. It's almost forty years old. That time they were in Spain on a coach tour. She's suntanned, wearing a red dress and looking so happy. Ove is standing next to her, holding her hand. He sits there for what must be an hour, just staring at that photo. Of all the imaginable things he most misses about her, the thing he really wishes he could do again is hold her hand in his. She had a way of folding her index finger into his palm, hiding it inside. And he always felt that nothing in the world was impossible when she did that. Of all the things he could miss, that's what he misses most.

Slowly he stands up. Goes into the living room. Up the steps of the ladder. And then once and for all he drills the hole and puts in the hook.

Then gets off the ladder and studies his work.

He goes into the hall and puts on his suit jacket. Feels in his pocket for the envelope. He's turned out all the lights. Washed up his coffee mug. Put up a hook in his living room. He's done.

He takes down the rope from the clothes-hanger in the hall. Gently, with the back of his hand, he caresses her coats one last time. Then he goes into the living room, ties a noose in the rope, threads it through the hook, climbs up on the stool, and puts his head in the noose.

Kicks the stool away.

Closes his eyes and feels the noose closing round his throat like the jaws of a large wild animal.

8

A MAN WHO WAS OVE AND A PAIR OF HIS
FATHER'S OLD FOOTPRINTS

She believed in destiny. That all the roads you walk in life, in one way or another 'lead to what has been predetermined for you'. Ove, of course, just started muttering under his breath and got very busy fiddling about with a screw or something whenever she started going on like this. But he never disagreed with her. Maybe to her destiny was 'something', that was none of his business. But to him, destiny was 'someone'.

It's a strange thing, becoming an orphan at sixteen. To lose your family long before you've had time to create your own to replace it. It's a very specific sort of loneliness.

Ove, conscientious and dutiful, completed his two-week stint on the railways. And to his own surprise he found that he liked it. There was a certain liberation in doing a job. Grabbing hold of things with his own two hands and seeing the fruit of his efforts. Ove hadn't ever disliked school, but he hadn't quite seen the point of it either. He liked mathematics, and was two academic years ahead of his classmates. As for the other subjects, quite honestly he was not so concerned about them.

But this was something entirely different. Something that suited him much better.

When he clocked off from his last shift on the last day he was downcast. Not only because he had to go back to school, but because it had only occurred to him now that he didn't know how to earn a living. Dad had been good in many ways, of course, but Ove had to admit he hadn't left much of an estate except a run-down house, an old Saab and a dented wristwatch. Alms from the church were out of the question, God should be bloody clear about that. Ove said as much to himself while he stood there in the changing rooms, maybe as much for his own benefit as God's.

'If you really had to take both Mum and Dad, keep your bloody money!' he yelled up at the ceiling.

Then he packed up his stuff and left. Whether God or anyone else was listening he never found out. But when Ove came out of the changing rooms, a man from the managing director's office was standing there waiting for him.

'Ove?' he asked.

Ove nodded.

'The director would like to express his thanks for doing such a good job over the past fortnight,' the man said, short and to the point.

'Thanks,' said Ove as he started walking away.

The man put his hand on Ove's arm. Ove stopped.

'The director was wondering whether you might have an interest in staying and carrying on doing a good job?'

Ove stood in silence, looking at the man. Maybe mostly to check if this was some kind of joke. Then he slowly nodded.

When he'd taken a few more steps the man called out behind him:

'The director says you are just like your father!'

Ove didn't turn around. But his back was straighter as he walked off.

And that's how he ended up in his father's old boots. He worked hard, never complained and was never ill. The old boys on his shift found him a little on the quiet side and a little odd on top of that. He never wanted to join them for a beer after work and he seemed uninterested in women as well, which was more than weird in its own right. But he was a chip off the old block and had never given them anything to complain about. If anyone asked Ove for a hand he got on with it, if anyone asked him to cover a shift for them, he did it without any fuss. As time went by, more or less all of them owed him a favour or two. So they accepted him.

When the old truck, the one they used to drive up and down the railway track, broke down one night twenty kilometres outside of town, in one of the worst downpours of the whole year, Ove managed to repair it with nothing but a screwdriver and half a roll of gauze tape. After that, as far as the old boys on the tracks were concerned, Ove was okay.

In the evenings he'd boil his sausages and potatoes, staring out the kitchen window as he ate. And the next morning he'd go to work again. He liked the routine, liked always knowing what to expect. Since his father's death he had begun more and more to differentiate between people who did what they should, and those who didn't. People who did and people who just talked. Ove talked less and less and did more and more.

He had no friends. But on the other hand he hardly had any enemies either, apart from Tom, who since his promotion to foreman took every opportunity to make Ove's life as difficult as possible. He gave him the dirtiest and heaviest jobs, shouted at him, tripped him up at breakfast, sent him under railway carriages for inspections and set them in motion while Ove lay unprotected on the sleepers. When Ove, startled, threw himself out of the way just in time, Tom laughed contemptuously and roared: 'Look out or you'll end up like your old man!'

Ove kept his head down, though, and his mouth shut. He saw no purpose in challenging a man who was twice his own size. He went to work every day and did justice to himself – that had been good enough for his father and so it would also have to do for Ove. His colleagues learned to appreciate him for it. 'When people don't talk so much they don't dish out the crap either,' one of his older workmates said to him one afternoon down on the track. And Ove nodded. Some got it and some didn't.

There were also some who got what Ove ended up doing one day in the director's office, while others didn't.

It was almost two years after his father's funeral. Ove had just turned eighteen. Tom had been caught out stealing money from the float in one of the carriages. Admittedly no one but Ove saw him take it, but Tom and Ove had been the only two people in the carriage when the money went missing. And, as a serious man from the director's office explained when Tom and Ove were ordered to present themselves, no one could believe Ove was the guilty party. And he wasn't, of course.

Ove was left on a wooden chair in the corridor outside the director's office. He sat there looking at the floor for fifteen minutes before the door opened. Tom stepped outside, his fists so clenched with determination that his skin was bloodless and white on his lower arms.

He kept trying to make eye contact with Ove; Ove just kept staring down at the floor until he was brought into the director's office.

More serious men in suits were spread around the room inside. The director himself was pacing back and forth behind his desk, his face highly coloured, and there was an insinuation that he was too angry to stand still.

'You want to sit down, Ove?' said one of the men in suits at last.

Ove met his gaze, and knew who he was. His dad had mended his car once. A blue Opel Manta. With the big engine. He smiled amicably at Ove and gestured cursorily at a chair in the middle of the floor. As if to let him know that he was among friends now and could relax.

Ove shook his head. The Opel Manta man nodded with understanding.

'Well then. This is just a formality, Ove. No one in here believes you took the money. All you need to do is tell us who did it.'

Ove looked down at the floor. Half a minute passed.

'Ove?'

Ove didn't answer. The harsh voice of the director broke the silence at long last. 'Answer the question, Ove!'

Ove stood in silence. Looking down at the floor. The facial

expressions of the men in suits shifted from conviction to slight confusion.

'Ove . . . you do understand that you have to answer the question. Did you take the money?'

'No,' said Ove with a steady voice.

'So who was it?'

Ove stood in silence.

'Answer the question!' ordered the director.

Ove looked up. Stood there with a straight back.

'I'm not the sort that tells tales about what other people do,' he said.

The room was steeped in silence for what must have been several minutes.

'You do understand, Ove . . . that if you don't tell us who it was, and if we have one or more witnesses who say it was you . . . Then we'll have to draw the conclusion that it was you?' said the director, not as amicable now.

Ove nodded, but didn't say another word. The director scrutinised him, as if he was a bluffer in a game of cards. Ove's face was unmoved. The director nodded grimly.

'So you can go, then.'

And Ove left.

Tom had put the blame on Ove when he was in the director's office some fifteen minutes earlier. During the afternoon, two of the younger men from Tom's shift, eager as young men are to earn the approval of older men, came forward and claimed that they had seen Ove take the money with their own eyes. If Ove had pointed out Tom it would have been one word against another. But now it was Tom's words against Ove's silence. The next morning he was told by the foreman to empty his locker and present himself outside the director's office.

Tom stood inside the door of the changing rooms and jeered at him as he was leaving.

'Thief,' hissed Tom.

Ove passed him without raising his eyes.

'Thief! Thief! Thief!' one of their younger colleagues, who

had testified against Ove, chanted happily across the changing rooms, until one of the older men in their shift gave him a slap across the ear that silenced him.

'THIEF!' Tom shouted demonstratively, so loudly that the words were still ringing in Ove's head several days after.

Ove walked out into the evening air without turning round. He took a deep breath. He was furious, but not because they had called him a thief. He would never be the sort of man who cared what other men called him. But the shame of losing a job to which his father had devoted his whole life burned like a red-hot poker in his breast.

He had plenty of time to think his life over as he walked one last time to the office, a bundle of work clothes clutched in his arms. He had liked working here. Proper tasks, proper tools, a real job. He decided that once the police had gone through the motions of whatever they did with thieves in this situation, he'd try to go somewhere where he could get himself another job like this one. He might have to travel far, he imagined. Most likely a criminal record needed a reasonable geographical distance before it started to pale and become uninteresting. He had nothing to keep him here, he realised. But at least he had not become the sort of man who told tales. He hoped this would make his father more forgiving about Ove losing his job, once they were reunited.

He had to sit on the wooden chair in the corridor for almost forty minutes before a middle-aged woman in a tight-fitting black skirt and pointy glasses came and told him he could come into the office. She closed the door behind him. He stood there, still with his work-clothes in his arms. The director sat behind his desk with his hands clasped together in front of him. The two men submitted one another to such a long examination that either of them could have been an unusually interesting painting in a museum.

'It was Tom who took that money,' said the director.

He did not say it as a question, just a short confirming statement. Ove didn't answer. The director nodded.

'But the men in your family are not the kind that tell.'

That was not a question either. And Ove didn't reply.

The director noticed that he straightened a little at the words 'the men in your family'.

The director nodded again. Put on a pair of glasses, looked through a pile of papers and started writing something. As if in that very moment Ove had disappeared from the room. Ove stood in front of him for so long that he quite seriously began to doubt whether the director was aware of his presence. The director looked up.

'Yes?'

'Men are what they are because of what they do. Not what they say,' said Ove.

The director looked at him with surprise. It was the longest sequence of words anyone at the railway depot had heard the boy say since he started working there two years ago. In all honesty, Ove did not know where they came from. He just felt they had to be said.

The director looked down at his pile of papers again. Wrote something there. Pushed a piece of paper across the desk. Pointed to where Ove should sign his name.

'This is a declaration that you have voluntarily given up your job,' he said. Ove signed his name. Straightened up, with something unyielding in his face.

'You can tell them to come in now, I'm ready.'

'Who?' asked the director.

'The police,' said Ove, clenching his fists at his sides.

The director shook his head briskly and went back to digging in his pile of papers.

'I actually think the witness testimonies have been lost in this mess.'

Ove moved his weight from one foot to another, without really knowing how to respond to this. The director waved his hand without looking at him.

'You're free to go now.'

Ove turned round. Went into the corridor. Closed the door

behind him. Felt light-headed. Just as he reached the front door the woman who had first let him in caught him up with energetic steps, and before he had time to protest she pressed a paper into his hands.

'The director wants you to know that you're hired as a night-cleaner on the long-distance train, report to the foreman there tomorrow morning,' she said sternly.

Ove stared at her, then at the paper. She leaned in closer.

'The director asked me to pass on another message: you did not take that wallet when you were nine years old. And he'll be deuced if you took anything now. And it would be a damned pity for him to be responsible for turfing a decent man's son into the street just because the son has some principles.'

And so it turned out that Ove became a night-cleaner instead. And if this hadn't happened, he would never have come off his shift that morning and caught sight of her. With those red shoes and the gold brooch and all her burnished brown hair. And that laughter of hers which, for the rest of his life, would make him feel as if someone was running around barefoot on the inside of his breast.

She often said that 'all roads lead to something you were always predestined to do' . And for her, perhaps, it was something.

But for Ove it was someone.

9

A MAN CALLED OVE BLEEDS A RADIATOR

They say the brain functions quicker while it's falling. As if the sudden explosion of kinetic energy forces the mental faculties to accelerate until the perception of the exterior world goes into slow motion.

So Ove had time to think of many different things.

Mainly radiators.

Because there are right and wrong ways of doing things, as we all know. And even though it was many years ago and Ove could no longer remember exactly what solution he'd considered to be the right one in the argument about which central heating system should be adopted by the Residents' Association, he did remember very clearly that Rune's approach to it had been wrong.

But it wasn't just the central heating system. Rune and Ove had known one another for almost forty years, and they had been at loggerheads for at least thirty-seven of them.

Ove could not in all honesty remember how it all started. It wasn't the sort of dispute where you did remember. It was more an argument where the little disagreements had ended up so entangled that every new word was treacherously booby-trapped, and in the end it wasn't possible to open one's mouth at all without setting off at least four unexploded mines from earlier conflicts. It was the sort of argument that had just run, and run and run. Until one day it just ran out.

It wasn't really about cars, properly speaking. But Ove drove a Saab, after all. And Rune drove a Volvo. Anyone could have seen it wouldn't work out in the long run. In the beginning, though, they had been friends. Or, at least, friends to the extent that men like Ove and Rune were capable of being friends. Mostly for the sake of their wives, obviously. All four of them had moved into the area at the same time, and Sonja and Anita became instant best friends as only women married to men like Ove and Rune can be.

Ove recalled that he had at least not disliked Rune in those early years, as far as he could remember. They were the ones who set up the Residents' Association, Ove as chairman and Rune as assistant chairman. They had stuck together when the council wanted to cut down the forest behind Ove and Rune's houses in order to build even more houses. Of course, the council claimed that those construction plans had been there for years before Rune and Ove moved into their houses, but one did not get far with Rune and Ove using that sort of argumentation. 'It's war, you bastards!' Rune had roared at them down the telephone line. And it truly was: endless appeals and writs and petitions and letters to newspapers. A year and a half later the Council gave up and started building somewhere else instead.

That evening Rune and Ove had drunk a glass of whisky each on Rune's patio. They didn't seem overly happy about winning, their wives pointed out. Both men were rather disappointed that the council had given up so quickly. These had been some of the most enjoyable eighteen months of their lives.

'Is no one prepared to fight for their principles any more?' Rune had wondered.

'Not a sausage,' Ove had answered.

And then they said a toast to unworthy enemies.

That was long before the coup d'état in the Residents' Association, of course. And before Rune bought a BMW.

'Idiot,' thought Ove on that day, and also today, all these years after. And every day in between, actually. 'How the heck are you supposed to have a reasonable conversation with someone who buys a BMW?' Ove used to ask Sonja when she wondered why the two men could not have a reasonable conversation any more. And at that point Sonja used to find no other course but to roll her eyes whilst muttering, 'You're hopeless.'

Ove wasn't hopeless, in his own view. He just had a sense of there needing to be a bit of order in the greater scheme of things. He felt one should not go through life as if everything was exchangeable. As if loyalty was worthless. Nowadays people changed their stuff so often that any expertise in how to make things last was becoming superfluous. Quality: no one cared about that any more. Not Rune or the other neighbours and not those managers in the place where Ove worked. Now everything had to be computerised, as if one couldn't build a house until some consultant in a too-small shirt figured out how to open a laptop. As if that was how they built the Coliseum and the pyramids of Giza. Christ, they managed to build the Eiffel Tower in 1889 but nowadays one couldn't come up with the bloody drawings for a one-storey house without taking a break for someone to run off and recharge their mobile telephone.

This was a world where one became outdated before one's time was up. An entire country standing up and applauding the fact that no one was capable of doing anything properly any more. The unreserved celebration of mediocrity.

No one could change tyres. Install a dimmer switch. Lay some tiles. Plaster a wall. Submit their own tax accounts. These were all forms of knowledge that had lost their relevance, and the sort of things Ove had once spoken of with Rune. And then Rune went and bought a BMW.

Was a person hopeless because they believed there should be some limits? Ove didn't think so.

And yes, he didn't exactly remember how that argument with Rune had started. But it had continued. It had been about radiators and central heating systems and parking slots and trees that had to be felled and snow clearance and lawnmowers and rat poison in Rune's pond. For more than thirty-five years they had paced about on their identical patios behind their identical houses, whilst throwing meaningful glares over the fence. And then one day about a year ago it all came to an end. Rune became ill. Never came out of the house any more. Ove didn't even know if he still had the BMW.

And there was a part of him that missed that bloody old sod.

So, as they say, the brain functions quicker when it's falling. Like thinking thousands of thoughts in a fraction of a second. In other words, Ove has a good deal of time to think after he's kicked the stool over and fallen and landed on the floor with a lot of angry thrashing. He lies there, on his back, looking up for what seems like half an eternity at the hook still up on the ceiling. Then, in shock, he stares at the rope, which has snapped into two long stumps.

This society, thinks Ove. Can't they even manufacture rope any more? He swears profusely while he furiously tries to untangle his legs. How can one fail to manufacture rope, for Christ's sake? How can you get *rope* wrong?

No, there's no quality any more, Ove decides. He stands up, brushes himself down, peers around the room and ground floor of his terraced house. Feels his cheeks burning, he's not quite sure if it's because of anger or shame.

He looks at the window and the drawn curtains, as if concerned that someone may have seen him.

Isn't that bloody typical, he thinks to himself. You can't even kill yourself in a sensible way any more. He picks up the snapped rope and throws it in the kitchen waste. Folds up the plastic sheeting and puts it in the IKEA bags. Puts back the hammer-action drill and the drill bits in their cases; then goes out and puts everything back in the shed.

He stands out there for a few minutes and thinks about how Sonja always used to nag at him to tidy the place up. He always refused, knowing that any new space would immediately be an excuse to go out and buy more useless stuff with which to fill it. And now it's too late for tidying, he confirms. Now there's no longer anyone who wants to go out and buy useless stuff.

Now the tidying would just result in a lot of empty gaps. And Ove hates empty gaps.

He goes up to the workbench, picks up an adjustable spanner and a little plastic water can. He walks out, locks the shed, and tugs at the door handle three times. Then goes down the little pathway between the houses, turns off by the last letter box and rings a doorbell. Anita opens the door. Ove looks at her without a word. Sees Rune sitting there in his wheelchair, vacantly staring out of the window. It seems that's all he's done these last few years.

'Where have you got the radiators, then?' mutters Ove.

Anita smiles a surprised little smile and nods with equally mixed eagerness and confusion.

'Oh, Ove, that's dreadfully kind of you, if it's not too much trou—'

Ove steps into the hall without letting her finish what she's saying, or removing his shoes.

'Yeah, yeah, this crappy day is already ruined anyway.'

10

A MAN WHO WAS OVE AND A HOUSE
THAT OVE BUILT

A week after his eighteenth birthday, Ove passed his driving test, responded to an advertisement and walked twenty-five kilometres to buy his first own car: a blue Saab 93. He sold his dad's old Saab 92 to pay for it. It was only marginally newer, admittedly, and quite a run-down Saab 93 at that, but a man was not a proper man until he had bought his own car, felt Ove. And so it was.

It was a time of change in the country. People moved and found new jobs and bought televisions, and the newspapers started talking about a 'middle class'. Ove didn't quite know what this was, but he was well aware that he was not a part of it. The middle classes moved into new housing developments with straight walls and carefully trimmed lawns, and it soon grew clear to Ove that his parental home stood in the way of progress. And if there was anything this middle class was not enamoured of, it was whatever stood in the way of progress.

Ove received several letters from the council about what was called 'the redrawing of municipal boundaries'. He didn't quite understand the content of these letters, but he understood that his parental home did not fit among the new-built houses in the street. The council notified him of their intention to force him to sell the land to them so the house could be demolished and another built in its place.

Ove didn't quite know what it was that made him refuse. Maybe because he didn't like the tone of that letter from the council. Or because the house was all he had left of his family.

Whatever the case, he parked his first very own car in the garden that evening and sat in the driver's seat for several hours, gazing at the house. It was, to be blunt, decrepit. His father's speciality had been machines, not building, and Ove was not much better himself. These days he only used the kitchen and the little room leading off it, while the entire first floor was slowly being turned into a recreational stamping ground for mice. He watched the house from the car, as if hoping that it might start repairing itself if he waited patiently enough. It lay exactly on the boundary between two municipal authorities, on a line on the map that would now be moved either one way or the other. It was the remnant of an extinguished little village at the edge of the forest, next to the shining residential development into which people wearing suits had now moved with their families.

The suits didn't like the lonely youth in the house due for demolition at the end of the street. The children were not allowed to play around Ove's house. Suits preferred to live in the vicinity of other suits, Ove had come to understand. He had nothing against that, of course – but they were the ones who had moved into his neighbourhood, not the other way around.

And so, filled with a kind of strange defiance that made Ove's heart beat a little faster for the first time in years, he decided not to sell his house to the council. He decided to do the opposite. Repair it.

Of course, he had no idea of how to do it. He didn't know a dovetail joint from a pot of potatoes. Realising that his new working hours left him entirely free in the daytime, he went to a nearby construction site and applied for a job. He imagined this must be the best possible place to learn about building and he didn't need much sleep anyway. The only thing they could offer him was a labouring job, said the foreman. Ove took it.

So he spent his nights picking up litter on the line heading south out of town; then, after three hours of sleep, used what time remained to dart up and down the scaffolding, listening to the men in hard hats talking about construction techniques. One day a week he was free, and then he dragged sacks of cement and wooden beams back and forth for eighteen hours at a stretch, perspiring and lonely, demolishing and rebuilding the only thing his parents had left him apart from the Saab and his father's wristwatch. Ove's muscles grew and he was a fast learner.

The foreman at the building site took a liking to the hard-working youth, and one Friday afternoon took Ove to the pile of discarded planks, made-to-measure timber that had cracked and was due for burning.

'If I happen to look the other way and something you need goes walking, I'll assume you've burned it,' said the foreman and walked off.

Once the rumours of his house-building had spread among his older colleagues, one or other of them occasionally asked Ove about it. When he knocked up the wall in the living room, a wiry colleague with wonky front teeth, after spending twenty minutes telling Ove what an idiot he was for not knowing better from the start, taught him how to calculate the load-bearing parameters. When he laid the floor in the kitchen, a more heavy-built colleague, with a missing little finger on one hand, after calling him a plonker three dozen times, showed him how to take proper measurements.

One afternoon, as he was about to head home at the end of his shift, Ove found a little toolbox full of used tools by his clothes. It came with a note that simply read: 'To the puppy.'

Slowly, the house took shape. Screw by screw and floorboard by floorboard. No one saw it, of course, but there was no need for anyone to see it. A job well done is a reward in its own right, as his father always used to say.

He kept out of the way of his neighbours as much as he could. He knew they didn't like him and he saw no reason to give them further ammunition. The only exception was an elderly man and his wife who lived next door to Ove. This man was the only one in their whole street who did not wear a tie.

Ove had religiously fed the birds every other day since his father died. He only forgot to do it one morning. When the following morning he came out to compensate for his omission, he almost collided head-first with the older man by the fence under the bird-table. His neighbour gave him an insulted glance; he had bird-seed in his hands. They did not say anything to one another. Ove merely nodded and the older man gave him a little nod back. Ove went back into his house and from that time on made sure he kept to his own days.

They never spoke to one another. But one morning when the older man stepped onto his front step, Ove was painting his fence. And when he was done with that, he also painted the other side of the fence. The older man didn't say anything about it, but when Ove went past his kitchen window in the evening they nodded at one another. And the next day there was a home-baked apple pie on Ove's front step. Ove had not eaten home-made apple pie since his mother died.

Ove received more letters from the council. They became increasingly threatening in their tone and displeased that he still hadn't contacted them about the sale of his property. In the end he started throwing the letters away without even opening them. If they wanted his father's house they could come here and try and take it, the same way Tom had tried to take that wallet from him all those years ago.

A few mornings later Ove walked past the neighbour's house and saw the elderly man feeding the birds in the company of a little boy. A grandchild of his, Ove realised. He watched them surreptitiously through the bedroom window. The way the older man and the boy spoke in low voices with each other, as if they were sharing some great secret. It reminded him of something.

That night he had his supper in the Saab.

A few weeks later, Ove drove home the last nail in his house and when the sun rose over the horizon he stood in the garden with his hands shoved into the pockets of his navy trousers, proudly surveying his work.

He'd discovered that he liked houses. Maybe mostly because they were understandable. They could be calculated and drawn on paper. They did not leak if they were made watertight, they did not collapse if they were properly supported. Houses were fair, they gave you what you deserved. Which, unfortunately, was more than one could say about people.

And so the days went by. Ove went to work and came home and had sausages and spuds. He never felt alone despite his lack of company. Then one Sunday, as Ove was moving some planks, a jovial man with a round face and an ill-fitting suit turned up at his gate. The sweat ran from his forehead and he asked Ove if there might be a glass of water of the cold variety going spare. Ove saw no reason to deny him this, and while the man drank it by his gate, some small talk passed between them. Or rather, it was mostly the man with the round face who did the talking. It turned out that he was very interested in houses. Apparently he was in the midst of doing up his own house in another part of town. And somehow the man with the round face managed to invite himself into Ove's kitchen for a cup of coffee. Obviously, Ove was not used to this kind of pushy behaviour, but after an hour-long conversation about house-building, he was prepared to admit to himself that it wasn't so unpleasant having a bit of company in the kitchen for a change.

Just before the man left he asked in passing about Ove's house insurance. Ove answered candidly that he'd never given it much thought. His father had not been very interested in insurance policies.

The jovial man with the round face was filled with consternation, and he explained to Ove that it would be a veritable catastrophe for him if something happened to the house. After listening carefully to his many admonishments, Ove felt bound to agree with him. He had never given much thought to it until then. Which made him feel rather stupid now.

The man then asked if he might use the telephone; Ove said that would be fine. It turned out that his guest, grateful for a stranger's hospitality on a hot summer's day, had found a way of repaying his kindness. For it transpired that he actually worked for an insurance company, and was able to pull some strings to arrange an excellent quotation for Ove.

Ove was sceptical at first. He asked again about the man's credentials, which he was happy to reiterate. He then spent a considerable amount of time negotiating a better price.

'You're a tough businessman,' laughed the man with the round face. Ove felt surprisingly proud when he heard this – *a tough businessman*. The man then glanced at his watch, thanked Ove and said he'd best be on his way. As he left he gave Ove a piece of paper with his telephone number and said that he'd very much like to come by another day and have some more coffee and talk some more about house renovation. This was the first time anyone had ever expressed a wish to be Ove's friend.

Ove paid the man with the round face the full year's premium in cash. They shook hands.

The man with the round face never contacted him again. Ove tried to call him on one occasion but no one answered. He felt a quick stab of disappointment but decided not to think about it again. At least when salesmen called from other insurance companies he was able to say without any bad conscience that he was already insured. And that was something.

Ove continued avoiding his neighbours. He didn't want any problems with them. But unfortunately the problems seemed to have decided to seek out Ove instead. A few weeks after his house repairs were finished, one of his suited neighbours was burgled. It was the second burglary in the area in a relatively short period. The suits got together early next morning to deliberate on that young rascal in the condemned house, who must have had something to do with it. They knew very well 'where he'd got the money for all that renovation'. In the evening someone stuck a note under Ove's door, on which it was written: 'Clear off if you know what's good for you!' The night after that a stone was thrown through his window. Ove picked up the stone and changed the glass in the window. He never confronted the suits. Saw no purpose in it. But he wasn't going to move either.

Early the next morning he was woken by the smell of smoke.

He was out of his bed in an instant; the first thing that came into his head was that whoever had thrown that stone had apparently not finished yet. On his way down the stairs he instinctively grabbed a hammer. Not that Ove had ever been a violent man. But you could never be sure, he decided.

He was wearing only his underpants when he stepped onto the front veranda. All that lugging of construction materials in the last months had turned Ove into an impressively muscular young man without him even noticing. His bare upper body and the hammer swinging in his clenched right fist made the group gathered in the street momentarily take their eyes off the fire, and instinctively take a step back.

And that was when Ove realised that it was not his house that was burning, but his neighbour's.

The suits stood in the street, staring like deer into headlights. The elderly man emerged out of the smoke, his wife leaning on his arm. She was coughing terribly. When the elderly man handed her over to one of the suits' wives, and then turned back towards the fire, several of the suits cried out to him, telling him to leave it. 'It's too late! Wait for the fire brigade!' they roared. The elderly man didn't listen. Burning material fell over the threshold as he tried to step inside into a sea of fire.

Ove stood in the face of the wind by his gate and saw how scattered glowing balls had already set the dry grass alight between his house and the neighbour's. For a few long-drawn-out seconds he evaluated the situation as best he could: the fire would be all over his house in a few minutes if he didn't charge off to get the water-hose at once. He saw the elderly man trying to push his way past an overturned bookcase on his way into the house. The suits shouted his name and

82

tried to make him stop, but the elderly man's wife was screaming out another name.

Their grandchild.

Ove weighed on his heels as he watched the embers stealing their way through the grass. In all honesty he was probably not thinking so much about what he wanted to do, but what his father would have done. And as soon as that thought had taken root there was not much choice about it.

He muttered, irritated, looking at his house a last time, instinctively calculating to himself how many hours it had taken to build it. And then he ran towards the fire.

The house was so filled with thick, sticky smoke that it was like being struck in the face with a shovel. The elderly man struggled to move a fallen bookcase, which was blocking a door. Ove threw it aside as if it was made of paper and cleared a way up the stairs. By the time they emerged into the light of dawn, the elderly man was carrying the boy in his soot-covered arms. Ove had long, bleeding grazes across his chest and arms.

The bystanders just ran around panicking, screaming. The air was pierced by sirens. Uniformed firemen surrounded them.

Still only wearing his underpants and with aching lungs, Ove saw the first flames climbing his own house. He charged across the lawn but was immediately stopped by a group of firemen. They were everywhere, all of a sudden.

Refused to let him through.

A man in a white shirt, some sort of chief fireman as Ove understood it, stood before him with his legs wide apart and explained that they couldn't let him try to extinguish the fire in his own house. It was much too dangerous. Unfortunately, the white shirt explained after that, the fire brigade could not put it out either until they had the appropriate permissions from the authorities.

It turned out that because Ove's house now lay exactly on the municipal boundary, clearance from the command centre was required on the shortwave radio before they could get to work. Permission had to be sought, papers had to be stamped.

'Rules are rules,' the man in the white shirt explained in a monotone voice, when Ove protested.

Ove tore himself free and ran in fury towards the water-hose. But it was futile – by the time the firemen got the all-clear signal, the house was already engulfed by fire.

Ove stood in his garden and watched, helpless and in sorrow, as it burned.

When a few hours later he stood in a telephone box calling the insurance company, he learned that they had never heard of the jovial man with the round face. There was no valid insurance policy on the house. The woman from the insurance company sighed, impatiently explaining that swindlers often went from door to door claiming to be from their company, and that she hoped at least Ove hadn't given him any cash.

Ove hung up, and clenched his fist in his pocket.

11

A MAN CALLED OVE AND A LANKY ONE WHO CAN'T OPEN A WINDOW WITHOUT FALLING OFF A LADDER

It's quarter to six and the first proper snowfall of the year has laid itself like a cold blanket over the slumbering community of terraced houses. Ove unhooks his jacket and goes outside for his daily inspection. With equal surprise and dissatisfaction, he sees the cat sitting in the snow outside his door. It seems to have been sitting there all night.

Ove slams the front door extra hard to scare it away. Apparently it doesn't have the common sense to take fright. Instead it just sits there in the snow, licking its stomach. Utterly unconcerned. Ove doesn't like that sort of behaviour in a cat. He shakes his head and plants his feet firmly on the ground. The cat gives him the briefest of glances, clearly uninterested, then goes back to licking itself. Ove waves his arms at it. The cat doesn't budge an inch.

'This is private land!' says Ove.

When the cat still fails to give him any sort of acknowledgement, Ove loses his patience and, in a sweeping movement, kicks one of his clogs towards it. Looking back, he couldn't swear that it wasn't intentional. His wife would have been furious if she'd seen it, of course.

It doesn't make much difference, anyway. The clog flies in a smooth arc and passes a good metre and a half to the left of its intended target, before bouncing softly against the side of the shed and landing in the snow. The cat looks nonchalantly first at the clog, and then at Ove.

In the end it stands up, strolls around the corner of Ove's shed and disappears.

Ove walks through the snow in his socks to fetch the clog. He glares at it, as if he feels it should be ashamed of itself for not having a better sense of aim. Then he pulls himself together and goes on his inspection tour.

Just because he's dying today doesn't mean that the vandals should be given free rein.

When he comes back to his house, he pushes his way through the snow and opens the door to the shed. It smells of white spirit and mould in there, exactly as it should in a shed. He steps over the Saab's summer tyres and moves the jars of unsorted screws out of the way. Squeezes past the workbench, careful not to knock over the pots of white spirit with brushes in them. Lifts aside the garden chairs and the globe barbecue. Puts away the rim-wrench and snatches up the snow shovel. Weighs it a bit in his hand, the way one might do with a two-handed sword. Stands there in silence, scrutinising it.

When he comes out of the shed with the shovel, the cat is sitting in the snow again, right outside his house. Ove glares in amazement at its audacity. Its fur is thawing out, dripping. Or what remains of its fur. There are more bald patches than fur on that creature. It also has a long scar running along one eye, down across its nose. If cats have nine lives this one is quite clearly working its way through at least the seventh or eighth of them.

'Clear off,' says Ove.

The cat gives him a judgemental stare, as if it's sitting on the decision-making side of the desk at a job interview.

Ove grips the shovel, scoops up some snow and throws it at the cat, which jumps out of the way and glares indignantly at him. Spits out a bit of snow. Snorts. Then turns around and pads off again, around the corner of Ove's shed.

Ove puts his snow shovel to work. It takes him fifteen minutes to free up the paving between the house and the shed. He works with care. Straight lines, even edges. People don't shovel snow that way any more. Nowadays they just clear a way, they use snow blowers and all sorts of things. Any old method will do, scattering snow all over the place. As if that was the only thing that mattered in life: pushing one's way forward.

When he's done, he leans for a moment against the shovel in a snowdrift on the little pathway. Balances his body weight on it and watches the sun rising over the sleeping houses. He's been awake for most of the night, thinking of ways to die. He has even drawn some diagrams and charts to clarify the various methods. After carefully weighing up the pros and cons, he's accepted that what he's doing today has to be the best of bad alternatives. Admittedly he doesn't like the fact that the Saab will be left in neutral and use up a lot of expensive petrol for no good reason afterwards, but it's simply a factor that he'll have to accept in order to get it done.

He puts the snow shovel back in the shed and goes into the house. Puts on his good navy suit again. It will get stained and foul-smelling by the end of all this, but Ove has decided that his wife just has to go along with it, at least when he gets there.

He has his breakfast and listens to the radio. Washes up and wipes down the top. Then goes round the house checking the radiators. Turns off all lights. Checks that the coffee percolator is unplugged. Puts on the blue jacket over his suit, then the clogs, and goes back into the shed; he returns with a long rolled-up plastic tube. Locks the shed and front door, tugs three times at each door handle. Then goes down the little pathway between the houses.

The white Skoda comes from the left and takes him by such surprise that he almost collapses in a snowdrift by the shed. Ove runs down the pathway in pursuit, shaking his fist.

'Can't you read, you bloody idiot!' he roars.

The driver, a slim man with a cigarette in his hand, seems to have heard him. When the Skoda turns off by the bike shed their eyes meet through the side window. The man looks directly at Ove and rolls down his window. Lifts his eyebrows, disinterested.

'Motor vehicles prohibited!' Ove repeats, pointing at the sign where the very same message is written. He walks towards the Skoda with clenched fists.

The man hangs his left arm out of the window and unhurriedly ashes his cigarette. His blue eyes are completely unmoved. He looks at Ove as one looks at an animal behind a fence. Devoid of aggression, totally indifferent. As if Ove was something the man might wipe off with a damp cloth.

'Read the si—' says Ove harshly as he gets closer, but the man has already rolled up his window.

Ove yells at the Skoda but the man ignores him. He doesn't even pull away with a wheelspin and screaming tyres; he simply rolls off towards the garages and then onward to the main road, as if Ove's gesticulation was of no more consequence than a broken streetlight.

Ove stands rooted to the spot, so worked up that his fists are trembling. When the Skoda has disappeared he turns round and walks back between the houses, so hurried that he almost stumbles over his own legs. Outside Rune and Anita's house, where the white Skoda has quite clearly been parked, are two cigarette butts on the ground. Ove picks them up as if they were clues in a high-level criminal case.

'Hello, Ove,' he hears Anita say, cautiously, behind him.

Ove turns towards her. She is standing on the step, wrapped in a grey cardigan. It looks as if it's trying to grab hold of her body, like two hands clutching a wet bar of soap.

'Yeah, yeah. Hello,' answers Ove.

'He was from the council,' she says, with a nod in the direction in which the Skoda drove off.

'Vehicles are prohibited in this area,' says Ove.

She nods cautiously, again.

'He said he has special permission from the council to drive to the house.'

'He doesn't have ANY bloody . . .' Ove begins, then stops himself and clamps his jaws around the words.

Anita's lips are trembling.

'They want to take Rune away from me,' she says.

Ove nods without answering. He is still holding the plastic tube in his hand. He pushes his other clenched fist into his pocket. For a moment he thinks about saying something, but then he looks down, turns round and leaves. He's already gone several metres when he realises that he has the cigarette butts in his pocket, but by then it's too late to do anything about it.

Blonde Weed is standing in the street. Mutt starts barking hysterically as soon as it catches sight of Ove. The door to the house behind them is open and Ove assumes they are standing there waiting for that thing known as Anders. Mutt has something like fur in her mouth; its owner grins with satisfaction. Ove stares at her as he goes past; she doesn't avert her eyes. Her grin gets even broader, as if she's grinning at Ove's expense.

When he passes between his house and that of the Lanky One and Pregnant Woman, he sees the Lanky One standing in the doorway.

'Hi there, Ove!' he calls out inanely.

Ove sees his ladder leaning up against the Lanky One's house. The Lanky One waves cheerfully. Apparently he's got up early today, or at least early by the standards of IT consultants. Ove can see that he's holding a blunt silver dining knife in one hand. And he realises he's most likely intending to use it to lever the jammed upstairs window. Ove's ladder, which the Lanky One is clearly about to scale, has been shoved at an angle into a deep snowdrift.

'Have a good day!'

'Yeah, yeah,' answers Ove without turning round as he trudges past.

Mutt is outside that Anders thing's house, barking furiously.

Out of the corner of his eye, Ove sees the Weed still standing there with a scorching smile in his direction. It disturbs Ove. He doesn't quite know the reason for it, but he feels a disturbance in his bones.

As he walks up between the houses, past the bicycle shed and into the parking area, he reluctantly admits to himself that he's walking around looking for the cat, but he can't seem to find it anywhere.

He opens his garage door, unlocks the Saab and then stands there, his hands in his pockets, for what must be in excess of a half-hour. He doesn't quite know why he's doing it, he just feels that something like this requires some kind of sanctified silence before one heads off.

He considers whether the paintwork of the Saab will become terribly dirty as a result of this. He supposes so. It's a pity and a shame, he realises, but not much can be done about it. He gives the tyres a couple of evaluating kicks. They're in fine order, they really are. Good for at least another three winters, he estimates, judging by his last kick. Which quickly reminds him about the letter in the inside pocket of his jacket, so he fishes it out to check whether he has remembered to leave instructions about the summer tyres. Yes, he has. It's written here under 'Saab + Accessories'. 'Summer tyres in the shed,' and then clear instructions that even a genuine moron could understand about where the rim bolts can be found in the boot. Ove slides the letter back into the envelope and puts it in the inside pocket of his jacket.

He glances over his shoulder into the parking area. Not because he's bothered about that damned cat, obviously. He just hopes nothing's happened to it, because then there'll be hell to pay from Ove's wife, he's quite sure about that. He just doesn't want a ticking off because of the damned cat. That's all.

The sirens of an approaching ambulance can be heard in the distance, but he barely takes any notice. Just gets into the driver's seat and starts the engine. Opens the back electric window about five centimetres. Gets out of the car. Closes the garage door. Fixes the plastic tube tightly over the exhaust pipe. Watches the exhaust fumes slowly bubbling out of the other end of the tube. Then feeds the tube through the open back window. Gets into the car. Closes the door. Adjusts the wing mirrors. Fine-tunes the radio one step forward and one step back. Leans back in the seat. Closes his eyes. Feels the thick exhaust smoke, cubic centimetre by cubic centimetre, filling the garage and his lungs.

It wasn't supposed to be like this. You work and pay off the mortgage and pay tax and do what you should. You marry. For better or for worse until death do us part, wasn't that what they agreed? Ove remembers quite clearly that it was. And she wasn't supposed to be the first one to die. Wasn't it bloody well understood that it was *his* death they were talking about? Well, wasn't it?

Ove hears a banging at the garage door. Ignores it. Straightens the creases of his trousers. Looks at himself in the reverse mirror. Wonders whether perhaps he should have put on a tie. She always liked it when he wore a tie. She looked at him then as the most handsome man in the world. He wonders if she will look at him now. If she'll be ashamed of him turning up in the afterlife unemployed and wearing a dirty suit. Will she think he's an idiot who can't even hold down an honest job without being phased out, just because his knowledge has been found wanting on account of some computer. Will she still look at him the way she used to, like a man who can be relied on? A man who can take responsibility for things and fix a water-heater if necessary. Will she like him as much now that he's just an old person with no purpose in the world?

There's more frenetic banging at the garage door. Ove stares sourly at it. More banging. Ove thinks to himself that it's enough now.

'That will do!' he roars and opens the door of the Saab so abruptly that the plastic tube is dislodged from between the window and the moulding and falls onto the concrete floor. Palls of exhaust fumes pour out in all directions.

The Pregnant Foreign Woman should probably have learned by now not to stand so close to doors when Ove is on the other side. But this time she can't avoid getting the garage door right in her face when Ove throws it open violently.

Ove sees her and freezes. She's holding her nose. Looking at him with that distinct expression of someone who just had a garage door slammed into her nose. The exhaust fumes come pouring out of the garage in a dense cloud, covering half of the parking area in a thick, noxious mist.

'I . . . you have to bloo . . . you have to watch out when the door's being opened . . .' Ove manages to say.

'What are you doing?' the Pregnant One manages to bite back at him, whilst watching the Saab with its engine idling and the exhaust spewing out of the mouth of the plastic tube on the floor.

'Me? . . . nothing,' says Ove indignantly, looking as if he'd prefer to shut the garage door again.

Thick red drops are forming in her nostrils. She covers her face with one hand and waves at him with the other.

'I need a lift to the hospital,' she says, tilting her head back.

Ove looks sceptical. 'What the hell? Pull yourself together. It's just a nosebleed.'

She swears in something Ove assumes is Farsi and clamps the bridge of her nose hard between her thumb and index finger. Then she shakes her head impatiently, dripping blood all over her jacket.

'Not because of the nosebleed!'

Ove's a bit puzzled by that. Puts his hands in his pockets.

'No, no. Well then.'

She groans.

'Patrick fell off the ladder.'

She leans her head back, so that Ove stands there talking to the underside of her chin.

'Who's Patrick?' Ove asks the chin.

'My husband,' the chin answers.

'The Lanky One?' asks Ove.

'That's him, yeah,' says the chin.

'And he fell off the ladder?' Ove clarifies.

'Yes. When he was opening the window.'

'Right. What a bloody surprise; you could see that one coming from a mile away . . .'

The chin disappears and the large brown eyes reappear. They don't look entirely pleased.

'Are we going to have a debate about this or what?'

Ove scratches his head, slightly bothered.

'No, no . . . but can't you drive yourself? In that little Japanese sewing machine you arrived in the other day?' he tries to protest.

'I don't have a driving licence,' she replies, mopping blood from her lip.

'What do you mean you don't have a driving licence?' asks Ove, as if her words are utterly inexplicable to him.

Again she sighs impatiently.

'Look, I don't have a driving licence and that's all, what's the problem?'

'How old are you?' Ove asks, almost fascinated now.

'Thirty,' she says impatiently.

'*Thirty*?! And no driving licence? Is there something wrong with you?'

She groans, holding one hand over her nose and snapping her fingers with irritation in front of Ove's face.

'Focus a bit, Ove! The hospital! You have to drive us to the hospital!'

Ove looks almost offended.

'What do you mean, "us"? You'll have to call an ambulance if the person you're married to can't open a window without falling off a ladder . . .'

'I already did! They've taken him to the hospital. But there was no space for me in the ambulance. And now because of the snow, every taxi in town is occupied and the buses are getting bogged down everywhere!'

Scattered streams of blood are running down one of her cheeks. Ove clamps his jaws so hard that he starts gnashing his teeth.

'You can't trust bloody buses. The drivers are always drunks,' he says quietly, his chin at an angle that might make someone believe he was trying to hide his words on the inside of his shirt collar.

Maybe she notices the way his mood shifts as soon as she mentions the word 'bus'. Maybe not. Anyway, she nods, as if this in some way clinches it.

'Right, then. So you have to drive us.'

Ove makes a courageous attempt to point threateningly at her. But to his own dismay he feels it's not as convincing as he might have hoped.

'There are no "have to"s round here. I'm not some bloody mobility service!' he manages to say at last.

But she just squeezes her index finger and thumb even harder round the bridge of her nose. And nods, as if she has not in any way listened to what he just said. She waves, with irritation, towards the garage and the plastic tube on the floor spewing out exhaust fumes thicker and thicker against the ceiling.

'I don't have time to fuss about this any more. Get things ready so we can leave. I'll go and get the children.'

'The CHILDREN???' Ove shouts after her, without getting any kind of answer.

She's already swanned off on those tiny feet that look wholly undersized for that large pregnant bump, disappearing round the corner of the bicycle shed and down towards the houses.

Ove stays where he is, as if waiting for someone to catch up with her and tell her that actually Ove had not finished talking. But no one does. He tucks his fists into his belt and throws a glance at the tube on the floor. It's actually not his responsibility if people can't manage to stay on the ladders they borrow off him – that's his own view.

But of course he can't avoid thinking about what his wife would have told him to do under the circumstances, if she'd been here. And of course it's not so difficult to work it out, Ove realises. Sadly enough.

At long last he walks up to the car and pokes off the tube

from the exhaust pipe with his shoe. Gets into the Saab. Checks his mirrors. Puts it into first and pulls out into the parking area. Not that he cares particularly about how the pregnant foreign woman gets to the hospital. But Ove knows very well that there'll be no end of nagging from his wife if the last thing Ove does in this life is to give a pregnant woman a nosebleed and then abandon her to take the bus.

And if the petrol is going to be used up anyway, he may as well give her a lift there and back. 'Maybe then that woman will leave me in peace,' thinks Ove.

But of course she doesn't.

12

A MAN WHO WAS OVE AND ONE DAY
HE HAD ENOUGH

People always said Ove and Ove's wife were like night and day. Ove realised full well, of course, that he was the night. It didn't matter to him. On the other hand it always amused his wife when someone said it, because she could then point out whilst giggling that people only thought Ove was the night because he was too mean to turn on the sun.

He never understood why she chose him. She only loved abstract things like music and books and strange words. Ove was a man entirely filled with tangible things. He liked screwdrivers and oil filters. He went through life with his hands firmly shoved into his pockets. She danced.

'You only need one ray of light to chase all the shadows away,' she said to him once, when he asked her why she had to be so upbeat the whole time.

Apparently some monk called Francis had written as much in one of her books.

'You don't fool me, darling,' she said with a playful little smile and crept into his big arms. 'You're dancing on the inside, Ove, when no one's watching. And I'll always love you for that. Whether you like it or not.'

Ove never quite fathomed what she meant by that. He'd never been one for dancing. It seemed far too haphazard and giddy. He liked straight lines and clear decisions. That was why he had always liked mathematics. There were right or wrong answers there. Not like the other hippy subjects they tried to trick you into doing at school, where you could 'argue your case'. As if that was a way of concluding a discussion: checking who knew more long words. Ove wanted what was right to be right, and what was wrong to be wrong.

He knew very well that some people thought he was nothing but a grumpy old sod without any faith in people. But, to put it bluntly, that was because people had never given him reason to see it another way.

Because a time comes in all men's lives when they decide what sort of men they're going to be: the kind that lets other people walk all over them, or not.

Ove slept in the Saab the nights after the fire. The first morning he tried to clear up among the ashes and destruction. The second morning he had to accept that this would never sort itself out. The house was lost, and all the work he had put into it.

On the third morning two men, wearing the same kind of white shirt as that chief fireman, turned up. They stood by his gate, apparently quite unmoved by the ruin in front of them. They didn't present themselves by name, only mentioned the name of the authority they came from. As if they were robots sent out by the mother ship.

'We've been sending you letters,' said one of the white shirts, holding out a pile of documents for Ove.

'Many letters,' said the other white shirt and made a note in a pad.

'You never answered,' said the first, as if he was reprimanding a dog.

Ove just stood there, defiant.

'Very unfortunate, this,' said the other, with a curt nod at what used to be Ove's house.

Ove nodded.

'The fire brigade says it was caused by a harmless electrical fault,' continued the first white shirt robotically, pointing at a paper in his hand.

Ove felt a spontaneous objection to his use of the word 'harmless'.

'We've sent you letters,' the second man repeated, waving his pad.

'The municipal boundaries are being redrawn.'

'The land where your house stands will be developed for a number of new constructions.'

'The land where your house stood,' corrected his partner.

'The council is willing to purchase your land at the market price,' said the first man.

'Well . . . a market price now that there's no longer a house on the land,' clarified the other.

Ove took the papers. Started reading.

'You don't have much of a choice,' said the first.

'This is not so much your choice as the council's,' said the other.

The first man tapped his pen impatiently against the papers, pointing at a line at the bottom where it said 'signature'.

Ove stood at his gate and read their document in silence. He became aware of an ache in his breast; it took a long, long time before he understood what it was.

Hate.

He hated those men in white shirts. He couldn't remember having hated anyone before, but now it was like a ball of fire inside. Ove's parents had bought this house. Ove had grown up here. Learned to walk. His father had taught him everything there was to know about a Saab engine here. And after all that, someone at a municipal authority decided something else should be built here. And a man with a round face sold insurance that was not insurance. A man in a white shirt prevented Ove from putting out a fire and now two other white shirts stood here talking about a 'market price'.

But Ove really did not have a choice. He could have stood there until the sun had completely risen, but he could not change the situation.

So he signed their document. While keeping his fist clenched in his pocket.

* * *

He left the plot where once his parental home had stood, and he never looked back. Rented a little room from an old lady in town. Sat and stared desolately at the wall all day. In the evening he went to work. Cleaned the train compartments. In the morning, he and the other workers were told not to go to their usual changing rooms, they had to go back to the head office to pick up new sets of work clothes.

As Ove was walking down the corridor he met Tom. It was the first time they had seen each other since Ove got blamed for the theft from the carriage. A more sensible man than Tom would probably have avoided eye contact. Or tried to pretend that the incident had never happened. But Tom was not a more sensible sort of man.

'Well, if it isn't the little thief!' he exclaimed with a combative smile.

Ove didn't answer. Tried to get past but got a hard elbow from one of the younger colleagues Tom surrounded himself with. Ove looked up. The younger colleague was smiling disdainfully at him.

'Hold on to your wallets, the thief's here!' Tom called out so loud that his voice echoed through the corridors.

With one hand, Ove took a firmer grip on the pile of clothes in his arm. But he clenched his fist in his pocket. Went into an empty changing room. Took off his dirty old work clothes, unclipped his father's dented wristwatch and put it on the bench. When he turned round to go into the shower, Tom was standing in the doorway.

'We heard about the fire,' he said. Ove could see that Tom was hoping he'd answer.

'That father of yours would have been proud of you! Not even he was useless enough to burn down his own bloody house!' Tom called out to him as he was stepping into the shower.

Ove heard his younger colleagues all laughing together. He closed his eyes, leaned his forehead against the wall and let the hot water flow over him. Stood there for more than twenty minutes. The longest shower he'd ever had.

When he came out, his father's watch was gone. Ove rooted among the clothes on the bench, searched the floor, fine-combed all the lockers.

A time comes in all men's lives when they decide what sort of men they are going to be. Whether they are the kind that let other people tread on them, or not.

Maybe it was because Tom had put the blame on him for the theft in the carriage. Maybe it was the fire. Maybe it was the bogus insurance agent. Or the white shirts. Or maybe it was just enough now. There and then, it was as if someone had removed a fuse in Ove's mind. Everything in his eyes grew a shade darker. He walked out of the changing room, still naked and with water dripping from his flexing muscles. Walked to the bottom of the corridor to the foremen's changing room, kicked the door open and cleared a way through the astonished press of men inside. Tom was standing in front of a mirror at the far end, trimming his bushy beard. Ove gripped him by the shoulder and roared so loudly that the sheet-metal-covered walls echoed.

'Give me back my watch!'

Tom, with a superior expression, looked down at his face. His dark figure towered over Ove like a shadow.

'I don't have your bloo—'

'GIVE IT HERE!' Ove bellowed before Tom had reached the end of the sentence, so fiercely that the other men in the room saw fit to move a little closer to their lockers.

A second later Tom's jacket had been ripped out of his hands with such power that he didn't even think of protesting. He just stood there, like a punished child, as Ove hauled out his wrist-watch from the inside pocket.

And then Ove hit him. Just once. It was enough. Tom collapsed like a sack of wet flour. By the time the heavy body hit the floor, Ove had already turned around and walked away.

A time like that comes for all men, when they choose what sort of men they want to be. And if you don't know the story you don't know the men.

* * *

100

Tom was taken to the hospital. Again and again he was asked what had happened, but Tom's eyes just flickered and he mumbled something about having 'slipped'. And strangely enough, none of the other men who'd been in the changing rooms at the time had any recollection of what had happened.

That was the last time Ove saw Tom. And, he decided, the last time he'd let anyone trick him.

He kept his job as a night cleaner, but he gave up his job at the construction site. He no longer had a house to build, and anyway he'd learned so much about construction by this point that the men in their hard hats no longer had anything to teach him.

They gave him a toolbox as a farewell present. This time with new-bought tools. 'To the puppy. To help you build something that lasts,' they'd written on a piece of paper.

Ove had no immediate use for it, so he carried it about aimlessly for a few days. Finally the old lady renting him a room took pity on him and started looking for things round the house for him to mend. It was more peaceful that way for both of them.

Later that year he enlisted for military service. He scored the highest possible mark for every physical test. The recruitment officer liked this taciturn young man who seemed as strong as a bear, and he pressed him to consider a career as a professional soldier. Ove thought it sounded good. Military personnel wore uniforms and followed orders. All knew what they were doing. All had a function. Things had a place. Ove felt he could actually be good as a soldier. In fact, as he went down the stairs to have his obligatory medical examination, he felt lighter in his heart than he had for many years. As if he had been given a sudden purpose. A goal. Something to be.

His joy lasted no more than ten minutes.

The recruitment officer had said that the medical examination was a 'mere formality'. But when the stethoscope was held against Ove's chest, something was heard that should not have been heard. He was sent to a doctor in the city. A week later he was informed that he had a rare congenital heart condition. He was exempted from any further military service. Ove called and protested. He wrote letters. He went to three other doctors in the hope that a mistake had been made. It was no use.

'Rules are rules,' said a white-shirted man in the army's administrative offices the last time Ove went there to try to overturn the decision. Ove was so disappointed that he did not even wait for the bus; instead he walked all the way back to the train station. He sat on the platform, more despondent than at any time since his father's death.

A few months later he would walk down that platform with the woman he was destined to marry. But at that precise moment, of course, he had no idea of this.

He went back to his work as a night-cleaner on the railways. Grew quieter than ever. The old lady whose room he rented eventually grew so tired of his gloomy face that she arranged for him to borrow a nearby garage. After all, the boy had that car he was always fiddling with, she said. Maybe he could keep himself entertained with all that?

Ove took his entire Saab to pieces in the garage the next morning. He cleaned all the parts, and then put them together again. To see if he could do it. And to have something to do.

When he was done with it, he sold the Saab at a profit and bought a newer but otherwise identical Saab 93. The first thing he did was to take it to pieces. To see if he could manage it. And he could.

His days passed like this, slow and methodical. And then one morning he saw her. She had brown hair and blue eyes and red shoes and a big yellow clasp in her hair.

And then there was no more peace and quiet for Ove.

13

A MAN CALLED OVE AND A CLOWN
CALLED BEPPO

'Ove's funny,' titters the three-year-old with delight.

'Yeah,' the seven-year-old mumbles, not at all as impressed. She takes her little sister by the hand and walks with grown-up steps towards the hospital entrance.

Their mother looks as if she's going to have a go at Ove, but seems to decide that there's no time for that. She waddles off towards the entrance, one hand on her pouting belly, as if concerned that the child may try to escape.

Ove walks behind, dragging his steps. He doesn't care that she thinks 'it's easier just to pay up and stop arguing'. Because it's actually about the principle. Why is that parking attendant entitled to give Ove a ticket for questioning why one has to pay for hospital parking? Ove is not the sort of man who'll stop himself from roaring: 'You're just a fake policeman!' at a parking attendant. That's all there is to say about it.

You go to hospital to die, Ove knows that. It's enough that the state wants to be paid for everything you do while you're alive. When it also wants to be paid for the parking when you go to die, Ove thinks that's about far enough. He explained this in so many words to the parking attendant. And that's when the parking attendant started waving his book at him. And that's when Parvaneh started raging about how she'd be quite happy to pay up. As if *that* was the important part of the discussion.

Women don't seem to get principles.

He hears the seven-year-old complaining in front of him that her clothes are smelling of exhaust. Even though they kept the Saab's windows rolled down all the way, it wasn't possible to get rid of the stench. Their mother had asked Ove what he'd really been doing in there in the garage, but Ove had just answered with a sound more or less like when you try to move a bathtub by dragging it across some tiles. Of course for the three-year-old it was the greatest adventure of her life to be able to drive along in a car with all its windows down although it was below zero outside. The seven-year-old, on the other hand, had burrowed her face into her scarf and vented a good deal more scepticism. She'd been irritated about slipping around with her bottom on the sheets of newspaper Ove had spread across the seat to stop them 'filthifying things'. Ove had also spread newspaper on the front seat, but her mother snatched it away before she sat down. Ove had looked more than advisably displeased about this, but managed not to say anything. Instead he continuously glanced at her stomach all the way to the hospital, as if anxious that she might suddenly start leaking over the upholstery.

'Stand still here now,' she says to the girls when they are in the hospital reception.

They're surrounded by glass walls and benches smelling of disinfectant. There are nurses in white clothes and colourful plastic slippers and old people dragging themselves back and forth in the corridors, leaning on rickety walkers. On the floor is a sign announcing that Lift 2 in Entrance A is out of order, and that visitors to Ward 114 are therefore asked to go to Lift 1 in Entrance C. Beneath that is another message, announcing that Lift 1 in Entrance C is out of order and visitors to Ward 114 are asked to go to Lift 2 in Entrance A. Under that message is a third message, announcing that Ward 114 is closed this month because of repairs. Under that message is a picture of a clown, informing people that Beppo the hospital clown is visiting sick children today.

'Where did Ove get to now?' Parvaneh bursts out.

'He went to the toilet, I think,' mumbles the seven-year-old.

'Clauwn!' says the three-year-old, pointing happily at the sign.

'Do you know you have to *pay* them here to go to the toilet?' Ove exclaims incredulously.

Parvaneh spins round and gives Ove a harassed look.

'Do you need change?'

Ove looks offended.

'Why would I need change?'

'For the toilet?'

'I don't need to go to the toilet.'

'But you said . . .' she begins, then stops herself and shakes her head. 'Forget it, just forget it . . . when does the parking ticket run out?' she asks instead.

'Ten minutes.'

She groans.

'Don't you understand it'll take longer than ten minutes?'

'In that case I'll go out and feed the meter in ten minutes,' says Ove, as if this was quite obvious.

'Why don't you just pay for longer and save yourself the bother?' she asks and looks like she wishes she hadn't as soon as the question crosses her lips.

'Because that's exactly what they want! They're not getting a load of money for time we might not even *use*!'

'Oh, I don't have the strength for this . . .' sighs Parvaneh and holds her forehead.

She looks at her daughters.

'Will you sit here nicely with Uncle Ove while Mum goes to see how Dad is? Please?'

'Yeah, yeah,' nods the seven-year-old grumpily.

'Yeeeees!' the three-year-old shrieks with excitement.

'What?' whispers Ove.

Parvaneh stands up.

'What do you mean "with Ove"? Where do you think you're going?' To his great consternation, the Pregnant One seems not to register the level of upset in his voice.

'You have to sit here and keep an eye on them,' she states curtly and disappears down the corridor before Ove can raise further objections.

Ove stands there staring at her. As if he was expecting her to come rushing back and crying out that she was only joking. But she doesn't. So Ove turns to the girls. And in the next second he looks as if he's just about to shine a desk lamp into their eyes and interrogate them on their whereabouts at the time of the murder.

'BOOK!' screams the three-year-old at once and rushes off towards the corner of the waiting room, where there's a veritable chaos of toys, games and picture books.

Ove nods and, having confirmed to himself that this three-year-old seems to be reasonably self-motivating, he turns his attention to the seven-year-old.

'Right, and what about you?'

'What do you mean, me?' she counters with indignation.

'Do you need food or do you have to go for a wee or anything like that?'

The child looks at him as if he just offered her a beer and a cigarette.

'I'm almost EIGHT! I can go to the toilet MYSELF!'

Ove throws out his arms abruptly.

'Sure, sure. So bloody sorry for asking.'

'Mmm,' she snorts.

'You swored!' yells the three-year-old as she turns up again, running to and fro between Ove's trouser legs.

He sceptically peruses this grammatically challenged little natural disaster. She looks up and her whole face smiles at him.

'Read!' she orders him in an excitable manner, holding up a book with her arms stretched out so far that she almost loses her balance.

Ove looks at the book more or less as if it just sent him a chain letter insisting that the book was really a Nigerian prince who had a 'very lucrative investment opportunity' for Ove and now only needed Ove's account number 'to sort something out'.

106

'Read!' she demands again, climbing the bench in the waiting room with surprising agility.

Ove reluctantly sits about a metre away on the bench. The three-year-old sighs impatiently and disappears from sight, her head reappearing seconds later under his arm with her hands leaning against his knee for support and her nose pressed against the colourful pictures in the book.

'Once upon a time there was a little train,' reads Ove, with all the enthusiasm of someone reciting a tax statement.

Then he turns the page. The three-year-old stops him and goes back. The seven-year-old shakes her head tiredly.

'You have to say what happens on that page as well. And do voices,' she says.

Ove stares at her.

'What bloo—'

He clears his throat mid-sentence.

'What voices?' he corrects himself.

'Fairytale voices,' replies the seven-year-old.

'You swored,' the three-year-old announces with glee.

'Did not,' says Ove.

'Yes,' says the three-year-old.

'We're not doing any bloo— We're not doing any voices!'

'Maybe you're no good at reading stories,' notes the seven-year-old.

'Maybe you're no good at listening to them!' Ove counters.

'Maybe you're no good at TELLING THEM!'

Ove looks at the book, very unimpressed.

'What kind of sh—nonsense is this anyway? Some talking train? Is there nothing about cars?'

'Maybe there's something about nutty old men instead,' mutters the seven-year-old.

'I'm not an "old man",' Ove hisses.

'Clauwn!' the three-year-old cries out jubilantly.

'And I'm not a CLOWN either!' he roars.

The older one rolls her eyes at Ove, not unlike the way her mother often rolls her eyes at Ove.

'She doesn't mean you. She means the clown.'

Ove looks up and catches sight of a full-grown man who's quite seriously got himself dressed up as a clown, standing in the doorway of the waiting room.

He's got a big stupid grin on his face as well.

'CLAAUUWN,' the toddler howls, jumping up and down on the bench in a way that finally convinces Ove that the kid is on drugs.

He's heard about that sort of thing. They have that Attention Deficit Hyperactivity Disorder and get to take amphetamines on prescription.

'And who's this little girl here, then? Does she want to see a magic trick, perhaps?' the clown exclaims helpfully and squelches over to them like a drunken moose, in a pair of large red shoes that, Ove confirms to himself, only an utterly meaningless person would prefer to wear rather than getting himself a proper job.

The clown looks gaily at Ove.

'Has Uncle got a five-crown piece, perhaps?'

'No, Uncle doesn't, perhaps,' Ove replies.

The clown looks surprised. Which isn't an entirely successful look for a clown.

'But . . . listen, it's a magic trick, you do have a coin on you don't you?' mumbles the clown in his more normal voice, which contrasts quite strongly with his character and reveals that behind this idiotic clown a quite ordinary idiot is hiding, probably all of twenty-five years old.

'Come on, I'm a hospital clown. It's for the children's sake. I'll give it back.'

'Just give him a five-crown coin,' says the seven-year-old.

'CLAAUUWN!' screams the three-year-old.

Ove peers down with exasperation at the tiny speech defect and wrinkles his nose.

'Right,' he says, taking out a five-crown piece from his wallet.

Then he points at the clown.

'But I want it back. Immediately. I'm paying for the parking with that.'

The clown nods eagerly and snatches the coin out of his hand.

Minutes later, Parvaneh comes back down the corridor to the waiting room. She stops, confusedly scanning the room from side to side.

'Are you looking for your girls?' a nurse asks sharply behind her.

'Yes,' Parvaneh answers, perplexed.

'There,' says the nurse in a not entirely appreciative way and points at a bench by the large glass doors leading onto the parking area.

Ove is sitting there, with his arms crossed, looking very angry.

On one side of him sits the seven-year-old, staring up at the ceiling with an utterly bored expression, and on the other side sits the three-year-old, looking as if she just found out she's going to have an ice cream breakfast every day for a whole month. On either side of the bench stand two particularly large representatives of the hospital's security guards, both with very grim facial expressions.

'Are these your children?' one of them asks. He doesn't look at all as if he's having an ice cream breakfast.

'Yes, what did they do?' Parvaneh wonders, almost terrified.

'*They* didn't do anything,' the other security guard replies, with a hostile stare at Ove.

'Me neither,' Ove mutters sulkily.

'Ove hit the clauwn!' the three-year-old shrieks delightedly.

'Sneak,' says Ove.

Parvaneh stares at him, agape, and can't even think of anything to say.

'He was no good at magic anyway,' the seven-year-old groans. 'Can we go home now?' she asks, standing up.

'Why . . . hold on . . . what . . . what clown?'

'The clauwn Beppo,' the toddler explains, nodding wisely.

'He was going to do magic,' says her sister.

'Rubbish magic,' says Ove.

'Like, he was going to make Ove's five-crown coin go away,' the seven-year-old elaborates.

'And then he tried to give back *another* five-crown coin!' Ove interjects, with an insulted stare at the nearby security guards, as if this should be enough of an explanation.

'Ove HIT the clauwn, Mum,' the three-year-old titters as if this was the best thing that ever happened in her whole life.

Parvaneh stares for a long time at Ove, the three-year-old, seven-year-old and the two security guards.

'We're here to visit my husband. He's had an accident. I'm bringing in the children now to say hello to him,' she explains to the guards.

'Daddy fall!' says the three-year-old.

'That's fine,' nods one of the security guards.

'But this one stays here,' confirms the other security guard and points at Ove.

'I hardly hit him. I just gave him a little poke,' Ove mumbles; adding, 'Bloody fake policemen,' just to be on the safe side.

'Honestly, he was no good at magic anyway,' says the seven-year-old grumpily in Ove's defence as they leave to visit their father.

An hour later they are back at Ove's garage. The Lanky One has one arm and one leg in plaster and has to stay at the hospital for several days, Ove has been informed by Parvaneh. When she told him, Ove had to bite his lip very hard to stop himself laughing. He actually got the feeling Parvaneh was doing the same thing. The Saab still smells of exhaust when he collects the sheets of newspaper from the seats.

'Please, Ove, are you sure you won't let me pay the parking fine?' says Parvaneh.

'Is it your car?' Ove grunts.

'No.'

'Well then,' he replies.

'But it feels a bit like it was my fault,' she repeats, concerned.

'You don't hand out parking fines. The council does. So it's the bloody council's fault,' says Ove and closes the door of the Saab. 'And those fake policemen at the hospital,' he adds, clearly still very upset that they forced him to sit without moving on that bench until Parvaneh came back to pick him up and they went home. As if he couldn't be trusted to wander about freely among the other hospital visitors.

Parvaneh looks at him for a long time in thoughtful silence. The seven-year-old gets tired of waiting and starts walking across the parking area towards the house. The three-year-old looks at Ove with a radiant smile.

'You're funny!' She smiles.

Ove looks at her and puts his hands in his trouser pockets.

'Uh huh, uh huh. You shouldn't turn out too bad yourself.'

The three-year-old nods excitedly. Parvaneh looks at Ove, looks at the plastic tube on the floor of his garage. Looks at Ove again, a touch worried.

'I could do with a bit of help taking the ladder away . . .' she says, as if she was in the middle of a much longer thought.

Ove kicks distractedly at the asphalt.

'And I think we have a radiator, as well, that doesn't work,' she adds; a passing thought. 'Would be nice of you if you could have a look at it. Patrick doesn't know how to do things like that, you know,' she says and takes the three-year-old by the hand.

Ove nods slowly.

'No. Might have known.'

Parvaneh nods. Then she suddenly gives off a satisfied smile. 'And you can't let the girls freeze to death tonight, Ove, right? It's quite enough that they had to watch you assault a clown, no?'

Ove gives her a dour glance. Silently, to himself, as if negotiating, he concedes that he can hardly let the children perish just because their no-good father can't open a window without falling off a ladder. There'd be a hellish amount of nagging from Ove's wife if he went and arrived in the next world as a newly qualified child murderer.

Then he picks up the plastic tube from the floor and hangs it up on a hook on the wall. Locks the Saab with the key. Closes the garage. Tugs at it three times to make sure it's closed. Then goes to fetch his tools from the shed.

Tomorrow's as good a day as any to kill oneself.

14

A MAN WHO WAS OVE AND
A WOMAN ON A TRAIN

She had a golden brooch pinned to her front, in which the sunlight reflected hypnotically through the train window. It was half past six in the morning, Ove had just clocked off his shift and was actually supposed to be taking the train home. But then he saw her on the platform with all her rich auburn hair and her blue eyes and all her effervescent laughter. And he got back on the train. Of course he didn't quite know himself why he was doing it. He had never been spontaneous before in his life. But when he saw her it was as if something malfunctioned.

He convinced one of the conductors to lend him his spare pair of trousers and shirt, so he didn't have to look like a train cleaner, and then Ove went to sit by Sonja. It was the single best decision he would ever make.

He didn't know what he was going to say. But he had hardly had time to sink into the seat before she turned to him cheerfully, smiled warmly and said 'hello'. And he found he was able to say 'hello' back to her without any significant complications. And when she saw that he was looking at the pile of books she had in her lap, she tilted them slightly so he could read their titles. Ove only understood about half the words.

'You like reading?' she asked him brightly.

Ove shook his head with some insecurity, but it didn't seem to concern her very much. She just smiled, said that she loved books more than anything, and started telling him excitedly what each of the ones in her lap was about. And Ove realised that he wanted to hear her talking about the things she loved for the rest of his life.

He had never heard anything quite as amazing as that voice. She talked as if she was continuously on the verge of breaking into giggles. And when she giggled she sounded the way Ove imagined champagne bubbles would have sounded if they were capable of laughter. He didn't quite know what he should say to avoid seeming uneducated and stupid, but it proved to be less of a problem than he had thought.

She liked talking and Ove liked keeping quiet. Retrospectively, Ove assumed that was what people meant when they said that people were compatible.

Many years later she told him that she had found him quite puzzling when he came to sit with her in that compartment. Abrupt and blunt in his whole being. But his shoulders were broad and his arms so muscular that they stretched the fabric of his shirt. And he had kind eyes. He listened when she talked, and she liked making him smile. Anyway the journey to school was so boring that it was pleasant just to have some company.

She was studying to be a teacher. Came on the train every day, after ten or twenty kilometres she changed to another train, then a bus. All in all, it was a one and a half hour journey in the wrong direction for Ove. Only when they crossed the platform that first time, side by side, and stood by her bus stop, did she ask what he was doing there. And when Ove realised that he was only five or so kilometres from the military barracks where he would have been had it not been for that problem with his heart, the words slipped out of him before he understood why.

'I'm doing my military service over there,' he said, waving vaguely.

'So maybe we'll see each other on the train going back as well. I go home at five . . .'

Ove couldn't think of anything to say. He knew, of course,

that one does not go home from military installations at five o'clock, but she clearly did not. So he just shrugged. And then she got on her bus and was gone.

Ove decided that this was undoubtedly very impractical in many ways. But there was not a lot to be done about it. So he turned round, found a signpost pointing out the way to the little centre of the tiny student town where he now found himself, at least a two-hour journey from his home. And then he started walking. After forty-five minutes he asked his way to the only tailor in the area, and, after eventually finding it, ponderously stepped inside to ask whether it would be possible to have a shirt ironed and a pair of trousers pressed and, if so, how long it would take. 'Ten minutes, if you wait,' came his answer.

'Then I'll be back at four,' said Ove and left. He wandered back down to the train station and lay down on a bench in the waiting hall. At quarter past three he went all the way back to the tailor's, had his shirt and trousers pressed while he sat waiting in his underwear in the staff toilet, then walked back to the station and took the train back with her for an hour and a half back to her station. And then travelled for another half-hour to his own station. He repeated the whole thing the day after. And the day after that. On the following day the man from the cash desk at the train station intervened and made it clear to Ove that he couldn't sleep here like some loafer, surely he could understand that? Ove saw the point he was making, but explained that there was a woman at stake here. When he heard this, the man from the ticket desk gave him a little nod and from then on let him sleep in the left luggage room. Even men at train station ticket desks have been in love.

Ove did the same thing every day for three months. In the end she grew tired of his never inviting her out for dinner. So she invited herself instead.

'I'll be waiting here tomorrow evening at eight o'clock. I want you to be wearing a suit and I'd like you to invite me out for dinner,' she said succinctly as she stepped off the train one Friday evening.

And so it was.

Ove had never been asked how he lived before he met her. But if anyone had asked him, he would have answered that he didn't.

On the Saturday evening he put on his father's old brown suit. It was tight round his shoulders. Then he ate two sausages and seven potatoes, which he prepared in the little kitchenette in his room, before doing his rounds of the house to put in a couple of screws, which the old lady had asked him to do.

'Are you meeting someone?' she asked, pleased to see him coming down the stairs. She had never seen him wearing a suit. Ove nodded gruffly.

'Yeah,' he said in a way that could either be described as a word or an inhalation. The older woman nodded and probably tried to hide a little smile.

'It must be someone very special if you've dressed yourself up like that,' she said.

Ove inhaled again and nodded curtly. When he was at the door, she called out from the kitchen.

'Flowers, Ove!'

Perplexed, Ove stuck his head round the partition wall and stared at her.

'She'd probably like some flowers,' the old woman declared with some emphasis.

Ove cleared his throat and closed the front door.

For more than fifteen minutes he stood waiting for her at the station in his tight-fitting suit and his new-polished shoes. He was sceptical about people who came late. 'If you can't depend on someone being on time, you shouldn't trust 'em with anything more important either,' he used to mutter when people came dribbling along with their clocking-in cards three or four minutes late, as if this didn't matter. As if the railway line would just lie there waiting for them in the morning and not have something better to do.

So for each of those fifteen minutes that Ove stood waiting at the station he was slightly irritated. And then the irritation turned into a certain anxiety, and after that he decided that Sonja had only been ribbing him when she suggested they should meet. He had never felt so silly in his entire life. Of course she didn't want to go out with him, how could he have got that into his head? His humiliation, when the insight dawned on him, welled up like a stream of lava and he was tempted to toss the flowers in the nearest bin and march off without turning round.

Looking back, he couldn't quite explain why he stayed. Maybe because he felt, in spite of it all, that an agreement to meet was an agreement. And maybe there was some other reason. Something a little harder to put your finger on. He didn't know it at that moment, of course, but he was destined to spend so many quarter-hours of his life waiting for her that his old father would have gone cross-eyed if he'd found out. And when she did finally turn up, in a long floral-print skirt and a cardigan so red that it made Ove shift his body weight from his right foot to his left, he decided that maybe her inability to be on time was not the most important thing.

The woman at the florist's had asked him 'what he wanted'. He informed her gruffly that this was a bit of a bloody question to ask. After all she was the one who sold the greens and he the one who bought them, not the other way round. The woman had looked a bit bothered about that, but then she asked if the recipient of the flowers had some favourite colour, perhaps? 'Pink,' Ove had said with great certainty, although he did not know.

And now she stood outside the station with his flowers pressed happily to her breast, in all that red cardigan of hers, making the rest of the world look as if it was made in greyscale.

'They're absolutely beautiful,' she smiled, in that candid way that made Ove stare down at the ground and kick at the gravel.

Ove wasn't much for restaurants. He had never understood why one would ever eat out for a lot of money when one could eat at home. He wasn't so taken with show-off furniture and elaborate cooking, and he was very much aware of his conversational shortcomings as well. Whatever the case, he had at least eaten in advance so he could afford to let her order whatever she wanted from the menu, while opting for the cheapest dish for himself. And at least if she asked him something he wouldn't have his mouth full of food. To him it seemed like a good plan.

While she was ordering, the waiter smiled ingratiatingly. Ove knew all too well what both he and the other diners in the restaurant had thought when they came in. She was too good for Ove, that's what they'd thought. And Ove felt very silly about that. Mostly because he entirely agreed with their opinion.

She told him with great animation about her studies, about books she'd read or films she'd seen. And when she looked at Ove she made him feel, for the first time, that he was the only man in the world. And Ove had enough integrity to realise that this wasn't right, he couldn't sit here lying any longer. So he cleared his throat, collected his faculties and told her the whole truth. That he wasn't doing his military service at all, that in fact he was just a simple cleaner on the trains who had a defective heart and who had lied for no other reason than that he enjoyed riding with her on the train so very much. He assumed this would be the only dinner he ever had with her, and he did not think she deserved having it with a fraudster. When he had finished his story he put his napkin on the table and got out his wallet to pay.

'I'm sorry,' he mumbled, shame-faced, and kicked his chair leg a little, before adding in such a low voice that it could hardly even be heard: 'I just wanted to know what it felt like to be someone you look at.' As he was getting up she reached across the table and put her hand on his.

'I've never heard you say so many words before,' she smiled.

He mumbled something about how this didn't change the facts. He was a liar. When she asked him to sit down again he obliged her and sank back into his chair. She wasn't angry, the way he thought she'd be. She started laughing. In the end she said it hadn't actually been so difficult working out that he wasn't doing his military service, because he never wore a uniform.

'Anyway, everyone knows soldiers don't go home at five o'clock on weekdays.'

Ove had hardly been as discreet as a Russian spy, she added. She'd come to the conclusion that he had his reasons for it. And she'd liked the way he listened to her. And made her laugh. And that, she said, had been more than enough for her.

And then she asked him what he really wanted to do with his life, if he could choose anything he wanted. And then he answered, without even thinking about it, that he wanted to build houses. Construct them. Draw the plans. Calculate the best way to make them stand where they stood. And then she didn't start laughing as he thought she would. She got angry.

'But why don't you *do* it, then?' she demanded to know.

Ove did not have a particularly good answer to that one.

On the Monday she came to his house with brochures for a correspondence course leading to an engineering qualification. The old landlady was quite overwhelmed when she looked at the beautiful young woman walking up the stairs with self-confident steps. Later she tapped Ove's back and whispered that those flowers were probably a very good investment. Ove couldn't help but agree.

When he came up to his room she was sitting on his bed. Ove stood sulkily in the doorway, with his hands in his pockets. She looked at him and laughed.

'Are we an item now?' she asked.

'Well, yes,' he replied hesitantly, 'I suppose it could be that way.'

And then it was that way.

She handed him the brochures. It was a two-year course, and it proved that all the time Ove had spent on learning about house building had not, after all, been wasted as he once believed. Maybe he did not have much of a head for studying in a conventional sense, but he understood numbers and he understood houses. That got him far. He took the examination after six

119

months. Then another. And another. Then he got his employment at the housing office and stayed there for more than a third of a century. Worked hard, was never ill, paid his mortgage, paid tax, did his duty. Bought a little two-storey terraced house in a recently constructed development in the forest. She wanted to get married so Ove proposed. She wanted children, which was fine with him, said Ove. And their understanding was that children should live in terraced housing developments among other children.

And less than forty years later there was no forest round the house any more. Just other houses. And one day she was lying there in a hospital and holding his hand and telling him not to worry. Everything was going to be all right. Easy for her to say, thought Ove, his breast pulsating with anger and sorrow. But she just whispered, 'Everything will be fine, darling Ove,' and leaned her arm against his arm. And then gently pushed her index finger into the palm of his hand. And then closed her eyes and died.

Ove stayed there with her hand in his for several hours. Until the hospital staff entered the room with warm voices and careful movements, explaining that they had to take her body away. Ove rose from his chair, nodded and went to the undertakers to take care of the documentation. On the Sunday she was buried. On the Monday he went to work.

But if anyone had asked, he would have told them that he never lived before he met her. And not after, either.

15

A MAN CALLED OVE AND A DELAYED TRAIN

The slightly porky man on the other side of the Plexiglas has backcombed hair and arms covered in tattoos. As if it isn't enough to look like someone has slapped a pack of margarine over his head, he has to cover himself in doodles as well. There's not even a proper motif, as far as Ove can see, just a lot of patterns. Is that something an adult person in a healthy state of mind would consent to? Going about with his arms looking like a pair of pyjamas?

'Your ticket machine doesn't work,' Ove informs him.

'No?' says the man behind the Plexiglas.

'What do you mean, "no"?'

'I mean . . . I'm asking, doesn't it work?'

'I just told you, it's broken!'

The man behind the Plexiglas looks dubious. 'Maybe there's something wrong with your card? Some dirt on the magnetic strip?' he suggests.

Ove looks as if the man behind the Plexiglas had just raised the possibility of Ove having erectile dysfunction. The man behind the Plexiglas goes silent.

'There's no dirt on my magnetic strip, you can be sure of that,' Ove splutters.

The man behind the Plexiglas nods. Then changes his mind and shakes his head. Tries to explain to Ove that the machine 'actually worked earlier in the day'. Ove dismisses this as utterly irrelevant, of course, because it is clearly broken now. The man behind the Plexiglas wonders if Ove has cash instead. Ove replies that this is none of his bloody business. A tense silence settles.

At long last the man behind the Plexiglas asks if he can 'check out the card'. Ove looks at him as if they just met in a dark alley and he's asked to 'check out' Ove's private parts.

'Don't try anything,' Ove warns as he hesitantly pushes it under the window.

The man behind the Plexiglas grabs the card and rubs it against his leg in a vigorous manner. As if Ove had never read in the newspaper about that thing they call 'skimming'. As if Ove was an idiot.

'What are you DOING?' Ove cries and bangs the palm of his hand against the Plexiglas window.

The man pushes the card back under the window.

'Try it now,' he says.

Ove thinks that any old fool could figure out that if the card wasn't working half a minute ago it isn't going to work now either. Ove points this out to the man behind the Plexiglas.

'Please?' says the man.

Ove sighs demonstratively. Gets out his card again, without taking his eyes off the Plexiglas. The card works.

'You see!' jeers the man behind the Plexiglas.

Ove glares at the card as if he feels it has double-crossed him, before he puts it back in his wallet.

'Have a good day,' the man behind the Plexiglas calls out behind him.

'We'll see,' mutters Ove.

For the last twenty years practically every human being he's met has done nothing but drone on at Ove about how he should be paying for everything by card. But cash has always been good enough for Ove; cash has in fact served humanity perfectly well for thousands of years. And Ove doesn't trust the banks and all their electronics.

But his wife insisted on getting hold of one of those cards in spite of it all, even though Ove warned her against it. And when she died the bank simply sent Ove a new card in his name, connected to her account. And now, after he's been buying flowers for her grave for the past six months there's a sum of 136 crowns and 54 öre left on it. And Ove knows very well that this money will disappear into the pocket of some bank director if Ove dies without spending it first.

But now when Ove actually wants to use that damned plastic card, it doesn't work of course. Or there are a lot of extra fees when he uses it in the shops. Which only goes to prove that Ove was right all along. And he's going to say as much to his wife as soon as he sees her, she had better be quite clear about that.

He had gone out this morning long before the sun had drummed up the energy to rise over the horizon, much less any of his neighbours. He had carefully studied the train timetable in the hall. Then he'd turned out the lights, switched off the radiators, locked his front door and left the envelope with all the instructions on the hall mat inside the door. He assumed that someone would find it when they came to take the house.

He fetched the snow shovel, cleared the snow away from the front of the house, put back the shovel in the shed. Locked the shed. Had Ove been a bit more attentive he would have noticed the fairly large cat-shaped cavity in the quite large snowdrift just outside his shed as he started heading off towards the parking area. But because he had more important things on his mind he did not.

Chastened by recent experiences, he did not take the Saab, but walked instead to the station. Because this time neither pregnant foreign women, blonde weeds, Rune's wife nor low-quality rope would be given any opportunity of ruining Ove's morning. He'd bled these people's radiators, loaned them his things, given them lifts to the hospital. But now he was finally on his way.

He checked the train timetable once more. He hated being late. It ruined the planning. Made everything out of step. His wife had been utterly useless at it, keeping to plans. But it was always like that with women. They couldn't stick to a plan even if you glued them to it, Ove had learned. When he was driving somewhere he drew up schedules and plans and decided where they'd fill up and when they'd stop for coffee, all in the interest of making the trip as time-efficient as possible. He studied maps and estimated exactly how long each leg of the journey would take and how they should avoid rush hour traffic and the short cuts to take that people with sat-navs wouldn't be able to make head nor tail of. Ove always had a clear travel strategy. His wife, on the other hand, always came up with insanities like 'going by a sense of feel' and 'taking it easy'. As if that was a way for an adult person to get anywhere in life. And then she always remembered that she had to make a call or had forgotten some scarf or other. Or she didn't know which coat to pack at the last moment. Or something else. She always forgot the Thermos of coffee on the draining board, which was actually the *only* important thing. There were four coats in those damned bags but no coffee. As if one could just turn off into a petrol station every hour and buy the burnt fox piss they were selling in there. And get even more delayed. And when Ove got disgruntled she always had to challenge the importance of having a time plan when driving somewhere. 'We're not in a hurry, anyway,' she'd say. As if *that* had anything to do with it.

Now, standing at the station platform, he presses his hands into his pockets. He isn't wearing his suit jacket. It's much too stained and smells too strongly of car exhaust, so he feels she'd probably have a crack at him if he were to turn up in that. She doesn't like the shirt and jumper he's wearing now, but at least they're clean and in a decent condition. It's almost fifteen degrees below zero. He hasn't yet changed the blue autumn jacket for the blue winter coat, and the cold is blowing straight through it. He's been a bit distracted of late, he has to admit. He hasn't given any real thought to how one is supposed to present oneself when arriving upstairs. Initially he thought one should be all spruced up and formal. Most likely there'll be some kind of uniform up there, to avoid confusion. He supposes there will be all sorts of people – foreigners, for instance, each one wearing stranger kit than the next. Presumably it will be possible to organise your clothes once you get there; surely there will even be some sort of wardrobe department?

The platform is almost empty. On the other side of the track are some sleepy-looking youths with oversize backpacks which, Ove decides, are most likely filled with drugs. Alongside them is a man in his forties in a grey suit and a black overcoat. He's reading the newspaper. A little further off are some small-talking women in their best years with county council logos on their chests and purple tresses of hair. They're chain-smoking long menthol cigarettes.

On Ove's side of the track it's empty but for three over-dimensioned municipal employees in their mid-thirties in workmen's trousers and hard hats, standing in a ring and staring down into a hole. Around them is a carelessly erected loop of cordon tape. One of them has a mug of coffee from 7-Eleven, another is eating a banana, the third is trying to poke his mobile without removing his gloves. It's not going so well. And the hole stays where it is. And still we're surprised when the whole world comes crashing down in a financial crisis, Ove thinks. When people do little more than standing around eating bananas and looking into holes in the ground all day.

He checks his watch. One minute left. He stands at the edge of the platform. Balancing the soles of his shoes over the edge. It's a fall of no more than one and a half metres, he estimates. One sixty, possibly. There's a certain symbolism in a train taking his life and he doesn't like this much. He doesn't think the train driver should have to see the awfulness of it. For this reason he has decided to jump when the train is very close, so it's the side of the first carriage that throws him onto the rails rather than the big windscreen at the front. He looks in the direction the train is coming from and slowly starts counting. It's important that the timing is absolutely right, he determines. The sun is just up; it shines obstinately into his eyes like a child who has just been given a torch.

And that's when he hears the first scream.

Ove looks up just in time to see the suit-wearing man in his black overcoat starting to sway back and forth, like a panda that's been given a Valium overdose. It continues for a second or so, then the suit-wearing man looks up blindly and his whole body is struck with some form of nervous twitching. His arms shake convulsively. And then, as if the moment is a long sequence of still photographs, the newspaper falls out of his hands and he passes out, falling off the edge onto the track with a thump, as if he were a crate of cement mixture.

The chain-smoking old girls with the county council logos on their breasts start shrieking in panic. The drug-taking youths stare at the track, their hands enmeshed in their backpack straps as if fearing that they might otherwise fall over. Ove stands on the edge of the platform on the other side and looks with irritation from one to the other.

'For Christ's sake,' fumes Ove to himself at long last as he jumps down onto the track. 'GRAB HOLD HERE WILL YOU!' he calls out to one of the backpackers on the platform. The stultified youth drags himself slowly to the edge. Ove hoists up the suit-wearing man in a way that men who have never put their foot in a gym yet have spent their entire lives carrying two concrete plinths under each arm tend to be able to do. He heaves up the body into the backpacker's arms in a way that Audi-driving men wearing neon-bright jogging pants are often incapable of doing.

'He can't stay here in the path of the train, you get that don't you!?'

The backpackers nod in confusion, and finally by their collective efforts manage to drag the suit-wearing body onto the platform. The county council women are still screaming, as if they sincerely believe this is a constructive approach under the circumstances. The man appears to be breathing, but Ove stays down there on the track. He hears the train coming. It's not quite the way he planned it, but it'll have to do.

Then he calmly goes into the middle of the track, puts his

hands in his pocket and stares into the headlights. He hears the warning whistle like a foghorn. Feels the track shaking powerfully under his feet, as if a testosterone-fuelled bull were trying to charge him. He breathes out. In the midst of that inferno of shaking and yelling and the chilling scream of the train's brakes he feels a deep relief.

At last.

To Ove, the moments that follow are elongated as if time itself has applied its brakes and made everything around him travel in slow-motion. The explosion of sounds is muted into a low hiss in his ears, the train approaching so slowly that it's as if it's being pulled along by two decrepit oxen. The headlights flash despairingly at him. And in the interval between two of the flashes, while he isn't blinded, he finds himself establishing eye contact with the train driver. He can't be more than twenty years old. One of those who still gets called 'the puppy' by his older colleagues.

Ove stares into the puppy's face. Clenches his fists in his pockets as if he's cursing himself for what he's about to do. But it can't be helped, he thinks. There's a right way of doing things. And a wrong way.

So the train is perhaps about fifteen metres away when Ove swears with irritation, and as calmly as if he was getting up to fetch himself a cup of coffee, steps out of the way and jumps up on the platform again.

The train has drawn level with him by the time the driver has managed to stop it. The puppy's terror has sucked all the blood out of his face. He is clearly holding back his tears. The two men look at each other through the locomotive window as if they had just emerged from some apocalyptic desert and now realised that neither of them were the last human beings on earth. One is relieved by this insight. And the other disappointed.

The boy in the locomotive nods carefully. Ove nods back with resignation.

Fair enough that Ove no longer wants his life. But the sort

of man who ruins someone else's by making eye contact with him seconds before his body is turned into blood paste against the said person's windscreen; damn it, Ove is not that sort of man. Neither his dad nor Sonja would ever have forgiven him for that.

'Are you all right?' one of the hard-hats calls out behind Ove.

'Another minute and you'd have been a goner!' yells one of the others.

They stand there staring at him, not at all unlike the way they were standing just now and staring into that hole. It seems to be their prime area of competence, in fact: to stare at things. Ove stares back.

'Another second, I mean,' clarifies the man who still has a banana in his hand.

'It could have gone quite badly, that,' sniggers the first hard-hat.

'Really badly,' the other one agrees.

'Could have died, actually,' clarifies the third.

'You're a real hero!'

'Saved their life!'

'His. Saved "his" life,' Ove corrects and hears Sonja's voice in his own.

'Would have died otherwise,' the third one reiterates, taking a forthright bite of his banana.

On the track is the train with all its red emergency lights turned on, puffing and screeching like a very fat person who's just run into a wall. A great number of examples of what Ove assumes must be IT consultants and other disreputable folk come streaming out and stand about dizzily on the platform. Ove puts his hands in his trouser pockets.

'I suppose now you'll have a lot of bloody delayed trains as well,' he says and looks with particular displeasure at the chaotic press of people on the platform.

'Yeah,' says the first hard-hat.

'Reckon so,' says the other.

'Lots and of lots of delays,' the third one agrees.

Ove makes a sound like a heavy bureau that's got a rusted-up hinge. He goes past all three of them without a word.

'Where you off to? You're a hero!' the first hard-hat yells at him, surprised.

'Yeah,' yells the other.

'A hero!' yells the third.

Ove doesn't answer. He walks past the man behind the Plexiglas, back out into the snow-covered streets and starts walking home.

The town slowly wakes up around him with its foreign-made cars and its statistics and credit card debt and all its other crap.

And so this day is also ruined, he confirms with bitterness.

As he is walking alongside the bicycle shed by the parking area, he sees the white Skoda coming past from the direction of Anita and Rune's house. A determined woman with glasses is sitting in the passenger seat, her arms filled with files and papers. Behind the wheel sits the man in the white shirt. Ove has to jump out of the way to avoid being run over as the car races round the corner.

The man lifts a smouldering cigarette towards Ove through the windscreen, and offers a superior half-smile. As if it's Ove's fault that he's in the way, but he's generous enough to let it go.

'Idiot!' Ove yells after the Skoda, but the man in the white shirt doesn't seem to react at all.

Ove memorises the registration number before the car disappears round the corner.

'Soon it'll be your turn, you old fart,' hisses a malevolent voice behind him.

Ove spins round with his fist instinctively raised, and finds himself staring at his own reflection in Blonde Weed's sunglasses. She's holding that damned mutt in her arms. It growls at him.

'They were from the social,' she jeers, with a nod towards the road.

In the parking area, Ove sees that imbecile Anders reversing his Audi out of his garage. It has those new, wave-shaped headlights, Ove notes, presumably designed so that no one at night will be able to avoid the insight that here comes a car driven by an utter shit.

'What business is it of yours?' Ove says to the Weed.

Her lips are pulled into the sort of grimace that comes as close to a real smile as a woman whose lips have been injected with environmental waste and nerve toxins is ever likely to achieve.

'It's my business because this time it's that bloody old man at the bottom of the road they're putting in a home. And after that it'll be you!'

She spits at the ground beside him and walks towards the Audi. Ove watches her, his chest puffing in and out under his shirt. As the Audi swings round she shows him the middle finger on the other side of the window. Ove's first instinct is to run after them and tear that German sheet metal monster, inclusive of imbeciles, weeds, growling mutts and wave-shaped headlights, to smithereens. But then suddenly he feels out of breath, as if he's been running full tilt through the snow. He leans forward, puts his hands on his knees and notices to his own fury that he's panting for air, and his heart racing.

He straightens up after a minute or so. There's a slight flickering effect in his right eye. The Audi has gone. Ove turns round and slowly heads back to his house, one hand pressed to his chest.

When he gets to his house he stops by the shed. Stares down into a cat-shaped hole in the snowdrift.

There's a cat at the bottom of it.

Might have bloody known.

16

A MAN WHO WAS OVE AND

A TRUCK IN THE FOREST

Before that day when the dour and slightly fumbling boy with the muscular body and the sad blue eyes sat down beside Sonja on the train, there were really only three things she loved unconditionally in her life: books, her father and cats.

She'd obviously had quite a lot of attention, it wasn't that. The suitors had come in all shapes and sizes. Tall and dark or short and blond and fun-loving and dull and elegant and boastful and handsome and greedy, and if they hadn't been slightly dissuaded by the stories in the village of Sonja's father keeping one or two firearms in the isolated wooden house out there in the woods, they would most likely have been a bit pushier too. But none of them had looked at her the way that boy looked at her when he sat down beside her on the train. As if she was the only girl in the world.

Sometimes, especially in the first few years, some of her girlfriends questioned the choice she had made. Sonja was very beautiful, as the people around her seemed to find it so important to keep telling her. Furthermore she loved to laugh and, whatever life threw at her, she was the sort of person who took a positive view of it. But Ove was, well, Ove was Ove. Something which the people around her also kept telling Sonja.

He'd been a grumpy old man since he started junior school, they insisted. And she could have someone so much better.

But to Sonja, Ove was never dour and awkward and sharp-edged. To her, he was the slightly dishevelled pink flowers at their first dinner. He was his father's slightly too tight-fitting brown suit across his broad, sad shoulders. He believed so strongly in things: justice and fair play and hard work and a world where right just had to be right. Not so one could get a medal or a diploma or a slap on the back for it, but just because that was how it was supposed to be. Not many men of his kind were made any more, Sonja had understood. So she was holding on to this one. Maybe he didn't write her poems or serenade her with songs or come home with expensive gifts. But no other boy had gone the wrong way on the train for hours every day just because he liked sitting next to her while she spoke.

And when she took hold of his lower arm, thick as her thigh, and tickled him until that sulky boy's face opened up in a smile, it was like a plaster cast cracking round a piece of jewellery, and when this happened it was as if something started singing inside Sonja. And they only belonged to her, those moments.

She didn't get angry with him that first night they had dinner, when he told her he'd lied about his military service. Of course she got angry with him on an immeasurable number of occasions after that, but not that night.

'They say the best men are born out of their faults and that they often improve later on, more than if they'd never done anything wrong,' she'd said gently.

'Who said that?' asked Ove and looked at the triple set of cutlery in front of him on the table, the way one might look at a box that had just been opened while someone said, 'Choose your weapon.'

'Shakespeare,' said Sonja.

'Is that any good?' Ove wondered.

'It's fantastic,' Sonja nodded, smiling.

'I've never read anything with him,' mumbled Ove into the tablecloth.

'By him,' Sonja corrected, and lovingly put her hand on his.

In their almost four decades together Sonja taught hundreds of pupils with learning difficulties to read and write, and she got them to read Shakespeare's collected works. In the same period she never managed to make Ove read a single Shakespeare play. But as soon as they moved into their terraced house he spent every evening for weeks on end in the toolshed. And when he was done, the most beautiful book cases she had ever seen were in their living room.

'You have to keep them somewhere,' he muttered and poked a little cut on his thumb with the tip of a screwdriver.

And she crept into his arms and said that she loved him.

And he nodded.

She only asked once about the burns on his arms.

And she had to piece together the exact circumstances of how he lost his parental home, from the succinct fragments on offer when Ove reluctantly revealed what had happened. In the end she found out how he got the scars. And when one of her girl-friends asked why she loved him she answered that most men ran away from an inferno. But men like Ove ran into it.

Ove did not meet Sonja's father more times than he could count on his fingers. The old man lived a long way north, a good way into the forest, almost as if he had consulted a map of all the population centres in the country before concluding that this was as far from other people as one could live.

Sonja's mother died in the maternity bed. Her father never remarried.

'I have a woman. She's just not home at the moment,' he spat out the few times anyone dared bring up the question.

Sonja moved to the local town when she started studying for her upper secondary examinations – all in humanities subjects – at a sixth form college. Her father looked at her with bound-less indignation when she suggested that he might like to come with her. 'What can I do there? Meet folk?' he growled. He always spoke the word 'folk' as if it was a swear word. So Sonja let him be. Apart from her weekend visits and his monthly trip in the truck to the grocery store in the nearest village, he only had Ernest for company.

Ernest was the biggest farm cat in the world. When Sonja was small she actually thought he was a pony. He came and went in her father's house as he pleased, but he didn't live there. Where he lived, in fact, was not known to anyone. Sonja named him Ernest after Ernest Hemingway. Her father had never bothered with books, but when his daughter sat reading the newspaper at the age of five he wasn't so stupid that he tried to avoid doing something about it. 'A girl can't read shit like that: she'll lose her head,' he stated as he pushed her towards the library counter in the village. The old librarian didn't quite know what he meant by that, but there was no doubt about the girl's quite outstanding intellect.

The monthly trip to the grocery store simply had to be extended to a monthly trip to the library, the librarian and father decided together, without any particular need to discuss it further. By the time Sonja passed her twelfth birthday she had read all the books at least twice. The ones she liked, such as *The Old Man and the Sea*, she'd read so many times that she'd lost count.

So Ernest ended up being called Ernest. And no one owned him. He didn't talk, but he liked to go fishing with her father, who appreciated his qualities. They would share the catch equally once they got home.

The first time Sonja brought Ove out to the old wooden house in the forest, Ove and her father sat in buttoned-up silence opposite each other, staring down at their food for almost an hour, while she tried to encourage some form of civilised conversation. Neither of the two men could quite understand what they were doing there, apart from the fact that it was important to the only woman either of them cared about. They had both protested about the whole arrangement, insistently and vociferously, but without success.

Sonja's father was negatively disposed from the very beginning.

All he knew about this boy was that he came from town and that Sonja had mentioned that he did not like cats very much. These were two characteristics, as far as he was concerned, that gave him reason enough to view Ove as unreliable.

As for Ove, he felt he was at a job interview, and he had never been very good at that sort of thing. So when Sonja wasn't talking, which admittedly she did almost all of the time, there was a sort of silence in the room that can only arise between a man who does not want to lose his daughter and a man who has not yet completely understood that he has been chosen to take her away from there. Finally Sonja kicked Ove's shinbone to make him say something. Ove looked up from his plate and noted the angry twitches around the edges of her eyes. He cleared his throat and looked around with a certain desperation to find something to ask this old man about. Because this was what Ove had learned: if one didn't have anything to say one had to find something to ask. If there was one thing that made people forget to dislike one, it was when they were given the opportunity to talk about themselves.

At long last Ove's gaze fell on the truck, visible through the old man's kitchen window.

'That's an L10, isn't it?' he said, pointing with his fork.

'Yup,' said the old man, looking down at his plate.

'Saab is making them now,' Ove stated with a short nod.

'Scania!' the old man roared, glaring at Ove.

And the room was once again overwhelmed by that silence which can only arise between a woman's beloved and her father.

Ove looked down grimly at his plate. Sonja kicked her father on his shin. Her father looked back at her grumpily. Until he saw those twitches around her eyes. He was not so stupid a man that he had not learned to avoid what tended to happen after them. So he cleared his throat irately and picked at his food.

'Just because some suit at Saab waved his wallet around and bought the factory it don't stop being a Scania,' he grunted in a low voice, which was slightly less accusing, and then moved his shinbones a little further from his daughter's shoe.

Sonja's father had always driven Scania trucks. He couldn't understand why anyone would have anything else. Then, after years of consumer loyalty, they merged with Saab. It was a treachery he never quite forgave them for.

Ove, who, in turn, had become very interested in Scania when they merged with Saab, looked thoughtfully out of the window whilst chewing his potato.

'Does it run well?' he asked.

'No,' muttered the old man irascibly and went back to his plate. 'None of their models run well. None of 'em are built right. Mechanics want half a fortune to fix anything on it,' he added, as if he was actually explaining it to someone sitting under the table.

'I can have a look at it if you'll let me,' said Ove and looked enthusiastic all of a sudden.

It was the first time Sonja could ever remember him actually sounding enthusiastic about anything.

The two men looked at each other for a moment. Then Sonja's father nodded. And Ove nodded curtly back. And then they rose to their feet, objective and determined, in the way two men might behave if they had just agreed to go and kill a third man. A few minutes later Sonja's father came back into the kitchen, leaning on his stick, and sank into his chair with his chronically dissatisfied mumbling. He sat there for a good while stuffing his pipe with care, then at last nodded at the saucepans and managed to say:

'Nice.'

'Thanks, Dad.' She smiled.

'You cooked it. Not me,' he said.

'The thanks was not for the food,' she answered and took away the plates, kissing her father tenderly on his forehead at the same time as she saw Ove diving in under the bonnet of the truck in the yard.

Her father said nothing, just stood up with a quiet snort and took the newspaper from the kitchen top. Halfway to his armchair in the living room he stopped himself, however, and stood there slightly unresolved, leaning on his stick.

'Does he fish?' he finally grunted without looking at her.

'I don't think so,' Sonja answered.

Her father nodded gruffly. Stood silent for a long while.

'I see. He'll have to learn, then,' he grumbled at long last, before putting his pipe in his mouth and disappearing into the living room.

Sonja had never heard him give anyone a higher compliment.

17

A MAN CALLED OVE AND A CAT ANNOYANCE
IN A SNOWDRIFT

'Is it dead?' Parvaneh asks in terror as she rushes forward as quickly as her pregnant belly will allow and stands there staring down into the hole.

'I'm not a vet,' Ove replies – not in an unfriendly way. Just as a point of information.

He doesn't understand where this woman keeps appearing from all the time. Can't a man calmly and quietly stand over a cat-shaped hole in a snowdrift in his own garden any more?

'You have to get him out!' she cries, hitting him on the shoulder with her glove.

Ove looks displeased and pushes his hands deeper into his jacket pockets. He is still having a bit of trouble breathing.

'Don't have to at all,' he says.

'Jesus, what's wrong with you?'

'I don't get along with cats very well,' Ove informs her and plants his heels in the snow.

But her gaze when she turns round makes him move a little further away.

'Maybe he's sleeping,' he offers, peering into the hole. Before adding: 'Otherwise he'll come out when it thaws.'

When the glove comes flying past him again he confirms to himself that keeping a safe distance was a very sound idea.

But the next thing he knows Parvaneh has dived into the

snowdrift; she emerges seconds later with the little deep-frozen creature in her thin arms. It looks like four ice lollies clumsily wrapped in a shredded scarf.

'Open the door!' she yells, really losing her composure now.

Ove presses the soles of his shoes into the snow. He has certainly not begun this day with the intention of letting either women or cats into his house, he'd like to make that very clear to her. But she comes right at him with the animal in her arms and a determination in her steps. It's really only a question of the speed of his reactions whether she walks through him or past him. Ove has never experienced a worse woman when it comes to listening to what decent people tell her. He feels out of breath again. He fights the impulse to clutch his breast.

She keeps going. He gives way. She strides past.

The small icicle-decorated package in her arms obstinately brings up a flow of memories in Ove's head before he can put a stop to them; memories of Ernest, fat, stupid old Ernest, so beloved of Sonja that you could have bounced five-crown coins on her heart whenever she saw him.

'OPEN THE DOOR THEN!' Parvaneh roars and looks round at Ove so abruptly that there's a danger of whiplash.

Ove hauls out the keys from his pocket. As if someone else has taken control of his arm. He's having a hard time accepting what he's actually doing. One part of him in his head is yelling 'NO' while the rest of his body is busy with some sort of teenage rebellion.

'Get me some blankets!' Parvaneh orders and runs across the threshold with her shoes still on.

Ove stands there for a few moments, catching his breath, before he ambles off after her.

'It's bloody freezing in here. Turn up the radiators!' Parvaneh tosses out the words as if this is something quite obvious, gesturing impatiently at Ove as she puts the cat down on his sofa.

'There'll be no turning up of radiators here,' Ove announces firmly. He parks himself in the living room doorway and wonders whether she might try to swat him again with the glove if he tells her at least to put some newspapers under the cat. When she turns to him again he decides to give it a miss. Ove doesn't know if he's ever seen such an angry woman.

'I've got a blanket upstairs,' he says at long last, avoiding her gaze by suddenly feeling incredibly interested in the hall lamp.

'Get it then!'

Ove looks as if he's repeating her words to himself, though silently, in an affected, disdainful voice; but he takes off his shoes and crosses the living room at a cautious distance from her glove striking range.

All the way up and down the stairs he mumbles to himself about why it has to be so damned difficult to get any peace and quiet in this street. Upstairs he stops and takes a few deep breaths. The pain in his chest has gone. His heart is beating normally again. It happens now and then, and he no longer gets stressed about it. It always passes. And he won't be needing that heart for very much longer, so it doesn't matter either way.

He hears voices from the living room. He can hardly believe his ears. Considering how they are constantly preventing him from dying, these neighbours of his are certainly not shy when it comes to driving a man to the brink of madness and suicide. That's for sure.

When Ove comes back down the stairs with the blanket in his hand, the overweight young man from next door is standing in the middle of his living room, looking with curiosity at the cat and Parvaneh.

'Hey, man!' he says cheerfully and waves at Ove.

He's only wearing a T-shirt, even though there's snow outside.

'Okay,' says Ove, silently appalled that you can pop upstairs for a moment only to find when you come back down that you've apparently started a bed and breakfast operation.

'I heard someone shouting, just wanted to check that everything was cool here,' says the young man jovially, shrugging his shoulders so that his back blubber folds the T-shirt into deep wrinkles.

Parvaneh snatches the blanket out of Ove's hand and starts wrapping the cat in it.

'You'll never get him warm like that,' says the young man pleasantly.

'Don't interfere,' says Ove, who, while perhaps not an expert at defrosting cats, does not appreciate at all having people marching into his house and issuing orders about how things should be done.

'Be quiet, Ove!' says Parvaneh and looks entreatingly at the young man. 'What shall we do, then? He's ice-cold!'

'Don't tell me to be quiet,' mumbles Ove.

'He'll die,' says Parvaneh.

'Die my arse, he's just a bit chilly . . .' Ove interjects, in a new attempt to regain control over the situation.

The Pregnant One puts her index finger over his lips and hushes him. Ove looks so absurdly irritated at this it's as if he's going to break into some sort of rage-fuelled pirouette.

When Parvaneh holds up the cat it has started shifting in colour from purple to white. Ove looks a little less sure of himself when he notices this. He glances at Parvaneh. Then reluctantly steps back and gives way.

The young, overweight man takes off his T-shirt.

'But what the . . . this has got to be . . . what are you DOING?' stutters Ove.

His eyes flicker from Parvaneh by the sofa, with the defrosting cat in her arms and water dripping onto the floor, to the young man standing there with his torso bare in the middle of Ove's living room, the fat trembling over his chest down towards his knees, as if he were a big pack of ice cream that had first melted and then been refrozen.

'Here, give him to me,' says the young man unconcernedly and reaches over with two arms thick as tree trunks towards Parvaneh.

When she hands over the cat he encloses it in his enormous embrace, pressing it against his chest as if trying to make a gigantic cat spring roll.

'By the way, my name's Jimmy,' he says to Parvaneh and smiles.

'I'm Parvaneh,' says Parvaneh.

'Nice name,' says Jimmy.

'Thanks! It means "butterfly".' Parvaneh smiles.

'Nice!' says Jimmy.

'You'll smother that cat,' says Ove.

'Oh, give it a rest will you, Ove,' says Jimmy.

'I reckon it would rather freeze to death in a dignified manner than be strangled,' he says to Jimmy, nodding at the dripping ball of fluff pressed into his arms.

Jimmy pulls his good-tempered face into a big grin.

'Chill a bit, Ove. You can say what you like about us fatties, but we're the dog's bollocks when it comes to pumping out a bit of heat!'

Parvaneh peers nervously over his blubbery upper arm and gently puts the palm of her hand against the cat's nose. Then she brightens.

'He's getting warmer,' she exclaims, turning to Ove in triumph.

Ove nods. He was about to say something sarcastic to her. Now he finds, uneasily, that he's relieved at the news. He distracts himself from this emotion by assiduously inspecting the TV remote control.

Not that he's concerned about the cat. It's just that Sonja would have been happy. Nothing more than that.

'I'll heat a bit of water,' says Parvaneh, and in a single snappy movement she slips past Ove and is suddenly standing in his kitchen, tugging at his kitchen cabinets.

'What the hell,' mumbles Ove as he lets go of the remote control and tears off in pursuit.

When he gets there, she's standing motionless and slightly confused in the middle of the floor with his electric kettle in her hand. She looks a bit overwhelmed, as if the realisation of what's happened has only just hit her.

It's the first time Ove has seen this woman run out of something to say. The kitchen has been cleared and tidied, but it's dusty.

It smells of stewed coffee, there's dirt in the crannies, and everywhere are Ove's wife's things. Her little decorative objects

142

in the window, her hair grips left on the kitchen table, her hand-writing on the Post-It notes on the fridge.

The kitchen is filled with those soft wheel marks. As if someone has been going back and forth with a bicycle, thousands of times.

The cooker and kitchen counter are noticeably lower than is usual.

As if the kitchen had been built for a child. Parvaneh stares at them the way people always do when they see it for the first time. Ove has got used to it. He rebuilt the kitchen himself after the accident. The council refused to help, of course.

Parvaneh looks as if she's somehow got stuck.

Ove takes the electric kettle out of her outstretched hands without looking into her eyes. Slowly he fills it with water and plugs it in.

'I didn't know, Ove,' she whispers, contrite.

Ove leans over the low sink with his back to her. She comes forward and puts her fingertips gently on his shoulder.

'I'm sorry, Ove. Really. I shouldn't have barged into your kitchen without asking first.'

Ove clears his throat and nods without turning round. He doesn't know how long they stand there. She lets her enervated hand rest on his shoulder. He decides not to push it away.

Jimmy's voice breaks the silence.

'You got anything to eat?' he calls out from the living room.

Ove's shoulder slips away from Parvaneh's hand. He shakes his head, wipes his face with the back of his hand and heads off to the fridge still without looking at her.

Jimmy clucks gratefully when Ove comes out of the kitchen and hands him a sausage sandwich. Ove parks himself a few metres away and looks a bit grim.

'So how is he, then?' he says with a curt nod at the cat in Jimmy's arms.

Water is dripping liberally onto the floor now, but the animal is slowly but surely regaining both its shape and colour.

'Seems better, no?' grins Jimmy as he wolfs down the sandwich in a single bite.

Ove gives him a sceptical look. Jimmy is perspiring like a bit of pork left on a sauna boiler. There's something mournful in his eyes when he looks back at Ove.

'You know it was . . . pretty bad with your wife, Ove. I always liked her. She made, like, the best chow in town.'

Ove looks at him, and for the first time all morning he doesn't look a bit angry.

'Yes. She . . . cooked very well,' he agrees.

He goes over to the window and, with his back to the room, tugs at the handle as if to check it. Pokes the rubber seal.

Parvaneh stands in the kitchen doorway, wrapping her arms around herself and her belly.

'He can stay here until he's completely defrosted, then you have to take him,' says Ove, shrugging towards the cat.

He can see in the corner of his eye how she's peering at him. As if she's trying to figure out what sort of hand he has from the other side of a casino table. It makes him uneasy.

'I'm afraid I can't,' she says after that. 'The girls are . . . allergic,' she adds.

Ove hears a little pause before she says 'allergic'. He scrutinises her suspiciously in the reflection in the window, but does not answer. Instead he turns to the overweight young man.

'So you'll have to take care of it,' he says.

Jimmy, who's not only sweating buckets now but also turning blotchy and red in his face, looks down benevolently at the cat. It's slowly started moving its stump of a tail and burrowing its dripping nose deeper into Jimmy's generous folds of upper arm fat.

'Don't think it's such a cool idea me taking care of the puss, sorry man,' says Jimmy and shrugs tremulously, so that the cat makes a circus tumble and ends up upside down. He holds out his arms. His skin is red, as if he's on fire.

'I'm a bit allergic as well . . .'

Parvaneh gives off a little scream, runs up to him, takes the cat away from him, quickly enfolding it in the blanket again.

'We have to get to a hospital!' she yells.

'I'm barred from the hospital,' Ove replies, without thinking about it.

When he peers in her direction and she looks ready to throw the cat at him, he looks down again and groans disconsolately. 'All I want is to die,' he thinks to himself and presses his toes into one of the floorboards.

It flexes slightly. Ove looks up at Jimmy. Looks at the cat. Surveys the wet floor. Shakes his head at Parvaneh.

'We'll have to take my car then,' he mutters.

He takes his jacket from the hook and opens the front door. After a few seconds he sticks his head back into the hall. Glares at Parvaneh.

'But I'm not bringing the car to the house because it's prohibit—'

She interrupts him with some words in Farsi that Ove can't understand. Nonetheless he finds them unnecessarily dramatic. She wraps the cat more tightly in the blanket and walks past him into the snow.

'Rules are rules, you know,' says Ove truculently as she heads off to the parking area, but she doesn't answer.

Ove turns round and points at Jimmy.

'And you put on a jumper. Or you're not going anywhere in the Saab, let's be clear about that.'

Parvaneh pays for the parking at the hospital. Ove doesn't make a fuss about it.

18

A MAN WHO WAS OVE AND
A CAT CALLED ERNEST

Ove didn't dislike this cat in particular. It's just that he didn't much like cats in general. He'd always perceived them as untrustworthy. Especially when, as in the case of Ernest, they were as big as mopeds. It was actually quite difficult to determine whether he was just an unusually large cat or an outstandingly small lion. And you should never befriend something if there's a possibility it may take a fancy to eating you in your sleep.

But Sonja loved Ernest so unconditionally that Ove managed to keep this kind of perfectly sensible observation to himself. He knew better than to speak ill of what she loved; after all, he understood very keenly how it was to receive her love when no one else could understand why he was worthy of it. So he and Ernest learned to get along reasonably well when they visited the cottage in the forest, apart from the fact that Ernest bit Ove once when he sat on his tail on one of the kitchen chairs. Or at least they learned to keep their distance. Just like Ove and Sonja's father.

Even if Ove's view was that this Cat Annoyance was not entitled to sit on one chair and spread his tail over another, he let it go. For Sonja's sake.

Ove learned to fish. In the two autumns that followed their first visit, the roof of the house for the first time ever did not leak. And the truck started every time the key was turned without

146

as much as a splutter. Of course Sonja's father was not openly grateful about this. But on the other hand he never again brought up his reservations about Ove 'being from town'. And this, from Sonja's father, was as good a proof of affection as any.

Two springs passed and two summers. And in the third year, one cool June night, Sonja's father died. And Ove had never seen anyone cry like Sonja cried then. The first few days she hardly got out of bed. Ove, for someone who had run into death as much as he had in his life, had a very paltry relationship to his feelings about it, and he pushed it all away in some confusion in the kitchen of the forest cottage. The pastor from the village church came by and ran through the details of the burial.

'A good man,' stated the pastor succinctly and pointed at one of the photos of Sonja and her father on the living room wall. Ove nodded. Didn't know what he was expected to say to that one. Then he went outside to see if anything on the truck needed fiddling with.

On the fourth day Sonja got out of bed and started cleaning the cottage with such frenetic energy that Ove kept out of her way, in the way that insightful folk avoid an oncoming tornado. He meandered about the farm, looking for things to do. He rebuilt the woodshed, which had collapsed in one of the winter storms. In the coming days he filled it with newly cut wood. Mowed the grass. Lopped overhanging branches from the surrounding forest. Late on the evening of the sixth day they called from the grocery store.

Everyone called it an accident, of course. But no one who had met Ernest could believe that he had run out in front of a car by accident. Sorrow does strange things to living creatures. Ove drove faster than he had ever driven on the roads that night. Sonja held Ernest's big head in her hands all the way. He was still breathing when they made it to the vet, but his injuries were far too serious, the loss of blood too great.

After two hours crouching at his side in the operating theatre, Sonja kissed the cat's wide brow and whispered, 'Goodbye, darling Ernest.' And then, as if the words were coming out of her mouth wrapped in whisks of cloud: 'And goodbye to you, my darling father.'

And then the cat closed his eyes and died.

When Sonja came out of the waiting room she rested her forehead heavily against Ove's broad chest.

'I feel so much loss, Ove. Loss, as if my heart was beating outside my body.'

They stood in silence for a long time, with their arms around each other. And at long last she lifted her face towards his, and looked into his eyes with great seriousness.

'You have to love me twice as much now,' she said.

And then Ove lied to her for the second – and last – time: he said that he would. Even though he knew it wasn't possible for him to love her any more than he already did.

They buried Ernest beside the lake where he used to go fishing with Sonja's father. The pastor was there to read the blessing. After that, Ove loaded up the Saab and they drove back on the small roads, with Sonja's head leaning against his shoulder. On the way he stopped in the first little town they passed through. Sonja had arranged to meet someone there. Ove did not know who. It was one of the traits she appreciated most about him, she often said long after the event. She knew no one else who could sit in a car for an hour, waiting, without demanding to know what he was waiting for or how long it would take. Which was not to say that Ove did not moan, because moaning was one thing he excelled at. Especially if he had to pay for the parking. But he never asked what she was doing. And he always waited for her.

Then when Sonja came out at last and got back inside, closing the Saab's door with a soft squeeze, which she knew was required to avoid a wounded glance from him as if she had kicked a living creature, she gently took his hand.

'I think we need to buy a house of our own,' she said softly.

'What's the point of that?' Ove wondered.

'I think our child has to grow up in a house,' she said and carefully moved his hand down to her belly.

Ove was quiet for a long time; a long time even by Ove's standards. He looked thoughtfully at her stomach, as if expecting it to raise some sort of flag. Then he straightened up, twisted the tuning button half a turn forward and half a turn back. Adjusted his wing mirrors. And nodded sensibly.

'We'll have to get a Saab estate, then.'

19

A MAN CALLED OVE AND A CAT THAT WAS BROKEN WHEN HE CAME

Ove spent most of yesterday shouting at Parvaneh that this damned cat would live in Ove's house over his dead body.

And now here he stands, looking at the cat. And the cat looks back.

And Ove remains strikingly non-dead.

It's all incredibly irritating.

A half-dozen times Ove has woken up in the night when the cat, with more than a little disrespect, has crawled up and stretched out next to him in the bed. And just as many times the cat has woken up when Ove, with more than a bit of brusqueness, has booted it down to the floor again.

Now, when it's gone quarter to six and Ove has got up, the cat is sitting in the middle of the kitchen floor. It sports a disgruntled expression, as if Ove owes it money. Ove stares back at it with a suspicion normally reserved for a cat that has rung his doorbell with a Bible in its paws, like a Jehovah's Witness.

'I suppose you're expecting food,' mutters Ove at last.

The cat doesn't answer. It just nibbles its remaining patches of fur and nonchalantly licks one of its paw pads.

'But in this house you don't just lounge about like some kind of consultant and expect fried sparrows to fly into your mouth.'

Ove goes to the sink. Turns on the coffee maker. Checks his watch. Looks at the cat. After leaving the hospital, Parvaneh had managed to get hold of a friend who was apparently a veterinarian. The veterinarian had come to have a look at the cat and concluded that there was 'serious frostbite and advanced malnutrition'. And then he'd given Ove a long list of instructions about what the cat needed to eat and its general care.

'I'm not running a cat repair company,' Ove clarifies to the cat. 'You're only here because I couldn't talk any sense into that pregnant woman.' He nods across the living room towards the window facing onto Parvaneh's house.

The cat, busying itself trying to lick one of its eyes, does not reply.

Ove holds up four little socks towards it. He was given them by the veterinarian. Apparently the Cat Annoyance needs exercise more than anything, and this is something Ove feels he may be able to help it achieve. The further from his wallpaper those claws are, the better. That's Ove's reasoning.

'Hop into these things and then we can go. I'm running late!'

The cat gets up elaborately and walks with long, self-conscious steps towards the door. As if walking on a red carpet. It gives the socks an initial sceptical look, but doesn't cause too much of a fuss when Ove quite roughly puts them on. When he's done, Ove stands up and scrutinises the cat from top to bottom. Shakes his head. A cat wearing socks – it can't be natural. The cat, now standing there checking out its new outfit, suddenly looks immeasurably pleased with itself.

Ove makes an extra loop to the end of the pathway. Outside Anita and Rune's house he picks up a cigarette butt. He rolls it between his fingers. That Skoda-driving man from the council seems to drive about in these parts as if he owned them. Ove swears and puts the butt in his pocket.

When they get back to the house, Ove reluctantly feeds the wretched animal, and once it's finished, announces that they've got errands to run. He may have been temporarily press-ganged into cohabiting with this little creature, but he'll be damned if he's going to leave a wild animal on its own in his house. So the

151

cat has to come with him. Immediately there's a disagreement between Ove and the cat about whether or not the cat should sit on a sheet of newspaper in the Saab's passenger seat. At first Ove sits the cat on two supplements of entertainment news, which the cat, much insulted, kicks onto the floor with its back feet. It makes itself comfortable on the soft upholstery. At this Ove firmly picks up the cat by the scruff of its neck, so that the cat hisses at him in a not so passive-aggressive manner, while Ove shoves three cultural supplements and book reviews under him. The cat gives him a furious look. Ove puts him down, but oddly enough it stays on the newspaper and only looks out of the window with a wounded, dismal expression. Ove concludes that he's won the battle, nods with satisfaction, puts the Saab into gear and drives onto the main road. Only then does the cat slowly and deliberately drag its claws in a long tear across the newsprint, and then puts both its front paws through the rip. While at the same time giving Ove a highly challenging look, as if to ask: 'And what are you going to do about it?'

Ove slams on the brakes of the Saab so that the cat, shocked, is thrown forward and bangs its nose against the dashboard. 'THAT's what I have to say about it!' Ove's triumphant expression seems to say. After that, the cat refuses to look at Ove for the rest of the journey and just sits hunched up in a corner of the seat, rubbing its nose with one of its paws in a very offended way. But while Ove is inside the florist's, it licks long wet streaks across Ove's steering wheel, safety belt and the inside of Ove's car door.

When Ove comes back with the flowers and discovers that his whole car is full of cat saliva he waves his forefinger in a threatening manner, as if it were a scimitar. And then the cat bites his scimitar. Ove refuses to speak to him for the rest of the journey.

When they get to the churchyard, Ove plays it safe and scrunches up the remains of the newspaper into a ball, with which he roughly pushes the cat out of the car. Then he gets the flowers out of the boot, locks the Saab with his key, makes a circuit around it and checks each of the doors. Together they climb the frozen gravelled slope leading up to the church turn-off and force their way through the snow, before they stop by Sonja. Ove brushes some snow off the gravestone with the back of his hand and gives the flowers a little shake.

'I've brought some flowers with me,' he mumbles. 'Pink. Which you like. They say they die in the frost but they only tell you that to trick you into buying the more expensive ones.'

The cat sinks down on its behind in the snow. Ove gives it a sullen look; then refocuses on the gravestone.

'Right, right . . . this is the Cat Annoyance. It's living with us now. Almost froze to death outside our house.'

The cat gives Ove an offended look. Ove clears his throat.

'He looked like that when he came,' he clarifies, a sudden defensive note in his voice. Then, with a nod at the cat and the gravestone:

'So it wasn't me who broke him. He was already broken,' he adds to Sonja.

Both the gravestone and the cat wait in silence beside him. Ove stares at his shoes for a moment. Grunts. Sinks onto his knees in the snow and brushes a bit more snow off the stone. Carefully lays his hand on it.

'I miss you,' he whispers.

There's a quick gleam in the corner of Ove's eye. He feels something soft against his arm. It takes a few seconds before he realises that the cat is gently resting its head in the palm of his hand.

20

A MAN CALLED OVE AND AN INTRUDER

For almost twenty minutes, Ove sits in the driver's seat of the Saab with the garage door open. For the first five minutes the cat stares at him impatiently from the passenger seat. During the next five it begins to look properly worried. In the end it tries to open the door itself; when this fails, it promptly lies down on the seat and goes to sleep.

Ove glances at it as it rolls onto its side and starts snoring. He has to concede that the Cat Annoyance has a very direct approach to problem-solving.

He looks out over the parking area again at the garage opposite. He must have stood out there with Rune a hundred times. They were friends once. Ove can't think of very many people in his life he could describe as such. Ove and Ove's wife were the first people to move into this street of terraced houses all those years ago, when it had only recently been built and was still surrounded by trees. That same day, Rune and Rune's wife moved in. Anita was also pregnant and, of course, immediately became best friends with Ove's wife in that way only women knew how. And just as all women who become best friends they both had the idea that Rune and Ove had to become best friends. Because they had so many 'interests in common'. Ove couldn't really understand what they meant by that. After all, Rune drove a Volvo.

Not that Ove exactly had anything against Rune apart from

that. He had a proper job and he didn't talk more than he had to. Admittedly he did drive that Volvo but, as Ove's wife kept insisting, this did not necessarily make a person immoral. So Ove put up with him. After a period he even lent him tools. And one afternoon, standing in the parking area, thumbs tucked into their belts, they got caught up in a conversation about lawnmower prices. When they parted they shook hands. As if the mutual decision to become friends was a business agreement.

When the two men later found out that all sorts of people were moving into the area, they sat down in Ove and Sonja's kitchen for consultations. By the time they emerged from these, they had established a shared framework of rules, signs clarifying what was permitted or not, and a newly set-up steering group for the Residents' Association. Ove was the chairman; Rune, the vice-chairman.

In the months that followed they went to the dump together. Grumbled at people who had parked their cars incorrectly. Bargained for better deals on paint and drainpipes at the iron-monger's, stood on either side of the man from the telephone company when he came to install telephones and jack plugs, brusquely pointing out where and how he should best go about it. Not that either of them knew exactly how telephone cables should be installed, but they were both well versed in keeping an eye on whippersnappers like this one, to stop them pulling a fast one. That was all there was to it.

Sometimes the two couples had dinner together. In so far as one could have dinner when Ove and Rune mostly just stood about in the parking area the whole evening, kicking the tyres of their cars and comparing their load capacity, turning radius and other significant matters. And that was all there was to it.

Sonja and Anita's bellies kept growing steadily, which, according to Rune, made Anita 'doolally in the brain'. Apparently he had to look for the coffee pot in the fridge more or less daily once she was in her third month. Sonja, not to be outdone, developed a temper that could flare up quicker than a pair of saloon doors in a John Wayne film, which made Ove reluctant to open his mouth at all. This, of course, gave further cause for irritation. When she wasn't breaking out in a sweat she was freezing. And as soon as Ove tired of arguing with her and agreed to turn up the radiators by a half-step she started sweating again, and he had to run round and turn them back down again. She also ate bananas in such quantities that the people at the supermarket must have thought Ove had started a zoo.

'The hormones are on the war path,' Rune said with an insightful nod during one of the nights when he and Ove sat in the outside space behind his house, while the women kept to Sonja and Ove's kitchen, talking about whatever it is women talk about.

Rune told him that he had found Anita crying her eyes out by the radio the day before, for no other reason than that it 'was a nice song'.

'A . . . nice song?' said Ove, perplexed.

'A nice song,' Rune answered.

The two men shook their heads in mutual disbelief and stared out into the darkness. Sat in silence.

'The grass needs cutting,' said Rune at last.

'I bought new blades for the mower.' Ove nodded.

'How much did you pay for them?'

And so their friendship went on.

In the evenings, Sonja played music for her belly, because she said it made the child move. Ove mostly just sat in his armchair on the other side of the room and pretended to be watching television while she was doing it. In his innermost thoughts he was worried about what it would be like once the child finally decided to come out. What if, for example, the kid disliked Ove because Ove *wasn't* so fond of music?

It's not that Ove was afraid. He just didn't know how to prepare himself for fatherhood. He had asked for some sort of manual but Sonja had just laughed at him. Ove didn't understand why. There were manuals for everything else.

He was doubtful about whether he'd be any good at being someone's dad. He didn't like children an awful lot. He hadn't even been very good at being a child. Sonja thought he should talk to Rune about it because they were 'in the same situation'. Ove couldn't quite understand what she meant by that. Rune was not in fact going to be the father of Ove's child, but an altogether different one. At least Rune agreed with Ove about the point of not having much to discuss, and that was something. So when Anita came over in the evenings and sat in the kitchen with Sonja, talking about the aches and pains and all those things, Ove and Rune made the excuse of having 'things' to talk about and went out to Ove's shed and just stood there in silence, picking at various bits on Ove's workbench.

Standing there next to each other with a closed door for a third night on the trot without knowing what they were supposed to do with themselves, they agreed that they needed to get busy with something before, as Rune put it, 'the new neighbours start thinking there's some sort of monkey business going on in here'.

Ove agreed that it might be best to do as he said. And so it was. They didn't talk much while they were doing it, but they helped each other with the drawings and measuring the angles and ensuring that the corners were straight and properly done. And late one evening when Anita and Sonja were in the fourth month, two light blue cots were installed in the prepared nurseries of their terraced houses.

'We can rub it down and repaint it pink if we get a girl,' mumbled Ove when he showed it to Sonja. Sonja put her arms around him, and he felt his neck getting all wet with her tears. Completely irrational hormones.

'I want you to ask me to be your wife,' she whispered.

And so it was. They married in the Town Hall, very simply. Neither of them had any family, so only Rune and Anita came. Sonja and Ove put on their rings and then all four of them went to a restaurant. Ove paid but Rune helped check the bill to make sure it 'had been done properly'. Of course it hadn't. So after conferring with the waiter for about an hour, the two men managed to convince him it would be easier for him if he halved the bill or they'd 'report him'. Obviously it was a bit hazy exactly who would report who for what, but eventually, with a certain amount of swearing and arm-waving, the waiter gave up and went into the kitchen and wrote them a new bill. In the meantime Rune and Ove nodded grimly at one another without noticing that their wives, as usual, had taken a taxi home twenty minutes earlier.

Ove nods to himself as he sits there in the Saab looking at Rune's garage door. He can't remember when he last saw it open. He turns off the headlights of the Saab, gives the cat a poke to wake it up and gets out.

'Ove?' says a curious, unfamiliar voice.

Suddenly an unknown woman, clearly the owner of the unfamiliar voice, has stuck her head into the garage. She's about forty-five, wearing tatty jeans and a green windcheater jacket that looks too large for her. She doesn't have any make-up on and her hair is in a ponytail. The woman blunders into his garage and looks around with interest. The cat steps forward and gives her a threatening hiss. She stops. Ove puts his hands in his pockets.

'Ove?' she bursts out again, in that exaggerated chummy way of people who want to sell you something, whilst pretending it's the very last thing on their mind.

'I don't want anything,' says Ove, nodding at the garage door – a clear gesture that she needn't bother about finding another door, it'll be just fine if she walks out the same way that she came.

She looks utterly unchastened by that.

'My name is Lena. I'm a journalist at the local newspaper and, well . . .' she begins, and then offers her hand.

Ove looks at her hand. And looks at her.

'I don't want anything,' he says again.

'What?'

'I suppose you're selling subscriptions. But I don't want one.'

She looks puzzled.

'Right . . . well, actually . . . I'm not selling the paper. I write

158

for it. I'm a *journalist*,' she repeats slowly, as if there were something wrong with him.

'I still don't want anything,' Ove reiterates as he starts shooing her out of the garage door.

'But I want to talk to *you*, Ove!' she protests and starts trying to force herself back inside.

Ove waves his hands at her as if trying to scare her away by shaking an invisible rug in front of her.

'You saved a man's life at the train station yesterday! I want to interview you about it,' she calls out excitedly.

Clearly she's about to say something else when she notices that she's lost Ove's attention. His gaze falls on something behind her. His eyes turn to slits.

'I'll be damned,' he mumbles.

'Yes . . . I'd like to ask y—' she begins sincerely, but Ove has already squeezed past her and started running towards the white Skoda that's turned up by the parking area and started driving down towards the houses.

The bespectacled woman is caught off guard when Ove charges forward and bangs on the window and she throws the file of documents into her own face. The man in the white shirt, on the other hand, is quite unmoved. He rolls down the window.

'Yes?' he asks.

'Vehicle traffic is prohibited in the residential area,' Ove hisses and points at each of the houses, at the Skoda, at the man in the white shirt and at the parking area.

'In this Residents' Association we park in the *parking* area!'

The man in the white shirt looks at the houses. Then at the parking area. Then at Ove.

'I have permission from the council to drive up to the houses. So I have to ask you to get out of the way.'

Ove is so agitated by his answer that it takes him many seconds even just to formulate some swear words by way of an answer. Meanwhile, the man in the shirt has picked up a pack of cigarettes from the dashboard, which he taps against his trouser leg.

'Would you be kind enough to get out of the way,' he asks Ove.

'What are you doing here?' Ove blurts out.

'That's nothing for you to worry yourself about,' says the man in the white shirt with a monotone voice, as if he's a computer-generated voicemail message letting Ove know that he's been placed in a telephone queue.

He puts the cigarette he's shaken out in his mouth and lights it. Ove breathes so heavily that his chest is pumping up and down under his jacket. The woman gathers up her papers and files and adjusts her glasses. The man just sighs, as if Ove is a cheeky child refusing to stop riding his skateboard on the pavement.

'You know what I'm doing here. We're taking Rune, in the house at the bottom, into care.'

He hangs his arm out of the window and flicks the ash against the wing mirror of the Skoda.

'Taking him into care?'

'Yes,' says the man, nodding indifferently.

'And if Anita doesn't want that?' Ove hisses, tapping his index finger against the roof of the car.

The man in the white shirt looks at the woman in the passenger seat and smiles resignedly. Then he turns to Ove again and speaks very slowly. As if otherwise Ove might not understand his words.

'It's not up to Anita to make that decision. It's up to the investigation team.'

Ove's breathing becomes even more strained. He can feel his pulse in his throat.

'You're not bringing this car into this area,' he says through gritted teeth.

His fists are clenched. His tone is pointed and threatening. But his opponent looks quite calm. He puts out the cigarette against the paintwork of the door and drops it on the ground.

As if everything Ove had said was nothing more than the inarticulate raving of a senile old man.

'And what exactly are you going to do to stop me, Ove?' says the man at long last.

The way he flings out his name makes Ove look as if someone just shoved a mallet in his gut. He stares at the man in the white shirt, his mouth slightly agape and his eyes scanning to and fro over the car.

'How do you know my name?'

'I know a lot about you.'

Ove only manages by a whisker to pull his foot out of the way of the wheel as the Skoda moves off again and drives down towards the houses. Ove stands there, in shock, staring after them.

'Who was that?' says the woman in the windcheater behind him.

Ove spins round.

'How do you know my name?' he demands to know.

She takes a step back. Pushes a few evasive wisps of hair out of her face without taking her eyes off Ove's clenched fists.

'I work for the local newspaper . . . we interviewed people on the platform about how you saved that man . . .'

'How do you know my name?' says Ove again, his voice shaking with anger.

'You swiped your card when you paid for your train ticket. I went through the receipts in the till,' she says and takes a few more steps back.

'And him!!! How does HE know my name?' Ove roars and waves in the direction in which the Skoda went, the veins on his forehead bulging.

'I . . . don't know,' she says.

Ove breathes violently through his nose and nails her with his eyes. As if trying to see whether she's lying.

'I have no idea, I've never seen that man before,' she promises.

Ove rivets his eyes into her even harder. Finally he nods grimly to himself. Then he turns round and walks towards his house. She calls out to him but he doesn't react. The cat follows him into the hall. Ove closes the door. Further down the road, the man in the white shirt and the woman with glasses ring the doorbell of Anita and Rune's house.

Ove sinks onto the stool in his hall. Shaking with humiliation.

He had almost forgotten that feeling. The humiliation of it. The powerlessness. The realisation that one cannot fight men in white shirts.

And now they're back. They haven't been here since he and Sonja came home from Spain. After the accident.

21

A MAN WHO WAS OVE AND
COUNTRIES WHERE THEY PLAY
FOREIGN MUSIC IN RESTAURANTS

Of course, the coach tour was her idea. Ove couldn't see the use of it. If they had to go anywhere why not just take the Saab? But Sonja insisted that coaches were 'romantic', and that sort of thing was incredibly important, Ove had learned. So that's how it ended up. Even though everyone in Spain seemed to think they were somehow exceptional because they went round yawning and drinking and playing foreign music in restaurants and going to bed in the middle of the day.

Ove did his best not to like any of it. But Sonja got so worked up about it all that in the end it inevitably affected him too. She laughed so loudly when he held her that he felt it through his whole body. Not even Ove could avoid liking it.

They stayed in a little hotel, with a little pool, and a little restaurant run by a man whose name, as Ove understood it, was Hosay. It was spelled 'José' but it seemed people weren't too particular about pronunciation in Spain. Hosay couldn't speak any Swedish but he was very interested in speaking anyway. Sonja had a little book, in which she looked things up, so she could say things like 'sunset' and 'ham' in Spanish. Ove felt it didn't stop being the butt end of a pig just because you said it another way, but he never mentioned this.

On the other hand he tried to point out to her that she shouldn't give money to the beggars in the street, as they'd only buy schnapps with it. But she kept doing it.

'They can do what they like with the money,' she said.

When Ove protested she just smiled and took his big hands in hers and kissed them, explaining that when a person gives to another person it's not just the receiver who's blessed. It's the giver.

On the third day she went to bed in the middle of the day. Because that was what people did in Spain, she said, and one should adopt the 'local customs of a place'. Ove suspected it was not so much about customs as her own preferences, and this suited her very well as an excuse. She already slept sixteen hours out of twenty-four since she got pregnant.

Ove occupied himself by going for walks. He took the road leading past the hotel into the village. All the houses were made of stone, he noted. Many of them didn't appear to have thresholds under their front doors, and there were no decent window seals to be seen. Ove thought it slightly barbaric. One couldn't bloody build houses like this.

He was on his way back to the hotel when he saw Hosay leaning over a smoking brown car at the side of the road. Inside sat two children and a very old woman with a shawl round her head. She didn't seem to be feeling very well.

Hosay caught sight of Ove and waved at him in an agitated manner with something almost like panic in his eyes. 'Sennjaur,' he called out to Ove, the way he'd done every time he spoke to him since their arrival. Ove assumed it meant 'Ove' in Spanish, but he hadn't checked Sonja's phrase book so carefully. Hosay pointed at the car and gesticulated wildly at Ove again. Ove stuck his hands into his trouser pockets and stopped at a safe distance, with a watchful look on his face.

'Hospital!' Hosay shouted again and pointed at the old woman in the car. In fact she didn't look in very good nick, Ove reaffirmed to himself. Hosay pointed to the woman and pointed under the bonnet at the smoking engine, repeating despairingly

'Hospital! Hospital!' Ove cast his evaluating eye on the spectacle and finally drew the conclusion that this smoking, Spanish-manufactured car must be known as a 'hospital'.

He leaned over the engine and peered down. It didn't look so complicated, he thought.

'Hospital,' Hosay said again and nodded several times and looked quite worried.

Ove didn't know what he was expected to say to that; clearly the whole matter of car makes was considered quite important in Spain, and certainly Ove could empathise with that.

'Saaaab,' he said, therefore, pointing demonstratively at his chest.

Hosay stared in puzzlement at him for a moment. Then he pointed at himself.

'Hosay!'

'I wasn't bloody asking for your name, I was only sayi—' Ove started saying, but he stopped himself when he was met on the other side of the bonnet by a stare as glazed as an inland lake.

Obviously this Hosay's grasp of Swedish was even worse than Ove's Spanish. Ove sighed and looked with some concern at the children in the back seat. They were holding the old woman's hands and looked quite terrified. Ove looked down at the engine again.

Then he rolled up his shirtsleeves and motioned for Hosay to move out of the way. Within ten minutes they were back on the road, and Ove had never seen anyone so relieved to have their car fixed.

However much she flicked through her little phrase book, Sonja never found out the exact reason why they weren't charged for any of the food they ate in José's restaurant that week. But she laughed until she was positively simmering every time the little Spanish man who owned the restaurant lit up like a sun every time he saw Ove, held out his arms and exclaimed: 'Señor Saab!!!'

Her daily naps and Ove's walks became a ritual. On the second day, Ove walked past a man putting up a fence, and stopped to explain that this was absolutely the wrong way to do it. The man couldn't understand a word of what he was saying, so Ove decided in the end that it would be quicker to show him how. On the third day he built a new exterior wall on a church building, with the assistance of the village priest. On the fourth day he went with Hosay to a field outside the village, where he helped one of Hosay's friends pull out a horse that had got stuck in a muddy ditch.

Many years later it occurred to Sonja to ask him about all that. When Ove at last told her, she shook her head both long and hard. 'So while I was sleeping you sneaked out and helped people in need . . . and mended their fences? People can say whatever they like about you, Ove. But you're the strangest superhero I ever heard about.'

On the bus on the way home from Spain she put Ove's hand on her belly and he felt the child kicking – faintly, as if someone had prodded the palm of his hand through a very thick oven glove. They sat there for several hours feeling the little bumps. Ove didn't say anything but Sonja saw the way he wiped his eyes with the back of his hand when he rose from his seat and mumbled something about needing 'the toilet'.

It was the happiest week of Ove's life.

It was destined to be followed by the very unhappiest.

22

A MAN CALLED OVE AND SOMEONE
IN A GARAGE

Ove and the cat sit in silence in the Saab outside the hospital.

'Stop looking at me as if this is my fault,' says Ove to the cat.

The cat looks back at him as if it isn't angry but disappointed.

It wasn't really the plan that he would be sitting outside this hospital again. He hates hospitals, after all, and now he's bloody been here three times in less than a week. It's not right and proper. But no other choice was available to him.

Because today went to pot from the very beginning.

It started with Ove and the cat, during their daily inspection, when they discovered that the sign forbidding vehicular traffic within the residential area had been run over. This inspired such colourful profanities from Ove that the cat looked quite embarrassed. Ove marched off in fury and emerged moments later with his snow shovel. Then he stopped, looking towards Anita and Rune's house, his jaws clamped so hard that they made a creaking sound.

The cat looked at him accusingly.

'It's not my fault the old sod went and got old,' he said more firmly.

When the cat didn't seem to find this to be in any way an acceptable explanation, Ove pointed at it with the snow shovel.

'You think this is the first time I've had a run-in with the council? That decision about Rune, do you think they've actually come to a real conclusion about it? They NEVER will! It'll go to appeal and then they'll drag it out and put it through their shitty bureaucratic grind! You understand? You think it'll happen quickly, but it takes months! Years! You think I'm going to stick around here just because that old sod went all helpless?'

The cat didn't answer.

'You don't understand! Understand?' Ove hissed and turned round.

He felt the cat's eyes on his back as he marched inside.

That is not the reason why Ove and the cat are sitting in the Saab in the parking area outside the hospital. But it does have a fairly direct connection with Ove standing there shovelling snow when that journalist woman in her slightly too large green jacket turned up outside his house.

'Ove?' she asked behind him, as if she was concerned that he may have changed his identity since she last came here to disturb him.

Ove continued shovelling without in any way acknowledging her presence.

'I only want to ask you a few question . . .' she tried.

'Ask them somewhere else. I don't want them here,' Ove answered, scattering snow about him in a way that made it difficult to tell whether he was shovelling or digging.

'But I only want t—' she said, but she was interrupted by Ove and the cat going into the house and slamming the door in her face.

Ove and the cat squatted in the hall and waited for her to leave. But she didn't leave. She started banging on the door and calling out: 'But you're a hero!!!'

'She's absolutely psychotic, that woman,' said Ove to the cat.

The cat didn't disagree.

When she carried on banging and shouting even louder, Ove didn't know what to do, so he threw the door open and put his finger over his mouth, hushing her up, as if in the next moment he was going to point out that this was actually a library.

She attempted to grin up at his face, waving something that Ove instinctively perceived as a camera of some sort. Or something else. It wasn't so easy knowing what cameras looked like any more in this bloody society.

Then she tried to step into his hall. Maybe she shouldn't have done that.

Ove raised his big hand and pushed her back over the threshold as a reflex, so that she almost fell head-first into the snow.

'I don't want anything,' said Ove.

She regained her balance and waved the camera at him, while yelling something. Ove wasn't listening. He looked at the camera as if it were a weapon, and then decided to flee. This person was clearly not a reasonable person.

So the cat and Ove stepped out of the door, locked it and headed off as quick as they could towards the parking area. The journalist woman jogged along behind them.

To be absolutely clear about it, though, no part of this bears any relation to why Ove is now sitting outside the hospital. But when Parvaneh stood knocking on the door of Ove's house, fifteen minutes or so later, holding her three-year-old by the hand, and when no one opened and then she heard voices from the parking area, this, so to speak, has a good deal to do with Ove sitting outside the hospital.

Parvaneh and the child came round the corner of the parking area and saw Ove standing outside his closed garage door with his hands sullenly shoved into his pockets. The cat was sitting at his feet looking guilty.

'What are you doing?' said Parvaneh.

'Nothing,' said Ove defensively.

Some knocking sounds were coming from the inside of the garage door.

'What was that?' said Parvaneh, staring at it with surprise.

Ove suddenly seemed extremely interested in a particular section of the asphalt under one of his shoes. The cat looked a bit as if it was about to start whistling and trying to walk away.

Another knock came from the inside of the garage door.

'Hello?' said Parvaneh.

'Hello?' answered the garage door.

Parvaneh's eyes widened.

'Christ . . . have you locked someone in the *garage*, Ove!?' Ove didn't answer. Parvaneh shook him as if trying to dislodge some coconuts.

'OVE!'

'Yes, yes. But I didn't do it on purpose, for God's sake,' he muttered and wriggled out of her grip.

Parvaneh shook her head.

'Not on purpose?'

'No, not on purpose,' said Ove, as if this should wrap up the discussion.

When he noticed that Parvaneh was obviously expecting some sort of clarification, he scratched his head and sighed.

'Her. Well. She's one of those journalist people. It wasn't bloody me who locked her in. I was going to lock myself and the cat in there. But then she followed us. And, you know. Things took their course.'

Parvaneh started massaging her temples.

'I can't deal with this . . .'

'Naughty,' said the three-year-old and shook her finger at Ove.

'Hello?' said the garage door.

'There's no one here!' Ove hissed back.

'But I can hear you!' said the garage door.

Ove sighed and looked despondently at Parvaneh. As if he was about to exclaim: 'You hear that, even garage doors are talking to me these days!'

Parvaneh waved him aside, walked up to the door, leaned her face up close and knocked tentatively. The door knocked back.

As if it expected to communicate by Morse code from now on. Parvaneh cleared her throat.

'Why do you want to talk to Ove?' she said, relying on the conventional alphabet.

'He's a hero!'

'A . . . what?'

'Okay, sorry. So: my name is Lena; I work at the local newspaper and I want to intervie—'

Parvaneh looks at Ove in shock.

'What does she mean, a hero?'

'She's just prattling on!' Ove protested.

'He saved a man's life; he'd fallen on the track!' yelled the garage door.

'Are you sure you've got the right Ove?' said Parvaneh.

Ove looked insulted.

'I see. So now it's out of the question that I could be a hero, is it?' he muttered.

Parvaneh peered at him suspiciously. The three-year-old tried to grab hold of what was left of the cat's tail, with an excitable, 'Kitty!' 'Kitty' did not look particularly impressed by this and tried to hide behind Ove's legs.

'What have you done, Ove?' said Parvaneh in a low, confidential voice, taking two steps away from the garage door.

The three-year-old chased the cat round his feet. Ove tried to figure out what he should do with his hands.

'Ah, so I hauled a suit off the rails, it's nothing to make a bloody fuss about,' he mumbled.

Parvaneh tried to keep a straight face.

'Or to have a giggle about, actually,' said Ove sourly.

'Sorry,' said Parvaneh.

The garage door called out something that sounded like: 'Hello? Are you still there?'

'No!' Ove bellowed.

'Why are you so terrifically angry?' the garage door wondered.

Ove was starting to look hesitant. He leaned towards Parvaneh.

'I . . . don't know how to get rid of her,' he said, and if

Parvaneh had not known better she might have concluded that there was something pleading in his eyes. 'I don't want her in there on her own with the Saab!' he whispered gravely.

Parvaneh nodded, in confirmation of the unfortunate aspects of the situation. Ove lowered a tired, mediating hand between the three-year-old and the cat before that situation went out of control round his shoes. The three-year-old looked as if she was ready to try to hug the cat. The cat looked as if it was ready to pick out the three-year-old in an identity parade at a police station. Ove managed to catch the three-year-old, who burst into peals of laughter.

'Why are you here in the first place?' Ove demanded to know of Parvaneh as he handed over the little bundle like a sack of potatoes.

'We're taking the bus to the hospital to pick up Patrick and Jimmy,' she answered.

She saw the way Ove's face twitched above his cheekbones when she said 'bus'.

'We . . .' Parvaneh began, as if articulating the beginnings of a thought.

She looked at the garage door; then looked at Ove.

'I can't hear what you're saying! Talk louder!' yelled the garage door.

Ove immediately took two steps away from it. At once, Parvaneh smiled confidently at him. As if she had just worked out the solution to a crossword.

'Hey, Ove! How about this: if you give us a lift to the hospital, I'll help you get rid of this journalist! Okay?'

Ove looked up. He didn't look a bit convinced. Parvaneh threw out her arms.

'Or I'll tell the journalist that I can tell a story or two about you, Ove,' she said whilst raising her eyebrows.

'Story? What story?' the garage door called out and started banging in an excitable manner.

Ove looked dejectedly at the garage door.

'This is blackmail,' he said desperately to Parvaneh.

Parvaneh nodded cheerfully.

'Ove ackatted de clauwn!' said the three-year-old and nodded in an initiated way at the cat, clearly because she felt that Ove's aversion to the hospital needed further explanation to whoever was not there the last time they went.

The cat seemed not to know what this meant. But if the clown had been anywhere near as tiresome as this three-year-old, the cat didn't take an entirely negative view of Ove hitting someone.

And so this is the reason why Ove is sitting here now. The cat looks personally let down by Ove for making it travel all the way in the back seat with the three-year-old. Ove adjusts the newspapers on the seats. He feels he's been tricked. When Parvaneh said she'd 'get rid of' the journalist, he didn't have a very clear idea of exactly how she'd manage it. Obviously he didn't have expectations of her being conjured away in a puff of smoke or knocked out with a spade or buried in the desert or anything of that kind.

In fact the only thing Parvaneh had done was to open the garage door, give that journalist her card and say, 'Call me and we'll talk about Ove.' Was that really a way of getting rid of anyone? Ove doesn't think, properly speaking, that it's a way of getting rid of anyone at all.

But now it's too late, of course. Now, damn it, he's sitting here waiting outside the hospital for the third time in less than a week. Blackmail, that's what it is.

Further to this, Ove has the cat's resentful stares to contend with. Something in its eyes reminds him of the way Sonja used to look at him.

'They won't be coming to take Rune away. They say they're going to do it, but they'll be busy with the process for many years,' says Ove to the cat.

Maybe he's also saying it to Sonja. And maybe to himself. He doesn't know.

'At least stop feeling so sorry for yourself. If it wasn't for me you'd be living with the kid and then you wouldn't have much

173

left of what you have now for a tail. Think about that!' he snorts at the cat, in an attempt to change the subject.

The cat rolls onto its side, away from Ove, and goes to sleep in protest. Ove looks out of the window again. He knows very well that the three-year-old isn't allergic at all. He knows very well that Parvaneh just lied to him so she wouldn't have to take care of the Cat Annoyance.

He's not some bloody senile old man.

23

A MAN WHO WAS OVE AND A COACH THAT
NEVER GOT THERE

'Every man needs to know what he's fighting for.' That was apparently what people said. Or at least it was what Sonja had once read out aloud to Ove from one of her books. Ove couldn't remember which one; there were always so many books around that woman. In Spain she had bought a whole bag of them, despite not even speaking Spanish. 'I'll learn while I'm reading,' she said. As if that was the way you did it. Ove told her he was a bit more about thinking for himself rather than reading what a lot of other clots had on their minds. Sonja just smiled and caressed his cheek.

Then he carried her absurdly oversized bags to the coach. Felt the driver smelling of wine as he went by, but concluded that maybe this was the way they did things in Spain and left it at that. Sat there in the seat as Sonja moved his hand to her belly and that was when he felt his child kicking, for the first and last time. He stood up and went to the toilet and when he was halfway down the aisle the bus lurched, scraped against the central barrier and then there was a moment of silence. As if time was taking a deep breath. Then: an explosion of splintering glass. The merciless screeching of twisting metal. Violent crunches as the cars behind the bus slammed into it.

And all the screams. He'd never forget them.

Ove was thrown about and only remembered falling on his

175

stomach. He looked round for her, terrified, among the tumult of human bodies, but she was gone. He threw himself forward, cutting himself under a rain of glass from the ceiling, but it was as if a furious wild animal was holding him back and forcing him down on the floor in unreflecting humiliation. It would pursue him every night for the rest of his life: his utter impotence in the situation.

He sat by her bed every moment of the first week. Until the nurses insisted that he shower and change his clothes. Everywhere they looked at him with sympathetic stares and expressed their 'condolences'. A doctor came in and spoke to Ove in an indifferent, clinical voice about the need to 'prepare himself for the likelihood of her not waking up again'. Ove threw that doctor through a door. A door that was locked and shut. 'She isn't dead,' he raved down the corridor. 'Stop behaving as if she was dead!' No one at the hospital dared make that mistake again.

On the tenth day, as the rain smattered against the windows and the radio spoke of the worst storm in several decades, Sonja opened her eyes in torturous little slits, caught sight of Ove, and stole her hand into his. Enfolded her finger in the palm of his hand.

Then she fell asleep and slept through the night. When she woke up again the nurses offered to tell her, but Ove grimly insisted that he was the one who would do it. Then he told her everything in a composed voice, while caressing her hands in his, as if they were very, very cold. He told her about the driver smelling of wine and the bus veering into the crash barrier and the collision. The smell of burnt rubber. The ear-splitting crashing sound.

And about a child that would never come now.

And she wept. An ancient, inconsolable despair that screamed and tore and shredded them both as countless hours passed. Time and sorrow and fury flowed together in stark, long-drawn darkness. Ove knew there and then that he would never forgive himself for having got up from his seat at that exact moment, for not being there to protect them. And knew that this pain was for ever.

But Sonja would not have been Sonja if she had let the darkness win. So, one morning, Ove did not know how many days had passed since the accident, expressing herself quite succinctly, she declared that she wanted to start having physiotherapy. And when Ove looked at her as if it was his own spine screaming like a tortured animal every time she moved, she gently leaned her head against his chest and whispered: 'We can busy ourselves with living or with dying, Ove. We have to move on.'

And that's how it was.

In the following months Ove met innumerable men in white shirts. They sat behind desks made of light-coloured wood in various municipal offices and they apparently had endless amounts of time to instruct Ove in what documents had to be filled in for various purposes, but no time at all to discuss the measures that were needed for Sonja to get better.

A woman was despatched to the hospital from one of the municipal authorities, where she bullishly explained that Sonja could be placed in 'a service home for other people in her situation'. Something about how 'the strain of everyday life' quite understandably could be 'excessive' for Ove. She didn't say it right out, but it was clear as crystal what she was driving at. She did not believe that Ove could see himself staying with his wife now. 'Under present conditions,' she kept repeating, nodding discreetly at the bedside. She spoke to Ove as if Sonja was not even in the room.

Admittedly Ove opened the door this time, but she was ejected all the same.

'The only home we're going to is our own one! Where we LIVE!' Ove roared at her, and in pure frustration and anger he threw one of Sonja's shoes out of the room.

Afterwards he had to go and ask the nurses, who'd almost been hit by it, if they knew where it had gone. Which of course made him even angrier. It was the first time since the accident that he heard Sonja laughing. As if it was pouring out of her, without the slightest possibility of stopping it, like she was being wrestled to the ground by her own giggling. She laughed and laughed and laughed until the vowels were rolling across the walls and floors, as if they meant to do away with the laws of time and space. It made Ove feel as if his chest was slowly rising out of the ruins of a collapsed house after an earthquake. It gave his heart space to beat again.

He went home and rebuilt the whole house, ripped out the old kitchen top and put in a new, lower one. Even managed to find a specially made cooker. Reconstructed the doorframes and fitted ramps over all the thresholds. The day after Sonja was allowed to leave the hospital she went back to her teacher training. In the spring she sat her examination. There was an advertisement in the newspaper for a teaching position in a school with the worst reputation in town, with the sort of class that no qualified teacher with all the parts of her brain correctly screwed together would voluntarily face. It was Attention Deficit Hyperactivity Disorder before Attention Deficit Hyperactivity Disorder had been invented. 'There's no hope for these boys and girls,' the headmaster soberly explained in the interview. 'This is not education, this is storage.' Maybe Sonja understood how it felt to be described as such. The vacant position only attracted one applicant, and she got those boys and girls to read Shakespeare.

In the meantime Ove was so weighed down with anger that Sonja sometimes had to ask him to go outside so he didn't demolish the furniture. It pained her infinitely to see his shoulders so loaded down with the will to destroy. Destroy that coach driver. The travel agency. The crash barrier of that motorway. The wine producer. Everything and everyone. Punch and keep punching until every bastard had been obliterated. That was all he wanted to do. He put that anger in his shed. He put it in the garage. He spread it over the ground during his inspection rounds. But that wasn't all. In the end he also started putting it in letters. He wrote to the Spanish government. To the Swedish authorities. To the police. To the court. But no one took responsibility. No one cared. They answered by reference to legal texts or other authorities. Made excuses. When the council refused to build a ramp at the stairs of the school where Sonja worked, Ove wrote letters and complaints for months. He wrote letters to newspapers. He tried to sue them. He literally inundated them with the unfathomable vengefulness of a father who had been robbed.

But everywhere, sooner or later, he was stopped by men in white shirts and strict, smug expressions on their faces. And one couldn't fight them. Not only did they have the state on their side, they *were* the state. The last complaint was rejected. The fighting was over because the white shirts had decided so. And Ove never forgave them that.

Sonja saw everything. She understood where he was hurting. So she let him be angry, let all that anger find its outlet somewhere, in some way. But on one of those early summer's evenings in May that always come along bearing gentle promises about the summer ahead, she rolled up to him, the wheels leaving soft marks on the parquet floor. He was sitting at the kitchen table writing one of his letters, and she took his pen away from him, slipped her hand into his and pressed her finger into his rough palm. Leaned her forehead tenderly against his chest.

'That's enough now, Ove. No more letters. There's no space for life with all these letters of yours.'

And she looked up, softly caressed his cheek, and smiled.

'It's enough now, my darling Ove.'

And then it was enough.

The next morning Ove got up at dawn, drove the Saab to her school, and with his own bare hands built the disabled ramp the council was refusing to put up. And after that she came home every evening for as long as Ove could remember and told him, with fire in her eyes, about her boys and girls. The ones who arrived in the classroom with police escorts yet when they left could recite four-hundred-year-old poetry. The ones who could make her cry and laugh and sing until her voice was bouncing off the ceilings of their little house. Ove could never make head

179

nor tail of those impossible kids, but he was not beyond liking them for what they did to Sonja.

Every human being needs to know what she's fighting for. That was what they said. And she fought for what was good. For the children she never had. And Ove fought for her.

Because that was the only thing in this world he really knew.

24

A MAN CALLED OVE AND A BRAT WHO PAINTS
IN COLOUR

The Saab is so full of people when Ove drives away from the hospital that he keeps checking the fuel gauge, as if he's afraid that it's going to break into a scornful dance. In his back mirror he sees Parvaneh unconcernedly giving the three-year-old paper and colour crayons.

'Does she have to do that in the car?' barks Ove.

'Would you rather have her restless, so she starts wondering how to pull the upholstery off of the seats?' Parvaneh says calmly.

Ove doesn't answer. Just looks at the three-year-old in his mirror. She's shaking a big purple crayon at the cat in Parvaneh's lap and yelling: 'DROORING!' The cat observes the child with great caution, clearly reluctant to make itself available as a decorative surface.

Patrick sits between them, turning and twisting his body to try and find a comfortable position for his plastered shinbone, which he's wedged up on the armrest between the front seats.

It's not easy, because he's doing his best not to dislodge the newspapers that Ove has placed both on his seat and under the plastered leg.

The three-year-old drops a colour crayon, which rolls forward under the passenger seat, where Jimmy, who has come along to help, is sitting. In what must surely be a move worthy of an Olympian acrobat for a man of his physique, Jimmy manages to bend forward and scoop up the crayon from the mat in front of him. He checks it out for a moment, grins, then turns to Patrick's propped-up leg and draws a large, smiling man on the plaster. The toddler shrieks with joy when she notices.

'So you're going to start making a mess as well?' says Ove.

'Pretty neat, isn't it?' Jimmy jeers and looks as if he's about to make a high-five at Ove.

Ove rolls his eyes.

'Sorry, man, couldn't stop myself,' says Jimmy and, somewhat shamefaced, gives back the crayon to Parvaneh.

There's a plinging sound in Jimmy's pocket. He hauls out a mobile phone as large as a full-grown man's hand and occupies himself with frenetically tapping the display.

'Whose is the cat?' Patrick asks from the back.

'Ove's kitty!' the three-year-old answers with rock-solid certainty.

'It is *not*,' Ove corrects her at once.

He sees Parvaneh smiling teasingly at him in the back mirror.

'Is so!' she says.

'No it ISN'T!' says Ove.

She laughs. Patrick looks very puzzled. She pats him encouragingly on the knee.

'Don't worry about what Ove is saying. It's absolutely his cat.'

'He's a bloody vagrant, that's what he is!' Ove corrects.

The cat lifts its head to find out what all the commotion is about, then concludes that all this is sensationally uninteresting and snuggles back into Parvaneh's lap. Or rather, her belly.

'So it's not being handed in somewhere?' Patrick wonders, scrutinising the feline.

The cat lifts its head a little, hissing briefly at him by way of an answer.

'What do you mean, "handed in"?' Ove says, cutting him short.

'Well . . . to a cat home or someth—' Patrick begins, but gets no further before Ove bawls:

'No one's being handed in to any bloody home!'

And with this, the subject is exhausted. Patrick tries not to look startled. Parvaneh tries not to burst out laughing. Neither really manage.

'Can't we stop off somewhere for something to eat?' Jimmy interjects and adjusts his seat position; the Saab starts swaying.

Ove looks at the group assembled around him, as if he's been kidnapped and taken to a parallel universe. For a moment he thinks about swerving off the road, until he realises that the worst case scenario would be that they all accompanied him into the afterlife. After this insight, he reduces his speed and increases the gap significantly between his own car and the one in front.

'Wee!' yells the three-year-old.

'Can we stop, Ove? Nasanin needs to pee,' Parvaneh calls out, in that manner peculiar to people who believe that the back seat of a Saab is two hundred metres behind the driver.

'Yeah! Then we can have something to eat at the same time.' Jimmy nods with anticipation.

'Yeah, let's do that, I need a wee as well,' says Parvaneh.

'McDonald's have toilets,' Jimmy informs them helpfully.

'McDonald's will be fine, stop there,' Parvaneh nods.

'There'll be no stopping here,' says Ove firmly.

Parvaneh eyes him in the rear-view mirror. Ove glares back. Ten minutes later he's sitting in the Saab, waiting for them all outside McDonald's. Even the cat has gone inside with them. The traitor. Parvaneh comes out and taps on Ove's window.

'Are you sure you don't want anything?' she says softly to him.

Ove nods. She looks a little dejected. He rolls up the window again. She walks round the car and hops in on the passenger side.

'Thanks for stopping.' She smiles.

'Yeah yeah,' says Ove.

She's eating French fries. Ove reaches forward and puts more newspaper on the floor in front of her. She starts laughing. He can't understand at what.

'I need your help, Ove,' she says suddenly.

Ove doesn't seem spontaneously or enormously enthusiastic.

'I thought you could help me pass my driving test,' she carries on.

'What did you say?' asks Ove, as if he must have heard her wrong.

She shrugs. 'Patrick will be in plaster for months. I have to get a driving license so I can give the girls lifts. I thought you could give me some driving lessons.'

Ove looks so confused that he even forgets to get upset.

'So in other words you don't have a driving license?'

'No.'

'So it wasn't a joke?'

'No.'

'Did you lose your license?'

'No. I never had one.'

Ove's brain seems to need a good few moments to process this information, which, to him, is utterly beyond belief.

'What's your work?' he asks.

'What's that got to do with it?' she replies.

'Surely it's got everything to do with it?'

'I'm an estate agent.'

Ove nods.

'And no driving license?'

'No.'

Ove shakes his head grimly, as if this is the very pinnacle of being a human being who doesn't take responsibility for anything. Parvaneh smiles that little teasing smile of hers again, scrunches up the empty French fries bag and opens the door.

'Look at it this way, Ove: do you really want *anyone* else to teach me to drive in the residential area?'

She gets out of the car and goes to the bin. Ove doesn't answer. He just snorts.

Jimmy shows up in the doorway.

'Can I eat in the car?' he asks, a piece of chicken sticking out of his mouth.

At first Ove thinks of saying no, but then realises they'll never get out of here at this rate. Instead, he spreads so many news-papers over the passenger seat and floor that it's as if he's preparing to give the car a respray.

'Just hop in, will you, so we can get home,' he groans and gestures at Jimmy.

Jimmy nods, upbeat. His mobile phone plings.

'And stop that noise – this isn't a bloody pinball arcade.'

'Sorry, man, work keep emailing me all the time,' says Jimmy, balancing his food in one hand and fiddling with the mobile in his pocket with the other.

'So you have a job, then?' says Ove.

Jimmy nods enthusiastically.

'I program iPhone apps.'

Ove has no further questions.

At least it's relatively quiet in the car for ten minutes until they roll into the parking area outside Ove's garage. Ove stops alongside the bicycle shed, puts the Saab into neutral without turning off the engine and gives his passengers a meaningful look.

'It's fine, Ove. Patrick can manage on his crutches from here,' says Parvaneh with unmistakable irony.

'Cars aren't allowed in the residential area,' says Ove.

Undeterred, Patrick extricates himself and his plaster-cast from the back seat of the car, while Jimmy squeezes out of the passenger seat, hamburger grease all over his T-shirt.

Parvaneh lifts out the three-year-old in her car seat and puts it on the ground. The girl waves something in the air, whilst yelling out some garbled words.

Parvaneh nods, goes back to the car, leans in through the front door and gives Ove a sheet of paper.

'What's that?' Ove asks, making not the slightest movement to accept it.

'It's Nasanin's drawing.'

'What am I supposed to do with that?'

'She's drawn you,' Parvaneh replies, and shoves it into his hands.

Ove gives the paper a reluctant look. It's filled with lines and swirls.

'That's Jimmy, and that's the cat and that's Patrick and me. And that's you,' explains Parvaneh.

When she says that last bit she points at a figure in the middle of the drawing. Everything else on the paper is drawn in black, but the figure in the middle is a veritable explosion of colour. A riot of yellow and red and blue and green and orange and purple.

'You're the funniest thing she knows. That's why she always draws you in colour,' says Parvaneh.

Then she closes the passenger door and walks off.

It takes several seconds before Ove collects himself enough to call out after her: 'What do you mean, "always"?'

But by then they have all started walking back to the houses.

Slightly offended, Ove adjusts the newspaper on the passenger seat. The cat climbs over from the back and makes itself comfortable on it. Ove reverses the Saab into the garage. Closes the door. Puts it into neutral without turning off the engine. Feels the exhaust fumes slowly filling the garage and gazes at the plastic tube hanging on the wall. For a few minutes all that can be heard is the cat's breathing and the engine's rhythmic stuttering. It would be easy, just sitting there and waiting for the inevitable. It's the only logical thing, Ove knows. He's been longing for it for a long time now. The end. He misses her so much that sometimes he can't bear existing in his own body. It would be the only rational thing, just sitting here until the fumes lull both him and the cat to sleep and bring this to an end.

But then he looks at the cat. And he turns off the engine.

The next morning they get up at quarter to six. Drink coffee and eat tuna fish respectively. When they've finished their inspection round, Ove carefully shovels snow outside his house. When he's done with that he stands outside his shed, leaning on his snow-shovel, looking at the line of terraced houses.

Then he crosses the road and starts clearing snow in front of the other houses.

25

A MAN CALLED OVE AND A PIECE OF
CORRUGATED IRON

Ove waits till after breakfast, once he's let the cat out. Only then does he take down a plastic bottle from the top shelf in the bathroom. He weighs it in his hand as if he's about to throw it somewhere, rattles it lightly to see if many pills are left.

Towards the end the doctors prescribed so many painkillers for Sonja. Their bathroom still looks like a storage facility for the Colombian mafia. Ove obviously doesn't trust medicine, has always been convinced its only real effects are psychological and, as a result, it only works on people with feeble brainstems.

But it's only just struck him that chemicals are not at all an unusual way of taking one's life.

He hears something outside the front door – the cat is back surprisingly quickly, scraping its paws by the threshold and sounding like it's been caught in a gin trap. As if it knows what's going through Ove's mind. Ove can understand that it's disappointed in him. He can't possibly expect it to understand his actions.

He thinks about how it would feel, doing it this way. He has never taken any narcotics. Has hardly even been affected by alcohol. Has never liked the feeling of losing control. He's come to realise over the years that it's this very feeling that normal folk like and strive for, but as far as Ove is concerned only a complete bloody airhead could find loss of control a state worth aiming for. He wonders if he'll feel nauseous, if he'll feel pain when his body's organs give up and stop functioning. Or will he just go to sleep when his body becomes unfit for purpose?

By now, the cat is howling out there in the snow. Ove closes his eyes and thinks of Sonja. It's not that he's the sort of man who gives up and dies; he doesn't want her to think that. But it's actually *wrong*, all this. She married him. And now he doesn't quite know how to carry on without the tip of her nose in the pit between his throat and his shoulder. That's all.

He unscrews the lid and distributes the pills along the edge of the washbasin. Watches them as if expecting them to transform into little murderous robots. Of course they don't. Ove is unimpressed. He finds it quite inexplicable how those little white dots could do him any harm, regardless of how many of them he takes. The cat sounds as if it's spitting snow all over Ove's front door. But then it's interrupted by another, quite different sound.

A dog barking.

Ove looks up. It's quiet for a few seconds, and then he hears the cat yowling with pain. Then more barking. And Blonde Weed roaring something.

Ove stands there gripping onto the washbasin. Closes his eyes as if he could blink the sound out. It doesn't work. Then at last he sighs and straightens up. Unscrews the lid of the bottle, pushes the pills back into it. Goes down the stairs. As he crosses the living room he puts the jar in the window. And through the window he sees Blonde Weed in the road, taking aim and then rushing towards the cat.

Ove opens the door exactly as she's about to kick the animal in the head with all her strength. The cat quickly dodges her needle-sharp heel and backs away towards Ove's toolshed. Mutt growls hysterically, saliva flying around its head as if it was a rabies-infected beast. There's fur in its jaws. Ove notes that this is the first time he can remember having seen Weed without her sunglasses. Malevolence glitters in her green eyes. She pulls back, preparing for another kick, then catches sight of Ove and stops herself mid-flow. Her lower lip is trembling with anger.

'I'll have that thing shot!' she hisses and points at the cat.

Very slowly Ove shakes his head without taking his eyes off her. She swallows. Something about his expression, as if sculpted from a seam of rock, makes her murderous assurance falter.

'It's a f-f-fucking street cat and . . . and it's going to die! It scratched Prince!' she stammers.

Ove doesn't say anything but his eyes turn black. And in the end even the dog backs away from him.

'Come on, Prince,' she says, disappearing around the corner as if Ove had physically shoved her from behind.

Ove stays where he is, breathing heavily. He presses his fist to his chest, feels the uncontrolled beating of his heart. He groans a little. Then he looks at the cat. The cat looks back at him. There's a new wound down its flank. Blood in its fur again.

'Nine lives won't last you very long, will they?' says Ove.

The cat licks its paw and looks as if it's not the sort of cat that likes to keep count. Ove nods and steps aside.

'Get inside, then.'

The cat traipses in over the threshold. Ove closes the door.

He stands in the middle of the living room. Everywhere, Sonja looks back at him. Only now does it strike him that he's positioned the photographs so they follow him through the house wherever he goes. She's on the table in the kitchen, hangs on the wall in the hall and halfway up the stairs. She's on the window shelf in the living room, where the cat has now jumped up and sits right beside her. It sends Ove a disgruntled look as it sweeps the pills onto the floor, with a crash. When Ove picks up the bottle, the cat looks at him in horror, as if about to shout, 'J'accuse!'

Ove kicks a little at a skirting board, then turns round and goes into the kitchen to put the pill bottle in a cupboard. Then he makes coffee and pours water in a bowl for the cat.

They drink in silence.

Ove picks up the empty bowl and puts it next to his coffee

cup in the sink. He stands with his hands on his hips for a good while. Then turns around and goes into the hall.

'Tag along, then,' he urges the cat without looking at it. 'Let's give that village cur something to think about.'

Ove puts on the navy winter jacket, steps into his clogs, and lets the cat walk out of the door first. He looks at the photo of Sonja on the wall. She laughs back at him. Maybe it's not so enormously important to die that it can't wait another hour, thinks Ove and follows the cat into the street.

He goes to Rune's house, where it takes several minutes before the door opens. There's a slow, dragging sound inside before anything happens with the lock, as if a ghost is approaching with heavy chains rattling behind it. Then, finally, it opens and Rune stands there looking at Ove and the cat with an empty stare.

'You got any corrugated iron?' wonders Ove, without allowing any time for smalltalk.

Rune gives him a concentrated stare for a second or two, as if his brain is fighting desperately to produce a memory.

'Corrugated iron?' he says to himself, as if tasting the word, like someone who's just woken up and is intensely trying to remember what he's been dreaming.

'Corrugated iron; that's it,' says Ove with a nod.

Rune looks at him, or rather he looks straight through him. His eyes have the gleam of a newly waxed bonnet. He's emaciated and hunchbacked; his beard is grey, bordering on white. This used to be a solid bloke commanding a bit of respect, but now his clothes hang on his body in rags. He's grown old: very, very old, Ove realises, and it hits him with a force he hadn't quite counted on. Rune's gaze flickers for a moment. Then his mouth starts twitching.

'Ove?' he exclaims.

'Yeah, well . . . one thing's for sure, I'm not the Pope,' Ove replies.

The baggy skin on Rune's face cracks into a sleepy smile. Both men, once as close as men of that sort could be, stare at

191

each other. One of them a man who refuses to forget the past, and one who can't remember it at all.

'You look old,' says Ove.

Rune grins.

Then Anita's anxious voice makes itself heard and in the next moment her small, drumming feet are bearing her at speed towards the door.

'Is there someone at the door, Rune? What are you doing there?' she calls out, terrified, as she appears in the doorway. Then she sees Ove.

'Oh . . . hello, Ove,' she says and stops abruptly.

Ove stands there with his hands in his pockets. The cat beside him looks as if it would do the same, if it had pockets. Or hands. Anita is small and colourless in her grey trousers, grey knitted cardigan, grey hair and grey skin. But Ove notices that her face is slightly red-eyed and swollen. Quickly she wipes her eyes and blinks away the pain. As women of that generation do. As if they stood in the doorway every morning, determinedly driving sorrow out of the house with a broom. Tenderly she takes Rune by the shoulders and leads him to his wheelchair by the window in the living room.

'Hello, Ove,' she repeats in a friendly, also surprised, voice when she comes back to the door. 'What can I do for you?'

'Do you have any corrugated iron?' he asks back.

She looks puzzled.

'Corrected iron?' she mumbles, as if the iron has somehow been wrong and now someone has to put it right.

Ove sighs deeply.

'Good God, corrugated iron.'

Anita doesn't look the slightest bit less puzzled.

'Am I supposed to have some?'

'Rune will have some in his shed, definitely,' says Ove and holds out his hand.

Anita nods. Takes down the shed key from the wall and puts it in Ove's hand.

'Corrugated. Iron?' she says again.

'Yes,' says Ove.

'But we don't have a metal roof.'

'What's that got to do with it?'

Anita shakes her head.

'No . . . no, maybe it doesn't, of course.'

'One always has a bit of sheet metal,' says Ove, as if this was absolutely beyond dispute.

Anita nods. As one does when faced with the undeniable fact that a bit of corrugated iron is the sort of thing that all normal, right-thinking people keep lying about in their sheds, just in case there's call for it.

'But don't you have any of that metal yourself, then?' she tries, mainly to have something to talk about.

'I've used mine up,' says Ove.

Anita nods understandingly. As one does when facing the indisputable fact that there's nothing odd about a normal man without a metal roof getting through his corrugated iron at such a rate that it runs out.

A minute later, Ove turns up triumphantly in the doorway, dragging a gigantic piece of corrugated iron, as big as a living room rug. Anita honestly has no idea how such a large piece of metal has even fitted in there without her knowing about it.

'Told you,' Ove says with a nod, giving her back the key.

'Yes . . . yes, you did, didn't you,' Anita feels obliged to admit.

Ove turns to the window. Rune looks back. And just as Anita turns round to go back into the house, Rune grins again, and lifts his hand in a brief wave. As if right there, just for a second, he knew exactly who Ove was and what he was doing there.

Anita stops hesitantly. Turns round.

'They've been here from Social Services again, they want to take Rune away from me,' she says without looking up.

Her voice cracks like dry newspaper when she speaks her husband's name. Ove fingers the corrugated iron.

'They say I'm not capable of taking care of him. With his illness and everything. They say he has to go into a home,' she says.

193

Ove carries on fingering the corrugated iron.

'He'll die if I put him in a home, Ove. You know that . . .' she whispers.

Ove nods and looks at the remains of a cigarette butt, frozen into the crack between two paving stones. Out of the corner of his eye he notices how Anita is sort of leaning slightly to one side. Sonja explained about a year ago that it was the hip replacement operation, he remembers. Her hands shake as well, these days. 'The first stage of multiple sclerosis,' Sonja had also explained. And a few years ago Rune got Alzheimer's as well.

'Your lad can come and give you a hand, then,' he mumbles in a low voice.

Anita looks up. Looks into his eyes and smiles indulgently.

'Johan? Ah . . . he lives in America, you know. He's got enough on his own plate. You know how young people are!'

Ove doesn't answer. Anita says 'America' as if it were the kingdom of heaven where her egoistic son had moved. Not once has Ove seen that brat here in the street since Rune sickened. Grown man now, but no time for his parents.

Anita jumps to attention, as if she's caught herself doing something disreputable. She smiles apologetically at Ove.

'Sorry, Ove, I shouldn't stand here taking up your time with my nattering.'

She goes back into the house. Ove stays where he is with the sheet of corrugated iron in his hand and the cat at his side. He mutters something to himself just before the door is closed. Anita turns round in surprise, peers out of the crack and looks at him.

'Pardon me?'

Ove twists without meeting her eyes. Then he turns round and starts to leave, while his words slip out of him involuntarily.

'I said if you have any more problems with those bloody radiators, you can come and ring my doorbell. The cat and me are at home.'

Anita's furrowed face pulls itself into a surprised smile. She takes half a step out of the door, as if she wants to say something more. Maybe something about Sonja, how deeply she misses her best friend. How she misses what they had, all four of them, when they first moved into this street almost forty years ago. How she even misses the way Rune and Ove used to argue. But Ove has already disappeared around the corner.

Back in his toolshed, Ove fetches the spare battery for the Saab and two large metal clips. He lays out the sheet of corrugated iron across the paving stones between the shed and the house and carefully covers it with snow.

He stands next to the cat, evaluating his creation for a long time. A perfect dog trap, hidden under snow, bursting with electricity, ready to bite. It seems a wholly proportionate revenge. The next time Blonde Weed passes by with that bloody Mutt of hers and the latter gets the idea of peeing on Ove's paving, it'll do so onto an electrified, conductive metal plate. And then let's see how amusing they find it, Ove thinks to himself.

The cat tilts its head and looks at the metal sheet.

'Like a bolt of lightning up your urethra,' says Ove.

The cat looks at him for a long time. As if to say: 'You're not serious, are you?' Eventually Ove sticks his hands in his pockets and shakes his head.

'No . . . no, I suppose not.' He sighs glumly.

And then he packs up the battery and clamps and corrugated iron and puts everything in the garage. Not because he doesn't think those morons deserve a proper electric shock. Because they do. But because he knows it's been a while since someone reminded him of the difference between being wicked because one has to be or because one can.

'It was a bloody good idea, though,' he concludes to the cat as they go back into the house.

The cat goes into the living room with the dismissive body language of someone mumbling: 'Sure, sure it was . . .'

And then they have lunch.

26

A MAN CALLED OVE AND A
SOCIETY WHERE NO ONE CAN
REPAIR A BICYCLE ANY MORE

Many people find it difficult living with someone who likes to be alone. It grates with those who can't handle it themselves. But Sonja didn't whine more than she had to. 'I took you as you were,' she used to say

But Sonja was not so silly that she didn't understand that even men like Ove like to have someone to talk to now and then. It had been quite a while since he'd had that.

'I won,' Ove says curtly when he hears the slamming of the post box.

The cat jumps off the window frame in the living room and goes into the kitchen. Bad loser, thinks Ove and goes to the front door. It's been years since he last made a bet with someone about what time the post would come. He used to make bets with Rune when they were on holiday in the summers, which grew so intensive that they developed complex systems of marginal extensions and half-minutes to determine who was most accurate. That was how it was back in those days. The post arrived at twelve o'clock on the dot, so one needed precise demarcations to be able to say who had guessed right. Nowadays it isn't like that. Nowadays the post can be delivered halfway through the afternoon any old way it pleases. The post office takes care of it when it feels like it and you just have to be grateful and that's it. Ove tried to make bets with Sonja after he and Rune stopped talking. But she didn't understand the rules. So he gave up.

The youth barely manages to avoid being knocked off the steps when Ove throws the door open. Ove looks at him in surprise. He's wearing a postman's uniform.

'Yes?' demands Ove.

The youth looks like he can't come up with an answer. He fiddles with a newspaper and a letter. And that's when Ove notices that it's the same youth who argued with him about that bicycle a few days ago, by the storage shed. The bicycle the youth said he was going to 'fix'. Of course Ove knows what that means. 'Fix' means 'steal and sell on the Internet' to these rascals, that's the long and short of it.

The youth looks, if possible, even less thrilled about recognising Ove than vice versa. He looks a little like a waiter sometimes does, when he's undecided about whether to serve you your food or take it into the kitchen and spit on it. The lad looks coolly at Ove before reluctantly handing the post over with a grumpy 'there y'go'. Ove accepts it without taking his eyes off him.

'Your letter box is mashed, so I was gonna give you these,' says the youth.

He nods at the folded-double pile of junk that used to be Ove's letter box until the Lanky One who can't reverse with a trailer reversed his trailer into it – then nods at the letter and newspaper in Ove's hand. Ove looks down at them. The newspaper is one of those local rags they hand out for nothing even when one puts up a sign quite expressly telling them to do no such bloody thing. And the letter is most likely advertising, Ove imagines. Admittedly his name and address have been written in longhand on the front, but that's a typical advertising trick. To make one think it's a letter from a real person, and then one opens it and in a flash one has been subjected to marketing. That trick won't work on Ove.

The youth stands there weighing on his heels and looking down at the ground. As if he's struggling with something inside that wants to come out.

'Was there something else?' Ove wonders.

He pulls his hand through his greasy, late-pubescent shock of hair.

'Ah, what the hell . . . I was just wondering if you have a wife called Sonja,' he manages to say.

Ove looks suspicious. The lad points at the envelope.

'I saw the surname. I had a teacher with that name. Was just wondering . . .'

He seems to be cursing himself for having said anything. He spins round on the spot and starts walking away. Ove clears his throat and kicks the threshold.

'Wait . . . that could be right. What about Sonja?'

The lad stops a metre further away.

'Ah, shit . . . I just liked her, that's all I wanted to say. I'm . . . you know . . . I'm not so good at reading and writing and all that.'

Ove almost says, 'I'd never have guessed,' but he leaves it. The youth twists awkwardly. Runs his hand through his hair, somewhat disoriented, as if he's hoping to find the appropriate words up there somewhere.

'She's the only teacher I ever had who didn't think I was thick as a plank,' he mumbles, almost choking on his emotion. 'She got me reading that . . . Shakespeare, you know. I didn't know I could even read, sort of thing. She got me reading the most hardcore thick book an' all. It felt really shit when I heard she died, you know.'

Ove doesn't answer. The youth looks down at the ground. Shrugs.

'That's it . . .'

He's silent. And then they both stand there, the fifty-nine-year-old and the teenager, a few metres apart, kicking at the snow. As if they were kicking a memory back and forth, a memory of a woman who insisted on seeing more potential in certain men than they saw in themselves. Neither of them know what to do with their shared experience.

'What are you doing with that bike?' says Ove at last.

'I promised to fix it up for my girlfriend. She lives there,' the youth answers, nodding at the house at the far end of their row, opposite Anita and Rune's place. The one where those recycling types live when they're not in Thailand or wherever they go.

'Or, you know. She's not my girlfriend yet. But I'm thinking I'm wanting her to be. Sort of thing.'

Ove scrutinises the youth as middle-aged men often scrutinise younger men who seem to invent their own grammar as they go along.

'So have you got any tools, then?' he asks.

The youth shakes his head.

'How are you going to repair a bike without tools?' Ove marvels, more with genuine surprise than agitation.

The youth shrugs.

'Dunno.'

'Why did you promise to repair it, then?'

The youth kicks the snow. Scratches his face with his entire hand, embarrassed.

'Because I love her.'

Ove can't quite decide what to say to that one. So he rolls up the local newspaper and envelope and slaps it into his palm, like a baton.

'I have to get going,' the youth mumbles almost inaudibly and makes a movement to turn round again.

'Come over after work, then, and I'll get the bike out for you.' Ove's words seem to pop up out of nowhere. 'But you have to bring your own tools,' he adds.

The youth brightens up.

'You serious, man?'

Ove continues slapping the paper baton into his hand. The youth swallows.

'Awesome! Wait . . . ah, shit . . . I can't pick it up today! I have to go to my other job! But tomorrow, man, I can come tomorrow. Is it cool if I pick it up tomorrow, like, instead?'

Ove tilts his head and looks as if everything that's just been said came from the mouth of a character in an animated film. The youth takes a deep breath and pulls himself together.

'What other job?' asks Ove, as if he's had an incomplete answer in the final of *Jeopardy*.

'I sort of work in a café in the evenings and at the weekends,' says the youth, with that new-won hope in his eyes about perhaps being able to rescue his fantasy relationship with a girlfriend who doesn't even know that she's his girlfriend – the sort of relationship that only a boy in late puberty with greasy hair can have.

'I need both jobs because I'm saving money,' he explains.

'For what?'

'A car.'

Ove can't avoid noticing how he straightens up slightly when he says 'car'. Ove looks dubious for a moment. Then he slowly but watchfully slaps the baton into his palm again.

'What sort of car?'

'I had a look at a Renault,' the youth says brightly, stretching a little more.

The air around the two men stops for a hundredth of a breath or so. An eerie silence suddenly envelops them. If this was a scene from a film, the camera would very likely have time to pan 360 degrees around them before Ove finally loses his composure.

'Renault? *Renault*? That's bloody FRENCH! You can't bloody well go and buy a FRENCH car!!!'

The youth seems just about to say something but he doesn't get the chance before Ove shakes his whole upper body as if trying to get rid of a persistent wasp.

'Christ, you puppy! Don't you know anything about cars?'

The youth shakes his head. Ove sighs deeply and puts his hand on his forehead as if he's been struck by a sudden migraine.

'And how are you going to get the bicycle to the café if you don't have a car?' he says at long last, visibly struggling to regain his composure.

'I hadn't . . . thought about that,' says the youth.

Ove shakes his head.

'Renault? Christ almighty . . .'

The youth nods. Ove rubs his eyes in frustration.

'Where's this sodding café you work at, then?' he mutters.

Twenty minutes later, Parvaneh opens her front door in surprise. Ove is standing outside, thoughtfully striking his hand with a paper baton.

'Have you got one of those green signs?'

'What?'

'You have to have one of those green signs when you're a learner driver. Do you have one or not?'

She nods.

'Yeah . . . yes I have, but wh—'

'I'll come and pick you up in two hours. We'll take my car.'

Ove turns round and tramps back across the little road without waiting for an answer.

27

A MAN CALLED OVE AND A DRIVING LESSON

It happened now and then in the almost forty years they lived in the row of terraced houses, that some thoughtless and recently moved-in neighbour was bold enough to ask Sonja what the real cause was for the deep animosity between Ove and Rune. Why had two men who had once been friends suddenly started hating one another with such overpowering intensity?

Sonja usually answered that it was quite straightforward. It was simply about how when the two men and their wives moved into their houses, Ove drove a Saab 96 and Rune a Volvo 244. A year or so later Ove bought a Saab 95 and Rune bought a Volvo 245. Three years later Ove bought a Saab 900 and Rune bought a Volvo 265. In the decades that followed, Ove bought another two Saab 900s and then a Saab 9000. Rune bought another Volvo 265 and then a Volvo 745, but a few years later he went back to a sedan model and acquired a Volvo 740. Whereupon Ove bought yet one more Saab 9000 and Rune eventually went over to a Volvo 760, after which Ove got himself a Saab 9000i and Rune part-exchanged to a Volvo 760 Turbo.

And then the day came when Ove went to the car dealer to look at the recently launched Saab 9-3, and when he came home in the evening, Rune had bought a BMW.

'A *BMW*!' Ove had roared at Sonja. 'How can you *reason* with a human being like that? *How?*'

And possibly it was not the entire explanation for why these two men loathed one another, Sonja used to explain. Either you understood it or you didn't. And if you didn't understand, there was no point even trying to clarify the rest.

Most people never did understand, Ove often commented. But then people had no idea of loyalty these days. The car was just 'a means of transport' and the road just a complication arising between two points. Ove is convinced this is why the roads are as bad as they are. If people were a little more careful with their cars they wouldn't drive like idiots, he thinks, watching with concern as Parvaneh pushes away the newspaper he has spread across her seat. She has to retract the driver's seat as far as it'll go, so she can manoeuvre her pregnant belly into the car; then bring it forward all the way so she can reach the wheel.

The driving lesson doesn't start so well. Or, to be precise, it begins with Parvaneh trying to get into the Saab with a bottle of fizzy juice in her hand. She shouldn't have done that. Then she tries to fiddle with Ove's radio to find 'a more entertaining channel'. She shouldn't have done that either.

Ove picks up the newspaper from the floor, rolls it up and starts nervously striking it against his hand, like a more aggressive version of a stress ball. She grabs the wheel and looks at the instruments like a curious child.

'Where do we start?' she yells eagerly, after at long last agreeing to hand over the juice.

Ove sighs. The cat sits in the back seat and looks as if it wished, with intensity, that cats knew how to strap on safety belts.

'Press the clutch pedal,' says Ove, slightly grim.

Parvaneh looks around her seat as if searching for something. Then she looks at Ove and smiles ingratiatingly.

'Which one's the clutch?'

Ove's face fills with disbelief.

She looks around the seat again, turns towards the seat belt fixture in the back rest, as if she may find the clutch there. Ove holds his forehead. Parvaneh's facial expression immediately sours.

203

'I told you I want a driving license for an automatic! Why did you make me use your car?'

'Because you're getting a proper license!' Ove cuts her short, emphasising 'proper' in a way that makes it plain that a license for an automatic is as much a 'proper driving license' as a car with an automatic gearbox is a 'proper car'.

'Stop shouting at me!' shouts Parvaneh.

'I'm not shouting!' Ove shouts back.

The cat curls up in the back seat, clearly anxious not to end up in the middle of this, whatever it is. Parvaneh crosses her arms and glares out of the side window. Ove strikes his paper baton rhythmically into the palm of his hand.

'The pedal on the far left is the clutch,' he grunts in the end.

After taking a breath so deep that he has to stop halfway for a rest before he inhales again, he continues:

'The one in the middle is the brake. On the far right is the accelerator. You release the clutch slowly until you find the point where it engages, then give it a bit of gas, release the clutch and move off.'

Parvaneh seems to accept this as an apology. She nods and calms down. Takes hold of the steering wheel, starts the car and follows his instructions. The Saab lurches forward with a little jump, then pauses before catapulting itself with a loud roar towards the guest parking and very nearly crashing into another car. Ove tugs at the handbrake. Parvaneh lets go of the steering wheel and yells in panic, covering her eyes with her hands until the Saab finally comes to an abrupt stop. Ove is puffing as if he had to make his way to the handbrake by forcing himself through a military obstacle course. His facial muscles twitch like a man whose eyes are being sprayed with lemon juice.

'What do I do now!?' roars Parvaneh when she realises that the Saab is two centimetres from the tail lights of the car in front.

'Reverse. You put it in reverse,' Ove manages to say through his teeth.

'I almost smashed into that car!' pants Parvaneh.

Ove peers over the edge of the bonnet. And then, suddenly, a sort of calm comes over his face. He turns and nods at her, very matter-of-fact.

'Doesn't matter. It's a Volvo.'

It takes them fifteen minutes to get out of the parking area and onto the main road. Once they're there, Parvaneh revs the first gear until the Saab vibrates like it's about to explode. Ove tells her to change gear and she replies that she doesn't know how. Meanwhile the cat seems to be trying to open the back door.

When they get to the first red light, a big black city jeep with two shaven-headed young men in the front pulls up so close to their rear bumper that Ove is pretty sure he'll have their registration number etched into his paintwork when they get home. Parvaneh glances nervously in the mirror. The city jeep revs its engine, as if giving vent to some sort of opinion. Ove turns round and looks out of the back window. The two men have tattoos all over their throats, he notes. As if the city jeep is not a clear enough advertisement for their stupidity.

The light turns green. Parvaneh brings up the clutch, the Saab splutters and the instrument panel goes black. Stressed, Parvaneh turns the key in the ignition, which only makes it grind in a heart-rending manner. The engine makes a roar, coughs and dies anew. The men with the shaved heads and tattooed throats sound the horn. One of them gestures.

'Press down the clutch and give it more gas,' says Ove.

'That's what I'm doing!' she answers.

'That's not what you're doing.'

'Yes I am!'

'Now you're shouting.'

'I'M NOT BLOODY SHOUTING!' she shouts.

The city jeep blares its horn. Parvaneh presses down the clutch. The Saab rolls backwards a few centimetres and bumps into the front of the city jeep. The Throat Tattoos are now hanging on the horn as if it's an air raid alarm.

Parvaneh tugs despairingly at the key, only to be rewarded by yet another stall. Then suddenly she lets go of everything and hides her face in her hands.

'Good Go . . . are you crying now?' Ove asks in amazement.

'I'M NOT BLOODY CRYING!' she howls, her tears spattering over the dashboard.

Ove leans back and looks down at his knee. Fingers the end of the paper baton.

'It's just such a strain, this, do you understand?' she sobs and leans her forehead against the wheel as if hoping it might be soft and fluffy. 'I'm sort of PREGNANT! I'm just a bit STRESSED, can no one show a bit of understanding for a pregnant bloody woman who's a bit STRESSED!!???'

Ove twists uncomfortably in the passenger seat. She punches the steering wheel several times, mumbles something about how all she wants is to 'drink some bloody lemonade', flops her arms over the top of the steering wheel, buries her face in her sleeves and starts crying again.

The city jeep behind them signals until it sounds as if the Finland ferry is about to run them down. And then something in Ove snaps. He throws the door open, gets out of the car, walks slowly round the city jeep and rips the driver's door open.

'Have you never been a learner driver or what?'

The driver doesn't have time to answer.

'You stupid little bastard!' Ove roars in the face of the shaven-headed young man with throat tattoos, his spittle cascading over their seats.

The Throat Tattoo doesn't have time to answer and Ove doesn't wait for him either. Instead he grabs the young man by his collar and pulls him up so hard that his body tumbles clumsily out of the car. He's a muscular sort, easily weighing in at a hundred kilos, but Ove holds his collar in an immovable steel grip. Evidently, Throat Tattoo is so surprised by the strength in the old man's grip that it doesn't occur to him to put up any resistance. Fury burns in Ove's eyes as he presses the probably thirty-five-years-younger man so hard against the side of the city jeep that the bodywork creaks. He places the tip of his index finger in the middle of the shaved head and positions his eyes so close to Throat Tattoo's face that they feel each other's breath.

'If you sound that horn one more time it'll be the LAST thing you do on this earth. Got it?'

Throat Tattoo allows his eyes to divert quickly towards his equally muscular friend inside the car, and then at the growing queue of other cars behind the city jeep. No one is making the slightest move to come to his assistance. No one beeps. No one moves. Everyone seems to be thinking the same thing: If a non-throat-tattooed man of Ove's age without any hesitation steps up to a throat-tattooed man of the age of this Throat Tattoo and presses him up against a car in this manner, then it's very likely not the throat-tattooed man one should be most worried about annoying.

Ove's eyes are black with anger. After a short moment of reflection, Throat Tattoo seems convinced by the argument that the old man unmistakably means business. The tip of his nose, almost unnoticeably, moves up and down.

Ove nods by way of confirmation and lets him back down on the ground. Then turns round, walks around the city jeep and gets back into the Saab. Parvaneh stares at him, with her mouth hanging open.

'Now you listen to me,' says Ove calmly while he carefully closes the door. 'You've given birth to two children and quite soon you'll be squeezing out a third. You've come here from a land far away and most likely you fled war and persecution and all sorts of other nonsense. You've learned a new language and got yourself an education and you're holding together a family of obvious incompetents. And I'll be damned if I've seen you afraid of a single bloody thing in this world before now.'

Ove rivets his eyes into her. Parvaneh is still agape. Ove points imperiously at the pedals under her feet.

'I'm not asking for brain surgery. I'm asking you to drive a car. It's got an accelerator, a brake and a clutch. Some of the greatest twits in world history have sorted out how it works. And you will as well.'

And then he utters seven words, which Parvaneh will always remember as the loveliest compliment he'll ever give her.

'Because you are not a complete twit.'

Parvaneh pushes a ringlet of hair out of her face, sticky with tears. Clumsily she once again grabs hold of the steering wheel with both hands. Ove nods, puts on his safety belt and makes himself comfortable.

'Now push the clutch down and do what I say.'

And that afternoon Parvaneh learns to drive.

28

A MAN WHO WAS OVE AND
A MAN WHO WAS RUNE

Sonja used to say that Ove was 'unforgiving'. For instance, he refused to go back to the local bakery eight years after they gave him the wrong change when he bought pastries once at the end of the 1990s. Ove called it 'having firm principles'. They were never quite in agreement when it came to words and their meanings.

He knows that she is disappointed that he and Rune could not keep the peace. He knows that the animosity between him and Rune to some extent ruined the possibility of Sonja and Anita becoming the great friends they could have been. But when a conflict has been going on for long enough it can be impossible to sort out, for the simple reason that no one can remember how it first started. And Ove didn't know how it first started.

He only knew how it ended.

A BMW. There must have been some people who understood it and some who didn't. There were probably people who thought there was no connection between cars and emotions. But there would never be a clearer explanation as to why these two men had become enemies for life.

Of course it had started innocently enough, not long after Ove and Sonja came back from Spain and the accident. Ove laid new paving stones in their little garden that summer, whereupon

Rune put up a new fence round his. Whereupon Ove put up an even higher fence round his garden, whereupon Rune went off to the builders' merchants and a few days later started boasting all over the street that he had 'built a swimming pool'. That was no bloody swimming pool, Ove raged to Sonja. It was a little splash pool for Rune and Anita's new-born urchin, that was all it was. For a while Ove had plans to report it to the planning department as an illegal construction, but at that point Sonja put her foot down and sent him out to 'mow the lawn' and calm himself down. And so Ove did just that, although it certainly did not calm him down very much at all.

The lawn was oblong, about five metres wide and ran along the back of Ove and Rune's houses and the house in-between, which Sonja and Anita had quickly named 'the neutral zone'. No one quite knew what that lawn was for or what function it was expected to fill, but when terraced housing was put up in those days, some city architect must have got the idea that there had to be lawns here and there, for no other reason than that they looked so very nice in the drawings. When Ove and Rune formed the Residents' Association and were still friends, the two men decided that Ove should be the 'grounds man' and responsible for keeping the grass mowed. It had always been Ove before. On one occasion the other neighbours had proposed that the Association should put out tables and benches on the lawn to create a sort of 'common space for all the neighbours', but obviously Ove and Rune put a stop to that at once. It would only turn into a bloody mess and lots of noise.

And as far as that went, it was all peace and joy. At least in so far as anything could be 'peace and joy' when men like Ove and Rune were involved.

Soon after Rune had built his 'pool', a rat ran across Ove's newly mown lawn and into the trees on the other side. Ove immediately called a 'crisis meeting' of the Association and demanded that all local residents put out rat poison around their houses. The neighbours protested, of course, because they had seen hedgehogs by the edge of the woods and were concerned that they might eat the poison. Rune also protested, because he was afraid that some of it would end up in his pool. Ove suggested to Rune that he button up his shirt and go see a psychologist about his delusions of living on the French Riviera. Rune made a malicious joke at Ove's expense, to the effect that Ove had probably only imagined seeing that rat. All the others laughed. Ove never forgave Rune for that. The next morning someone had thrown birdseed all over Rune's outside space, and Rune had to use a spade to chase away a dozen rats as big as vacuum cleaners in the next few weeks. After that Ove got permission to put out poison, even though Rune mumbled that he'd pay him back for this.

Two years later Rune won the Great Tree Conflict, when he gained permission at the annual meeting to saw down a tree blocking his and Anita's evening sun on one side. The same tree on the other side screened off Ove and Sonja's bedroom from blinding morning sunlight. Further, he managed to block Ove's furious motion that the Association would then have to pay for Ove's new awning.

However, Ove got his revenge during the Snow Clearance Skirmish of the following winter, in which Rune wanted to anoint himself 'Chief of Snow Shovelling' and at the same time lumber the Residents' Association with the purchase of a gigantic snow slinger. Ove had no intention of letting Rune walk round with some bloody contraption at the expense of the Association and spray snow over Ove's windows, which he made crystal clear at the Steering Group meeting.

Rune was still chosen to be responsible for snow clearance, but to his great annoyance he had to spend all winter shovelling the snow by hand between the houses. The outcome of this, of course, was that he consistently shovelled outside all the houses in their row except Ove and Sonja's. Just to annoy Rune, in mid-January Ove hired a gigantic snow slinger to clear the ten square metres outside his door. Rune was incandescent about it, Ove remembers with delight to this day.

Of course, Rune found a way of paying him back the following summer, by buying one of those monstrous lawn tractors. Then, by a combination of treachery, lies and conspiracies, he managed to get approval at the Annual Meeting to take over Ove's lawn-mowing responsibilities on the grounds that he had 'slightly more adequate equipment than the one who was in charge of it before'.

As a partial restitution, Ove managed some four years later to stop Rune's plans of putting in new windows in his house, because after thirty-three letters and a dozen angry telephone calls the Planning Department gave up and accepted Ove's argument that this would 'ruin the harmonized architectural character of the area'.

In the following three years, Rune refused to speak of Ove as anything but 'that bloody red-tapist'. Ove took it as a compliment. And the next year he changed his own windows.

When the next winter set in, the steering group decided that the area needed a new collective heating system. Quite coincidentally, of course, Rune and Ove happened to have diametrically different views on what sort of heating system was required, which was jokingly referred to by the other neighbours as 'the battle of the water pump'. It grew into an eternal struggle between the two men.

And so it continued.

But, as Sonja used to say, there were also some other moments. There weren't many of them, but women like Sonja and Anita knew how to make the most of them. Because there hadn't always been burning conflict. One summer in the 1980s, for instance, Ove had bought a Saab 9000 and Rune a Volvo 760. And they were so pleased with this that they kept the peace for several weeks. Sonja and Anita even managed to get all four of them together for dinner on a few occasions. Rune and Anita's son, who'd had time to turn into a teenager by this stage, with all the divinely sanctioned charmlessness and impoliteness this entailed, sat at one end of the table like an irritable accessory. That boy was born angry, Sonja used to say with sadness in her voice, but Ove and Rune managed to get along so well that they even had a little whisky together at the end of the evening.

Unfortunately, at their last dinner that summer Ove and Rune had the idea of having a barbecue. And obviously they started feuding at once about the most effective way of lighting Ove's globe grill. Within fifteen minutes the argument had escalated so much in volume that Sonja and Anita agreed it might be best to eat their dinner separately after all. The two men had time to buy and sell a Volvo 760 (Turbo) and a Saab 9000i before they spoke to one another again.

Meanwhile, the neighbours came and went in the row of houses. In the end there had been so many new faces in the doorways of the other terraced houses that they all merged in a sea of grey. Where before there had been forest, there were only construction cranes. Ove and Rune stood outside their houses, hands obstinately shoved into their trouser pockets, like ancient relics in a new age, while a parade of uppity estate agents barely able to see over their grapefruit-size tie knots patrolled the little road between the houses and kept their eyes on them – like vultures watching ageing water buffaloes. They could hardly wait to move some bloody consultants' families into their houses, both Ove and Rune knew that very well.

Rune and Anita's son moved away from home when he was twenty, in the early 1990s. Apparently he went to America, Ove found out from Sonja. They hardly saw him again. From time to time Anita had a telephone call around the time of Christmas, but 'he was so busy with his own things now', as Anita said when she tried to keep her spirits up, even though Sonja could see that she had to hold back her tears. Some boys leave everything behind and never look back. That was all there was to it.

Rune never said anything about it. But to anyone who had known him a long time, it was as if he grew a few centimetres shorter in the years that followed. As if he sort of crumpled with a deep sigh and never really breathed properly again.

A few years later Rune and Ove fell out for the hundredth time about that collective heating system. Ove stormed out of a Residents' Association meeting, in a fury, and never returned.

The last battle the two men fought was a bit into the noughties when Rune bought one of those automated robotic lawnmowers, which he'd ordered from Asia, and left it to whizz about on the lawn behind the houses. Rune could even remotely program it to cut 'special patterns', Sonja said in an impressed tone of voice one evening when she came home from visiting Anita. Ove soon twigged that this 'special pattern' was the habit of that robotic little shit to consistently rumble back and forth all night outside Ove and Sonja's bedroom window. One evening Sonja saw Ove fetch a screwdriver and walk out of the veranda door. Next morning the little robot, quite inexplicably, had driven right into Rune's pool.

The month after, Rune went into the hospital for the first time. He never bought another lawnmower. Ove did not know himself how their animosity had begun, though he knew very well that it ended there and then. Afterwards it was only memories for Ove, and a lack of them for Rune.

And there were very likely people who thought one could not interpret men's feelings by the cars they drove.

But when they moved into the terrace, Ove drove a Saab 96 and Rune a Volvo 244. After the accident Ove bought a Saab 95 so he'd have space for Sonja's wheelchair. That same year Rune bought a Volvo 245 to have space for a pram. Three years later Sonja got a more modern wheelchair and Ove bought a hatchback, a Saab 900. Rune bought a Volvo 265 because Anita had started talking about having another child.

Then Ove bought two more Saab 900's and after that his first Saab 9000. Rune bought a Volvo 265 and eventually a Volvo 745 estate. But no more children came. One evening Sonja came home and told Ove that Anita had been to the doctor.

And a week later a Volvo 740 stood parked in Rune's garage. The saloon model.

Ove saw it when he washed his Saab. In the evening Rune found a half-bottle of whisky outside his door. They never spoke about it.

Maybe their sorrow over children that never came should have brought the two men closer. But sorrow is unreliable in that way. When people don't share it there's a good chance that it will drive them apart instead.

Maybe Ove never forgave Rune for having a son that he could not even get along with. Maybe Rune never forgave Ove for not being able to forgive him for it. Maybe neither of them forgave themselves for not being able to give the women they loved more than anything what they wanted more than anything. Rune and Anita's lad grew up and cleared out of home as soon as he got the chance. And Rune went and bought a sporty BMW, one of those cars that only has space for two people and a handbag. Because now it was only him and Anita, as he told Sonja when they met in the parking area. 'And one can't drive a Volvo all of one's life,' he said with an attempt at a half-hearted smile. She could hear that he was trying to swallow his tears. And that was the moment when Ove realised that a part of Rune had given up for ever. And for that maybe neither Ove nor Rune forgave him.

So there were certainly people who thought that feelings could not be judged by looking at cars. But they were wrong.

29

A MAN CALLED OVE AND A BENDER

'Seriously, where are we going!?' Parvaneh wonders, out of breath.

'To fix something,' Ove answers curtly, three steps ahead of her, with the cat half-jogging at his side.

'What thing?'

'A thing!'

Parvaneh stops and catches her breath.

'Here!' Ove calls out and stops abruptly in front of a little café.

A scent of fresh-baked croissants comes through the glass door. Parvaneh looks at the parking area on the other side of the street where they left the Saab. In the end they could not have parked closer to the café. At first Ove had been absolutely convinced that the café was at the other end of the block. That was when Parvaneh had suggested they could possibly park on that side, but the notion was abandoned once they found that parking cost one crown more per hour.

Instead they had parked here and walked all around the block looking for the café. Because Ove, as Parvaneh had soon realised, was the sort of man who, when he was not quite certain where he was going, just carried on walking straight ahead, convinced that the road would eventually fall into line. And now when they find that the café is directly opposite the spot where they parked, Ove looks as if this was his plan all along. Parvaneh mops some sweat off her cheek.

A man with a ragged, dirty beard is leaning against a wall halfway down the street. He has a paper cup in front of him. Outside the café Ove, Parvaneh and the cat meet a slim boy aged about twenty who has what looks very much like black soot around his eyes. It takes Ove a moment to realise it's the boy who was standing behind the lad with the bicycle when Ove met him the first time. He looks a little cautious; although he smiles at Ove, Ove can't think of anything to do but nod back. As if wanting to clarify that while he has no intention of returning the smile, he is prepared to acknowledge receipt of it.

'Why didn't you let me park next to the red car?' Parvaneh wants to know as they open the glass door and step inside.

Ove doesn't answer.

'I would have managed it!' she says self-confidently.

Ove shakes his head wearily. Two hours ago she didn't know where the clutch was, now she's irritated because he won't let her squeeze into a narrow parking space.

Once they're inside the café, Ove sees in the corner of his eye how the slim soot-eyed boy offers the sandwiches to the vagrant.

'Hi there, Ove!' a voice calls out so eagerly that it cracks into falsetto in the high notes.

Ove turns round and sees the lad from the bike shed. He's standing behind a long, polished counter at the front of the premises, wearing a baseball cap, Ove notes. Indoors.

The cat and Parvaneh make themselves at home, the latter mopping sweat from her forehead although it's ice-cold in there. Colder than outside in the street, actually. She pours herself some water from a jug on the counter. The cat unconcernedly laps up some of it from her glass when she isn't looking.

'Do you know each other?' Parvaneh asks with surprise, looking at the youth.

'Me and Ove are sort of mates.' The youth nods.

'Are you? Me and Ove are sort of mates, too!' Parvaneh grins, tenderly imitating his enthusiasm.

Ove stops at a safe distance from the counter. As if someone might give him a hug if he gets too close.

'My name's Adrian,' says the youth.

'Parvaneh,' says Parvaneh.

'You want something to drink?' he asks them.

'A latte for me please,' says Parvaneh, in a tone of voice as if she's suddenly having her shoulders massaged. She dabs her forehead with a napkin. 'Preferably an iced latte if you have it!'

Ove shifts his weight from his left foot to his right and peers round the premises. He's never liked cafés. Sonja, of course, loved them. Could sit in them for an entire Sunday 'just looking at people', as she put it. Ove used to try and sit there with her, reading a newspaper. Every Sunday they did it. He hasn't put his foot in a café since she died. He looks up and realises that Adrian, Parvaneh and the cat are waiting for his answer.

'Coffee, then. Black.'

Adrian scratches his hair under the cap.

'So . . . espresso?'

'No. Coffee.'

Adrian transfers his scratching from hair to chin.

'What . . . like black coffee?'

'Yes.'

'With milk?'

'If it's with milk it's not black coffee.'

Adrian moves a couple of sugar bowls on the counter. Mainly to have something to do, so he doesn't look too silly. A bit late for that, thinks Ove.

'Normal filter coffee. Normal bloody filter coffee,' Ove repeats.

Adrian nods.

'Oh, that . . . Well. I don't know how to make it.'

Ove points aggressively at the percolator in the corner, only barely visible behind a gigantic silver spaceship of a machine, which, Ove understands, is what they use for making espresso.

'Oh that one, yeah,' says Adrian, as if the penny has just dropped. 'Ah . . . I don't really know how that thing works.'

'Should have bloody known . . .' mutters Ove as he walks round the counter and takes matters into his own hands.

'Can someone tell me what we're doing here?' calls Parvaneh.

'This lad here has a bicycle that needs repairing,' explains Ove as he pours water into the jug.

'The bicycle hanging off the back of the car?'

'You brought it here? Thanks, Ove!'

'You don't have a car, do you?' he replies, while rummaging around a cupboard for coffee filters.

'Thanks, Ove!' says Adrian and takes a step towards him, then comes to his senses and stops before he does something silly.

'So that's your bicycle?' Parvaneh smiles.

'Kind of – it's my girlfriend's. Or the one I want to be my girlfriend . . . sort of thing.'

Parvaneh grins.

'So me and Ove drove all this way just to give you a bike so you can mend it? For a girl?'

Adrian nods. Parvaneh leans over the counter and pats Ove on the arm.

'You know, Ove, sometimes one almost suspects you have a heart . . .'

'Do you have tools here or not?' Ove says to Adrian, snatching his arm away.

Adrian nods.

'Go and get them then. The bike's on the Saab in the car park.'

Adrian nods quickly and disappears into the kitchen. After a minute or so he comes back with a big tool box, which he quickly takes to the exit.

'And you be quiet,' Ove says to Parvaneh.

She smirks in a way that suggests she has no intention of keeping quiet.

'I only brought the bicycle here so he wouldn't mess about in the sheds back home . . .' Ove adds.

'Sure, sure,' says Parvaneh with a laugh.

'Oh hey,' says Adrian as the soot-eyed boy appears again a moment later. 'This is my boss.'

219

'Hi there – ah, what . . . sorry, what are you doing?' asks the 'boss', looking with some interest at the spry stranger who has barricaded himself behind the counter of his café.

'The kid's going to fix a bicycle,' answers Ove as if this was something plain and obvious. 'Where do you keep the filters for real coffee?'

The soot-eyed boy points at one of the shelves. Ove squints at him.

'Is that make-up?'

Parvaneh hushes him up. Ove looks insulted.

'What? What's wrong with asking?'

The boy smiles a little nervously.

'Yes, it's make-up,' he nods, rubbing himself round his eyes. 'I went dancing last night,' he says, smiling gratefully as Parvaneh with the deftness of a fellow conspirator hauls out a wet-wipe from her handbag and offers it to him.

Ove nods and goes back to his coffee-making.

'And do you also have problems with bicycles and love and girls?' he asks absent-mindedly.

'No, no, not with bicycles anyway. And not with love either, I suppose. Well, not with girls, anyway.' He chuckles.

Ove turns on the percolator and, once it begins to splutter, turns round and leans against the inside of the counter as if this is the most natural thing in the world in a café where one doesn't work.

'Bent, are you?'

'OVE!' says Parvaneh and slaps him on the arm.

Ove snatches back his arm and looks very offended.

'What?!'

'You don't say . . . you don't call it that,' Parvaneh says, clearly unwilling to spell out the word again.

'Queer?' Ove offers.

Parvaneh tries to hit his arm again but Ove is too quick.

'Don't talk like that!' she orders him.

Ove turns to the sooty boy, genuinely puzzled.

'Can't one say bent? What are you supposed to say nowadays?'

'You say homosexual. Or an LGBT person,' Parvaneh interrupts before she has time to stop herself.

'Ah, you can say what you want, it's cool.' The boy smiles as he walks round the counter and puts on an apron.

'Right, good. Good to be clear. One of those gays, then,' mumbles Ove. Parvaneh shakes her head apologetically; the boy just laughs. 'Well then,' says Ove with a nod, and starts pouring himself a coffee while it's still going through.

Then he takes the cup and without another word goes outside into the parking area. The sooty boy doesn't comment on his taking the cup outside. It would seem a little unnecessary, under the circumstances, when this man within five minutes of his arrival at the boy's café has already appointed himself as barista and interrogated him about his sexual preferences.

Adrian is standing outside, by the Saab, looking as if he just got lost in a forest.

'Is it going well?' asks Ove rhetorically, taking a sip of coffee and looking at the bicycle, which Adrian hasn't even unhooked yet from the back of the car.

'Nah . . . you know. Sort of. Well,' Adrian begins, compulsively scratching his chest.

Ove observes him for half a minute or so. Takes another mouthful of his coffee. Nods irritably, like someone squeezing an avocado and finding it overly ripe. He forcefully presses his cup of coffee into the hands of the boy, and then steps forward to unhitch the bicycle. Turns it upside down and opens the toolbox which the youth has brought from the café.

'Didn't your dad ever teach you how to fix a bike?' he says without looking at Adrian, while he hunches over the punctured tyre.

'My dad's banged up,' Adrian replies almost inaudibly and scratches his shoulder, looking round as if he'd like to find a big black hole to sink into. Ove stops himself, looks up, and gives him an evaluating stare. The boy stares at the ground. Ove clears his throat.

'It's not so bloody difficult,' he mutters at long last and gestures at Adrian to sit on the ground.

It takes them ten minutes to repair the puncture. Ove barks monosyllabic instructions; Adrian remains silent throughout. But he's attentive and dextrous and in a certain sense does not make a complete fool of himself, Ove has to admit. Maybe he's not quite as fumbling with his hands as he is with words. They wipe off the dirt with a rag from the boot of the Saab, avoiding eye contact with each other.

'I hope the lady's worth it,' says Ove and closes the boot.

Now it's Adrian's turn to look nonplussed.

When they go back into the café, there's a short cube-shaped man in a stained shirt standing on a stepladder, tinkering with something that Ove suspects is a fan heater. The sooty boy stands below the stepladder with a selection of screwdrivers held aloft. He keeps mopping the remnants of make-up around his eyes, peering at the fat man on the ladder and looking a little on the nervous side. As if worried that he may be caught out. Parvaneh turns excitedly to Ove.

'This is Amel! He owns the café!' she says in a suitably gushing manner. She points to the cubic man on the ladder.

Amel doesn't turn round, but he emits a long sequence of hard consonants that, even though Ove does not understand them, he suspects to be various combinations of four-letter words and body parts.

'What's he saying?' asks Adrian.

The sooty boy twists uncomfortably.

'Ah . . . he . . . something about the fan heater being a bit of a fairy . . .'

He looks over at Adrian; then quickly turns his face down.

'What's that?' asks Ove, wandering over to him.

'He means it's worthless, like a homo,' he says in such a low voice that only Ove catches his words.

Parvaneh, on the other hand, is busy pointing at Amel with delight.

'You can't hear what he's saying but you sort of know that almost all of it is swear words! He's like a dubbed version of you, Ove!'

Ove doesn't look particularly delighted. Nor does Amel.

He stops tinkering with the fan heater and points at Ove with the screwdriver.

'The cat? Is that your cat?'

'No,' says Ove.

Not so much because he wants to point out that it isn't his cat, but because he wants to clarify that it's no one's cat.

'Cat out! No animals in café!' Amel slashes at the consonants so that they hop about like naughty children caught inside the sentence.

Ove looks with interest at the fan heater above Amel's head. Then at the cat on the bar stool. Then at the toolbox, which Adrian is still holding in his hand. Then at the fan heater again. And at Amel.

'If I repair that for you, the cat stays.'

He offers this more as a statement than a question. Amel seems to lose his self-possession for a few moments. By the time he regains it, in a way he could probably not explain afterwards, he has become the man holding the stepladder rather than the man standing on the stepladder. Ove digs about up there for a few minutes, climbs down, brushes the palm of his hand against his trouser leg and hands the screwdriver and a little adjustable spanner to the sooty boy.

'You fixed!' cries Amel suddenly as the fan heater splutters back to life.

In an effusive manner, he grabs Ove's shoulders.

'Whisky? You want? In my kitchen I have the whisky!'

Ove checks his watch. It's quarter past two in the afternoon. He shakes his head whilst looking a little uncomfortable, partly about the whisky and partly because of Amel, who is still holding on to him. The sooty boy disappears through the kitchen door behind the counter, still frenetically rubbing his eyes.

* * *

Adrian catches up with Ove and the cat on their way back to the Saab.

'Ove, mate, you won't say anything about Mirsad being . . .'

'Who?'

'My boss,' says Adrian. 'The one with the make-up.'

'The bent person?' says Ove.

Adrian nods.

'I mean his dad . . . I mean Amel . . . he doesn't know Mirsad is . . .'

Adrian fumbles for the right word.

'A bender?' Ove adds.

Adrian nods. Ove shrugs. Parvaneh comes wagging along behind them, out of breath.

'Where did you get to?' Ove asks her.

'I gave my change to him,' says Parvaneh, with a nod at the man with the dirty beard by the house wall.

'You know he'll only spend it on schnapps,' Ove states.

Parvaneh opens her eyes wide with something Ove strongly suspects to be sarcasm. 'Really? Will he? And I was *sooo* hoping he would use it to pay off his student loans from his university education in particle physics!'

Ove snorts and opens the Saab. Adrian stays where he is on the other side of the car.

'Yes?' Ove wonders.

'You won't say anything about Mirsad, will you? Seriously?'

'Why the hell would I say anything?' Ove points at him with exasperation. 'You! You want to buy a French car. Don't worry so much about others, you have enough problems of your own.'

30

A MAN CALLED OVE AND
A SOCIETY WITHOUT HIM

Ove brushes the snow off the gravestone. Digs determinedly into the frozen ground and carefully replenishes the flowers. He stands up, dusts himself off, and looks helplessly at her name, feeling ashamed of himself. He who always used to nag at her about being late. Now he stands here himself, apparently quite incapable of following her as he'd planned.

'It's just been bloody mayhem,' he mumbles to the stone.

And then he's silent again.

He doesn't know what happened to him after her funeral. The days and weeks floated together in such a way, and in such utter silence, that he could hardly describe what exactly he was doing. Before Parvaneh and that Patrick reversed into his post box he could barely remember saying a word to another human being since Sonja died.

Some evenings he forgets to eat. That's never happened before, as far as he can remember. Not since he sat down with her on that train almost forty years ago. As long as Sonja was there they had their routines. Ove got up at quarter to six, made coffee, went off for his inspection. By half past six Sonja had showered and then they had breakfast and drank coffee. Sonja had eggs; Ove had bread. At five past seven, Ove carried her into the passenger seat of the Saab, stowed her wheelchair in the boot and gave her a lift to school. Then he drove to work. At quarter to ten they took coffee breaks separately. Sonja took milk in her coffee; Ove had it black. At twelve they had lunch. At quarter to three another coffee break. At quarter past five Ove picked up Sonja in the school forecourt, hoisted her into the passenger seat and the wheelchair into the boot. By six o'clock they were at the kitchen table having their dinner, usually meat and potatoes and sauce. Ove's favourite meal. Then she solved crosswords with her legs drawn up beneath her on the sofa while Ove pottered about in the toolshed and watched the news. At half past nine Ove carried her upstairs to the bedroom. She nagged him for years about moving into the empty downstairs guest room, but Ove refused. After a decade or so she realised that this was his way of showing her that he had no intention of giving up. That God and the universe and all the other things would not be allowed to win. That the swine could go to hell. So she stopped nagging.

On Friday nights they sat up until half past ten watching television. On Saturdays they had a late breakfast, sometimes as late as eight. Then they went out to do their errands. The builder's merchant, furniture shop and garden centre. Sonja would buy potting soil and Ove liked to look at tools. They only had a small terraced house with a tiny outside space, yet there always seemed to be something to plant and something to build. On the way home they'd stop for ice cream. Sonja would have one with chocolate and Ove one with nuts. Once a year they raised the price by one crown per ice cream and then, as Sonja put it, Ove would 'have a tantrum'. When they got back to the house she'd roll out of the little terrace door onto the patio and Ove would help her out of the chair and gently put her on the ground so she could do some gardening in her beloved flowerbeds. In the meantime Ove would fetch a screwdriver and disappear into the house. That was the best thing about the house. It was never finished. There was always a screw somewhere for Ove to tighten.

On Sundays they went to a café and drank coffee. Ove read the newspaper and Sonja talked. And then it was Monday.

And one Monday she was no longer there.

And Ove didn't know exactly when he became so quiet. He'd always been taciturn, but this was something quite different. Maybe he had started talking more inside his own head. Maybe he was going insane (he did wonder sometimes). It was as if he didn't want other people to talk to him, he was afraid that their chattering voices would drown out the memory of her voice.

He lets his fingers run gently across the gravestone, as if running them through the long tassels of a very thick rug. He's never understood young people who bang on about 'finding themselves'. He used to hear that non-stop from all those thirty-year-olds at work. All they ever talked about was how they wanted more 'leisure time', as if that was the only point of working: to get to the point when one didn't have to do it. Sonja used to laugh at Ove and call him 'the most inflexible man in the world'. Ove refused to take that as an insult. He thought there should be some order in things. There should be routines and one should be able to feel secure about them. He could not see how it could be a bad attribute.

Sonja used to tell people about the time that Ove, in a moment of temporary mental dislocation in the middle of the 1980s, had been persuaded by her to get himself a red Saab, even though in all the years she'd known him he'd always driven a blue one. 'They were the worst three years of Ove's life,' Sonja tittered. Since then, Ove had never driven anything but a blue Saab. 'Other wives get annoyed because their husbands don't notice when they have their hair cut. When I have a haircut my husband is annoyed with me for days because I don't look the same,' Sonja used to say.

That's what Ove misses most of all. Having things the same as usual.

People need a function, he believes. And he has always been functional, no one can take that away from him.

*　　*　　*

It was thirteen years since Ove bought his blue Saab 9-5 Estate. Not long after, the Yanks at General Motors bought up the last Swedish-held shares in the company. Ove closed the newspaper that morning with a long string of swear words that continued into a good part of the afternoon. He never bought a car again. He had no intention of placing his foot in an American car, unless his foot and the rest of his body had first been placed in a coffin, they should be bloody clear about that. Sonja had of course also read the article and she had certain objections to Ove's exact version of events regarding the company's nationality, but it made no difference. Ove had made up his mind and now he was fixed on it. He was going to drive his car until either he, or it, broke down. Either way, proper cars were not being made any more, he'd decided. There was only a lot of electronics and crap inside them now. Like driving a computer. You couldn't even take them apart without the manufacturers whining about 'invalid guarantees'. So it was just as well. Sonja said once that the car would break down with sorrow the day Ove was buried. And maybe that was true.

'But there was a time for everything,' she also said. Often. For example when the doctors gave her the diagnosis four years ago. She found it easier to forgive than Ove did. Forgive God and the universe and everything. Ove got angry instead. Maybe because he felt someone had to be angry on her behalf, when everything that was evil seemed to assail the only person he'd ever met who didn't deserve it.

So he fought the whole world. He fought with hospital personnel and he fought with specialists and chief physicians. He fought with men in white shirts and the council representatives who in the end grew so numerous that he could barely remember their names. There was an insurance policy for this, another insurance policy for that, there was one contact person because Sonja was ill and another because she was in a wheelchair. Then a third contact person so she did not have to go to work and a fourth contact person to try and persuade the bloody authorities that this was precisely what she wanted: to go to work.

And it was impossible to fight men in white shirts. And one could not fight a diagnosis.

Sonja had cancer.

'We have to take it as it comes,' said Sonja. And that was what they did. She carried on working with her darling trouble-makers for as long as she could, until Ove had to push her into the classroom every morning because she no longer had the strength to do it herself. After a year she was down to seventy-five per cent of her full working week. After two years she was on fifty per cent. After three years she was on twenty-five per cent. When she finally had to go home she wrote a long personal letter to each of her students and exhorted them to call her if they ever needed anyone to talk to.

Almost everyone did call. They came to visit in long lines. One weekend there were so many of them in the terraced house that Ove had to go outside and sit in his toolshed for six hours. When the last of them had left that evening he went round the house carefully assuring himself that nothing had been stolen. As usual. Until Sonja called out to him not to forget to count the eggs in the fridge. Then he gave up. Carried her up the stairs while she laughed at him. He put her in the bed, and then, just before they went to sleep, she turned to him. Hid her finger in the palm of his hand. Burrowed her nose under his collarbone.

'God took a child from me, darling Ove. But he gave me a thousand others.'

In the fourth year she died.

Now he stands there running his hand over her gravestone. Again and again. As if he's trying to rub her back to life.

'I'm really going to do it this time. I know you don't like it. I don't like it either,' he says in a low voice.

He takes a deep breath. As if he has to steel himself against her trying to convince him not to do it.

'See you tomorrow,' he says firmly and stamps the snow off his shoes, as if not wanting to give her a chance to protest.

Then he takes the little path down to the parking area, with the cat padding along beside him. Out through the black gates, round the Saab, which still has the learner plate stuck to the back door. He opens the passenger door. Parvaneh looks at him, her big brown eyes filled with empathy.

'I've been thinking about something,' she says carefully, as she puts the Saab into gear and pulls off.

'Don't.'

But she can't be stopped.

'I was just thinking that maybe I could help you clean out the house. Maybe put Sonja's things in boxes and . . .'

She hardly has time to speak Sonja's name before Ove's face darkens, anger stiffening it into a mask.

'Not another word,' he roars, with a booming sound inside the car.

'But I was only thi—'

'Not another bloody WORD. Have you got it!?'

Parvaneh nods and goes silent. Shaking with anger, Ove stares out of the window all the way home.

31

A MAN CALLED OVE REVERSES WITH A
TRAILER. AGAIN.

The next morning, after letting the cat out, he fetches Sonja's father's old rifle from the attic. He's decided that his dislike of weapons could never be greater than his dislike of all the empty places she has left behind in their silent little house. It is time now.

But it seems that someone, somewhere, knows the only way of stopping him is to put something in his way that makes him angry enough not to do it.

For this reason, he stands now in the little road between the houses, his arms defiantly crossed, looking at the man in the white shirt and saying:

'I am here because there was nothing good on the TV.'

The man in the white shirt has been observing him without the slightest hint of emotion through the entire conversation. In fact, whenever Ove has met him, he has been more like a machine than a person. Just like all the other white shirts Ove has run into in his life. The ones that said Sonja was going to die after the coach accident, the ones that refused to take their responsibility afterwards and the ones who refused to hold others responsible. The ones who would not build a mobility ramp at the school. The ones who did not want to let her work. The ones that went through paragraphs of small print to root out some clause, meaning they wouldn't have to pay out any insurance money. The ones who wanted to put her in a home.

They had all had the same empty eyes. As if they were nothing but shiny shells walking round, grinding away at normal people and pulling their lives to pieces.

But when Ove says that thing about there being nothing good on the TV, he sees a little twitch at the temple of the white shirt. A flash of frustration, perhaps. Amazed anger, possibly. Pure disdain, very likely. It's the first time Ove has noticed that he's managed to get under the skin of the white shirt. Of any white shirt at all.

The man snaps his jaws shut, turns round and starts to walk away. Not with the measured, objective steps of a council employee in full control, but something else. With anger. Impatience. Vengefully.

Ove can't remember anything having made him feel so good in a long, long time.

Of course, he was supposed to have died today. He had been planning to calmly and peacefully shoot himself in the head just after breakfast. He'd tidied the kitchen and let the cat out and made himself comfortable in his favourite armchair. He'd planned it this way because the cat routinely asked to be let out at this time. One of the few traits of the cat that Ove was highly appreciative of was its reluctance to crap in other people's homes. Ove was a man of the same ilk.

But then of course Parvaneh came banging on his door as if it was the last functioning toilet in the civilised world. As if that woman had nowhere to wee at home. Ove put the rifle away behind the radiator so she wouldn't see it and start interfering. He opened the door and she more or less had to press her telephone into his hand by violent means before he accepted it.

'What is this?' Ove wanted to know, the telephone held between his index finger and his thumb, as if it smelled bad.

'It's for you,' groaned Parvaneh, holding her stomach and

mopping sweat from her forehead even though it was minus degrees outside. 'That journalist.'

'What do I want with her telephone?'

'God. It's not her telephone, it's my telephone. She's on the line!' Parvaneh said impatiently.

Then, before he could protest, she squeezed past him and headed for his toilet.

'Yes,' said Ove, lifting the telephone to within a few centimetres of his ear, slightly unclear about whether he was still talking to Parvaneh or the person at the other end.

'Hi!' yelled the journalist woman, Lena. Ove felt it might be wise to move the phone further away from his ear. 'So, are you ready to give me an interview now?' she went on in a gung-ho tone.

'No,' said Ove, holding the telephone in front of him to work out how to hang up.

'Did you read the letter I sent you? Or the newspaper? Have you read the newspaper? I thought I'd let you see it, so you can form an impression of our journalistic style!'

Ove went into the kitchen. Picked up the newspaper and letter that Adrian fellow had brought over a few days earlier.

'Have you got it?' roared the journalist woman.

'Calm yourself down. I'm reading it, aren't I!' Ove said out loud to the telephone and leaned over the kitchen table.

'I was just wondering if—' she continued valiantly.

'Can you CALM DOWN, woman!' Ove raged.

Suddenly, out the window, Ove noticed a man in a white shirt in a Skoda, driving past his house.

'Hello?' the journalist woman called just before Ove flew out of the front door.

'Oh dear, dear,' Parvaneh mumbled anxiously when she came out of the toilet and just about caught sight of him careering along between the houses.

The man in the white shirt got out of the Skoda on the driver's side outside Rune and Anita's house.

'It's enough now! You hear? You're NOT driving your car

inside the residential area! Not another bloody METRE! You got it?' shouted Ove in the distance, long before he'd even reached him.

The little man in the white shirt, in a most superior manner, adjusted the cigarette packet in his breast pocket while calmly meeting Ove's gaze.

'I have permission.'

'Like hell you do!'

The man in the white shirt shrugged. As if to chase away an irritating insect more than anything.

'And what exactly are you going to do about it, Ove?'

The question actually caught Ove off balance. Again. He stopped, his hands trembling with anger, at least a dozen pieces of invective at his disposal. But to his own surprise he could not bring himself to use any of them.

'I know who you are, Ove. I know everything about all the letters you've written about your wife's accident and your wife's illness. You're something of a legend in our offices, you should know,' said the man in the white shirt, his voice quite unwavering.

Ove's mouth opened into a crack. The man in the white shirt nodded at him.

'I know who you are. And I'm only doing my job. A decision is a decision. You can't do anything about it, you should have learned that by now.'

Ove took a step towards him but the man put up a hand against his chest and pressed him back. Not violently. Not aggressively. Just softly and firmly, as if the hand did not belong to him but was directly controlled by some robot at the computer centre of a municipal authority.

'Go and watch some telly instead. Before you have more problems with that heart of yours.'

On the passenger side of the Skoda the determined woman, wearing an identical white shirt, stepped out with a pile of paper in her arms. The man locked the car with a loud bleep. Then he turned his back on Ove as if Ove had never stood there talking to him.

Ove stayed where he was, his fists clenched at his sides and his chin jutting out as if he were an outraged bull elk. The white shirts disappeared into Anita and Rune's house. It took a minute before he recovered himself enough to even turn round. But then he did so with determined fury and started walking towards Parvaneh's house. Parvaneh was standing halfway up the little road.

'Is that useless husband of yours at home?' Ove growled, walking past her without waiting for an answer.

Parvaneh didn't have time to do more than nod before Ove, in four long strides, reached their front door. Patrick opened it, standing there on crutches, plaster apparently covering half of his body.

'Hi, Ove!' he called out cheerfully, trying to wave with a crutch, with the immediate effect that he lost his balance and stumbled into the wall.

'That trailer you had when you moved in. Where did you get it?' Ove demanded.

Patrick leaned with his functioning arm against the wall. Almost as if he wanted it to look as if he'd meant to stumble into it.

'What? Oh . . . *that* trailer. I borrowed it off a guy at work . . .'

'Call him. You need to borrow it again.'

And this was the reason why Ove did not die today. Because he was detained by something that made him sufficiently angry to hold his attention.

When the man and woman in the white shirts come out of Anita and Rune's house almost an hour later, they find that their little white car with the council logo has been boxed into the little cul-de-sac by a large trailer. A trailer which someone, while they were inside the house, must have parked exactly so it blocks the entire road behind them. One could almost think it had been done on purpose.

The woman looks genuinely puzzled. But the man in the white shirt immediately walks up to Ove.

235

'Have you done this?'

Ove crosses his arms and looks at him coldly.

'No.'

The man in the white shirt smiles in a superior manner. The way men in white shirts, who are used to always having things their own way, smile when someone tries to disagree with them.

'Move it at once.'

'I don't think so,' says Ove.

The man in the white shirt sighs, as if the threatening statement he makes after that was directed at a child.

'Move the trailer, Ove. Or I'll call the police.'

Ove shakes his head nonchalantly, pointing at the sign further down the road.

'Motor vehicles prohibited inside the residential area. It says so clearly on the sign.'

'Don't you have anything better to do than standing out here pretending to be the foreman?' groans the man in the white shirt.

'There was nothing good on TV,' says Ove.

And that's when there's a little twitch at the temple of the man in the white shirt. As if his mask has slipped a little, just a fraction. He looks at the trailer, his boxed-in Skoda, the sign, Ove standing in front of him with his arms crossed. The man seems to consider for an instant whether he might try to force Ove by violence, but he realises in another instant that this would very likely be an extremely bad idea.

'This was very silly of you, Ove. This was very, very silly,' he hisses finally.

And his blue eyes, for the first time, are filled with genuine fury. Ove's face does not betray the slightest emotion. The man in the white shirt walks away, up towards the garages and the main road, with the sort of steps that make it clear that this will not be the end of this story.

The woman with the papers hurries off after him.

One might have expected Ove to watch them with a look of triumph in his eyes. He would probably have expected this himself, in fact. But instead he just looks sad and tired. As if he hasn't slept in months. As if he hardly has the strength to keep his arms up any longer. He lets his hands glide into his pockets and goes back home. But no sooner has he closed the door than someone starts banging on it again.

'They're going to take Rune away from Anita,' says Parvaneh urgently, snatching the front door open before Ove has even reached the handle.

'Pah,' Ove snorts tiredly.

The resignation in his voice clearly takes both Parvaneh and Anita, who's standing behind her, by surprise. Maybe it also surprises Ove. He inhales quickly through his nose. Looks at Anita. She's greyer and more sunken than ever; her eyes are red, swollen.

'They say they'll come and pick him up this week, and that I can't manage to take care of him myself,' she says, in a voice so fragile that it hardly manages to get past her lips.

'We have to do something!' cries Parvaneh, grabbing him.

Ove snatches his arm back and avoids her eyes.

'Pah! They won't come to get him for years and years. This'll go to appeal and then it'll go through all the bureaucratic shit,' says Ove.

He tries to sound more convinced and sure of himself than he actually feels. But he doesn't have the strength to care about how he's coming across. He just wants them to leave.

'You don't know what you're talking about!' roars Parvaneh.

'You're the one who doesn't know what you're talking about, you've never had anything to do with the county council, you don't know what it's like fighting them,' he answers in a mono-tone voice, his shoulders slumped.

'But you have to talk . . .' she begins to say in a faltering voice. It's as if all the energy in Ove's body is draining out of him even as he stands there.

Maybe it's the sight of Anita's worn-out face. Maybe it's the insight that a simple battle won is nothing in the greater scheme of things. A boxed-in Skoda makes no difference. They always come back. Just like they did with Sonja. Like they always do. With their clauses and documents. Men in white shirts always win. And men like Ove always lose people like Sonja. And nothing can bring her back to him.

In the end, there is nothing left but a long series of weekdays with nothing more meaningful than oiling the kitchen counters. And Ove can't cope with it any more. He feels it in that moment more clearly than ever. He can't fight any more. Doesn't want to fight any more. Just wants it all to stop.

Parvaneh keeps trying to argue with him, but he just closes the door. She hammers at it but he doesn't listen. He sinks down on the stool in the hall and feels his hands trembling. His heart thumps so hard that it feels like his ears are about to explode. The pressure on his chest, as if an enormous darkness has put its boot over his throat, doesn't begin to release till more than twenty minutes later.

And then Ove starts to cry.

32

A MAN CALLED OVE ISN'T RUNNING A
DAMNED HOTEL

Sonja said once that to understand men like Ove and Rune, one had to understand from the very beginning that they were men caught in the wrong time. Men who only required a few simple things from life, she said. A roof over their heads, a quiet street, the right make of car, and a woman to be faithful to. A job where you had a proper function. A house where things broke at regular intervals, so you always had something to tinker with.

'All people want to live dignified lives, dignity just means something different to different people,' Sonja had said. To men like Ove and Rune dignity was simply that they'd had to manage on their own when they grew up, and therefore saw it as their right not to become reliant on others when they were adults. There was a sense of pride in having control. In being right. In knowing what road to take and how to screw in a screw, or not. Men like Ove and Rune were from a generation in which one was what one did, not what one talked about.

She knew, of course, that Ove didn't know how to bear his nameless anger. He needed labels to put on it. Ways of categorising. So when men in white shirts at the council, whose names no normal person could keep a track of, tried to do everything Sonja did not want – make her stop working, move her out of her house, imply that she was worth less than a healthy person who was able to walk, and assert that she was dying – Ove fought them. With documents and letters to newspapers and appeals, right down to something as unremarkable as a mobility ramp at a school. He fought so doggedly for her against men in white shirts that in the end he began to hold them personally responsible for all that happened to her – and to the child.

And then she left him alone in a world where he no longer understood the language.

Later that night, once Ove and the cat have had their dinner and watched the TV for a while, he turns out the lamp in the living room and goes upstairs. The cat follows watchfully at his heels, as if sensing that he's going to do something it hasn't been informed about. It sits on the bedroom floor while Ove gets undressed and looks as if it's trying to figure out a magic trick.

Ove goes to bed and lies still while the bloody cat, on Sonja's side of the bed, takes more than an hour to go to sleep. Obviously, he does not go to such lengths because of some lingering sense of obligation to the cat; he just doesn't have the energy for a row. He can't be expected to explain the concept of life and death to an animal that can't even take care of its own fur.

When the cat finally rolls onto its back on Sonja's pillow and starts snoring with an open mouth, Ove sneaks out of bed as light-footedly as he can. Goes down into the living room, gets out the rifle from the hiding place behind the radiator. He gets out four heavy-duty tarpaulins he's fetched in from the toolshed and hidden in the broom cupboard so the cat doesn't notice them. Starts taping them up on the walls in the hall. Ove, after some consideration, has decided that this will probably be the best room for the deed, because it has the smallest surface area. He's assuming that there's a good deal of splattering when one shoots oneself in the head, and he's loath to leave more of a mess behind than he has to. Sonja always hated it when he made a mess.

He's wearing his going-out shoes and suit again. It's dirty and still smells of car exhaust, but it'll have to do. He weighs the rifle in his hands, as if checking its centre of gravity. As if this will play a decisive role in the future of the venture. He turns and twists it, tries to angle the barrel almost as if intending to fold the weapon double. Not that Ove knows very much about weapons, but one wants to know if it's a decent bit of kit one's got, more or less. And because Ove supposes one can't test the quality of a rifle by kicking it, he decides it can be done by bending and pulling at it, to see what happens.

While he's doing this, it strikes him that it was probably a fairly bad idea to put on his best gear. Will be an awful lot of blood on the suit, Ove imagines. Seems silly. So he puts down the rifle, goes into the living room, gets undressed, carefully folds up the suit and puts it neatly beside his going-out shoes. Then he gets out the letter with all the instructions for Parvaneh and writes 'Bury me in my suit' under the heading 'Funeral Arrangements' and puts the letter on top of the pile of clothes. He has already stated clearly and unmistakably that there should not be any fuss in other respects. No exaggerated ceremony and rubbish like that. Shove him in the ground next to Sonja, that's all. The spot has already been prepared and paid for, and Ove has put cash in the envelope for the transport.

So, wearing nothing but his socks and underwear, Ove goes back into the hall and picks up his rifle. He catches sight of his own body in the hall mirror. He hasn't seen himself in this way for probably thirty-five years. He's still quite muscular and robust. Certainly in better shape than most men of his age. But something's happened to his skin that makes him look like he's melting, he notes. It looks terrible.

It's very quiet in the house. In the whole neighbourhood, actually. Everyone's sleeping. And only then does Ove realise that the cat will probably wake at the sound of the shot. Will probably scare the living daylights out of the poor critter, Ove admits. He thinks about this for a good while before he determinedly puts away the rifle and goes into the kitchen to turn on the radio. Not that he needs music to take his own life, and not that he likes the idea of the radio clicking its way through units of electricity when he's gone. But because if the cat wakes up from the bang, it may end up thinking that it's just a part of one of those modern pop songs the radio plays all the time these days. And then go back to sleep. That is Ove's train of thought.

There's no modern pop song on the radio, Ove hears, when he comes back into the hall and picks up the rifle again. It's the local news bulletin. So he stays where he is for a moment and listens. Not that it's so important to listen to the local news when you're about to shoot yourself in the head, but Ove thinks there's no harm in keeping yourself updated. They talk about the weather. And the economy. And the traffic. And the importance of local property owners staying vigilant over the weekend because of a large number of burglary rings on the rampage all over town. 'Bloody hooligans,' Ove mutters and grips the rifle a little more firmly when he hears that.

From a purely objective point of view, the fact that Ove was wielding a gun was something two other hooligans, Adrian and Mirsad, would ideally have been aware of before they unconcernedly trotted up to Ove's front door a few seconds later. They would then quite likely have understood that when Ove heard their creaking steps in the snow he would not immediately think to himself, 'Guests, how nice!' but rather 'Well I'll be damned!' And they'd probably also know that Ove, wearing nothing but socks and underpants, with a three-quarter-century-old hunting rifle in his hands, would kick the door open like an ageing, half-naked, suburban Rambo. And maybe then Adrian would not have screamed in a high-pitched voice that went right through every window in the street, nor would he have turned round in panic and run into the toolshed, almost knocking himself unconscious.

It takes a few confused cries and a good deal of tumult before Mirsad has time to clarify his identity as that of a normal hooligan, not a burglar hooligan, and for Ove to get to grips with what is happening. Before then he has had time to wave his rifle at them, making Adrian scream like an air raid warning.

'Shush! You'll wake the bloody cat!' Ove hisses angrily while Adrian reels backwards, a swelling large as a medium-sized pack of ravioli on his forehead.

'What in the name of God are you doing here?' he raves, the gun still firmly fixed on them. 'It's the middle of the bloody night!'

Mirsad is holding a big bag in his hand, which he gently drops into the snow. Adrian impulsively holds his hands up as if he's about to be robbed, and almost loses his balance and falls into the snow again.

'It was Adrian's idea,' Mirsad begins, looking down into the snow.

'Mirsad came out today, you know!' Adrian blurts out.

'What?'

'He . . . came out, you know. Told everyone he was . . .' says Adrian, but he seems slightly distracted, partly by the fact that a fuming old man in his underpants is pointing a gun at him, and partly because he is increasingly convinced that he's sustained some sort of concussion injury.

Mirsad straightens up and nods at Ove with more determination.

'I told my dad I'm gay.'

Ove's eyes grow slightly less threatening. But he doesn't lower his rifle.

'My dad hates gays. He always said he'd kill himself if he found out that any of his children were gay,' Mirsad goes on.

After a moment's silence he adds:

'He didn't take it so well. You might say.'

'He throwed him out!' Adrian interjects.

'Threw,' Ove corrects.

Mirsad picks up his bag from the ground and nods anew at Ove.

'This was a stupid idea. We shouldn't have disturbed—'

'Disturbed me with what?' Ove cuts him short.

Now he's standing here in his underpants in minus degrees he might as well at least find out the reason why, it seems to him.

Mirsad takes a deep breath. As if he's physically shoving his pride down his throat.

'Dad said I was sick and not welcome under his roof with my . . . "unnatural ways",' he says, swallowing hard before he manages to spit out the word "unnatural".

'Because you're a bender?' Ove clarifies.

Mirsad nods.

'I don't have any relatives here in town. I was going to stay the night at Adrian's, but his mum's new boyfriend is staying . . .'

He goes quiet. Looks like he's feeling very silly.

'It was an idiotic idea,' he says in a low voice and makes a move to turn round and leave.

Adrian, on the other hand, seems to be rediscovering a desire for discussion, and he stumbles eagerly through the snow towards Ove.

'What the hell, Ove! You've got a load of space in there! So we thought maybe he could kip here tonight?'

'Here? This is not a damned hotel!' says Ove, raising the rifle so that Adrian's chest collides right into the barrel.

Adrian freezes. Mirsad takes two quick steps forward through the snow and puts his hand on the rifle.

'We had nowhere else to go, sorry,' he says in a low voice while gently turning the barrel away from Adrian.

Ove looks like he's coming to his senses slightly. He lowers his weapon to the ground. When he almost imperceptibly takes a half-step backwards into the hall, as if he's only now become aware of the cold that envelops his not-so-well-dressed body, he notices, in the corner of his eye, the photo of Sonja on the wall. The red dress. The coach trip in Spain when she was pregnant. He asked her so many times to take that bloody photo down, but she refused. Said it 'was a memory worth as much as any other'.

Obstinate woman.

*   *   *

So this should have been the day Ove *finally* died. Instead it became the evening before the morning when he woke not only with a cat but also a bent person living in his terraced house. Sonja would have liked it, most likely. She liked hotels.

33

A MAN CALLED OVE AND AN INSPECTION
TOUR THAT IS NOT THE USUAL

Sometimes it is difficult to explain why some men suddenly do the things they do. Sometimes, of course, it's because they know they'll do them sooner or later anyway, and so they may as well just do them now. And sometimes it's the pure opposite – because they realise they should have done them long ago. Ove has probably known all along what he has to do, but all people at root are time optimists. We always think there's enough time to do things with other people. Time to say things to them. And then something happens and then we stand there holding on to words like 'if'.

As he marches down the stairs the next morning, he stops in the hallway. It hasn't smelled like this in the house since Sonja died. Watchfully he takes the last few steps down, lands on the parquet floor and stands in the doorway of the kitchen, his body language that of a man who has just caught a thief red-handed.

'Is that you who's been toasting bread?'

Mirsad nods anxiously.

'Yes . . . I hope that's okay. Sorry. I mean, is it?'

Ove notices that he's made coffee too. The cat is on the floor eating tuna. Ove nods, but doesn't answer the question.

'Me and the cat have to go for a little walk around our road,' he clarifies instead.

'Can I come?' asks Mirsad quickly.

Ove looks at him a little as if Mirsad has stopped him in a pedestrianized arcade, dressed up as a pirate and asked him to guess under which of the three teacups he's hidden the silver coin.

'Maybe I can help?' Mirsad continues eagerly.

Ove goes into the hall and shoves his feet into his clogs.

'It's a free country,' he mutters as he opens the door and lets out the cat.

Mirsad interprets this as 'Of course you can!!' and quickly puts on his jacket and shoes and goes after Ove.

'Hey guys!' Jimmy hollers as they reach the pavement. He turns up, puffing energetically behind Ove in a fiercely green tracksuit that's so tight around his body that Ove wonders at first if it's in fact a garment or a body painting.

'Jimmy!' says Jimmy, panting, and offering Mirsad his hand.

The cat looks as if it would like to rub itself lovingly against Jimmy's legs, but seems to change its mind, bearing in mind that the last time it did something similar Jimmy ended up in hospital. Instead it opts for the next best available thing and rolls about in the snow. Jimmy turns to Ove.

'I usually see you walking round about this time, so I was gonna check with you if you're cool with me tagging along. I've decided to start exercising, you know!'

He nods with such satisfaction that the fat under his chin sways between his shoulders like a mainsail in stormy conditions. Ove looks highly dubious.

'Do you usually get up at this time?'

'Shit, no, man. I haven't even gone to bed yet!' he laughs.

And this is why a cat, an overweight allergy sufferer, a bent person and a man called Ove make the inspection round that morning.

Mirsad explains in brief that he and his father are not getting along and that he's temporarily staying with Ove; Jimmy expresses disbelief that Ove is up at this time every single morning.

'Why did you have a fight with the old man, then?' asks Jimmy.

'That's none of your business!' Ove barks.

Mirsad gives Ove a grateful glance.

'But serious, man. You do this *every* morning?' Jimmy asks cheerfully.

'Yes, to check if there have been any burglaries.'

'For real? Are there a lot of burglaries round here?'

'There are never lots of burglaries before the first burglary,' Ove mutters and heads off towards the guest parking.

The cat looks at Jimmy as if unimpressed by his fitness drive. Jimmy pouts and touches his stomach, in the apparent belief that he has already lost some weight.

'Did you hear about Rune, then?' he calls out, hastening his steps into a half-jog behind Ove.

Ove doesn't answer.

'Social Services are coming to pick him up, you know,' Jimmy explains once he's caught up.

Ove opens his pad and starts noting down the registration plates of the cars. Jimmy evidently takes his silence as an invitation to keep talking.

'You know, the long and short of it is Anita applied for more home help. Rune is just screwed and she couldn't deal with it any more. So then the Social did some investigation and some bloke called and said they'd decided she couldn't handle it. And they were going to put Rune in one of those institutions, you know. And then Anita said they could forget about it, she didn't even want home help any more. But then that guy got really aggro and started getting totally uncool with her. Going on about how she couldn't take the investigation back now and she was the one who had asked them to look into it. And now the investigation had made a decision and that was all there was to it, you know. Doesn't matter what she says 'cos the Social guy is just running his own race, know what I mean?'

Jimmy goes silent and nods at Mirsad, in the hope of getting some kind of reaction.

'Uncool . . .' Mirsad declares hesitantly.

'BLOODY uncool!' nods Jimmy, until his upper body shakes.

Ove puts his pen and pad in the inside pocket of his jacket and steers his steps towards the bin room.

'Ah, it'll take them for ever to make those kinds of decisions. They say they're taking him now, but they won't pull their finger out for another year or two,' he snorts.

Ove knows how that damned bureaucracy works.

'But . . . the decision is made, man,' says Jimmy and scratches his hair.

'Just sodding appeal it! It'll take years!' says Ove grumpily as he strides past him.

Jimmy looks at him as if trying to evaluate whether it's worth the exertion of following him.

'But she has done! She's been writing letters and things for two years!'

Ove doesn't stop when he hears that. But he slows down. He hears Jimmy's heavy steps bearing down on him in the snow.

'Two years?' he asks without turning round.

'More or less,' says Jimmy.

Ove looks like he's counting the months in his head.

'That's a lie. Then Sonja would have known about it,' he says dismissively.

'I wasn't allowed to say anything to Sonja. Anita didn't want me to. You know . . .'

Jimmy goes silent. Looks down at the snow. Ove turns round. Raises his eyebrows.

'I know what?'

Jimmy takes a deep breath.

'She . . . thought you had enough troubles of your own,' he says in a low voice.

The silence that follows is so thick you could split it with an axe. Jimmy does not look up. And Ove doesn't say anything. He goes inside the bin room. Comes out. Goes into the bicycle shed. Comes out. The penny seems to have dropped. Jimmy's last words hang like a veil over his movements and an unfathomable anger builds up inside Ove, picking up speed like a tornado inside his chest. He tugs at doors with increasing violence. Kicks the thresholds. And when Jimmy in the end mumbles something about, 'Now it's all screwed, man, now they'll put Rune in a home, you know,' Ove slams a door so hard that the entire bin room shakes. He stands in silence with his back to them, panting more and more heavily.

'Are you . . . okay?' asks Mirsad.

Ove turns round and points with anything but controlled fury at Jimmy.

'Was that how she put it? She didn't want to ask for Sonja's help because we had "enough troubles of our own"?'

Jimmy nods anxiously. Ove stares down at the snow, his chest heaving under his jacket. He thinks about how Sonja would have taken it if she'd found out. If she'd known that her best friend had not asked for her help because Sonja had 'enough problems'. She would have been heartbroken.

Sometimes it's hard to explain why some men suddenly do the things they do. And Ove had probably known all along what he had to do, who he had to help before he could die. But we are always optimists when it comes to time, we think there will be time to do things with other people. And time to say things to them.

Time to appeal.

Again Ove turns to Jimmy with a grim expression.

'Two years?'

Jimmy nods. Ove clears his throat. For the first time he looks unsure.

'I thought she'd just started. I thought I . . . had more time,' he mumbled.

Jimmy looks as if he's trying to figure out who Ove is talking to. Ove looks up.

'And they're coming to get Rune now? Seriously? No bureaucratic rot and appeals and all that shit. You're SURE about this?'

Jimmy nods again. He opens his mouth to say something, but Ove has already started moving off. He makes off between the houses with the movements of a man about to take his revenge for a deadly injustice in a Western. Turns off at the house by the bottom, where the trailer and the white Skoda are still parked, banging at the door with such force that it's difficult to tell whether it will open before he reduces it to woodchips. Anita opens, in shock. Ove steps right into her hall.

'Have you got the papers from the authorities here?'

'Yes, but I tho—'

'Give them to me!'

In retrospect, Anita will tell the other neighbours that she had not seen Ove so angry since 1977, when there was talk of a merger between Saab and Volvo.

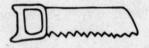

34

A MAN CALLED OVE AND A BOY IN THE
HOUSE NEXT DOOR

Ove has brought along a blue plastic deckchair to push into the snow and sit on. This could take a while, he knows. It always does when he has to tell Sonja something she won't like. He carefully brushes away all the snow from the gravestone, so they can see each other properly.

In just short of forty years a lot of different kinds of people have had time to pass through their row of terraced houses. The house between Ove's and Rune's has been lived in by quiet, loud, curious, unbearable and hardly noticeable kinds of people. Families have lived there whose teenage children pissed on the fence when they were drunk, or families who tried to plant non-approved bushes in the garden and families who got the idea that they wanted to paint their house pink. And if there was one single thing Ove and Rune agreed on, irrespective of how much they were feuding at the time, it was that whoever currently populated the neighbour's house tended to be utter imbeciles.

At the end of the 1980s the house was bought by a man who was apparently some sort of bank manager – as 'an investment' Ove heard him boast to the estate agent. He, in turn, rented the house to a series of tenants in the coming years. One summer, to three young men who made an audacious attempt to redefine it as a free zone for a veritable parade of drug addicts, prostitutes and criminal elements. The parties went on around the clock, broken glass from beer bottles covered the little walkway between the houses like confetti and the music boomed out so loud that the pictures fell off the wall in Sonja and Ove's living room.

Ove went over to put a stop to the nuisance, and the young men jeered at him. When he refused to go, one of them threatened him with a knife. When Sonja tried to make them see sense the following day, they called her a 'paralysed old bag'. The evening after they played louder than ever, and when Anita in pure desperation stood outside and shouted at them, they threw a bottle that went right through her and Rune's living room window.

And that was obviously quite a bad idea.

Ove immediately began working on his plans for revenge by examining the financial doings of their landlord. He called lawyers and the tax authorities to put a stop to the letting of the house, and he intended to persist with it even if he had to take the case 'all the bloody way to the Supreme Court', as he put it to Sonja. But he never had time to get that idea off the ground.

Late one night he saw Rune walking towards the parking area with his car keys in his hand. When he came back he had a plastic bag, the contents of which Ove could not determine, in his hand. And the following day the police came and took away the three young men in handcuffs and charged them with possession of a large amount of drugs, which, after an anonymous tip-off, had been found in their shed.

Ove and Rune were both standing in the street when it happened. Their eyes met. Ove scratched his chin.

'Me, I wouldn't even know where to buy narcotics in this town,' said Ove thoughtfully.

'In the street behind the train station,' said Rune with his hands in his pockets. 'At least that's what I've heard,' he added with a grin.

Ove nodded. They stood smiling there in the silence for a long time.

'Car running well?' asked Ove eventually.

'Like a Swiss watch,' smiled Rune.

They were on good terms for two months after that. Then, of course, they fell out again over the heating system. But it was nice while it lasted, as Anita said.

The tenants came and went in the following years, most with a surprising amount of forbearance and acceptance from Ove and Rune. Perspective can make a great deal of difference to people's reputation.

One summer halfway through the 1990s, a woman moved in with a chubby boy of about nine, whom Sonja and Anita immediately took to their hearts. The boy's father had left them when the boy was newborn, Sonja and Anita were told. A bull-necked man of about forty who lived with them now, and whose breath the two women tried to ignore for as long as possible, was her new love. He was rarely at home, and Anita and Sonja avoided asking too many questions. They supposed that the girl saw qualities in him that they, perhaps, did not understand. 'He has taken care of us, and you know how it is, it's not easy being a single mother,' she said with a brave smile at some point, and the women from the neighbouring houses left it at that.

The first time they heard the bull-necked man shouting through the walls they decided that each and every one must be allowed to mind their own business in their home. The second time they thought that all families row sometimes, and maybe this was nothing more serious than that.

When the bull-necked man was away the next time, Sonja invited in the woman and the boy for coffee. The woman explained with a strained laugh that the bruises were because she had thrown open a kitchen cabinet too quickly. In the evening Rune met the bull-necked man in the parking area. He got out of his car in a clear state of intoxication.

In the two nights that followed, the neighbouring houses on either side overheard how the man was shouting in there and things were being thrown at the floor. They heard the woman giving a short cry of pain, and when the sound of the weeping nine-year-old lad pleading with the man to stop came through the wall, Ove went outside and stood in front of his house. Rune was already waiting.

They were in the midst of one of their worst ever power struggles in the steering group of the Residents' Association. Had not even spoken to each other for almost a year. Now they just briefly glanced at one another, and then went back into their houses without a word. Two minutes later they met fully dressed at the front. They rang the bell; the thug lashed out at them as soon as he opened the door, but Ove's fist struck the bridge of his nose. The man lost his footing, got up, grabbed a kitchen knife and ran at Ove. He never got there. Rune's massive fist slugged him like a mallet. In his heyday he was quite a piece, that Rune. Highly unwise to get involved in fisticuffs with him.

The next day the man left the terrace and never came back. The young woman slept with Anita and Rune for two weeks before she dared go home again with her boy. Then Rune and Ove went into town and went to the bank, and in the evening Sonja and Anita explained to the young woman that she could see it as a gift or a loan, whichever she preferred. But it wasn't open for discussion. And so it was that the young woman stayed on in the house with her son, a chubby, computer-loving little boy whose name was Jimmy.

Now Ove leans forward and looks with great seriousness at the gravestone.

'I just thought I'd have more time, somehow. To do . . . everything.'

She doesn't answer.

'I know how you feel about causing trouble, Sonja. But this time you have to understand. One can't reason with these people.'

He pokes his thumbnail into the palm of his hand. The gravestone stays where it is without saying anything, but Ove doesn't need words to know what she would have thought. The silent approach has always been her preferred trick when there are disputes with him. Whether she's alive or dead.

255

In the morning, Ove had called that Social Services Authority or whatever the hell it was called. He'd called from Parvaneh's house because he no longer had a telephone line. Parvaneh had advised him to be 'friendly and approachable'. It hadn't started so well, because before long Ove had been connected to the 'responsible officer'. Which was the smoking man in the white shirt. He directly demonstrated a significant level of agitation about the little white Skoda, which was still parked at the bottom of the road outside Rune and Anita's house. And yes, Ove could have established a better negotiating position if he'd immediately apologised about it and maybe even agreed that it was regrettable that he'd intentionally put the man in the white shirt in this non-vehicular predicament. It would certainly have been better than the alternative, which was to hiss: 'So maybe you've learned to read signs now! Illiterate bastard!'

Ove's next move involved trying to convince the man that Rune should not be put in a home. The man informed Ove that 'Illiterate bastard!' was a very bad choice of words for bringing up that subject. After this, there was a long series of impolite phrases on both ends of the telephone line, before Ove declared in clear terms that things could not be allowed to work like this. One couldn't just come along and remove people from their homes and transport them to institutions any old way one liked, just because their sense of memory was getting a bit defective. The man at the other end answered coldly that it didn't matter very much where they put Rune now 'in the state he was in' because for him it 'would probably make a very marginal difference where he was'. Ove roared a series of invectives back. And then the man in the white shirt said something very stupid.

'The decision has been made. The investigation has been going on for two years. There's nothing you can do, Ove. Nothing. At all.'

And then he hung up.

Ove looked at Parvaneh. Looked at Patrick. Slammed Parvaneh's mobile into their kitchen table and boomed that they needed a 'New plan! Immediately!' Parvaneh looked deeply unhappy but Patrick nodded at once, grabbed his crutches and hobbled quickly out the door. As if he'd just been waiting for Ove to say that. Five minutes later, to Ove's deep dissatisfaction, he came back with that silly fop Anders from the neighbouring house. With Jimmy cheerfully tagging along.

'What's he doing here?' said Ove, pointing at the fop.

'I thought you needed a plan?' said Patrick, nodding at the fop and looking very pleased with himself.

'Anders is our plan!' Jimmy threw in.

Anders looked around the hall a little awkwardly, apparently slightly dissuaded by Ove's expression. But Patrick and Jimmy insistently pushed him into the living room.

'Go on, tell him,' Patrick prompted.

'Tell me what?'

'Okay, so I heard you had some problems with the owner of that Skoda, yeah?' began Anders, giving Patrick a nervous glance. Ove nodded impatiently for him to continue.

'Well, I don't think I've ever told you what sort of company I have, have I?' Anders went on tentatively.

Ove put his hands in his pockets. Adopted a slightly more relaxed position. And then Anders told him. And even Ove had to admit that it sounded almost more than decently opportune.

'Where are you keeping that blonde bimbo . . .' he started saying once Anders had finished, but he stopped himself when Parvaneh kicked his leg. 'Your girlfriend,' he corrected himself.

'Oh. We split up. She moved out,' said Anders and looked at his shoes.

Whereupon he had to explain that apparently she'd become a bit upset about Ove feuding so much with her and the dog. But her annoyance had been small beer compared to her agitation when Anders found out that Ove called her dog 'Mutt' and had not quite been able to stop himself smiling about it.

And so it came to pass that when the chain-smoking man in the white shirt turned up in their road that afternoon accompanied by a police officer to demand that Ove release the white Skoda from its captivity, both the trailer and the white Skoda were already gone. Ove stood outside his house with his hands calmly tucked into his pockets, while his adversary finally lost his composure altogether and started roaring expletives at him. Ove maintained that he had no idea how this had happened, but pointed out in a friendly manner that none of this would have happened in the first place if he'd just respected the sign that made it clear that cars were prohibited in the area. He obviously left out the detail that Anders owned a car towing company, and that one of his tow trucks had picked up the Skoda at lunchtime and then placed it in a large gravel pit forty kilometres outside town. And when the police officer tactfully asked if he had really not seen anything, Ove looked right into the eyes of the man in the white shirt and answered:

'I don't know. I may have forgotten. You start losing your memory at my age.'

When the police looked around and then wondered why Ove was standing about here in the street if he had nothing to do with the disappearance of the Skoda, Ove just innocently shrugged his shoulders and peered at the man in the white shirt.

'There's still nothing good on the TV.'

Anger drained the man's face of colour until, if possible, his face was even whiter than his shirt. He stormed off, raging that this was 'far from over'. And of course it wasn't. Only an hour or so later, Anita opened the door to a courier, who gave her a recorded delivery letter from the council. Signed, confirmed, with the time and date of the 'transfer into care'.

And now Ove stands by Sonja's gravestone and manages to say something about 'how sorry he is'.

'You get so damned worked up when I fight with people, I know that. But the reality of it is this. You'll just have to wait a bit longer for me up there. I don't have time to die right now.'

Then he digs up the old, frozen, pink flowers out of the

ground, plants the new ones, straightens up, folds up his deckchair and walks towards the parking area whilst muttering something that sounds suspiciously like 'because there's a bloody war on'.

35

A MAN CALLED OVE AND SOCIAL
INCOMPETENCE

When Parvaneh, with panic in her eyes, runs right into Ove's hall and continues into the toilet without even bothering to say 'good morning', Ove immediately disputes how one can become so acutely in need of a pee in the space of the twenty seconds it takes her to walk from her own house to his. But 'hell has no fury like a pregnant woman in need', Sonja once informed him. So he keeps his mouth shut.

The neighbours are saying he's been 'like a different person' these last days, that they've never seen him so 'engaged' before. But as Ove irritably explains to them, that's only because Ove has never bloody engaged himself in their particular business before. He's always been a bloody 'engaged' person.

Patrick says the way he walks between the houses and slams the doors the whole time is like 'a really angry avenging robot from the future'. Ove doesn't know what he means by that. But, anyway, he's spent hours at a time in the evenings sitting with Parvaneh and Patrick and the girls, while Patrick to the best of his abilities has tried to get Ove not to put angry fingerprints all over Patrick's computer monitor whenever he wants to show them something. Jimmy, Mirsad, Adrian and Anders have also been there. Jimmy has repeatedly tried to get everyone to call Parvaneh and Patrick's kitchen 'The Death Star' and Ove 'Darth Ove'. They've considered countless plans over the last few days – including planting marijuana in the white-shirted-man's shed, as Rune might have suggested – but after a few nights Ove seems to give up. He nods grimly, demands to use the telephone, and shuffles off into the next room to make a call.

He didn't like doing it. But when there's a war on there's a war.

Parvaneh comes out of the toilet.

'Are you done?' Ove wonders, as if he's suspecting this to be some sort of half-time interval.

She nods, but just as they're on their way out of the door she notices something in his living room and stops. Ove is standing in the doorway but he knows very well what she's staring at.

'It's . . . Pah! What the hell, it's nothing special,' he mumbles and tries to wave her out of the door.

When she fails to move he gives the edge of the doorframe a hard kick.

'It was only gathering dust. I sanded it down and repainted it and applied another layer of lacquer, that's all. It's no big bloody deal,' he grumbles, irritated.

'Oh, Ove,' whispers Parvaneh.

Ove occupies himself checking the threshold with a couple of kicks.

'We can rub it down and repaint it pink. If it's a girl, I mean,' he mutters.

Clears his throat.

'Or if it's a boy. Boys can have pink nowadays, can't they?'

Parvaneh looks at the light blue cot, her hand across her mouth.

'If you start crying now you're not having it,' warns Ove.

And when she starts crying anyway, Ove sighs – 'bloody women' – and turns round and starts walking down the road.

The man in the white shirt extinguishes his cigarette under his shoe and bangs on Anita and Rune's door about half an hour later. He's brought along three young men in nurse uniforms, as if he's expecting violent resistance. When frail little Anita opens the door, the three young men look a touch ashamed of themselves more than anything, but the man in the white shirt takes a step towards her and waves his document in the air as if holding an axe in his hands.

'It's time,' he informs her with a certain impatience and tries to step into the hall.

But she places herself in his way. As much as a person of her size can place herself in anyone's way.

'No!' she says without budging an inch.

The man in the white shirt stops and looks at her. Shakes his head tiredly at her and tightens the skin round his nose until it almost seems to be swallowed up in his cheek-flesh.

'You've had two years to do this the easy way, Anita. And now the decision has been made. And that's all there is to it.'

He tries to get past her again but Anita stays where she is on her threshold, immovable as an ancient standing stone.

She takes a deep breath without breaking their eye contact.

'What sort of love is it if you hand someone over when it gets difficult?' she cries, her voice shaking with sorrow. 'Abandon someone when there's resistance? Tell me what sort of love that is!'

The man pinches his lips. There's a nervous twitch round his cheekbones.

'Rune doesn't even know where he is half the time, the investigation has showed th—'

'But I KNOW!' Anita interrupts and points at the three nurses. 'I KNOW!' she cries at them.

'And who's going to take care of him, Anita?' he asks rhetorically, shaking his head. Then he takes a step forward and gestures for the three nurses to follow him into the house.

'I'm going to take care of him!' answers Anita, her gaze as dark as a burial at sea.

The man in the white shirt just carries on shaking his head as he pushes past her. And only then does he see the shadow rising up behind her.

'And so will I,' says Ove.

'And I will,' says Parvaneh.

'And me!' say Patrick, Jimmy, Anders, Adrian and Mirsad with a single voice as they push their way into the doorway until they're falling over each other.

The man in the white shirt stops. His eyes narrow into slits.

Suddenly a woman wearing beaten-up jeans and a slightly too big green windcheater turns up at his side with a Dictaphone in her hand.

'I'm from the local newspaper,' Lena announces, 'and I'd like to ask you a few questions.'

The man in the white shirt looks at her for a long time. Then he turns his gaze on Ove. The two men stare at one another in silence. Lena, the journalist, produces a pile of papers from her bag. She presses this into his arms.

'These are all the patients you and your section have been in charge of in recent years. All the people like Rune who have been taken into care and put in homes against their own and their families' wishes. All the irregularities that have taken place at geriatric residential care where you have been in charge of the placements. All the points where rules have not been followed and correct procedures have not been observed,' she states.

She does so in a tone as if she was just handing over the keys of a car he'd just won in the lottery. Then she adds, with a smile:

'The great thing about scrutinising bureaucracy when you're a journalist, you see, are that the first people to break the laws of bureaucracy are always the bureaucrats themselves.'

The man in the white shirt does not spare a single look at her. He keeps staring at Ove. Not a word comes from either of them. Slowly, the man in the white shirt clamps his jaws together.

Patrick clears his throat behind Ove and jumps out of the terraced house on his crutches, nodding at the pile of papers in the man's arms.

'We've also got your bank statements from the last seven years. And all the train and air tickets you've bought with your card and all the hotels you've stayed in. And all the web history from your work computer. And all your email correspondence, both work and personal . . .'

The eyes of the man in the white shirt wander from one to the other. His jaws so tightly clamped together that the skin on his face is turning pale.

'Not that there *would* be anything you want to keep secret,' says Lena with a smirk.

'Not at all,' Patrick agrees.

'But you know . . .'

'Once you start really digging into someone's past . . .'

'. . . you usually find something they'd rather keep to themselves,' says Lena.

'Something they'd rather . . . forget,' Patrick clarifies, with a nod towards the living room, from where Rune's head sticks out of one of the armchairs.

The TV is on in there. A smell of fresh-brewed coffee comes through the door. Patrick points one of his crutches, giving a little poke at the pile of paper in the man's arms, so that a sprinkling of snow settles over the man's white shirt.

'I'd especially take a look at that internet history, if I were you,' he explains.

And then they all stand there. Anita and Parvaneh and that journalist woman and Patrick and Ove and Jimmy and Anders and the man in the white shirt and the three nurses, in the sort of silence that only exists in the seconds before all the players in a poker game who have bet everything they've got put their cards on the table.

Finally, after a sequence that, for all involved, feels like being held under water with no possibility of breathing, the man in the white shirt starts slowly leafing through the papers in his arms.

'Where did you get all this shit?' he hisses, his shoulders hoisted up around his neck.

'On the InterNET!' rages Ove, abrupt and furious as he steps out of Anita and Rune's terraced house with his fists clenched by his hips.

The man in the white shirt looks up again. Lena clears her throat and pokes helpfully at the pile of paper.

'Maybe there's nothing illegal in all these old records, but my editor is pretty certain that with the right kind of media scrutiny it would take months for your section to go through all the legal processes. Years, maybe . . .' Gently she puts her hand once again on the man's shoulder. 'So I think it might be easiest for everyone concerned if you just leave now,' she whispers.

And then, to Ove's sincere surprise, the little man does just that. He turns round and leaves, followed by the three nurses. He goes round the corner and disappears the way shadows do when the sun reaches its apex in the sky. Or like villains at the ends of stories.

Lena nods, self-satisfied, at Ove. 'I told you no one has the stomach for a fight with journalists!'

Ove shoves his hands into his pockets.

'Don't forget what you promised me,' she grins.

Ove groans.

'Did you read the letter I sent you, by the way?' she asks.

He shakes his head.

'Do it!' she insists.

Ove answers with something that might either be a 'yeah, yeah' or a fierce exhalation of air through the nostrils. Difficult to judge.

When Ove leaves the house an hour later he's been sitting in the living room, talking quietly and one-to-one with Rune for a long time. Because he and Rune need to 'talk without disruption', Ove explains irritably before he drives Parvaneh, Anita and Patrick into the kitchen.

And if Anita hadn't known better, she could have sworn that in the minutes that followed she heard Rune laughing out loud several times.

36

A MAN CALLED OVE AND A WHISKY

It is difficult to admit that one is wrong. Particularly when one has been wrong for a very long time.

Sonja used to say that Ove had only admitted he was wrong on one occasion in all the years they had been married, and that was in the early 1980s after he'd agreed with her about something that later turned out to be incorrect. Ove himself maintained that this was a lie, a damned lie. By definition he had only admitted that she was wrong, not that he was.

'Loving someone is like moving into a house,' Sonja used to say. 'At first you fall in love with all the new things, amazed every morning that all this belongs to you, as if fearing that someone would suddenly come rushing in through the door to explain that a terrible mistake had been made, you weren't actually supposed to live in a wonderful place like this. Then over the years the walls become weathered, the wood splinters here and there, and you start to love that house not so much because of all its perfection, but rather its imperfections. You get to know all the nooks and crannies. How to avoid getting the key caught in the lock when it's cold outside. Which of the floorboards flex slightly when one steps on them or exactly how to open the wardrobe doors without their creaking. These are the little secrets that make it your home.'

Ove, of course, suspected that he represented the wardrobe

door in the example. And from time to time he heard Sonja muttering that 'sometimes I wonder if there's anything to be done, when the whole foundations are wonky from the very start' when she was angry with him. He knew very well what she was driving at.

'I'm just saying surely it depends on the cost of the diesel engine? And what its consumption is per kilometre?' says Parvaneh unconcernedly, slowing the Saab down by a red light and trying, with some grunts, to settle herself more comfortably in her seat.

Ove looks at her with boundless disappointment, as if she really hasn't listened to anything he's said. He's made an effort to educate this pregnant woman in the fundamentals of owning a car. He's explained that one has to change one's car every three years to avoid losing money. He has painstakingly run through what all people who know anything are well aware of, namely that one has to drive at least twenty thousand kilometres per year to save any money by opting for a diesel rather than a petrol-driven engine. And what does she do? She starts blabbering, disagreeing as usual, debating things like 'surely you don't save money by buying a car new' and it must depend on 'how much the car costs'. And then she says 'Why?'

'Because!' says Ove.

'Right,' says Parvaneh, rolling her eyes in a way that makes Ove suspect she is not accepting his authority on the topic as one might reasonably expect her to.

A few minutes later she's stopped in the parking area on the other side of the street.

'I'll wait here,' she says.

'Don't touch my radio settings,' orders Ove.

'As if I would,' she brays, with a sort of smile that Ove has begun to dislike in the last few weeks.

'It was nice that you came over yesterday,' she adds.

Ove replies with one of his sounds that aren't words as such, more a sort of clearing of his air passages. She pats him on the knee.

'The girls are happy when you come over. They like you!'

Ove gets out of the car without answering. There wasn't much wrong with the meal last night, he can stretch to admitting that. Although Ove doesn't feel there's a need to make such a palaver about cooking, as Parvaneh does. Meat and potatoes and sauce are perfectly adequate. But if one has to complicate things like she does, Ove could possibly agree that her rice with saffron is reasonably edible. It is. So he had two portions of it. And the cat had one and a half.

After dinner, while Patrick washed up, the three-year-old had demanded that Ove read her a bedtime story. Ove found it very difficult to reason with the little troll, because she didn't seem to understand normal argumentation, so he followed her with dissatisfaction through the hall towards her room and sat on her bedside, reading to her with his usual 'Ove-excitement', as Parvaneh once described it, although Ove didn't know what the hell she meant by that. When the three-year-old fell asleep with her head partly on his arm and partly on the open book, Ove had put both her and the cat in the bed and turned out the light.

On the way back through the hall he'd gone past the seven-year-old's room. She was sitting in front of her computer, of course, tapping and carrying on. This seemed to be all kids did these days, as Ove understood it. Patrick had explained that he'd 'tried to give her newer games but she only wanted to play that one', which made Ove more favourably disposed both to the seven-year-old and her computer game. Ove liked people who didn't do what Patrick told them to do.

There were drawings everywhere on the walls in her room. Black and white pencil sketches, mostly. Not at all bad, considering they had been created by the absence of deductive faculties and highly undeveloped motor function of a seven-year-old, Ove was willing to admit. None of them were of people. Only houses. Ove found this extremely engaging.

He stepped into the room and stood beside her. She looked up from the computer with the dour facial expression this kid always seemed to lug about with her, and in fact she didn't seem too pleased about his presence. But when Ove stayed where he was, she pointed at last to an upside-down storage box, made of plastic, on the floor. Ove sat down on it. And she started quietly explaining to him that the game was about building houses and then making cities out of the houses.

'I like houses,' she muttered quietly.

Ove looked at her. She looked at him. Ove put his index finger on the screen, leaving a large fingerprint, pointing at an empty space of the town and asking her what happened if she clicked that spot. She moved her cursor there and clicked, and in a flash the computer had put up a house there. Ove looked fairly suspicious about it. Then he made himself comfortable on the plastic box and pointed at another empty space. Two and a half hours later Parvaneh stomped in angrily and threatened to pull out the plug if they didn't call it a night at once.

Just as Ove stood in the doorway getting ready to leave, the seven-year-old carefully tugged at his shirtsleeve and pointed at a drawing on the wall right next to him. 'That's your house,' she whispered, as if it was a secret between her and Ove.

Ove nodded. Maybe they weren't totally worthless after all, those two kids.

He leaves Parvaneh in the parking area, crosses the street, opens the glass door and steps in. The café is empty. The fan heater overhead coughs as if it's full of cigar smoke. Amel stands behind the counter in a stained shirt, wiping glasses with a white towel.

His stocky body has sunk into itself, as if at the end of a very long breath. His face bears that combination of deep sorrow and inconsolable anger which only men of his generation and from his part of the world seem capable of mastering. Ove stays where he is, in the centre of the floor. The two men watch one another for a minute or so. One of them a man who can't bring himself to turf out a homosexual youth from his house, and the other who couldn't stop himself. Eventually Ove nods grimly and sits down on one of the bar stools.

He folds his hands together on the counter and gives Amel a dry look.

'I wouldn't be averse to that whisky now if it's still on offer.'

Amel's chest rises and falls in a couple of jerky breaths under the stained shirt. At first he seems to be considering opening his mouth, but then he thinks again. In silence he finishes wiping his glasses. Folds up the towel and puts it next to the espresso machine. Disappears into the kitchen without a word. Comes back with two glasses and a bottle, the letters on the label illegible to Ove. Puts these down on the counter between them.

It is difficult to admit that one is wrong. Particularly when one has been wrong for a very long time.

37

A MAN CALLED OVE AND A LOT OF
BASTARDS STICKING THEIR NOSES IN

'I'm sorry about this,' Ove creaks. He brushes the snow off the gravestone. 'But you know how it is. People have no respect at all for personal boundaries any more. They charge into your house without knocking and cause a right carry-on, you can hardly even sit on the crapper in peace any more,' he explains, while he digs the frozen flowers out of the ground and presses down the new ones through the snow.

He looks at her as if he's expecting her to nod her agreement. But she doesn't, of course. The cat sits next to Ove in the snow and looks like it absolutely agrees. Especially with that bit about not being to go to the toilet in peace.

Lena had come by Ove's house in the morning to drop off a copy of the newspaper. He was on the front cover, looking like the archetypal grumpy old sod. He'd kept his word and let her interview him. But he wasn't smiling like a donkey for the camera; he told them that in no uncertain terms.

'It's a fantastic interview!' she insisted proudly.

Ove didn't respond, but this did not seem to concern her. She looked impatient and sort of paced on the spot, whilst glancing at her watch as if in a hurry.

'Don't let me hold you up,' muttered Ove.

She managed a teenager's repressed titter by way of an answer.

'Me and Anders are going skating on the lake!'

Ove merely nodded at this point, taking this as confirmation that the conversation was over, and closed the door. He put the newspaper under the doormat; it would come in handy for absorbing the snow and slush brought in by the cat and Mirsad.

Back in the kitchen, he began clearing up all the advertising and free newspapers that Adrian had left with the day's post (Sonja may have managed to teach the rascal to read Shakespeare, but apparently he could not understand a three-word sign that said NO JUNK MAIL).

At the bottom of the pile he found the letter from Lena, the one Adrian had delivered that first time he rang Ove's doorbell.

Back then the youth rang the doorbell, at least – nowadays he ran in and out of the door as if he lived here, Ove grumbled as he held the letter up to the kitchen lamp like a banknote being checked. Then he got out a table knife from the kitchen drawer. Even though Sonja went mad every time he used a table knife to open an envelope rather than fetching the letter opener.

Dear Ove,

I hope you'll excuse me contacting you like this. Lena at the newspaper has let me know that you don't want to make a big thing out of this but she was kind enough to give me your address. Because for me it was a big thing, and I don't want to be the sort of person who does not say that to you, Ove. I respect that you don't want to let me thank you personally but at least I want to introduce you to some people who will always be grateful to you for your courage and selflessness. People like you are not made any more. Thanks is too small a word.

It was signed by the man in the black suit and grey overcoat, the one Ove hoisted off the track after he passed out. Lena had told Ove that the swooning fit had been caused by some sort of complicated brain disease. If they hadn't discovered it and started treating it when they did, it would have claimed his life within a few years. 'So in a way you saved his life twice over,' she'd exclaimed in that excitable tone of voice that made Ove regret a little not having left her locked up inside the garage while he still had the chance.

He folded up the letter and put it back in the envelope. Held up the photo. Three children, the oldest a teenager and the others more or less the same age as Parvaneh's oldest daughter, looked back at him. Or rather, they weren't really looking, they were sort of lying about in a pile, each with a water rifle and apparently laughing until they were practically screaming. Behind them stood a blonde woman of about forty-five, with a wide grin and her arms stretched out like a large bird of prey and an overflowing plastic bucket in each hand. At the bottom of the pile lay the man in the black suit, but wearing a blue polo shirt, and trying in vain to shield himself from the downpour.

Ove threw away the letter along with the advertising, tied up the bag, put it by the front door, went back into the kitchen, got out a magnet from the bottom drawer and put up the photo on the fridge. Right next to the riotous colour drawing that the three-year-old had made of him on the way back from the hospital.

Ove brushes his hand over the gravestone again, even though he's already brushed off all the snow that can be brushed off.

'Well, yes, I told them one might like a bit of peace and quiet like a normal human being. But they don't listen, they don't,' he moans, waving his arms tiredly towards the gravestone.

'Hi, Sonja,' says Parvaneh behind him, with a cheerful wave so that her big mittens slip off her hands.

'Hajj!' the three-year-old hollers happily.

'"Hi", you're supposed to say "hi",' the seven-year-old corrects.

'Hi, Sonja,' say Patrick, Jimmy, Adrian and Mirsad, all nodding in turn.

Ove stamps the snow off his shoes and nods, with a grunt, at the cat beside him.

'Yeah. And the cat you already know.'

Parvaneh's belly is now so big that she looks like a giant

tortoise when she heaves herself down into a squatting position, one hand on the gravestone and the other hooked around Patrick's arm. Not that Ove dares bring up the giant tortoise metaphor, of course. There are more pleasant ways of killing oneself, he feels. And that's speaking as someone who's already tried quite a few of them.

'This flower is from Patrick and the children and me,' says Parvaneh with a friendly smile at the stone.

Then she holds up another flower and adds:

'And this one's from Anita and Rune. They send loads of love.'

The multifarious gathering turns round to go back to the parking area, but Parvaneh stays by the gravestone. When Ove wants to know why, she just says, 'Never you bloody mind!' to him with the sort of smile that makes Ove want to throw things at her. Nothing hard, perhaps. But something symbolic.

He replies with a snort in the lower octave range, then finds, after a certain amount of inner deliberation, that a discussion with both of those women at the same time would be redundant from the very start. He starts going back to the Saab.

'Girls' talk,' says Parvaneh succinctly when at last she comes back to the parking area and gets into the driver's seat. Ove doesn't know what she means by that, but he decides to leave it alone. Nasanin's big sister helps her with her belt, in the back seat. In the meantime Jimmy, Mirsad and Patrick have managed to squeeze into Adrian's new car in front of them. A Toyota. Hardly an optimal choice of car for any kind of thinking person, Ove had pointed out to him many times while they stood there at the dealership. But at least it wasn't French. And Ove managed to get the price reduced by almost eight thousand crowns and made sure that the kid got winter tyres thrown in for the same price. So it seemed acceptable, in spite of it all.

When Ove got to the dealership the bloody kid had been checking out a Hyundai. So it could have been worse.

Once they make it back to their terrace, they go their separate ways. Ove, Mirsad and the cat wave at Parvaneh, Patrick, Jimmy and the children and turn off round the corner by Ove's toolshed.

It's difficult to judge how long the stocky man has been waiting outside Ove's house. Maybe all morning. He has the determined look of a straight-backed sentry posted somewhere in the field, in the wilderness. As if he's been cut from a thick tree trunk and the below-zero temperature is of no concern to him. But when Mirsad comes walking round the corner and the stocky man catches sight of him, he quickly comes to life.

'Hello,' he says, stretching, shifting his body weight back to the first foot.

'Hello, Dad,' mumbles Mirsad.

That evening Ove has his dinner with Parvaneh and Patrick, while a father and son talk about disappointments and hopes and masculinity in two languages in Ove's kitchen. Maybe most of all they speak of courage. Sonja would have liked it, Ove knows that much. But he tries not to smile so much that Parvaneh notices.

Before the seven-year-old goes to bed she presses a paper into Ove's hand, on which is written 'Birthday Party Invitation'. Ove reads through it as if it were a legal transfer of rights for a leasehold agreement.

'I see. And then you'll be wanting presents, I expect?' he huffs at last.

She looks down at the floor and shakes her head.

'You don't have to buy anything. I only want one thing anyway.'

Ove folds up the invitation and puts it in the back pocket of his trousers. Then, with a degree of authority, presses the palms of his hands against his sides.

'Right?'

'Mum says it's too expensive anyway so it doesn't matter,' she says without looking up, and then shakes her head again.

Ove nods conspiratorially, like a criminal who has just made a sign to another criminal that the telephone they are using is wiretapped. He and the girl look round the hall to check that neither her mother nor her father have their nosy ears around some corner, surreptitiously listening to them. And then Ove leans forward and the girl forms her hands in a funnel round her face and whispers into his ear

'An iPad.'

Ove looks a little as if she just said, 'An awyttsczyckdront!'

'It's a sort of computer. There are special drawing programs for it. For children,' she whispers a little louder.

And something is shining in her eyes.

Something that Ove recognises.

38

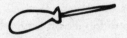

A MAN CALLED OVE AND THE END OF
A STORY

Broadly speaking there are two kinds of people. Those who understand how extremely useful white cables can be, and those who don't. Jimmy is the first of these. He loves white cables. And white telephones. And white computer monitors with fruit on the back. That's more or less the sum of what Ove has absorbed during the car journey into town, when Jimmy natters on excitedly about the sorts of things every rational person ought to be so insuperably interested in; until Ove at last sinks into a sort of deeply meditative state of mind, in which the overweight young man's babbling turns to a dull hissing in his ears.

As soon as the young man thundered into the passenger seat of the Saab with a large mustard sandwich in his hand, Ove obviously wished he hadn't asked for Jimmy's help with this. Things are not improved by Jimmy aimlessly shuffling off to 'check a few leads' as soon as they enter the shop.

If you want something done you have to do it yourself, as usual, Ove confirms to himself as he steers his steps alone towards the cashier. And not until Ove roars, 'Have you been frontally lobotomised or what!?' to the young man who's trying to show him the shop's range of portable computers does Jimmy come hurrying to his aid. And then it's not Ove but rather the shop assistant who needs to be aided.

'We're together,' Jimmy nods to the assistant with a glance

that sort of functions as a secret handshake to communicate the message, 'Don't worry, I'm one of you!'

The sales assistant takes a long frustrated breath and points at Ove.

'I'm trying to help him but . . .'

'You're just trying to fob me off with a load of CRAP, that's what you're doing!' Ove yells back at him without letting him get to a full stop, and menacing him with something he spontaneously snatches off the nearest shelf.

Ove doesn't quite know what it is, but it looks like a white electrical plug of some sort and it feels like the sort of thing he could throw very hard at the sales assistant if the need arises. The sales assistant looks at Jimmy with a sort of twitching around his eyes that Ove seems adept at generating in people with whom he comes into contact. This is so frequent that one could possibly name a syndrome after him.

'He didn't mean any harm, man,' Jimmy tries to say pleasantly.

'I'm trying to show him a MacBook and he's asking me what sort of car I drive,' the sales assistant bursts out, looking genuinely hurt.

'It's a relevant question,' mutters Ove, with a firm nod at Jimmy.

'I don't have a car! Because I think it's unnecessary and I want to use more environmentally friendly modes of transport!' says the sales assistant in a tone of voice pitched somewhere between intransigent anger and the foetal position.

Ove looks at Jimmy and throws out his arms, as if this should explain everything.

'You can't reason with a person like that,' he nods and evidently expects immediate support. 'Where the hell have you been, anyway?'

'I was just checking out the monitors over there, you know,' explains Jimmy.

'Are you buying a monitor?' asks Ove.

'No,' says Jimmy and looks at Ove as if it was a really strange question, more or less in the way that Sonja used to ask, 'What's that got to do with it?' when Ove asked her if she really 'needed' another pair of shoes.

The sales assistant tries to turn around and steal away, but Ove quickly puts his leg forward to stop him.

'Where are you going? We're not done here.'

The sales assistant looks deeply unhappy now. Jimmy pats him on the back, to encourage him.

'Ove here just wants to check out an iPad – can you sort us out?'

The sales assistant gives Ove a grim look.

'Okay, but as I was trying to ask him earlier, what model do you want? The 16-, 32- or 64-gigabyte?'

Ove looks at the sales assistant as if he feels the latter should stop regurgitating random combinations of letters.

'There are different versions with different amounts of memory,' Jimmy translates for Ove as if he were an interpreter for the Department of Immigration.

'And I suppose they want a hell of a lot of extra money for it,' Ove snorts back.

Jimmy nods his understanding of the situation and turns to the sales assistant.

'I think Ove wants to know a little more about the differences between the various models.'

The sales assistant groans.

'Well, do you want the normal or the 3G model, then?'

Jimmy turns to Ove.

'Will it be used mainly at home or will she use it outdoors as well?'

Ove pokes his torch finger into the air and points it dead straight at the sales assistant.

'Hey! I want her to have the BEST ONE! Understood?'

The sales assistant takes a nervous step back. Jimmy grins and opens his massive arms as if preparing himself for a big hug.

'Let's say 3G, 128-gig, all the bells and whistles you've got. And can you throw in a cable?'

A few minutes later Ove snatches the plastic bag with the iPad box from the counter, mumbling something about 'eight-thousandtwohundredandninetyfivecrowns and they don't even throw in a keyboard!' followed by 'thieves', 'bandits' and various obscenities.

And so it turns out that the seven-year-old gets an iPad that evening from Ove. And a lead from Jimmy.

She stands in the hall just inside the door, not quite sure what to do with that information, and in the end she just nods and says, 'Really nice . . . thanks.' Jimmy nods expansively.

'You got any snacks?'

She points to the living room, which is full of people. In the middle of the room is a birthday cake with eight lit candles, towards which the well-built young man immediately navigates. The girl who is now an eight-year-old stays in the hall, touching the iPad box with amazement. As if she hardly dares believe that she's actually got it in her hands. Ove leans towards her.

'That's how I always felt every time I bought a new car,' he says in a low voice.

She looks round to make sure no one can see; then she smiles and gives him a hug.

'Thanks, Granddad,' she whispers and runs into her room.

Ove stands quietly in the hall, poking his house keys against the calluses on one of his palms. Patrick comes limping along on his crutches in pursuit of the eight-year-old. Apparently he's been given the evening's most thankless task: that of convincing his daughter that it's more fun sitting there in a dress, eating cake with a lot of boring grown-ups than staying in her room listening to pop music and downloading apps onto her new iPad. Ove stays in the hall with his jacket on and stares emptily at the floor for what must be almost ten minutes.

'Are you okay?'

Parvaneh's voice tugs gently at him as if he is coming out of a deep dream. She's standing in the opening to the living room with her hands on her globular stomach, balancing it in front of her as if it were a large laundry basket. Ove looks up, slightly hazy in his eyes.

'Yeah, yeah, of course I am.'

'You want to come in and have some cake?'

'No . . . no. I don't like cake. I'll just take a little walk with the cat.'

Parvaneh's big brown eyes hold onto him in that piercing way, as they do more and more often these days, and which always makes him very unsettled. As if she's filled with dark premonitions.

'Okay,' she says at last, without any real conviction in her voice. 'Are we having a driving lesson tomorrow? I'll ring your doorbell at eight,' she suggests after that.

Ove nods. The cat strolls into the hall with cake in its whiskers.

'Are you done now?' Ove snorts at it, and when the cat looks ready to confirm that it is, Ove glances at Parvaneh, fidgets a little with his keys and agrees in a low voice:

'Right. Tomorrow morning at eight, then.'

The dense winter darkness has descended when Ove and the cat venture out into the little walkway between the houses. The laughter and music of the birthday party well out like a big warm carpet between the walls. Sonja would have liked it, Ove thinks to himself. She would have loved what was happening to the place with the arrival of this crazy, pregnant foreign woman and her utterly ungovernable family. She would have laughed a lot. And God, how much Ove missed that laugh.

He walks up towards the parking area with the cat. Checks all the signposts by giving them a good kick. Tugs at the garage doors. Makes a detour over the guest parking and then comes back. Checks the bin room. As they come back between the houses alongside Ove's toolshed, Ove sees something moving down by the last house on Parvaneh and Patrick's side of the road. At first Ove thinks it's one of the party guests, but soon he sees that the figure is moving by the shed belonging to the dark house of that recycling family. They, as far as Ove knows, are still in Thailand. He squints into the gloom to be sure that the shadows are not deceiving him, and for a few seconds he actually doesn't see anything. But then, just as he's ready to admit that his eyesight is not what it used to be, the figure reappears. And behind him, another two. And then he hears the unmistakable sound of someone tapping with a hammer at a window that's covered in insulation tape. Which is how one minimises the noise when the glass shatters. Ove knows exactly what it sounds like; he learned how to do it on the railways when they had to knock out broken train windows without cutting their fingers.

'Hey? What are you doing?' he calls through the darkness.

The figures down by the house stop moving. Ove hears voices.

'Hey you!' he bellows and starts running towards them.

He sees one of them take a couple of steps towards him, and he hears one of them shouting something. Ove increases his pace and charges at them like a human battering ram. He has time to think to himself that he should have brought something from the toolshed to fight with, but now it's too late. In the corner of his eye he notices one of the figures swinging something long and narrow in one fist, so Ove decides he has to hit that bastard first.

When there's a stabbing feeling in his breast he thinks at first that one of them has managed to attack him from behind and thump a fist into his back. But then there's another stab. Worse than ever, as if someone was skewering him from the scalp down, methodically working a sword all the way through his body until it comes out through the soles of his feet. Ove gasps for air but there's no air to be had. He falls in the middle of a stride, tumbles with his full weight into the snow. Perceives the dulled pain of his cheek scraping against the ice, and feels how something seems to be squeezing the insides of his chest in a big, merciless fist. Like an aluminium tin being crushed in the hand.

Ove hears the running steps of the burglars in the snow, and realises that they are fleeing. He doesn't know how many seconds pass, but the pain in his head, like a long line of fluorescent tubes exploding, is unbearable. He wants to cry out but there's no oxygen in his lungs. All he hears is Parvaneh's remote voice through the deafening sound of pulsating blood in his ears. Perceives the tottering steps when she stumbles and slips through the snow, her disproportionate body on those tiny feet. The last thing Ove has time to think before everything goes dark is that he has to make her promise that she won't let the ambulance drive down between the houses.

Because vehicular traffic is prohibited in the residential area.

39

A MAN CALLED OVE

Death is a strange thing. People live their whole lives as if it does not exist, and yet it's often one of the great motivations for living. Some of us, in time, become so conscious of it that we live harder, more obstinately, with more fury. Some need its constant presence to even be aware of its antithesis. Others become so preoccupied with it that they go into the waiting room long before it has announced its arrival. We fear it, yet most of us fear more than anything that it may take someone other than ourselves. For the greatest fear of death is always that it will pass us by. And leave us there alone.

People had always said that Ove was 'bitter'. But he wasn't bloody bitter. He just didn't go round grinning the whole time. Did that mean one had to be treated like a criminal? Ove hardly thought so. Something inside a man goes to pieces when he has to bury the only person who ever understood him. There is no time to heal that sort of wound.

And time is a curious thing. Most of us only live for the time that lies right ahead of us. A few days, weeks, years. One of the most painful moments in a person's life probably comes with the insight that an age has been reached when there is more to look back on than ahead. And when time no longer lies ahead of one, other things have to be lived for. Memories, perhaps. Afternoons in the sun with someone's hand clutched in one's own. The fragrance of flowerbeds in fresh bloom. Sundays in a café. Grandchildren, perhaps. One finds a way of living for the sake of someone else's future. And it wasn't as if Ove also died when Sonja left him. He just stopped living.

Grief is a strange thing.

When the hospital staff refused to let Parvaneh accompany Ove's stretcher into the operating theatre, it took the combined efforts of Patrick, Jimmy, Anders, Adrian, Mirsad and four nurses to hold her back, and her flying fists. When a doctor told her to consider the fact that she was actually pregnant and cautioned her to sit down and 'take it easy', Parvaneh overturned one of the wooden benches in the waiting room so that it landed on his foot. And when another doctor came out of a door with a clinically neutral facial expression and a curt way of expressing himself about 'preparing yourselves for the worst', she screamed out loud and collapsed on the floor like a shattered porcelain vase. Her face buried in her hands.

Love is a strange thing. It takes you by surprise.

It's half past three in the morning when a nurse comes to get her. She has refused to leave the waiting room. Her hair is one big mess, her eyes bloodshot and caked with streams of dried tears and mascara. When she steps into the little room at the bottom of the corridor she looks so weak at first that a nurse rushes forward to stop the pregnant woman crumbling to pieces as she crosses the threshold. Parvaneh supports herself against the doorframe, takes a deep breath, smiles an infinitely faint smile at the nurse and assures her that she's 'okay'. She takes a step into the room and remains there for a second, as if for the first time that night she can take in the full enormity of what has happened.

Then she goes up to the bed and stands next to it with fresh tears in her eyes. With both palms she starts thumping Ove's arm.

'You're *not* dying on me, Ove,' she weeps. 'Don't even think about it.' Ove's fingers move weakly; she grabs them with both hands and puts her forehead in the palm of his hand.

'I think you'd better calm yourself down, woman,' Ove whispers hoarsely.

And then she hits him on the arm again. And then he sees the wisdom of keeping quiet for a while. But she stays there with his hand in hers and slumps into the chair, with that mix of agitation, empathy and sheer terror in those big brown eyes of hers. At this point he lifts his other hand and strokes her hair. He has tubes going up his nose and his chest moves strenuously under the covers. As if his every breath is one long impulse of pain. His words come out wheezing.

'You didn't let those sods bring the ambulance into the residential area, did you?'

It takes about forty minutes before any of the nurses finally have the guts to go back into the room. A few moments later a bespectacled young doctor wearing plastic slippers who, in Ove's view, has the distinct appearance of someone with a stick up his bottom, comes into the room and stands dozily by the bed. He looks down at a paper.

'Parr . . . nava . . .?' He broods, and gives Parvaneh a distracted look.

'Parvaneh,' she corrects.

The doctor doesn't look particularly concerned.

'You're listed here as the "next of kin",' he says, glancing briefly at this emphatically Iranian thirty-year-old woman on the chair, and this emphatically un-Iranian Swede in the bed.

When neither of them make the slightest effort to explain how this can be, other than Parvaneh giving Ove a little shove and sniggering, 'Aaah, next of kin!' and Ove responding, 'Shut it will you!' the doctor sighs and continues.

'Ove has a heart problem . . .' he begins in an anodyne voice, following this up with a series of terms that no human being with less than ten years of medical training or an entirely unhealthy addiction to certain television series could ever be expected to understand.

When Parvaneh gives him a look studded with a long line of question marks and exclamation marks, the doctor sighs again in that way young doctors with glasses and plastic slippers and a stick up their bottom often do when confronted by people who do not even have the common bloody decency to attend medical school before they come to the hospital.

'His heart is too big,' the doctor states crassly.

Parvaneh stares blankly at him for a very long time. And then she looks at Ove in the bed, in a very searching way. And then she looks at the doctor again as if she's waiting for him to throw out his arms and start making jazzy movements with his fingers and crying out: 'Only joking!'

And when he doesn't do this she starts to laugh. First it's more like a cough, then as if she's holding back a sneeze and before long it's a long, sustained, raucous bout of giggling. She holds onto the side of the bed, waves her hand in front of her face as if to fan herself into stopping, but it doesn't help. And then at last it turns into one loud, long-drawn belly laugh that bursts out of the room and makes the nurses in the corridor stick their heads through the door and ask in wonder, 'What's going on in here?'

'You see what I have to put up with?' Ove hisses wearily at the doctor, rolling his eyes while Parvaneh, overwhelmed with hysterics, buries her face in one of the pillows.

The doctor looks as if there was never a seminar on how to deal with this type of situation, so in the end he clears his throat loudly and sort of brings his foot down with a quick stamping motion, in order to remind them of his authority, so to speak. It doesn't do much good, of course, but after many more attempts, Parvaneh gets herself into order enough to manage to say: 'Ove's heart is too big; I think I'm going to die.'

'It's me who's bloody dying!' Ove objects.

Parvaneh shakes her head and smiles warmly at the doctor. 'Was that all?'

The doctor closes his file with resignation.

'If he takes his medication we can keep it under control. But it's difficult to be sure about things like this. It could take a few months or a few years.'

Parvaneh gives him a dismissive wave.

'Oh don't concern yourself about that. Ove is quite clearly UTTERLY RUBBISH at dying!'

Ove looks quite offended by that.

Four days later Ove limps through the snow to his house. He's supported on one side by Parvaneh and on the other by Patrick. One is on crutches and the other knocked up, that's the support you get, he thinks. But he doesn't say it; Parvaneh just had a tantrum when Ove wouldn't let her reverse the Saab down between the houses a few minutes ago. 'I KNOW, OVE! Okay! I KNOW! If you say it one more time I swear to God I'll set fire to your bloody sign!' she shouted at him. Which Ove felt was a little overly dramatic, to say the least.

The snow creaks under his shoes. The windows are lit up. The cat sits outside the door, waiting. There are drawings spread across the table in the kitchen.

'The girls drew them for you,' says Parvaneh and puts his spare keys in the basket next to the telephone.

When she sees Ove's eyes reading the letters in the bottom corner of one of the drawings, she looks slightly embarrassed.

'They . . . sorry, Ove, don't worry about what they've written! You know how children are. My father died in Iran. They've never had a . . . you know . . .'

Ove takes no notice of her, just takes the drawings in his hand and goes to the kitchen drawers.

'They can call me whatever they like. No need for you to stick your bloody nose in.'

And then he puts up the drawings one by one on the fridge. The one that says 'To Granddad' gets the top spot. She tries not to smile. Doesn't succeed very convincingly.

'Stop sniggering and put the coffee on instead. I'm fetching down the removals crates from the attic,' Ove mumbles and limps off towards the stairs.

So, that evening, Parvaneh and the girls help him clean up his house. They wrap each and every one of Sonja's things in newspaper and carefully pack all her clothes into boxes. One memory at a time. And at half past nine when everything is done and the girls have fallen asleep on Ove's sofa with newsprint on their fingertips and chocolate ice cream around the corners of their mouths, then Parvaneh's hand suddenly grips Ove's upper arm like a voracious metal claw. And when Ove growls 'OUCH!' she growls back 'SHUSH!'

And then they have to go back to the hospital.

It's a boy.

A MAN CALLED OVE AND AN EPILOGUE

Life is a Curious Thing.

Winter turns to spring and Parvaneh passes her driving test. Ove teaches Adrian how to change tyres. The lad may have bought a Toyota, but that doesn't mean he's *entirely* beyond help, Ove explains to Sonja when he visits her one Sunday in April. Then he shows her some photographs of Parvaneh's little lad. Four months old and as fat as a seal pup. Patrick has tried to force one of those mobile phone camera things on him, but Ove doesn't trust them. So he walks round with a thick wad of paper copies inside his wallet instead, held together by a rubber band. Shows everyone he meets. Even the people who work at the florist's.

Spring turns to summer and by the time autumn sets in, the annoying journalist, Lena, moves in with that Audi-driving fop Anders. Ove drives the removal van; he has no faith in those jackasses being able to reverse it between the houses without ruining his letter box, so it's just as well. Of course, Lena doesn't believe in 'marriage as an institution', Ove tells Sonja with a snort that seems to suggest there have been certain discussions about this along the terrace, but the following spring he comes to the grave and shows her another wedding invitation.

Mirsad wears a black suit and is literally shaking with

nervousness. Parvaneh has to give him a shot of tequila before he goes into the Town Hall. Jimmy is waiting inside. Ove is his best man, and has bought a new suit for the occasion. They have the party at Amel's café; the stocky man tries to give a speech three times but he's too overwhelmed by emotion to manage more than a few stuttering words. On the other hand he names a sandwich after Jimmy, which Jimmy says is the most magnificent present he's ever had. He continues living in his mother's house with Mirsad. The following year they adopt a little girl. Jimmy brings her along to Anita and Rune's every afternoon, without fail, at three o'clock when they have coffee.

Rune doesn't get better. In certain periods, he is virtually uncontactable for days at a time. But every time that little girl runs into his and Anita's house with her arms reaching out for Anita, a euphoric smile fills his entire face. Without exception.

Even more houses are built in the area. In a few years it goes from a quiet backwater to a city district. Which obviously doesn't make Patrick more competent when it comes to opening windows or assembling IKEA wardrobes. One morning he turns up at Ove's door with two men more or less the same age as himself, who apparently are also not so good at it. Both own houses a few streets down, they explain. They're restoring them but they've run into problems with joists over partition walls. They don't know what to do. But Ove knows, of course. He mutters something that sounds a little like 'fools' and goes over to show them. The next day another neighbour turns up. And then another. And then another. Within a few months Ove has been everywhere, fixing this and that in almost every house within a radius of four streets. Obviously he always grumbles about people's incompetence. But when he's by himself by Sonja's grave he does mumble on one occasion that, 'Sometimes it can be quite nice having something to get on with in the daytime'.

Parvaneh's daughters celebrate their birthdays and before anyone can explain how it happened, the three-year-old has become a six-year-old, in that disrespectful way often noted in three-year-olds.

Ove goes with her to school on her first day. She teaches him to insert smileys into an SMS, and he makes her promise never to tell Patrick that he's got himself a mobile. The eight-year-old, who in a similar, disrespectful way has now turned ten, holds her first pyjama party. Their little brother disperses his toys all over Ove's kitchen. Ove builds a splash pond for him in his outside space but when someone calls it a splash pond Ove snorts that 'Actually it's a bloody pool, isn't it!' Anders is voted in again as the chairman of the Residents' Association. Parvaneh buys a new lawnmower for the lawn behind the houses.

Summers turn to autumns and autumns to winters and one icy-cold Sunday morning in November, almost four years to the day since Parvaneh and Patrick reversed that trailer into Ove's letter box, Parvaneh wakes up as if someone just placed a frozen hand on her brow. She gets up, looks out of her bedroom window and checks the time. It's quarter past eight. The snow hasn't been cleared outside Ove's house.

She runs across the little road in her dressing gown and slippers, calling out his name. Opens the door with the spare key he's given her, charges into the living room, stumbles up the stairs in her wet slippers and, with her heart in her mouth, fumbles her way into his bedroom.

Ove looks like he's sleeping very deeply. She has never seen his face looking so peaceful. The cat lies at his side with its little head carefully resting in the palm of his hand. When it sees Parvaneh it slowly, slowly stands up, as if only then fully accepting what has happened; then climbs into her lap. They sit together on the bedside and Parvaneh caresses the thin locks of hair on Ove's head until the ambulance crew gets there and, with tender and gentle words and movements, explain that they have to take the body away. Then she leans forward and whispers, 'Give my love to Sonja and thank her for the loan,' into his ear. Then she takes the big envelope from the bedside table on which it is written, in longhand, 'To Parvaneh,' and goes back down the stairs.

It's full of documents and certificates, original plans of the house, instruction booklets for the video player, the service booklet for the Saab. Bank account numbers and insurance policy documents. The telephone number of a lawyer to whom Ove has 'left all his affairs'. A whole life assembled and entered into files. The closing of accounts. At the top is a letter for her. She sits down at the kitchen table to read it. It's not long. As if Ove knew she'll only drench it in tears before she gets to the end.

> Adrian gets the Saab. Everything else is for you to take care of. You've got the house keys. The cat eats tuna fish twice per day and doesn't like shitting in other people's houses. Please respect that. There is a lawyer in town who has all the bank papers and so on. There is an account with 11 563 013 crowns and 67 öre. From Sonja's dad. The old man had shares. He was mean as hell. Me and Sonja never knew what to do with it. Your kids should get a million each when they turn eighteen, and Jimmy's girl should get the same. The rest is yours. But please don't let Patrick bloody take care of it. Sonja would have liked you. Don't let the new neighbours drive in the residential area.
> *Ove*

At the bottom of the sheet he's written in capitals 'YOU ARE NOT A COMPLETE IDIOT!' And after that, a smiley, as Nasanin has taught him.

There are clear instructions in the letters about the funeral, which mustn't under any circumstances 'be made a bloody fuss of'. Ove doesn't want any ceremony, he only wants to be thrown in the ground next to Sonja and that's all. 'No people. No messing about!' he states firmly and clearly to Parvaneh.

More than three hundred people come to the funeral.

When Patrick, Parvaneh and the girls come in there are people standing all along the walls and aisles. Everyone holds lit candles with 'Sonja's Fund' engraved on them. Because that is what Parvaneh has decided to use Ove's money for: a charity fund for orphaned children. Her eyes are swollen with tears, her throat is so dry that she has felt as if she's panting for air for several days now. The sight of the candles eases something in her breathing. And when Patrick sees all the people who have come to say their farewells to Ove, he elbows her gently in her side and grins with satisfaction.

'Shit. Ove would have hated this, wouldn't he?'

And then she laughs. Because he really would have.

In the evening she shows a young, recently married couple around Ove and Sonja's house. The woman is pregnant. Her eyes glitter as she walks through the rooms, the way eyes glitter when a person imagines her child's future memories unfolding there on the floor. Her husband is obviously much less pleased with the place. He's wearing a pair of carpenter's trousers and he mostly goes round kicking the skirting boards suspiciously and looking annoyed. Parvaneh obviously knows it doesn't make any difference, she can see in the girl's eyes that the decision has already been made. But when the young man asks in a sullen tone about 'that garage place' mentioned in the advert, Parvaneh looks him up and down carefully, nods drily and asks what car he drives. The young man straightens up for the first time, smiles an almost undetectable smile and looks her right in the eye with the sort of indomitable pride that only one word can convey.

'Saab.'

ACKNOWLEDGEMENTS

Jonas Cramby. Brilliant journalist and a real gentleman. Because you discovered Ove and gave him a name that first time, and for so generously allowing me to carry on with his story.

John Häggblom. My editor. Because in a gifted and scrupulous manner you advised me on all my linguistic failings, and because you patiently and humbly accepted all the times I totally ignored your advice.

Rolf Backman. My father. Because I hope I am unlike you in the smallest possible number of ways.

A MAN CALLED OVE
Reading Group Questions

🔧 Does it matter if you don't know (or get on with) your neighbours?
Should Ove just be left to mind his own business?

🔧 Ove and Sonja seem to prove that opposites attract; is this still true?

🔧 Should the State and the 'men in white shirts' have attempted to take care
of Rune and Sonja, even if they didn't have their permission?
To what extent is care a social responsibility rather than a personal choice?

🔧 Often the greatest heroes don't get the glory. Ove spends his whole life refusing
to 'make a fuss', even when he saves lives and shows incredible generosity. Are we too
obsessed with glory and recognition now that we live in the Age of Celebrity?

🔧 Why are men of a certain age so grumpy all the time?
Did Ove make you think twice about a typical 'grumpy old man'?

🔧 Ove has worked hard all his life, paid his taxes, never had a loan,
always kept his car clean. Yet one day society seems to forget about him.
Do we need to re-think our attitude towards later middle age?

🔧 In terms of technology, relationships and lifestyles, 'things aren't
what they used to be'. Is this for better or for worse?

HOW OVE

1. Which of the following sayings are you most likely to use?

- a) Rules are rules
- b) The early bird catches the worm
- c) Live and let live

2. A person must have ...

- a) Compassion
- b) Corrugated iron
- c) Principles

3. You find £20 in your street. What do you do?

- a) Pocket it
- b) Leave it
- c) Ask the neighbours if it's theirs

4. Your computer stops working. What do you do?

- a) Turn it off and on again
- b) Ring a helpline
- c) Hit it repeatedly

5. The best car is:

- a) A BMW
- b) A Volvo
- c) A Saab

ARE YOU? QUIZ

6. Sometimes, you just wished people would . . .

- a) Leave you alone
- b) Learn how to do things properly
- c) Take a chill pill

7. You least like:

- a) Fastidious people
- b) Idiots who can't drive properly
- c) Animals peeing on your garden path

8. Which do you value most?

- a) Your holiday memorabilia
- b) Your music collection
- c) Your driving licence

9. How do you show people you care?

- a) Buy them flowers
- b) Invite them for dinner
- c) Fix their radiators

10. What do you like to do first thing in the morning?

- a) Have a lie in
- b) Check your emails
- c) Inspect the neighbourhood

Mostly As:

You may be pleased to learn you are not like Ove at all!
You are far more laid back and accepting of other people, and no-one
could call you grumpy. And you clearly like a bit of fun.

Mostly Bs:

You have some Ove tendencies... Perhaps you like a certain amount
of order and try to live a moral life. But thankfully you haven't
reached Ove's obsessive levels yet!

Mostly Cs:

You are Ove! You believe the world should have order and that people
should follow rules. After all, what would happen if people just went
around doing what they pleased?

MEET THE AUTHOR:
FREDRIK BACKMAN

If I hadn't become a writer, I would have wanted to be ... a fork lift driver at a fruit warehouse. That's where I worked before people started giving me money for writing stuff, and I was pretty good at that.

My favourite food is ... the one that someone else cooked and my doctor doesn't know I'm eating right now. It could be deep fried. It's probably deep fried.

One thing that people may not know about me is ... that I never answer that question since that would mean people would know those things that there was probably a real good reason I didn't tell them in the first place.

My favourite hobby is ... ha ha be serious! I don't have hobbies. I have kids. They have hobbies.

First published on the Radio 2 Book Club website

FREDRIK BACKMAN

my grandmother sends her regards and apologises

Everyone remembers the smell of their grandmother's house. Everyone remembers the stories their grandmother told them. But does everyone remember their grandmother flirting with policemen? Driving illegally? Breaking into a zoo in the middle of the night? Firing a paintball gun from a balcony in her dressing gown?

Seven-year-old Elsa does.

Some might call Elsa's granny 'eccentric', or even 'crazy'. Elsa calls her a superhero. And granny's stories, of knights and princesses and dragons and castles, are her superpower. Because, as Elsa is starting to learn, heroes and villains don't always exist in imaginary kingdoms; they could live just down the hallway. As Christmas draws near, even the best superhero grandmothers may have one or two things they'd like to apologise for. And, in the process, Elsa can have some breath-taking adventures of her own …

'Firmly in league with the likes of Roald Dahl and Neil Gaiman. A touching, sometimes funny, often wise portrait of grief.'
Kirkus

sceptre

FREDRIK BACKMAN

BRITT-MARIE WAS HERE

For as long as anyone can remember, Britt-Marie has been an acquired taste. It's not that she's judgemental, or fussy, or difficult – she just expects things to be done in a certain way. A cutlery drawer should be arranged in the right order, for example (forks, knives, then spoons). We're not animals, are we?

But behind the passive-aggressive, socially awkward, absurdly pedantic busybody is a woman who has more imagination, bigger dreams and a warmer heart than anyone around her realises.

So when Britt-Marie finds herself unemployed, separated from her husband of twenty years, left to fend for herself in the miserable provincial backwater that is Borg – of which the kindest thing one can say is that it has a road going through it – and somehow tasked with running the local football team, she is a little unprepared. But she will learn that life may have more to offer her than she's ever realised, and love might be found in the most unexpected of places.

'Impressive [and] heart-warming … there are unexpected delights to being stuck with Britt-Marie.'
Literary Review

sceptre

sceptre